SOMETHING TO PROVE

"Well, well, well, the rumors *are* true. If it isn't Hell-on-Wheels."

Helena spun toward the amused baritone. She was getting much quicker at putting names to faces, but she wouldn't have needed any help matching the twenty-year-old Ryan Tanner with the version standing in front of her now. Sun-streaked blond hair, strong jaw, green eyes with cute little crinkles from being outside . . . There was something just so damn wholesome about him that he could be the centerfold for *Cute Boys Next Door* magazine. In jeans, a black polo shirt, and work boots, he certainly didn't look like he belonged in the mayor's office, but it did give him an almost edgy sex appeal—not hurt at all by the way the sleeves of his shirt strained against his biceps.

Under different circumstances . . . hummina. But that mocking "Hell-on-Wheels" comment had her hackles up. "It's just Helena these days."

"I'm sure the chief will be glad to hear it. He's new and all, but he's very committed to keeping Magnolia Beach orderly and peaceful."

And there it was. She'd rather hoped that Ryan had outgrown his holier-than-Helena attitude. *Be an adult. Let it go.* "I doubt I'll have time to make his acquaintance, but please pass along my regards."

Ryan walked around Julie's desk and pulled some papers out of an in-box. "What brings you to the mayor's office? I don't think even *you've* been in town long enough to cause any trouble."

Don't take the bait. "I'm looking for you, actually."

Ryan's eyebrows went up in surprise. "Then maybe we should step into my office."

Something to Prove

A Magnolia Beach Novel

KIMBERLY LANG

A SIGNET ECLIPSE BOOK

SIGNET ECLIPSE
Published by the Penguin Group
Penguin Group (USA) LLC, 375 Hudson Street,
New York, New York 10014

USA | Canada | UK | Ireland | Australia | New Zealand | India | South Africa | China
penguin.com
A Penguin Random House Company

First published by Signet Eclipse, an imprint of New American Library,
a division of Penguin Group (USA) LLC

First Printing, June 2015

Copyright © Kimberly Kerr, 2015

SIGNET ECLIPSE and logo are trademarks of Penguin Group (USA) LLC.

ISBN 978-0-451-47103-1

Printed in the United States of America
10 9 8 7 6 5 4 3 2 1

This book is dedicated to the memory of Randy Marsh, English teacher extraordinaire, who taught me the power of words and gave me a love of language and literature that put me on the path to become a writer. I like to think he'd be proud of me.

And to L. G. Wilson, who taught me both the importance of making an impassioned argument and the value of knowing when to just keep my mouth shut. Critical thinking is such an important skill. Thank you for not expelling me before I mastered it.

Chapter 1

If I'd known I was going to attract this much attention, I'd have worn lipstick.

Forcing herself to smile, Helena Wheeler waved at the elderly couple frowning down at her from their porch swing. Mr. and Mrs. Riley had been ancient twelve years ago, and though she assumed they'd been long dead by now, she realized they might be living proof that time really did stand still in Magnolia Beach, Alabama.

The Rileys weren't the only ones staring and muttering. Grannie's house sat three blocks off Magnolia Beach's main drag, and at least a dozen people had done shocked double takes as she'd passed. In a way, it was almost gratifying. She must not have changed all that much, which was heartening for someone staring down her thirty-second birthday and beginning to pay a bit more attention to those commercials talking about fine lines and wrinkles. The flip side, of course, was the hushed whispers that came after those double takes. She didn't have to hear them to realize that folks rather expected her not to have changed at all.

As Grannie would say, though, she was merely reaping what she'd sown. She couldn't really expect anything else.

They probably have the high school on lockdown already. She snorted. Like she even knew where to find a pig these days.

Well, she certainly couldn't terrorize the town on the weak cup of instant decaf she'd gulped this morning in an effort to fool herself into waking up. Her first stop would be the diner for coffee. Then, and only then, would she have the strength to tackle the mile-long to-do list that was tucked into her purse.

Magnolia Beach was just a small coastal Alabama town, with the geography—Heron Bayou on the west, Heron Bay on the south, and Mobile Bay on the east—forcing pretty much everything into one central location. That was part of its charm, the community's easy accessibility and friendly layout as much of a tourist attraction as the white sugar-sand beaches of the Mobile Bay side and the marina of the Heron Bay shore. Helena was immune to that "charm," but it did make today's errands much easier because she wouldn't have to drive and park.

Turning right onto Front Street from Lister Street—officially the place where Magnolia Beach's residential area became the so-called business district—Helena stopped and took a deep breath to ready herself for the next leg of this gauntlet. Then she smiled to herself. She'd forgotten how pretty Magnolia Beach was from this exact point. From here, it was a straight shot to Heron Bay, an unobstructed, perfect view all the way to where the Gulf's green water met blue sky at the horizon.

To her left, Grace Baptist still squared off with First Methodist—a name both hopeful and ridiculous at the same time since it was still the only Methodist church in Magnolia Beach. Grace Baptist had the Bible verse of the week up on its sign, and out of habit, Helena began trying to mentally rearrange the letters into something else. When nothing came to her, she realized that particular skill had gone rusty from disuse. *Pity. I used to be really good at that.*

The Frosty Freeze was shuttered, its picnic tables empty, but that would change once school let out for the day. There were more people on Front Street than cars—mothers with babies in strollers and toddlers following behind, old women doing their grocery shopping, men with rods on their shoulders heading to fish off the jetty, and the occasional tourist with camera in hand, taking pictures of the small-town goodness of a modern Mayberry.

In other words, Front Street looked much the same as it always had. Sure, there were a few new stores and fresh coats of paint on some of the buildings, but otherwise ... Helena was certain she'd still be able to get through town blindfolded.

She reached for her sunglasses. It was truly a beautiful day—sunny and warm, with just a hint of cool in the breeze to remind her it was actually September. It was exactly the kind of weather that Yankee snowbirds came south to the Gulf to experience.

And Magnolia Beach ... Those blue skies, the occasional white puffy cloud overhead, the tidy main street with American flags hanging off the buildings ... If she were designing the travel brochure for the town, *this* would be the picture.

In a way, she'd missed it. Not Magnolia Beach, of course, but she'd missed the water, the smell of salty air, and breezes off the ocean. As much as she loved Atlanta, she was still a beach girl at heart. Maybe one day, she'd relocate back to the coast—not to Magnolia Beach, but maybe someplace down along the Florida panhandle.

But those were plans for a different day.

The bells dinged as she pushed through the front door of Marge's Diner, triggering a Pavlovian-like craving for Ms. Marge's three-berry pie. Habit nearly sent her to the big booth in the back corner—assigned seating so Ms. Marge could "keep an eye on her" from the kitchen—but she angled to the shiny, stainless-steel counter instead. The breakfast rush was over, and only a few tables with their classic red-and-white checkered tablecloths still had customers seated at them. She kept her sunglasses on and her head low. Fortunately, Magnolia Beach's beaches and the marina attracted enough tourists that one lone woman wouldn't draw much attention—until someone recognized her *and* decided to speak to her at least. And she *really* needed coffee before that happened.

The bored-looking young woman behind the counter barely seemed old enough to be out of high school, and she glanced at Helena without a glimmer of recognition.

Perfect.

"What can I get ya?"

Helena thought longingly of the fabulous coffee shop right across the street from her place in Little Five Points, and the craving for one of their special double espresso hazelnut lattes nearly brought her to her knees. She pushed the thought aside. This was Magnolia Beach. "Just coffee, please. Black."

The coffee wasn't the best, but it was hot and strong, and her brain perked up the minute it hit her tongue.

"Helena?"

And so it begins.

Swiveling on the stool, she located the voice and found herself looking at a tall, lanky man who was staring back at her with surprise—not judgment. There was something so familiar—the shock of dark hair, the bright blue eyes. . . . "Tate!"

Tate Harris caught her as she launched herself off the stool and lifted her off her feet in a hug that squeezed the breath out of her.

"It really *is* you." The blue eyes narrowed into a scold. "I can't believe you'd come to town and not let me know."

"I just got in last night. You were definitely on my list of folks to find as soon as I got settled in."

Tate grinned. "I should hope so." He gave her another squeeze. "God, I've missed you."

Helena's heart contracted a little. Although he was a year younger, Tate had always been her friend, defender, and partner in crime—the Boy Wonder to her Batman. But that awkward teenager was gone, and the intervening years had been *very* good to him. "Look at you. All grown-up."

"And you're as beautiful as ever. Welcome home." Then

the smile faded, and concern took its place. "Ms. Louise didn't take a turn for the worse, did she?"

"Grannie is fine," she assured him. "The doc says she's healing well and should be able to come home in a couple of weeks."

Tate guided her back to her stool and ordered a cup of coffee for himself. The waitress suddenly didn't look so bored as she poured Tate's coffee. He grinned at her, and she blushed before she went back to filling saltshakers and casting the occasional glance Tate's way. "That's good news. She gave us all quite a scare."

"And me." Guilt settled on her shoulders. Grannie had lain at the foot of the stairs for nearly two days with a broken hip, a broken ankle, three cracked ribs, and a concussion before her neighbor, Mrs. Wilson, had found her.

"So that's why you're here."

"Yeah. I wanted her to come to Atlanta for a while after she's out of the convalescent home, but she pitched a holy fit at the idea. And since there's no way she'll be able to handle everything herself once they *do* release her, I had to come here." She shrugged.

He patted her arm. "You're a good granddaughter."

"I'm trying. I've got a lot to make up for."

Tate snorted but didn't say anything. He knew what she was up against.

"The Rileys and a few other folks have already given me the hairy eyeball today. I'm just hoping they don't break out the pitchforks and torches."

"It won't be that bad."

A spark of hope lit in her chest, surprising her. "You think folks are willing to—" She stopped as Tate shook his head.

"Jesus may forgive, but people don't forget. You, Miss Hell-on-Wheels, are half local legend, half cautionary tale told to keep kids on the straight and narrow path."

"I wasn't *that* bad," she muttered into her coffee.

"Uh, yeah. You were."

She lifted her chin. "Those were merely youthful indiscretions. And it was a long time ago. People do grow up and change, you know."

Tate nodded sagely. "That sounds like an excellent story. You should stick to it."

She returned the nod as regally as she could. "I shall." Tate grinned, and she leaned forward eagerly. "So tell me all about you. How've you been? Job? Wife? Kids?"

"Fine, yes, no, and no." He checked his watch and drained the last of his coffee. "All the other details will have to wait because I'm about to be very late for work. But we should go to dinner or something and catch up."

"I'd like that." And she meant it. The fact she'd missed Tate landed on her chest with a thud that surprised her with its weight.

"Everything's pretty much where you left it, but if you need anything while you're getting settled back in, just let me know." He scribbled a phone number onto the back of a business card and pushed it her way.

Helena did the same. "But I do have one thing you could help me with now."

Tate paused.

"You know what Grannie's house is like—all those stairs—and my first project is to get someone in to do some renovations before Grannie comes home. She's adamant that I call 'that Tanner boy' and get him to do it, but she didn't mention *which* Tanner boy, and there's so damn many of them."

Tate nodded. "You want Ryan."

Figures. Not that there was a Tanner in Magnolia Beach that she did have fond memories of, but why did it have to be Ryan? "Oh yay," she grumbled into her cup.

Tate laughed. "What happened to growing up and changing?"

"I certainly hope that's true in Ryan's case."

The grin got bigger. "Oh, this is going to be interesting. I don't have his number on me, but if you run down to the mayor's office, the secretary, Julie, can get it for you."

Throwing a couple of dollars onto the counter, she followed Tate outside. "Why would the mayor's secretary be keeping up with Ryan Tanner?" Magnolia Beach was a small town where everyone pretty much knew everyone else—and all their business—but even Magnolia Beach had limits.

"Because Ryan's the mayor, sweetcheeks."

It was a little hard to picture someone she went to high school with as the *mayor*, but she wasn't really that shocked. Ryan certainly wasn't the first Tanner to hold the office, and if his election to student body president was any indication, he'd probably swept into office in a landslide vote. He'd always been golden—not that it was hard for a Tanner to be popular in Magnolia Beach. They were *the* local family, with doctors, lawyers, business owners, and even a county sheriff hanging off the branches of the family tree.

"I gotta go," Tate said, squeezing her hand, "but I'll give you a call later. And, by the way," he said, leaning in close, "I'd never say this within earshot of Ms. Marge, but if you want a good cup of coffee, head over to Latte Dah on Williams Street. It's where the old yarn store used to be. Their coffee could fuel rockets to Mars."

"Morning, Dr. Harris." A lady Helena didn't recognize spoke as she passed, and Tate nodded politely in reply.

"Bye, Helena. Welcome home." Then, with a quick wave, he was gone.

Helena stood still for a moment, trying to process this new information. *Tate Harris is a doctor?* She fished the business card out of her pocket, and sure enough, Tate J. Harris had DVM after his name.

Grannie had told her Tate was working at the vet's office, but she'd made it sound like he was a vet tech or something—not the vet himself. *Good for him.* He'd always talked about vet school, but the cost alone had made it seem like a pipe dream, at best. She didn't know if she should be proud *of* him or *for* him, but it made her smile either way.

And Magnolia Beach had a coffee shop now? Wow. *That* was big news. She couldn't quite wrap her head around the idea.

Grannie liked to give updates on life in Magnolia Beach—hell, Helena knew all about Mrs. Potter's roses and that new high school teacher with the tattoo—but maybe she should start steering those conversations in more *practical* directions.

I wonder what else I don't know.

The short walk to the squat brick building that doubled as the city hall and police station told her the answer to her question was "a hell of a lot." There was a yoga studio tucked in between the barbershop and the post office now, and a day spa next door to Bryson's Shoe Store with a menu of services that rivaled most Atlanta spas, only the prices were much more affordable.

Helena felt like a tourist in her own hometown.

The glass doors on the front of the city hall building displayed the Magnolia Beach seal and all twenty of their weekly office hours. Helena paused with her hand on the door.

She'd never been in through this entrance before. Now, the side entrance into the police station was a different story. . . . She felt oddly grown-up. At the same time, she felt seventeen again.

One of the problems with coming back to Magnolia Beach was all the people who never left, many of them people she didn't really want to see. While that list was certainly a long one, Ryan Tanner sat firmly in the top ten. While they hadn't been archenemies, they certainly hadn't been friends. Popular football players from "good" families didn't exactly hang with delinquents and those from the wrong side of the tracks—not that Magnolia Beach was big enough to really have a "right" and "wrong" side of the tracks, but the idea was the same.

I'm not going to him for a favor. This was a business transaction, and she was an adult now. They didn't need to be friends or anything else for her to hire him.

With one last deep breath, she pulled the door open.

A petite blonde sat behind a desk, her fingers clattering over the keyboard. She looked up as Helena entered, a big smile on her face. "Hi. Can I help . . ."

The words trailed off as the smile disappeared and her eyes widened. The woman visibly pulled back as her eyes darted side to side.

Good Lord. You'd think I'd walked in here with a snake wrapped around my neck. The nameplate on the desk said JULIE SWENSON, but Julie *Lane* probably had a laundry list of grievances against Helena dating back to kindergarten. The "Swenson" told Helena that Julie had married her high school boyfriend, Mike, and the rumors about Mike and Helena at homecoming—she repressed a shudder at the thought—probably fueled part of Julie's reaction as well. *Oh, honey, I've never been* that *drunk.*

She tried for a neutral, friendly tone. "Hi, Julie. You look great."

"This is a surprise, Helena. In town for a short visit?"

There was such hope in the question that Helena took a little pleasure in squashing it. She might have been horrible to Julie, but thinking back, she remembered that Julie had deserved much of it. "Not too short. Grannie will be well enough to come home soon, and I'm going to be looking after her. I'm not really sure how long I'll be staying."

Julie looked like she had something nasty-tasting in her mouth. "That's very kind of you. I hope Ms. Louise heals quickly."

She hadn't planned on rekindling old animosities on this trip, but it seemed inevitable. "You and me both." She forced a cool smile. "And that brings me to why I'm here. I need to get in touch with Ryan Tanner about some work to be done to Grannie's house before she comes home. Tate Harris said you could get me the number?"

"Well, well, well, the rumors *are* true. If it isn't Hell-on-Wheels."

Helena spun toward the amused baritone. She was getting much quicker at putting names to faces, but she wouldn't have needed any help matching the twenty-year-old Ryan Tanner with the version standing in front of her now. Sun-streaked blond hair, strong jaw, green eyes with cute little crinkles from being outside . . . There was something just so damn *wholesome* about him that he could be the centerfold for *Cute Boys Next Door* magazine. In jeans, a black polo shirt, and work boots, he certainly didn't look like he belonged in the mayor's office, but it did give him an almost edgy sex appeal—not hurt at all by the way the sleeves of his shirt strained against his biceps.

Under different circumstances . . . hummina. But that mocking "Hell-on-Wheels" comment had her hackles up. "It's just Helena these days."

"I'm sure the chief will be glad to hear it. He's new and all, but he's very committed to keeping Magnolia Beach orderly and peaceful."

And there it was. She'd rather hoped that Ryan had outgrown his holier-than-Helena attitude. *Be an adult. Let it go.* "I doubt I'll have time to make his acquaintance, but please pass along my regards."

Ryan walked around Julie's desk and pulled some papers out of an in-box. "What brings you to the mayor's office? I don't think even *you've* been in town long enough to cause any trouble."

Don't take the bait. "I'm looking for you, actually."

Ryan's eyebrows went up in surprise. "Then maybe we should step into my office."

"It's not official Magnolia Beach business. I need to talk to you about my grandmother."

His attitude changed. It was subtle, but it was there all the same. Ryan indicated she should go into his office anyway. Somehow, she'd been expecting it to be dated and stuck in time, but it was modern, with nice but not-too-expensive-looking furniture. Ryan's eyes were concerned as he asked, "How is Ms. Louise?"

There was something very heartening about how much everyone seemed to care about Grannie. Her hospital room had remained full of fresh flowers, and she'd had a steady stream of visitors at the convalescent center. That knowledge had helped mitigate her own guilt at not being able to be there every day.

Growing up, Helena never understood why Grannie loved living in Magnolia Beach, but then again, Grannie had never done anything to irritate the people. Well, besides having a hellion for a grandchild, of course. But even then, everyone had considered Helena to be Louise's personal cross to bear and kept Grannie as a permanent fixture on the church's prayer list for her patience and attempts to rein Helena in.

"She's chomping at the bit to be released."

"I'm not surprised. When will she be coming home?"

"Two, maybe three, weeks. That's why I'm here."

"So you'll be staying awhile?" Ryan's eyebrows went up again, as if he were calculating the cost of adding an additional officer or the possible property damage. Helena reminded herself not to be annoyed.

"A little while." She sat in the guest chair in front of his desk. "Grannie is going to need a lot of help when she comes home. Which brings me back to you. She can't come home until the house is ready for her. I need ramps built and one of those walk-in bathtubs installed downstairs. We need some grab bars, stuff like that throughout the house, because I don't want her falling again." Just the thought put a sick feeling in her stomach. "Grannie wants you, specifically, to do the work."

Ryan leaned against his desk. "Tell Ms. Louise that I'm flattered."

"But . . . ?" she prompted.

"No but. I'll be happy to do it."

"Great. That's a big relief." And it was. The construction on the house was the biggest weight on her shoulders right now. And since she really didn't have the time to vet a parade of contractors, she'd go with Grannie's assurance that he was the best in Magnolia Beach. "I have some errands to run this morning, but I'll be home after that. You can come by anytime this afternoon or tonight to take a look and give me some estimates."

Ryan pulled out his phone and checked something. "Sometime after five okay?"

"That'll be great." She started to offer the address, but caught herself. "I think you know how to get to the house."

"That I do." There was that smirk again.

Helena was desperate to ask him what was so damn funny, but she restrained herself. "Then I'll see you this evening, Mayor Tanner." She stood and hitched her bag over her shoulder.

He nodded, and Helena showed herself to the door. "Welcome back to Magnolia Beach, Hell-on-Wheels," Ryan called from behind her. "Stay out of trouble, okay?"

She had to bite her tongue to keep from taking the bait this time. With a nod to Julie on her way out, she pushed through the glass doors and into the sunshine.

Lord have mercy. If this morning was the baseline for what life was going to be like for her the next few weeks . . .

Magnolia Beach had a lot of new businesses. She sincerely hoped one of them was a liquor store.

Ryan watched as Helena left in what could best be called a mild huff. Maybe he shouldn't have needled her like that. It wasn't his best move, but since the other choice had been to drop his tongue to his toes, he'd probably made the *better* choice out of self-preservation.

Helena had been the stuff of teenage fantasy: pretty, but not unapproachably beautiful, wild and possibly dangerous, inspiring fear and envy and disdain at the same time. She ran with a crowd of mostly older boys—many of them delinquents themselves—giving her a scary-sharp edge and a mouth that could cut you down to size without missing a beat.

The combination had been both alluring and detracting, much talked about in locker rooms and over illicit beers on the beach. So while Helena might have inspired the fantasies and starred in the dreams of many Magnolia Beach boys, very few had had the courage to act. They all knew she was way out of their league. Hitting on Helena seemed like a good way to have your head handed back to you.

He'd managed to stay out of her direct line of fire—most of the time—mainly because they'd run in different social circles. And though those circles didn't overlap, they did grate against each other pretty regularly with the expected antagonistic results. He knew Helena hadn't cared for him back then, but any chance he might have ever had to change her mind had ended when she up and left with a deckhand from one of the charter boats.

She never came back. Until now.

That allure should have faded over time, so the fresh rush of temptation had rocked him back on his heels. She'd certainly grown up pretty—the big brown eyes and dark hair were just as he remembered, but there was something . . . *softer* about her. More approachable.

She'd been casually dressed—jeans, a V-neck tee that just hinted at cleavage, minimal makeup—but that didn't have a girl-next-door effect. And the spike in his blood pressure wasn't adolescent at all.

Damn.

Julie stuck her head around the door. "Well, she's back. Can you believe it?"

"You thought she wouldn't come home?"

"I'm just surprised. Lord knows, she hasn't set foot in town for anything else. Not that I'm complaining, mind you," she added, "but it seems like she just fell off the face of the earth."

That was somewhat true. Helena's legendary status had only grown in her absence—mainly because it was a *complete* absence. Ms. Louise was always quick to mention a gift sent by Helena, and her neighbors had given her rides to the Mobile airport for what she called her "girl trips," but for the most part, even Ms. Louise had stayed silent about Helena's life after Magnolia Beach. "I think an injured grandmother who needs care trumps everything else."

"Ms. Louise has friends and neighbors who would be happy to help."

"It's not the same thing as family."

Julie shook her head sadly. "And even there the poor woman hasn't had much luck, has she?"

In a town the size of Magnolia Beach, where everything was everyone's business and fence-row gossip was the local pastime, it was considered a real shame that someone as well-liked and good as Ms. Louise had been dealt a rather poor hand: widowed young, then left to raise Helena on her own after her son died and Helena's mother ran off. Not that anyone would say that to her face, though. People shook their heads over Helena but maintained that Ms. Louise had done the best she could, considering the circumstances. "I don't think Helena is a bad grandchild, only one who lives far away."

It wasn't uncommon or anything; Magnolia Beach was a small town, and many of its young people left, never to return. As mayor, though, he was working hard to make Magnolia Beach a place they'd want to come back to.

Julie merely shrugged.

"Well, Helena's here now, when it counts, so give her credit for that much."

Julie's mouth twisted, and Ryan bit back a smile. Old grudges died hard, it seemed. Everyone knew about Mike and Helena at homecoming, and Julie obviously wasn't ready to let that go just yet.

"No one ever accused her of lacking nerve—that's for sure. *Anyway*," Julie said, her tone changing the subject rather nicely as she put a folder on his desk, "there's not much happening here today. Just a few things you need to sign." She left, leaving the door open behind her.

A few moments later, he heard the clatter of her fingers flying over her keyboard and figured e-mails were pinging into in-boxes all over town, heralding Helena's return.

Shaking his head, he flipped open the file. A couple of permits, the winners' certificates for the school's spelling bee, the minutes from the last council meeting. An average day and the reason this job was only part-time at best. Magnolia Beach was a good place, with good people, and it pretty much rolled along without much hassle or drama.

That was part of its charm.

And since he sincerely doubted Helena would find time to set fire to the football equipment shed again, he could enjoy the minor shake-up she'd cause by being here.

His mayoral duties completed for the day, he had a full half hour before he needed to be anywhere else, so he logged on to check his e-mail. With nothing important awaiting him there, either, he went online to Google Helena's name.

Seconds before he could, though, Julie stuck her head around the door. "Your brother just called—"

"Adam or Eli?" he asked without looking up.

"Adam. He said to let you know that your uncle Dave just left his office and will be here in about one minute."

Damn it. He quickly closed the search window and stood. "That's not much warning."

"He said it would give you enough time to prepare yourself but not enough time to escape," she said with a smirk.

Hard on her words, he heard the front door open. Julie shrugged a halfhearted apology and stepped aside as his uncle Dave's burly frame filled the doorway.

"I was just out for my walk and thought I'd stop in to say hello." Without waiting for an invitation, Uncle Dave came in and sat.

Ryan believed in an open-door policy, and there was a high level of casualness to the position of mayor of Magnolia Beach, but this was no spur-of-the-moment drive-by visit. His uncle had been mayor for too many years and had never quite let the job go. He was just lucky Uncle Dave deigned to sit in the guest chair instead of behind the desk. These casual "just stopped in to say hello" visits had led to the last two mayors severely limiting their terms.

It hadn't taken Ryan long to understand why, but he

had it worse than his predecessors. It was different when it was family. As his uncle liked to remind him when he protested, someone who'd changed his diapers was not going to be put off easily. And that basically included an entire generation of Magnolia Beach residents.

At least Uncle Dave didn't beat around the bush. "Word has it you're going to sign off on that new cell tower."

Not again. "I am aware of your objections, but it has to be done. We're trying to attract people to Magnolia Beach, and folks just don't like to go places where they can't get a good cell signal. They don't like to be disconnected from the world."

"I think it would be a selling point. To really get away from it all. That is the purpose of vacations."

"You said the same thing when we put in the town Wi-Fi, and it's proven itself a good investment."

"It'll be an eyesore."

"So are many necessities of modern life. But you'll be glad to know that the council chose a site specifically not to mar the view." The cell tower itself wasn't the problem, and Ryan knew it. The real problem was that the new cell tower was another step in his larger plan to improve Magnolia Beach, and *that* made some people nervous.

Uncle Dave began mumbling about how it would give them all brain cancer, and Ryan crossed that topic off his mental list. They could now move on to the prospects of the football team, people flying flags improperly, and, his perennial favorite, the length of his hair. Ryan furrowed his brow and pointedly gave his watch a worried look, hoping he would take the hint.

No such luck. Uncle Dave sat back in the chair and got comfortable. "I hear Hell-on-Wheels rolled back into town today. And that she was looking for you."

He hadn't been expecting *that* particular topic. *Good to know the Magnolia Beach grapevine is in full working order, though.* "I hear she prefers to just go by Helena these days. And, yes, she found me. There's some work that needs to be done on Ms. Louise's house, and I've agreed to do it. Hopefully Ms. Louise will get to come home soon."

"Glad to hear it. It'll be good to have her back. I'm looking forward to seeing how she turned out."

Ryan had only been half listening, nodding along, pretending to be busy, but that last bit had his head snapping up. He thought Uncle Dave had been talking about Ms. Louise. "How who turned out? Helena?"

"Of course Helena. I remember when the sheriff hauled her and that Paul Chatham in, both of them soaked to the bone, covered in mud, and madder than wet hens. . . ." He trailed off into chuckles. "He knew they'd been up to something, but he just couldn't prove what. The man was half-crazed for weeks trying to find a crime to fit the suspects." The chuckles morphed into full-belly laughs that had tears rolling down his cheeks. "Definitely a pistol, that girl. Always loaded and no safety. She kept everyone on their toes."

Ryan thought he was doing an admirable job of keeping his jaw from dropping open. "Yet you're the one who hauled her in front of the town council over the water tower incident." Uncle Dave certainly hadn't found *that* quite so amusing at the time.

Uncle Dave shrugged. "It had to be done. I thought it might put the fear of God in her before she got into some kind of real trouble."

Who is this man, and what has he done with my uncle? "*Real* trouble? Defacing town property wasn't *real* trouble?"

Uncle Dave waved him off. "It was just teenage mischief, and not even maliciously done. And, anyway, I'd been trying to get the council to approve the funds to repaint that tower for months. Helena helped me along. Once she painted over her artwork, the rest of the thing looked so bad, the council had to release the money." He raised an eyebrow. "Speaking of which . . . it's looking like it could use a fresh coat again."

Ryan was still stuck at the dismissal of Helena's petty-crime spree as "teenage mischief," so it took him a second to catch up to the conversation. "I'll add it to the list," he managed.

"Good." Uncle Dave pushed himself to his feet. Now that he had said his piece, his visit was over. "And when you see Helena again, you tell her I said welcome home." With a wave, he was gone.

Ryan sat back in his chair and scrubbed a hand across his face. This had been the oddest morning.

But he didn't have time to mull it over, as his phone was buzzing and he had to stop for supplies before meeting his crew at the Jones place. And he didn't have the time now to look up Helena, either, as curious as he was, and that annoyed him more than he expected.

He stopped by Julie's desk to return the signed papers, but Julie merely nodded and waved, her attention more focused on whoever was on the other end of the phone balanced between her ear and shoulder. Her voice was low, but he still heard "Helena" and "unbelievable."

He smiled. He could get supplies, go to the Jones place for a while, and then stop by the post office in a couple of hours. By then, the grapevine would have done its job and Anna Grace would have all the available information on Helena Wheeler, down to her shoe size, ready to share.

Living in a small town had its perks.

Chapter 2

Helena cursed as the download failed again and reached for her beer. Grannie might be able to function with a dial-up modem that dated from 1996, but Helena was going to have to get the cable guys out here with some technology from *this* century. She always bragged about how she was fortunate enough to be able to work from anywhere—assuming that "anywhere" had high-speed Internet access. But that wasn't Grannie's.

Frustrated, she shut down the laptop. Tomorrow, she'd go in search of somewhere with free Wi-Fi. Maybe that coffee shop Tate mentioned would have it.

Leaving the laptop on the table, she took her beer to the front porch. Pretty much all the houses looked the same here, all built in the mid to late sixties after Hurricane Betsy flooded the area in 1965. The beach-style clapboard bungalows had wide porches and postage-stamp-sized yards, and only the paint colors and different flowers in the beds made it possible to tell them apart. There were children playing ball in the street while parents washed their cars in the driveways, and she could smell hamburgers grilling not far away. *Idyllic. Charming. Monotonous.*

I miss my life already. She'd only been away from it for a day, but the long weeks she'd spend here, in Magnolia Beach, stretched ahead of her like a desolate desert highway.

Oh, there were other things she could be doing—she had a nice, long list—but she closed her eyes and set the swing in motion instead. It was hard to dredge up a real sense of urgency when she was still pitying herself for having to be here at all.

Misha, the friend who was keeping her plants alive in Atlanta, had taken on the role of life coach, earnestly encouraging her to use this time to both reconnect with her past and discover something new about herself. It had been all she could do not to laugh in Misha's face. She didn't *want* to reconnect with her past. Hell, that Helena felt like a completely different person, a stranger—self-centered, selfish, and really angry at the whole world. That wasn't someone she'd like to get to know again. A lot of it had been relatively harmless adolescent trouble, the consequence of the dangerous mix of small-town boredom and a still-developing frontal lobe, but there was a line, and she'd been dancing right along it. No one wanted to be the one to send Ms. Louise's granddaughter off to juvie, though—and she'd been smart enough not to do anything too damn dumb or felonious—so she'd done a hell of a lot of community service. So much of it that it was practically her first job. She could still remember that horrid orange safety vest she'd been forced to wear—and the mocking attitude of the deputy when he'd written Hell-on-Wheels across the back in black permanent marker.

She vaguely wondered if that vest was still around someplace. She snorted at the thought. They'd probably tucked it inside her permanent record.

Hence her avoidance of Magnolia Beach, a small town with an ability to carry a big grudge. The cards had been stacked against her from the get-go: Her mother had been an unknown entity, some wild thing her father found and knocked up on a trip to Jacksonville, and most people worried that even the influence of a God-fearing, good woman like Louise Wheeler might not be able to counteract Helena's questionable DNA. Her mother hadn't lasted long in Magnolia Beach after her father died, leaving when Helena was just a couple of months old, but those few months had made an impression on the local population—and not in a good way. The first time Helena stepped out of line, all her mother's sins had been remembered and reexamined. And since everyone claimed apples didn't fall far from their trees, most people assumed Helena was on the exact same path of trouble and bad news. Talk about a self-fulfilling prophecy.

She'd been lucky, though, getting it under control before her life became a cautionary tale suitable for an after-school special, but there was no pride or triumph in her story. She just wanted to forget it.

As for discovering something new about herself . . . That was a laugh. She'd been on that journey, *thankyouverymuch*. There was only so much introspection a person could do. Parental rejection leading to anger issues and attention-seeking behavior, blah, blah, blah—she'd done the therapy *and* had a shelf full of self-help books. She owned a business, paid her taxes, and donated to charities. She might not be *respectable*, but she was about as close as she was going to get. And that would just have to be enough for these people.

So, at best, she was going to discover how long she could survive being back in a town where the traffic lights went blinky at eleven o'clock—all three of them.

With a sigh and a strong mental shake, she drained the last of her drink. She could sit here and feel sorry for herself, or she could just deal. Since hosting a pity party wasn't going to change things, she'd deal.

Just like she'd always done.

But one look around Grannie's house, full of fifty-some-odd years' worth of stuff, was almost enough to send her back for another drink or a hide under the covers. "Clean out the sunroom" seemed like a manageable-enough task on paper, but in reality . . .

The knock at the door seemed like a small gift from God. She could postpone without feeling like she was procrastinating. Getting estimates from Ryan Tanner would also count as being productive.

But it was Tate at the door, not Ryan, and he greeted her with another hug that lifted her off her feet.

"Someone's been working out," she teased. "Come on in."

Tate looked around and smiled. "I haven't been in here in so long. It looks exactly the same, though."

She nodded. "Grannie's not one for change. Can I get you a beer? Can you stay awhile?" She sounded desperate, but perhaps she was. Just being back here was messing with her head. Plus, it was too quiet: The sound of children playing in the streets was actually a little creepy for someone more used to the city and traffic noise of her neighborhood.

"I was actually going to see if you wanted to go get that dinner I promised you."

That sounded divine, but . . . "I can't. I'm waiting on Ryan Tanner to come by to give me some estimates."

"When?"

"Sometime after five." She looked at the clock, saw it was five forty-five, shrugged, and went to the fridge. Tate shook his head when she offered him a beer, so she poured him a glass of tea instead. "He's worse than the cable company."

"Well, he's got football practice, so there's no telling what time he'll get here."

She leaned against the counter. "Isn't he a little old for that?"

"Ryan's one of the coaches now."

"Somehow, that doesn't surprise me." *He probably runs a scout troop, too. Wonder what the adult equivalent of "teacher's pet" is?* It was a little scary how quickly she'd reverted to her seventeen-year-old self. She took a long swallow of her beer.

"Hey, now, we've been to the state championships twice since he started coaching—something that hasn't happened since . . . well, since Ryan was still playing, probably."

"Go, Pirates," she deadpanned.

"Still not a football fan, huh?"

"I could not care less if I tried."

Tate gasped, hand to his chest in fake horror. "That's unnatural."

She made a face at him. "I actually want to hear about you, and what you've been up to, *Dr.* Harris."

"That's really all I've been up to. I was in school forever, then came back here and took over Doc Masters's practice when he retired last year."

"I'm so proud." He gave her a look, so she clarified, "No, I really am proud of you. That's great."

He accepted that with a nod. "And you?"

"I do graphic design. An online one-woman thing."

"I knew you'd end up doing something artsy."

"I've got pretty steady work, so I'm lucky. I love it *and* it pays the bills."

"Perfect combo." He tapped his glass against her bottle.

"Exactly." She stared him down. "But you . . . no wife, no kids? What's up with that?"

He nearly choked on his drink. "I could ask the same of you," he said, deflecting the question.

She shook her head in mock sadness. "Alas, the state of Georgia won't let me have a wife."

Tate laughed. "Then we'll just call that a topic neither of us wishes to discuss."

"Good call. What about Ellie and Sam?" She was suddenly hungry for news, which was strange. She hadn't even thought about most of these people in ages, and now that made her sad. And a little ashamed.

"Ellie's in Mobile—married, two kids, happy. Sam got divorced last year and moved back here. I'm sure she'd love to see you."

Tate had practically raised his sisters, and she could hear in his voice that he still adored them. "That's great, and I'd love to catch up with Sam if there's time." Carefully, she asked, "What about your parents?"

"Mom's still in the same place. The old man died about eight years ago," he said flatly.

Glad to hear it, she thought, but said, "I didn't know," instead. She wouldn't offer sympathy, and she knew Tate didn't expect it. Mr. Harris had been an evil, hateful man who only got worse when he drank. And it was a well-known secret how he took it out on his kids. She wasn't the least bit sorry the man was dead, and she wouldn't mouth platitudes she knew Tate didn't need or want to hear.

Tate quickly changed the subject. "So when are you going to let me take you to dinner and show you the sights of Magnolia Beach?"

"Magnolia Beach has sights?" she teased.

"A few. You've probably seen most of them, but we do have some nice restaurants now and a bar with live music three nights a week."

"Goodness, when will we have time to fit it all in?" At Tate's shrug, she added, "Well, my dance card isn't exactly full these days, so pretty much whenever is good for you. I should probably wait to make any concrete plans until I hear what Ryan's going to do and when he's going to do it. . . ." On cue, she heard Ryan call her name from the porch. "Speak of the devil. Come on in," she shouted as she headed back that way.

Ryan already had one foot in the door. Another difference between life here and in Atlanta. She'd already quit locking her door, and the only thing strange about a man letting himself into her house was that it actually wasn't strange at all. That, and the fact she'd reverted back to old habits so quickly. Hell, that was downright disturbing.

"Sorry I'm running late," Ryan said with an apologetic grin. "The boys were acting up, and there were laps that had to be run. . . ." He trailed off and cocked his head sideways. "Tate. I didn't expect to see you here."

Tate's nod was brief and quick. "Ryan."

There was an odd moment of tension Helena didn't quite understand. "What? Surprised there's at least one person who's glad I'm back?"

"Oh, there are several, I'm sure," Ryan said wryly. "Some might even surprise you."

She laughed. "Well, that would be a pleasant surprise, indeed." Setting down her beer, she turned to Tate. "It's my turn to cut things short. Sorry."

"No problem. Thanks for the tea." Tate set his glass on the table next to hers, then leaned in to plant a kiss on her cheek. "I'll call you tomorrow about that dinner."

"You'd better."

With another of those brisk nods in Ryan's direction, Tate was gone. Ryan watched him leave.

Helena picked up the list of work for Ryan she'd started earlier. "Okay, let's start with the—"

"That was fast."

"Excuse me?"

"You're back less than twenty-four hours and you already have a date with Tate Harris?"

That was so far out of left field that she laughed. "What— are you jealous or something?"

Ryan's head snapped around. "Huh?"

"Unless *you* have a thing for Tate, why would you even care?" she asked.

"Tate Harris is considered quite the eligible bachelor in Magnolia Beach. You'll make a whole *new* set of enemies if you poach him."

It hadn't occurred to her that Tate would be an "eligible bachelor," but it did make sense now that Ryan mentioned it. He'd grown up to be downright adorable *and* successful. "I'm not 'poaching' anyone. And even if I wanted to poach, Magnolia Beach's womenfolk could have him back in just a few weeks."

An eyebrow went up. "Just a few weeks, huh?"

"Believe me when I say I do not intend to stay a second longer than absolutely necessary. I have a life in Atlanta, thank you very much, and I can't wait to get back to it as soon as humanly possible."

"Ah, well, *that's* the spirit."

The sarcasm grated. She held the list in his direction. "Shall we?"

He nodded at the bottle in her other hand. "Are you

not going to offer me a beer first? Tsk, tsk, what's happened to your manners?"

"The rest of the world doesn't normally offer alcoholic beverages to random tradesmen, you know." But even as she said it, she was already heading to the fridge.

Ryan accepted the bottle with a nod of thanks, and she held the list in his direction again.

This time, he took it, but he didn't bother to look at it. "Let's start at the front of the house."

She followed him out the front door onto the porch, but before he could start talking, he was interrupted by a high-pitched yapping bark. A small black smudge jumped out of the open window of Ryan's truck and ran to sit at his feet, growling a warning at her. She jumped back a step. "What the hell?"

Ryan inclined his head toward it. "And that's Tank."

Tank was quite possibly the strangest-looking dog she'd ever seen. He was one of those hairless breeds, which gave him a rather ratlike appearance. He had a bit of an overbite and the little-dog antsiness that made his toenails click against the wooden planks as he danced around Ryan's ankles. He was tiny, maybe five or six pounds, tops, and he alternated between shooting her dirty looks and staring adoringly up at Ryan. "Tank?"

"Tank doesn't let his size affect his ego. He thinks he's bigger than he is."

Tank couldn't do her any real damage, but those teeth looked sharp nonetheless and would probably hurt if he got ahold of her. "He belongs to you?"

"I think I belong to him, actually. He just showed up on my porch one day, and when I opened the door, he wandered in like he owned the place."

"That's sweet." Especially since Ryan seemed more like a yellow Lab kind of guy. "Hysterical, but sweet."

"He comes with me to work sometimes, but he's happy hanging under the truck in the shade. He won't bother you. So, you'll need a ramp. . . ."

Over the next half hour, Helena developed a grudging admiration for Ryan. He obviously knew his stuff—

pointing out missing items on her list and coming up with different ways to solve the most obvious problems—and some of the not so obvious ones, too. For what seemed like the fiftieth time, she said, "I hadn't thought about that."

"This isn't my first rodeo, you know. We have a lot of retirees down here, not to mention the snowbirds who arrive every October. Adaptations to accommodate an aging population are a booming business." He looked at his notes. "Do you have a budget in mind?"

"Of course."

After a moment's pause, Ryan added, "And that number would be . . . ?"

His attitude gave her great pleasure to be able to say, "Something we'll discuss after I've seen your bid."

"You think I'll inflate the numbers?" Insult was stamped across his face.

She shrugged. "I think it's unwise to tell anyone how much you're willing to pay until you've seen how much they want to charge."

"Wow. There's some trust issues for you."

"It has nothing to do with trust or the lack thereof. It's just good business. Or didn't they teach you that up at Auburn's business school?" It was all she could do not to laugh at the look on his face. "I made a trip to the post office for some stamps. The new girl—Anna Grace?—is a true font of information."

Ryan looked a little exasperated. "She takes after her aunt."

Although she didn't know why she cared, she still asked, "When did Mrs. Trunbill finally retire?"

"Just a few years ago."

"Lord, she must have been eighty or something."

Ryan shook his head. "Sixty-five."

"Really?" That didn't seem possible.

"People just look older when you're younger."

"I guess." Old gossip popped back into her mind. "Is it true that Mrs. Trunbill sent letters to every male in town who had a *Playboy* subscription, threatening to tell their mothers about it?"

"She could have gotten fired for doing something like that," he said, looking distinctly uncomfortable.

"That wasn't my ques— *Oooh*, not only is it true, but you got one, didn't you?"

Ryan cleared his throat, but his neck and ears were reddening. "So, that front ramp . . ."

"There's nothing to be ashamed of. I understand most men only read it for the articles." She was trying to keep a straight face, but she felt the giggles bubbling up inside her. "And, from what I hear, the photography is really . . . artistic."

"You tell me. Isn't art *your* thing?"

It was a clever turning of the tables. "Excuse me?"

"You're an artist of some sort, aren't you?" She felt her eyebrows go up, and he smirked. "You're not the only one who went to the post office today."

Ugh. She'd forgotten the grapevine would work both ways. "I'm a graphic designer. I design brochures and bookmarks and logos and stuff. It's artistic, but not exactly art in the conventional sense."

"So you'll be able to work while you're here?"

Why would he care? "Eventually, yeah."

"Eventually?"

She couldn't keep the sigh out of her voice. "Grannie's still on dial-up, so downloading files is a bit of a problem at the moment."

"The town Wi-Fi probably doesn't reach this far," he said casually, as if this weren't shocking news or any-thing. "If you take your laptop down to the diner—or anywhere on Front Street, really—you should have a good signal."

She was still processing the first part of that state-ment. "Magnolia Beach has Wi-Fi?" Jeez, she'd thought the coffee shop was progress.

"Yes, we do," he said smugly. "Welcome to this cen-tury."

"Glad the town could join the rest of the world."

"Like I said, you'd be surprised at how much things have changed around here."

There was a challenge in Ryan's voice, but Helena wasn't exactly sure why—mayoral pride, maybe? "I'm more surprised at how much they *haven't* changed, actually. Hell, it still looks exactly the same."

"So you're saying if things don't *look* different, they can't actually *be* different?" An eyebrow went up as Ryan looked her over from head to toe. "You don't look all that different, Hell-on-Wheels. Are you saying that you haven't changed, either? Should I put the chief and deputy sheriff on alert?"

That was a low blow. She couldn't even defend herself without sounding ridiculous and there was no way in hell she was giving Ryan Tanner that pleasure. She cleared her throat. "So, I can assume you'll get all the proper permits that might be needed, and that all the work will be up to code?"

He shot her a look that called her a chicken more clearly than words ever could. "Of course."

She drained the last of her beer and went to get another. She was going to need it.

Ryan was having a hard time focusing on the figures in front of him. While there was nothing new or unusual about what needed to be done at Ms. Louise's, he'd figured it three times already and come up with three different sets of numbers.

He might as well pull an estimate straight out of his ass at this point. It couldn't be much further off-base than the mess he had in front of him.

Dear Lord, it was downright embarrassing the way he'd lost a decade of maturity—and slid a few rungs down the evolutionary ladder—just by being around Helena. He would have thought that at thirty-three, he'd be a bit more suave. Instead, he'd shown up at her house to find Tate Harris asking her out—on her first damn day back in town—and he'd been slammed with something he could only classify as jealousy.

Which made zero sense.

But there *was* something different about her, something he couldn't quite pin down, and it bothered him that he couldn't.

When his phone rang, he checked the caller ID and sighed. "Hi, Mom."

"I saw your light on. Is everything all right?"

His mother had to stand in the far back corner of her yard and crane her neck at an unnatural angle to see his house from hers, yet she insisted on pretending it was nothing more than a casual glance. *I have to move.* "It's late, Mom, and you're up. Maybe I should be asking you if everything's all right."

"I got up to let the dog out." The irritation in her voice called him out for sassing her.

"And I'm trying to get some work done."

"At midnight?"

"They don't call it 'burning the midnight oil' for nothing."

Concern replaced the irritation. "You're working too hard," she said, a truly ironic statement from a small-town doctor's wife who should really be used to work at any and all odd hours.

He rolled his eyes, safe in the knowledge she couldn't see him do it. "No, just working enough. In fact, I'm about to go to bed."

"I hear you're going to be doing some work on Louise Wheeler's house."

And now we get to the point of this call. "I am. She'll be coming home in a couple of weeks."

"That's good news."

He waited.

"And how's Helena?"

"Good, I think. We mainly talked about the job, but she seems healthy and happy."

"That's good to hear. I'm glad for her."

Maybe Mom's been drinking tonight. "Really, Mom? You never liked her."

He could almost hear his mother's lips pressing together in irritation. "I thought she was bad news, I won't deny that. But I'm not going to wish her ill now."

"That's very kind of you." *I don't know who this woman is.*

"Everyone deserves a chance at redemption. I think we should just all wait and see."

Somehow he couldn't picture Helena on a quest for redemption in the eyes of the citizens of Magnolia Beach. In fact, she seemed completely unapologetic for her youth, and he'd be a little disappointed in her if she tried to make amends. That like-it-or-not-I-don't-care-either-way attitude commanded respect for her strength, if nothing else.

He stood and stretched, then turned out the lamp on his desk. That should give his mother a hint. "Well, everyone can rest easy because she's not in town for long. Just until Ms. Louise gets settled."

"Then everything will work out just fine. Now, I'm going to go back to bed, and I think you should do the same."

"I'm headed there now."

"Good night, sweetheart. Sleep well."

"You, too, Mom." He left the phone on the desk and headed for the bedroom.

There were many benefits to living in small towns, but when the return of one teenage delinquent became the biggest news of the week . . . Good God.

He felt a little sorry for her.

But he couldn't shake his head and tsk-tsk at the gossips with long memories and nothing better to do, especially when he was just as bad. There were those who condemned her and those who were fascinated by her, and those camps hadn't shifted much in the intervening years.

She wasn't going to have an easy time of it.

Of course, neither were the men in Camp Fascination. And Ryan was honest enough to admit he was flying the flag there, too, these days. It didn't make a lot of sense, and might actually prove he needed some kind of therapy, but it was true, nonetheless.

The question was, what was he going to do about it?

Chapter 3

Latte Dah was everything Tate had promised and far more than Helena had dared hope for. Adorable, but not at all cheesy, with comfy-looking chairs and quiet corners, a pastry case that added five inches to her thighs just looking at the contents, and a board of coffee descriptions that nearly brought tears to her eyes. As she stood in line, she watched the barista hand over a cappuccino with a perfect heart in the foam, and Helena wanted to crawl over the counter to hug her.

Thank you, God, for small favors. She might just survive the next few weeks after all.

Helena watched the woman closely, searching for the familiar, but as far as she could tell, she'd never met her before. *Bonus.* She had a riot of curls held back from her face with a headband and a wide sunny smile that she turned on Helena. "And what can I get for you?"

Helena took a deep breath, letting the rich aromas filter into her bloodstream, then sighed happily. "One of everything. With an extra shot."

Her smile widened. "It *is* possible to overdose on caffeine, you know." Then her voice dropped conspiratorially. "But since you seem to be a serious drinker, I can make you my special triple-shot cappuccino. It's practically rocket fuel."

"That's what I heard. Hook me up."

"I'm glad my reputation precedes me." She stuck a hand over the counter. "I'm Molly. The proud owner of Latte Dah."

"It's very nice to meet you—*and* Latte Dah. I'm Helena."

Molly's eyebrows went up. "And it's great to meet *you*. Welcome home."

She was buoyed enough by the thought of that triple-shot cappuccino to be amused instead of annoyed. "Wow. News travels *really* damn fast in this town."

"Tate Harris was in this morning. He told me you might be coming by," she said by way of explanation. "Your coffee's on him, by the way."

"What a sweetie."

Molly looked down quickly and reached for a cup. "That he is."

Hmm. Did Molly have a thing for Tate? She was as adorable as her shop—petite and blond with a heart-shaped face and big brown eyes. A familiar—but forgotten—pang hit her stomach, awakening her inner Mama Bear. Tate was special, and he deserved someone equally as amazing. "So, how long have you been in town?"

"About two years. I'm originally from Fuller, up near Florence." Molly's hands were efficient and sure as she worked and talked at the same time. "But they already had a coffee shop, so I moved here."

"And how do you like it?"

"I love it." She cut her eyes sideways at Helena. "I know it's not for everyone, though."

There was no sense pretending she didn't know what Molly was getting at. "Very true. But the feeling is mutual. I don't really want to be here any more than folks want me here." She planted that seed in case Molly was the type to spread a little gossip herself.

"You might be surprised. I know Tate's glad you're back."

"I don't think Tate Harris has the most unbiased of opinions, though."

"Maybe not, but you're not the only person who's ever

gone someplace else to start over and reinvent themselves." Helena watched as Molly created beautiful leaves in the foam of her drink. Molly shrugged. "Magnolia Beach has grown some, even in just the time I've been here. You might find a kindred spirit or two."

There was something in Molly's voice that made Helena smile. "Not missing Fuller much, are you?"

"Not a damn bit." Molly was biting back a smile of her own as she handed over the cup. "Want a lemon bar to go with that? They're from Miller's Bakery."

She nearly drooled at the thought. Mrs. Miller made the best lemon bars in the state. "Oh yes, *please*."

"That's a sign of a native, right there. There's not a single person in this town who can resist one. Grab a seat. I'll bring it to you."

All traces of Mrs. Logan's yarn store were gone. The walls were a soothing shade of blue, a perfect backdrop for the beach-themed art and historical Magnolia Beach photos that covered the walls. Shelves with magazines and newspapers and knickknacks for sale helped create more private spaces, perfect for smaller groups to meet or a budding novelist to write.

The overstuffed chairs would be perfect for curling up with a magazine on a rainy day, but today wasn't rainy and Helena didn't have time to flip through magazines. Instead, she set up camp at a marble-topped table surrounded by mismatched chairs and pulled out her laptop.

Molly came over a minute later with the lemon bar and set it in front of her. "We have a coffee club that gets you discounts on the 'Bean of the Month,' a writers' group that meets every Thursday afternoon, and an open-mike night every other Saturday. The Wi-Fi password is 'coffee,' all lowercase. I hope you'll make yourself at home, Helena."

"Thank you." And she meant it. It was nice to know that not everyone was going to judge her based on what they had heard—and Helena didn't doubt that in Molly's case it was an earful. She put in her headphones and logged into her e-mail.

As she waited for the browser to load, she shook a bit of the powdered sugar off the lemon bar and took a bite. It melted on her tongue, the buttery cookie and grab-your-tonsils tartness even better than she remembered. And chased with Molly's special cappuccino . . . *Ah*, she might have just died and gone to heaven. Tasty, caffeinated heaven.

Client e-mails and files automatically sorted into their proper folders, leaving only a few e-mails in her box—including one from Ryan Tanner with the estimates for the job attached. She clicked it open first.

It was less than she expected. Way less, actually. Even accounting for the cost of living in Magnolia Beach versus Atlanta, it seemed too good to be true. A closer look showed him charging next to nothing for the labor.

They'd talked about the schedule, the need to get this done quickly versus the commitments he already had, and how Ryan would have to work odd hours around those commitments. She'd prepared herself for overtime and additional labor charges, so this couldn't be right.

Was this some kind of joke? A lowball bid to be inflated later when the work was half-done and she'd have no choice but to accept? So much for small-town honesty.

She grabbed her phone and stepped outside. Ryan answered on the third ring.

"I got your bid."

"And hello to you, too, Helena. If the bid's acceptable, I'll get started this week."

"What the hell?"

"I don't know what you mean." He sounded genuinely confused.

She took a deep breath, trying to keep her temper under control and her dealings with Ryan professional. Or as professional as she could manage. "There's no way that's what it'll cost."

"Accusing me of padding again?"

"No. It looks like you underbid. By a lot."

"And since when do you know how much a job like that should cost?"

"I'm not ignorant," she snapped.

"I never said you were, Helena."

"Then what?"

She could almost hear the shrug. "Consider it a friends and family discount."

She bit her tongue to keep from flaying him. This was even worse than potential shady dealings. She and Grannie might never have been the wealthiest of families in Magnolia Beach, but they weren't poor trailer trash, either. She didn't need his discount. "But we are neither friends nor family."

"I wasn't referring to you. I was referring to Ms. Louise."

"Who is also not your family—and not your friend, either. We'll pay the going rate."

"That's my bid. You're welcome to get others, but from what I understand, Ms. Louise was rather adamant that I do the work." He sounded downright smug, and it was a good thing for him that he wasn't within striking distance.

She had to lower her voice as people walking by were beginning to give her strange looks. "Since you claim to be such good friends with my grandmother, you should be well aware that she doesn't want or need your charity."

"Jesus, it's not charity. It's the price I want to charge for the job you want me to do. Why is that such a problem for you?"

Because she had her pride. And a healthy skepticism for things too good to be true. She wasn't about to let him collect more stars for his crown for doing the damn job she was hiring him for and *paying* him to do. More importantly, she didn't want to be in any kind of debt to Ryan Freakin' Tanner—or anyone else for that matter. Even the simplest small-town kindness always had strings attached. But she said none of that. "It just is. I'd rather pay the full price. I assure you I can afford it."

"And I assure *you* that I can afford to do this job for the quoted price."

She had to pry her jaw apart to speak. "I insist."

She heard his sigh. "So do I."

"Ryan Tanner—"

"If you're so concerned about charity," he interrupted, "then take whatever you think the difference would be and donate it to the charity of your choice. In Ms. Louise's honor, of course."

There was a challenge in his voice that made her eye begin to twitch. She now had to decide whether or not to stand her ground with Ryan and tell Grannie she'd chosen someone else to do the work. Assuming, of course, that there was another general contractor in Magnolia Beach who could do it.

The other option just rankled her. Why the hell would Ryan turn down money unless he thought she couldn't afford it? She could—albeit not *easily*—but it was none of his goddamn business either way.

Ah, screw it. If Ryan Tanner wanted to give away his time and money, it was no skin off her nose.

"Well, Helena? Are we on?"

She swallowed hard—it wasn't her pride she was forcing down, but somehow it still managed to feel like it. "We're on. I'm amazed you're able to stay in business, but consider your bid accepted."

"Then I'll call you tomorrow. You'll need to make some decisions on paint and such."

"You have my number, and you know where I live. The sooner we can get this done, the better."

She hung up and made a face at the phone. Wrenching open the door to Latte Dah, she stomped back over to the table, where her computer had gone to sleep and her coffee had gotten cold. *Damn it. He even ruined my coffee.*

Molly came over, her forehead wrinkled in concern. "Everything okay?"

She forced herself to smile. "Nothing another cup of coffee and another lemon bar wouldn't fix." She'd go for a run later to burn off the calories—and maybe some frustration, too.

Molly patted her shoulder in sympathy and support. "We've all had those kinds of phone calls, and on those days, I'm sorry I don't have a liquor license."

"Oh, that would make this place heaven on earth. I'd never leave."

Molly laughed as she took away the cold cup, and a moment later Helena heard the cappuccino machine sputter back to life. Shaking off her anger, she put her earbuds in and turned her music up as she went back to work.

Just a couple of e-mails below the one from Ryan was one from Tate she hadn't noticed earlier.

Busy tonight. Dinner tomorrow?

She hadn't come back to Magnolia Beach to socialize—and after last night's exploration of the house told her exactly what she was in for, God knew she had plenty to occupy her time—but this was Tate. And she really wanted to go.

She glanced up and nodded her thanks as Molly brought a fresh coffee and set it in front of her. If she went to dinner, she could also get a little intel on Molly from Tate—maybe figure out if Molly did have a thing for Tate and whether or not he returned the sentiment.

Yikes. There must be something in the air in Magnolia Beach. She'd been here less than two days, and she was already being sucked back into small-town happenings.

This was definitely going to send her back into therapy.

Ryan looked at his phone, half hoping Siri would pipe up with an explanation of the workings of Helena's mind for him, but had no such luck. He wasn't sure what about this had gotten her panties in a twist, but it seemed no good deed went unpunished. He was just trying to be nice, for God's sake.

To Ms. Louise, of course.

A crash and a curse pulled him sharply back into the moment, and he ran to see what had happened. Unsurprisingly, a red-faced Tucker stood over an overturned wheelbarrow, the scrap and trash he'd been taking to the Dumpster now littering the Joneses' front yard.

Tank barked at the racket, then sat and stared at Tucker disapprovingly as Ryan counted slowly to ten and Tucker stammered an explanation. He'd hired Tucker at his aunt's pleading to give him something productive to do while Tucker was "finding himself" after an unsuccessful freshman year at Troy State. Ryan was sympathetic to Tucker's situation—going from being a big trophy fish in a little pond to a tiny minnow in the ocean was a hard blow to the ego and difficult to recover from. *That*, Ryan knew from experience.

Sympathy was one thing, however; reality was another. And the reality of hiring his cousin was a steady, dangerous rise in his blood pressure. Nineteen-year-old arrogance combined with clumsiness and feelings of immortality were just a recipe for disaster. "Clean it up. Be sure to run a magnet to get all the nails out of the grass. The Jones kids should be able to go barefoot in their own yard. If one of them ends up with a nail in his foot, it's your hide on the line."

Tucker nodded, righting the wheelbarrow and dropping to his knees to clean up the mess.

"Good Lord. Tell me you don't let him loose with power tools."

That comment came from behind him, and he answered without even needing to turn around. "God, no. Aunt Claire would never forgive me if Tucker amputated something."

"It would ruin Christmas, you know."

"And we can't have that." Satisfied that Tucker was taking the cleanup seriously enough, he turned to Jamie. "What are you doing here?"

"I just dropped off my mom at your mom's, and she asked me to bring you this." Rolling his eyes, he held out a plastic container. "Pound cake."

Ryan looked at it suspiciously. His cousin wouldn't have been pressed into food delivery service without a good reason. "Are there strings?"

"Why else would Aunt Mary send me to deliver baked goods unless she wanted something?"

"And that would be?"

"I honestly don't know. I rushed out of there before I could get the details."

"I'm glad you're fast on your feet, then."

Jamie grinned. "Years of practice."

Ryan opened the container and took out a piece before offering it to Jamie. The cake was delicious, moist, and flavored with just a hint of maternal interference, as always. Mom would call him later with whatever it was she wanted, so he could enjoy this guilt-free for now. He broke off a small piece and tossed it to Tank.

"A couple of the guys are coming over to play poker tomorrow night. Want to come?"

"Can't," he said around a mouthful of cake. "I've got to install cabinets at the Millers' tomorrow, and then I'm headed to Ms. Louise's to get started on her place."

Jamie gave a low whistle. "That's some dangerous territory."

"How?"

"Hell-on-Wheels, of course."

Ryan laughed. "Really? You're still holding a high school grudge? Quit being such a baby."

"She didn't humiliate *you* in front of the entire school," he grumbled.

Ryan shook his head. "You won't get any sympathy from me. You brought that on yourself. And it was quite a fair revenge, considering what you did to her."

Jamie didn't have an answer for that. "Still . . ."

He tossed the now-empty container into the cab of his truck. "Seriously, grow up."

An eyebrow went up. "When did you become Helena's champion?"

"What?"

"You two weren't exactly friends."

"True, but unlike *some* people, I've outgrown my adolescence."

Jamie looked at him carefully. "So *that's* how it is."

"So that's how what is?"

"You've got a little crush on her, don't you?"

"You're crazy."

"I don't think so. Why else would you be pulling overtime at Ms. Louise's if not to get into Helena's good graces?"

"I'm just trying to get a nice old lady back into her home."

"Uh-huh."

"What?"

"That's a good story. You should stick to it."

Good Lord. "I don't need a 'story.' It's a job. Nothing more, nothing less."

"And you're doing it all yourself?"

"You think I should send Tucker over to do it? I'm trying to get Ms. Louise back into her house, not get the place condemned."

"How much are you charging for the overtime?" Jamie cocked his head when Ryan hesitated. "Since I'm the person who does your books, it's a fair question for me to ask."

Note to self: Get new accountant. "I admit I'm giving Ms. Louise a hefty discount, but she's a nice lady who's in a bad spot right now and deserves to get into her home as soon as possible."

If there was such a thing as a sarcastic nod, Jamie had it down pat. "Okay, then. Get your Good Deeds Done for the Elderly merit badge." He dropped his voice. "I hear Hell-on-Wheels grew up pretty, though."

"Go away. I'm trying to work here." For once, Ryan was glad he'd hired Tucker on this summer, as he'd just managed to drop the magnet on his foot, giving credence to Ryan's otherwise lame excuse to get rid of Jamie. "Saving that boy from himself is a full-time job in and of itself."

Jamie let it go. "Good luck with that. And if you change your mind about the poker, there will be a seat at the table for you. Otherwise, see you at the game Friday." With a wave, he was gone.

While Ryan appreciated the pound cake, he could've

done without the visit from Jamie and his insinuations. It was a sad state of affairs when a single man couldn't be around a single woman without someone making more of it. And while a man would have to be blind or dead *not* to see the attraction of Helena's charms—regardless of her reputation with the locals—it was scary to think folks were already expecting him to be charmed by them. Especially since he hadn't made up his own mind on the matter yet.

Just another joy of living in Magnolia Beach.

Chapter 4

A person would think, for practicality's sake if nothing else, that a bridge from Dauphin Island to Fort Morgan would be a good thing. It wasn't like it was a long, impossible stretch of water or anything, and it would certainly cut down on the travel time from the west side to the east side of Mobile Bay. Helena figured the lack of a bridge probably had something to do with boat access or something, but surely some smart person could figure out a way around that—like making it a drawbridge or just really tall, maybe. Instead, the hassle of lining up for the ferry and chugging slowly across the pass made a short-as-the-crow-flies trip into a nearly two-hour affair.

But the ferry ride brought back a touch of nostalgia, too, of high school weekends spent in Gulf Shores—where, in her teenage mind at least, the parties were better, the boys were cuter, and life in general was more exciting than in Magnolia Beach. She smiled to herself. The suspicion that life was better somewhere else was exactly the feeling that fueled small-town boredom and inspired frustrated wanderlust in the teenage population. Unfortunately, she hadn't figured that out until she found herself in Rome, Georgia, with a guy who wasn't nearly as cool or as cute once the summer was over and reality crashed down along with the fall temperatures.

Did she have regrets? Sure. But she didn't regret leaving—only the manner in which she did. But, then, if she hadn't left when and how she did, she probably wouldn't be where she was today, and she was really okay with today.

Well, not *today*, exactly. There were a lot of places she'd rather be than here right now.

But the ferry ride did offer a nice, calming view, and Helena returned to her car in time to disembark feeling refreshed from the sea air—even if she looked rather windblown.

From the ferry dock, it was only a few miles to the New Day Convalescent Center, a tidy stucco building that looked more like a hotel than a care facility. She hadn't chosen this place—hell, she hadn't even known about Grannie's fall until she was about to be moved here because Grannie hadn't wanted to worry her—but she couldn't complain. The staff was friendly and well trained, and when she'd come down the first time a couple of weeks ago, she'd been pleasantly surprised and relieved to find that it was clean, welcoming, and not nearly as depressing as the TV news exposés on elder abuse in nursing homes had led her to expect.

As she signed in at the visitor desk, the nurse informed her that Grannie was still in physical therapy and not back to her room yet. There was something in her voice, though, that had Helena's antennae twitching.

"I thought y'all had changed her PT time so she wouldn't miss her afternoon soaps." *That* had taken three phone calls to the home's administrator and medical adviser to arrange, but in the end, even they'd agreed it was a worthwhile schedule change just to stem the complaints. You didn't interrupt Grannie's stories for anything less than a genuine blood or fire emergency. *Everyone* knew that.

"We *had*," the nurse began carefully, "but we're having some . . . difficulties now."

Helena's heart began to beat faster as the adrenaline

kicked in, and she braced herself for bad news. "Difficulties?"

"Mrs. Wheeler is fine," the nurse assured her, and the panic ebbed some. "But since you have a few minutes before she's ready to receive visitors, maybe you'd like to speak with Dr. Abrams."

"Of course." If Grannie was physically fine, then something else was going on, and Helena went through a mental list as she followed the nurse down the hallway to Dr. Abrams's impressively decorated office.

Dr. Abrams stood as she entered. "Miss Wheeler. Good to see you again." He motioned for her to sit.

"Is everything all right with Grannie? Your nurse mentioned difficulties." Maybe it was a problem with the insurance or something. Adulthood had certainly slapped her in the face with paperwork and decisions she had to make as Grannie's next of kin, but . . .

"Mrs. Wheeler is fine. The difficulties are more mental than physical."

That brought her up short. *Mental?* Grannie might not be as physically robust as she used to be, but she'd never shown any signs of losing any of her mental capacities. The woman was still scary sharp, with a memory an elephant would envy. "I'm not sure what you mean."

He looked like he was choosing his words carefully. "Mrs. Wheeler is starting to tire of being here."

"No offense, but she tired of being here about two days after she arrived."

"Yes, but, until recently, she was cooperative. An active participant in her own recovery."

"And now she's not?"

"She wants to go home, and she seems to think the best way to achieve that is to irritate us to the point we'll kick her out." The doctor's mouth curved up a bit as he said it, as if he saw the humor in the situation.

Mercy. She'd always known she'd pay for her upbringing, but she'd expected it would be with the antics of her own loinfruit—not a role reversal with Grannie. As she sat across from Dr. Abrams, listening to his list of examples of Grannie's "recent uncooperativeness," she felt a stab of remorse for all the times Grannie had been called down to the school. And the police station. And the sheriff's office. And that one time to the Coast Guard station . . .

She sighed. "I'll talk to her."

"Good. If we can get Mrs. Wheeler actively participating in her recovery again, she should be able to go home in a couple of weeks." He smiled, but there was something oily about it. "Which is what everyone wants."

"I'll take care of it." She picked up her bag and the chrysanthemums she'd cut from Grannie's front flower bed and let herself out of Dr. Abrams's office. As she made her way to Grannie's room, she felt as if every staff member she passed were giving her annoyed looks over Grannie's antics.

Oh, paybacks are hell.

She knocked on Grannie's door at the same time she opened it, sticking her head through the opening to say, "You decent?"

Grannie was in a recliner near the window, looking a little tired but overall much better and less fragile than she had when Helena last visited. Her beautiful white hair was back to being perfectly coiffed, her blue eyes were bright, and she'd painted her nails a perky shade of pink to match the caftan she wore. "Helena!" She looked surprised but then opened her arms wide for a hug. "It's good to see you, baby. What on earth are you doing here?"

Helena hugged her carefully, not sure what might still be sore, and inhaled the familiar scent of Shalimar and talc. "I came to see how you were doing, of course. Why is that so surprising?"

"Well, you said you were coming down, but I thought you'd need a few days to settle in at the house before you came to visit."

"I've come home. Why would I need time to settle in to my own home?" It was a small lie, but one she wouldn't feel bad about. She stuck the chrysanthemums in a vase and carried them to the windowsill where they'd be in Grannie's line of sight. "These are blooming like crazy right now."

"I shudder to think of what my beds must look like."

"Actually, they look great." She stacked the magazines she'd brought on the small side table and filled the candy bowl with the hard toffees Grannie loved. "Mrs. Wilson has been sending her grandsons over to keep the grass cut and the weeds out of your flowers."

"That's very kind of Margaret and the boys."

Helena took the chair next to Grannie's and squeezed her hand gently. "Everyone loves you, Grannie, and they just want you to concentrate on getting better."

"I'll be fine once I get out of here."

"Which brings me to my next topic." She leveled a stern look at Grannie—the same look Grannie had leveled at her many, many times. There was no need to beat around the bush. "Dr. Abrams says you're being difficult."

Grannie was the picture of genteel, Southern pearl-clutching dismay. "I am not being difficult."

"You can't be released until the doctors say so, and if you're not cooperating with them—"

"I'll recuperate better in my own home."

"Which isn't ready for you, anyway. Ryan's starting the work tomorrow, but it's going to take him some time to finish."

"How long?"

"I don't know. He's very busy and working us in around his other projects, so a definite finish date isn't set."

Grannie didn't seem pleased to hear that.

"So you might as well make the best of your time here so you'll be ready as soon as the house is."

Grannie patted Helena's arm. "You're a sweet girl, Helena, coming to take care of your old grandmother."

Nice dodge, Grannie. "You're worth it, and you're certainly not old. If there's a reason you're unhappy here— *other* than simply being here," she amended quickly, "tell me, and I'll do my best to get it fixed or find another place for you to go to."

"You could just take me home now, you know." She lowered her voice and leaned forward as far as her still-healing rib fractures allowed. "Grab my things, and we'll make a run for it."

"Grannie . . ." She shook her head. "I'm not busting you out of here against all medical advice and taking you on the lam."

An eyebrow arched up. "Well, that's a new song you're singing."

It was Helena's turn for some pearl clutching. "That's unfair. I'm a responsible adult these days, remember?" Shooting a pointed glance at Grannie's ankle cast and walker, she added, "Like *you* could make a run for it anyway."

"I'd like to give it a try," Grannie retorted with a wink, then moved on to other topics, adding more items to Helena's to-do list and asking careful questions about the reception Helena was receiving back in Magnolia Beach.

Helena, equally as careful, gave vague answers and steered the conversation in other directions. Grannie did not need to be worrying about *her* right now.

After a few minutes, though, Helena couldn't help but notice Grannie becoming increasingly distracted and glancing at the clock. Then she produced a compact from the pocket of her caftan, checked her hair, and powdered her nose.

Helena didn't have time to comment on that, because seconds after Grannie put the compact away, there were three sharp knocks on her door, followed almost immediately by a silver-haired gentleman—well-tanned, good-looking, nicely dressed, with a wide, white smile—walking right in with a booming "Hello, gorgeous!"

Grannie just beamed and waved him in, lifting her cheek for his kiss. "Hello there, handsome." Helena felt her eyebrows hit her hairline. Grannie's voice had dropped an octave into what could only be described as a purr. As

Grannie's eyes locked with his for a long moment, Helena shifted awkwardly, feeling like she was witnessing something she shouldn't. After what felt like an eternity, Grannie finally seemed to remember she was there. "I want you to meet my granddaughter, Helena."

Still in a mild state of shock, Helena stood. The man tucked a cribbage board under his arm and took her hand in both of his. "It's wonderful to finally meet you, Helena. Louise has told me so much about you."

Funny, I haven't heard a single thing about you. She shot a look at Grannie, who frowned her into remembering her manners. "It's nice to meet you, too, Mr. . . . ?"

"Calvin Parker. But please, call me Cal."

"Cal's been fabulous company for me the last few weeks. I'd have gone simply stir-crazy without him."

"You . . . um . . ." She wasn't sure how to word it. "You are . . . on the staff here?" *Damn, that sounded a little too hopeful.*

"Oh, no, no, no. Knee replacement," he said, tapping his left one. "But soon I'll be ready to take Louise dancing."

Oh my God. Did Grannie just bat her eyelashes at him? "Well, uh . . ." She had to stop to clear her throat. "Thank you for keeping Grannie company. It relieves my mind to know she's made friends here."

"Oh, it's been my pleasure," Cal said, giving Grannie another long look. "But they're kicking me out of here in a day or so. I'm going to miss her terribly."

"Not for long," Grannie assured him. "Helena's going to bust me out of here."

Now Cal was frowning at her. "Don't encourage her, Helena. Louise needs to focus on getting better."

She felt unjustly vilified. "I happen to agree. The doctor says it should be another couple of weeks before she's ready to go."

"See, sweetheart, it's not that long. And I'll come see you as often as I can." Cal turned to Helena. "I live over in Bayou La Batre, so it's a bit of drive."

Since Bayou La Batre was only about fifteen minutes

from Magnolia Beach, and she'd just made the drive . . .
"Yes, I know."

*Well, this explained Grannie's sudden desire to leave
this place.* She cut her eyes in Grannie's direction, but
Grannie was too busy making cow eyes at Cal to notice.

"Louise and I usually play cribbage in the afternoons.
Would you like to join us?"

Although Grannie was smiling, Helena could see the
No, you don't in her eyes. She was almost ornery enough
to say yes, but she'd never hear the end of it if she did.

"I'd love to," she started, just to watch Grannie's
eyes narrow, "but I've got a lot to do to get things ready
for Grannie's return. I should probably head on home
now."

"Another time, then," Cal said with just the required
touch of disappointment in his voice, but he was already
setting up the game.

She picked up her purse and gave Grannie another
kiss on the cheek. "Bye, Grannie. Love you."

"Love you too, baby," she answered, giving her a look
that clearly said, *We'll talk about this later.*

Damn right we will. "Nice meeting you, Cal."

"And you, Helena. I'm sure I'll see you again soon."

Oh goody.

She was thankful the grounds of the New Day Center
were designed around the limitations of their guests—
flat, well signed, and easy to navigate—because Helena's
head was spinning too much to pay attention to where
her feet were going.

Grannie has a boyfriend?

There'd been that nice Mr. Costa back when Helena
was still in junior high who'd taken Grannie to lunch on
Sundays after church or to the occasional movie, but
other than that, Grannie had never really *dated*. Her life
had revolved around work and church and her bridge
club, and, honestly, Helena had never questioned that
until now.

But now there was a Cal. She cranked the engine and

pulled out of the parking lot. *Smilin' white-toothed Cal with his brand-new dancin' knee.*

And he was definitely younger than Grannie. Maybe in his late sixties? *I should have stopped at the nurses' station and gathered a little intel on this man.* Grannie was seventy-five—even though she told people she was seventy. Jeez, her grandmother was practically a cougar.

A cougar who wanted out of the nursing home because Smilin' Cal was going home to the other side of the bay.

She kept turning this new, quite *shocking* information over in her mind until she was back on the ferry, headed slowly back to Dauphin Island.

Grannie has a boyfriend.

It was shocking news, yes, but Helena was pleased at the same time. Grannie deserved to be happy.

Even if she was a little weirded out about it.

I wonder if the staff knows about their romance? Was that even allowed between patients? Or were Grannie and Cal sneaking around, arranging clandestine meetings and creeping down the hallways in the middle of the night to . . .

No!

She shook her head hard to get rid of the image. There was no way she could imagine her grandmother and Cal . . .

Ugh.

There were some places the human mind should just not go. And grandparent sex was pretty much at the top of that list.

But the *worst* part settled into her mind a few minutes later.

Her seventy-five-year-old grandmother was probably getting more action than she was.

Ryan was just finishing staking out the ramp to Ms. Louise's porch when Helena pulled into the driveway, dodging his truck and the piles of various supplies he'd stacked on the concrete. As she climbed out of the car, he did a double take. That dark hair was pulled up in a ponytail against the heat again, but today Helena was in a flowing cotton sundress, arms and legs bare. It was a much different look than he remembered.

But it suited her nicely. *Too* nicely.

She surveyed his handiwork as she walked toward him. "If you run that ramp through her rosebushes, Grannie will kill you, you know."

The statement, which should have sounded snappy and snarky, lacked any punch at all. As she got closer, sliding her sunglasses up onto her head, he noticed Helena's face was pinched, her eyebrows pulling together as if she were worried or unhappy. He knew from her e-mail this morning that she was going to Fort Morgan to visit her grandmother, so this didn't bode well. "How's Ms. Louise?" he asked carefully.

Tank appeared from his shady spot under the rose-bushes and trotted over to greet her—a little less aggressively this time than last—and after a moment, Helena squatted down to pet him.

"Oh, she's *splendid*." Helena made a sound suspiciously like a snort. "Better than some people half her age, in fact."

"That was a long drive for a quick visit, then."

"Tell me about it."

Something was going on. "Do you want to tell me about it?"

"Not particularly." It was an absent comment, thrown his direction as she eyeballed the outline of the ramp. "I'm serious, though. You didn't say anything about digging up the rosebushes."

"Just the one bush. And I'll move it around to the side of the porch."

"If it dies . . ."

He sighed. "It won't."

"If you say so. It's your head on the block, not mine." Pausing, Helena cocked her head and looked at him strangely. "I didn't realize you were starting work today. I thought you were just dropping off the paint chips."

"I know you want this done as soon as possible, so I'm working you in around other projects." He followed her up onto the porch into the shade. "The Millers' new kitchen cabinets are the wrong color and had to go back to the company, so I'm here today."

"That's kind of you," she said, but she seemed only partly involved in the conversation. Unlocking the front door, she looked back over her shoulder at him. "If you're going to be coming and going at odd hours, I should probably give you a key. I just ask that you knock before you come in."

"Is something wrong, Helena? You seem ... distracted."

"There are just some things in life that are difficult to wrap your head around." She shrugged as she pushed the door open and cool air came rushing out. "Come on in, and I'll get you that key."

He followed her in, carefully wiping his feet on the mat first. In the kitchen, Helena opened a drawer, searched for a moment, and then tossed a key ring his way. He caught it and tucked it in his pocket. Helena hadn't even waited to see if he had, pulling open the fridge door as soon as the key was airborne and grabbing a beer. She stopped and tilted her head in his direction. "It's early, I know, but do you want one?"

Drinking this early in the day? Something was definitely up. "No, thanks. Beer and power tools don't mix. Maybe later."

With another of those shrugs, she took a long drink from the bottle and leaned against the counter. Then she crossed her arms and asked, "You probably know everybody in the next three counties, right?"

"Not *every*—"

She didn't wait for him to finish. "What about a Calvin Parker over in Bayou La Batre?"

He had to think for a minute. "I know a Cal Parker. He's Adam's age, maybe a little younger, runs his family's body shop now...." He trailed off as Helena shook her head.

"Too young. Any chance that Cal's a junior?"

"I think he's named for his grandfather. Why?"

"Because I think Cal Senior is putting the moves on my grandmother."

Ryan was glad he'd refused that beer, or else he'd be spitting it across Ms. Louise's black-and-white linoleum right now. "What?"

Helena made a face and took another long swallow of her beer. "You heard me."

Well, being faced with her grandmother dating might explain Helena's mood, and while the shock of it might bring a dozen questions to mind, honestly, the idea of Ms. Louise dating wasn't something he really wanted to think about too much. He should probably offer to listen if she wanted to talk, but he really didn't want her to take him up on the offer. Especially since visions of his own recently widowed grandmother . . . *No. Stopping that train of thought right there.*

He realized his poker face might not be all that great when he heard Helena snort again.

"Right there with you." She rubbed her eyes and pinched the bridge of her nose. "I mean, I'm happy for her, of course, but it's not something I was quite prepared to face today. Jeez, talk about straight out of left field."

"Want me to call Cal—the younger one—and maybe ask him . . ." *Ask him what? Is your grandfather a player? What are his intentions toward Ms. Louise?* No part of that was any of his business, and Cal would think he was crazy.

"No, but thanks." She sighed heavily. "I'm just going to have to readjust my thinking. And it's good, right? I worry about her being lonely, so it'll make leaving here easier, knowing that she's got someone who really cares for her." Helena shook her head as if to clear it. "Okay, sorry about that. Moving on. Please feel free to come in and get drinks or whatever. Just sing out when you do so I don't have a heart attack. I'm going to go work for a while and let you get back to what you're doing."

Just like that, Helena was gone, her footsteps echoing through the house as she took the stairs two at a time. A moment later, he heard footsteps over his head, then the groan of squeaky springs as though she'd flopped onto the bed. And he just stood there, feeling dismissed out of hand. It was an unusual feeling, one he hadn't experienced since . . . well, since the *last* time Helena had done it.

He shook his head. Honestly, what did he expect? Helena had hired him to do a job, not to be her friend, and letting him get back to work would be the correct thing to do in this situation.

But why did it sting a little?

He moved the rosebush in question, the thorns cutting the crap out of his arms in the process, and carefully re-planted it with a hope and a prayer it didn't die. He got the holes for the footings dug and the concrete poured just about the time the sun started to set. *Now* he was ready for that beer, and he was just about to go into the house and get one—and hopefully talk to Helena again—when another car pulled into the driveway, and Tate Harris got out.

He liked Tate; he really did. He was a good man, a great vet, and an asset to the community, but Ryan was getting damn tired of seeing him on Helena's porch. Especially since anyone could see that all Tate lacked was a big bouquet of flowers to complete the "going court-ing" look he was sporting—freshly shaved, pressed shirt, hair still a little damp.

Ryan wiped an arm across his sweaty forehead and pulled off his dirty work gloves. "Tate."

"Wow, you're making progress already. Does Ms. Lou-ise know you're digging up her rosebushes, though?"

Good Lord. He had to build a handicap-accessible ramp to code if the woman ever wanted to get into her house again. God forbid some flowers might have to be sacrificed in the process. "Just one bush. And it's not like she doesn't have more of them."

"Hey, Tate! Right on time."

Ryan looked over his shoulder, and something hot and heavy landed in his stomach. Helena stood in the doorway, holding the screen open. The ponytail was gone, and her hair rioted in loose curls around her face and over her shoulders. She wore another sundress, only this one was made of a silky fabric that hugged her curves in a way that made his mouth go dry.

He heard a quiet sucking sound to his left that said Tate was having a similar reaction. But Tate was quicker to recover. "Whoa, you clean up nice, girl."

Helena grinned at him. "So do you." As she pulled the door shut behind her, she turned to Ryan. "I'm going out for a while. Could you just lock up when you leave?"

"I'm pretty much done for today."

"Oh, okay. Then I'll see you later." She was smiling—much happier than she'd been earlier—as she tucked her hand under Tate's arm. "Where are you taking me?"

"It's a surprise," Tate answered.

"I remember what happened the *last* time you said that, and I am way overdressed to be chasing down Mr. Cutter's goats."

Goats on the loose rang a bell. It figured Helena and Tate had something to do with it.

Tate assessed her outfit. "I would pay money to see you try in those shoes."

In response, she elbowed him in the ribs and Tate "oofed," causing Helena to giggle.

He'd never heard Helena giggle. In fact, he wasn't sure he'd ever heard her laugh, either—at least not in the happy, amused way. Sarcastic, bitter laughs, at the expense of others? Yeah. But happy giggles? No way.

Helena and Tate were still arguing good-naturedly when the car doors closed, and he couldn't hear their conversation anymore.

This was a different Helena. But Tate didn't seem surprised by it, so it was a side of her he obviously knew. But then, they'd been friends before she left, so Tate knew Helena in a way Ryan bet no one else in town did.

Including him. He knew *of* her, *about* her and her reputation, but now he was dealing with a grown-up Helena, who was not the person he expected her to be.

He could rationalize his newfound attraction to the

old Helena—he was older, less self-important, long past the cliques and drama of high school. Fascination didn't require reason.

But *this* Helena? A giggling, playful friend, defender of her grandmother's virtue as well as her rosebushes? *This* Helena complicated things. Because now he wasn't just fascinated by her.

He actually liked her.

Chapter 5

Bubba's Bait Shop turned out to be a sushi bar owned and run by Bubba Mallory, whom Helena remembered as a quiet kid more interested in chess and history than most boys named "Bubba" tended to be. A sushi restaurant in Magnolia Beach was surprising enough, but the real surprise was how ridiculously good the sushi was.

The last piece of her tiger roll sat on her plate and she eyed it longingly, but she just couldn't take another bite—she was about to explode already. Not wanting it to go to waste, she pushed it in Tate's direction, since he seemed to be able to eat his weight in sushi without a problem.

That wasn't the most unusual part of the evening, though. While she recognized a few faces, Tate seemed to know almost everyone in the place. She slapped a smile on her face, reminding herself that she wasn't a kid anymore and didn't care what these people thought of her. She also tried to ignore the sideways glances that came her way and the either overbright or overcautious greetings of those people who actually did speak to her.

Tate, however, seemed universally loved. People spoke to him; they waved; women batted their eyelashes at him. It bordered on surreal.

Finally, she leaned across the table. "Okay, I *have* to ask. How come I'm getting the stink eye for past sins, yet you seem to be forgiven and beloved?"

Tate grinned at her. "Consensus *may* be that I was young and foolish and simply led astray by an older, wilder woman."

Helena felt her jaw drop.

"Of course," he continued with mock gravity, "once the bad influence was removed, I repented, reformed, and made quite a success of myself."

She'd often wondered if Tate might get beyond their past and get redemption without her around, but having it confirmed irritated her more than she wanted to admit. "That's a load of horse shit. Like I could drag you up onto the school roof if you were kicking and screaming the whole way," she added in a grumble.

"Well, you weren't here to offer an alternate theory."

There was something in Tate's voice that panged her heart and her conscience, and the little voice that had been nagging her for two days had to be addressed. "Yeah. And I want to apologize for that."

"I'm sure the people of Magnolia Beach will be happy to hear it."

"Screw the 'people of Magnolia Beach.' I couldn't care less either way what they think. I owe the apology to *you*."

Tate's eyes widened.

Direct and honest. She owed Tate that much. "I'm sorry I took off like that, with so little warning. And I'm sorry I didn't call you or keep in touch."

He nodded, then asked, "Why didn't you?"

Tate was trying to keep it light, but she could hear the hurt in his voice and it made her feel worse. She knew him too well, knew he'd never tell her how deep the wound went. The guilt she'd held at bay by telling herself he was better off landed hard. She'd left him here with an abusive parent and their messed-up friends to pick up the debris of their adventures alone. He deserved an explanation. "At first . . ." She sighed. "Well, at first I was feeling like a big shot. I hated Magnolia Beach, and this was my chance to be freed from it. Then when things went to hell with Charlie, I didn't want to admit to anyone I'd failed. That I'd hitched my star to a loser.

I had no money, no job, no place to live. . . . I just couldn't admit it to anyone. I didn't want the pity or the 'I told you so's,' so I handled it myself. By the time I started to get my act together, it felt like it was too late. That bridge had been burned already, and I figured people would be happier if I just stayed gone." She looked him in the eye. "Some of that is true, I know—many people were probably happy that I just faded away. And I admit that all I wanted to do was forget everything about Magnolia Beach, so I intentionally shut out everything and everyone—including Grannie for a while. But I shouldn't have lumped you in with the others around here. I should have called, worked harder to keep in touch."

"I missed you," he said quietly.

"I missed you, too. You don't even know how much." She reached across the table to squeeze his hand. "I'm so, *so* sorry."

He returned the squeeze. "Well, I'm glad you're here now."

She was forgiven. Just like that. A huge weight lifted off her shoulders. She didn't really deserve it, but it felt good all the same. "And you now have my cell number, my e-mail address, my Twitter handle. . . ."

"I hope that doesn't mean that when you leave this time, you'll put Magnolia Beach back in the No-Go Zone."

"Let's see how this trip works out first. I may still get run out of town on the rails."

He chuckled and everything was normal again. "Making new enemies already? That was fast."

"No, just the old ones." She thought about Julie Lane, now Swenson. "Mainly because some folks just can't grow up and let go. But I may have made a *new* friend."

He looked impressed. "That bodes well. Who?"

"Molly from Latte Dah. Well, I wouldn't say she's a friend *yet*, but I'm hopeful." *Time to tactfully pry.* "Do you know her?"

He shook his head. "I know her, of course, but not well. She adopted a kitten that was abandoned at the clinic a few months ago and has spoiled it rotten on chicken and catnip. And she makes great coffee, too."

"Oh, that she definitely does." Helena didn't have to fake the enthusiasm behind that statement. "I'll probably become one of her best customers. But she seems really sweet, too."

Tate merely nodded and signaled for the check.

"And she's as cute as a button. I've always wanted curly hair like hers."

"I like your hair the way it is."

But we're not talking about me, doofus. "Thanks. But while I'd like to make at least one new friend, I wouldn't want her reputation to suffer from hanging around me too much."

"I think Molly can handle it." The check arrived, and Tate lost all interest in that topic of conversation.

Well, my prying skills suck.

He barely glanced at the check before he tucked bills inside. "My treat. Trust me," he added when she protested. "I can afford it."

"Only if you let me get it next time."

"We'll see. Want to walk down to the beach?"

It was a gorgeous night, and the desire to feel sand between her toes nearly overwhelmed her. *Yep, still a beach girl at heart.* "Rain check? My trip to see Grannie today meant I got no work done, and I've got to get some stuff ready to send to my clients before they take their business elsewhere. How about dinner tomorrow night, though?"

Tate shook his head. "Magnolia Beach plays Orange Beach tomorrow night. It's a home game. Most every place worth eating at will be closing early."

"Seriously? They still do that?" Some people might think that was charming, but from a business point of view, it seemed stupid to close early on a Friday night. Then she remembered the average turnout for a home game. . . . The concession stand was probably the only food place in town doing any business anyway.

"Of course." He offered her a hand as she slid out of the booth, then used it to guide her toward the door. "Should I pick you up?"

"For what?"

"The game."

She snorted. "You've got to be kidding me. I don't even *like* football."

"Still a rebel."

"Since when do *you* like football, anyway?" Tate had been slight and scrawny and not into sports at all as a teenager, and he'd hated the teasing from the jocks and coaches alike.

"Since I became an adult and figured out that it's not just a game, darlin'. It's a social obligation, especially for those of us who are pillars of the community."

She nearly choked. "*You're* a pillar? Since when?"

"Since I became the town vet. It comes with the territory. Doc Masters sat me down when I took over the clinic to go over all my new civic responsibilities. I'm now an enthusiastic supporter of the Magnolia Beach school system's athletic programs."

Helena tried to stifle a laugh and ended up making a strange snorting sound instead. "Wow. Your enthusiasm is nearly overwhelming."

"Hush." He closed her door and walked around to the driver's side. As the engine roared to life, he looked at her. "So you'll come to the game with me?"

"Not on your life." She forced her face into seriousness. "After all, a pillar like you shouldn't be seen with a bad influence like me. Think of the impressionable children."

"Think of the impression *you* can make—as a responsible, adult woman, showing your support for kids and the community. It's a scene right out of your redemption montage."

That sounded horrible, actually. "What makes you think I'm looking for redemption?"

Tate grinned at her. "The fact you're jealous of mine, of course."

"I am not."

He snorted. "It certainly seems like it."

She lifted her chin. "It wouldn't work anyway."

"Why do you think that?"

"Weren't you just telling me about Jesus forgiving, but no one forgetting?"

He shrugged. "You can't make people forget the past, but you can give them new ideas to replace the old ones."

When did Tate get so insightful? "I think I'd rather try to stay under the radar—at least for now. Let people ease into the idea, maybe."

Tate let the subject drop, making small talk on the short drive back to Grannie's, but Helena had deeper thoughts pressing on her now. Seeing Ryan rip out rosebushes and stake out ramps made everything very real, and Tate was only driving it home—however unwittingly. Until now, she'd been working with an idea, a concept, but the reality was settling in. Grannie wasn't getting any younger, and her health, while still good *now*, would become an issue sooner or later. Grannie's ability to travel would be curtailed, and Helena wouldn't be able to avoid Magnolia Beach forever. She was going to have to do something to make that easier for everyone to accept.

She just wasn't sure what.

And it annoyed her to have to consider it. She'd made her stand, earned her reputation. She wasn't proud of all she'd done, but she had too much pride to go begging for forgiveness now.

She hugged Tate once he pulled into Grannie's driveway. "G'night. Thanks for dinner."

"My pleasure. If you change your mind about the game, let me know."

"I won't," she assured him.

Grannie's house was dark and quiet. She should have left a light on or something, as it was weird to be here alone. Kicking off her shoes, she left them in the middle of the floor since Grannie wasn't here to yell at her about it, grabbed a glass of wine, and padded barefoot up the stairs to change.

She'd had a long day already, and the temptation to

drink herself to sleep was fierce, but she had a long night of work ahead of her, too.

Nobody ever said any of this was going to be easy.

Gunshots woke her up.

Helena sat straight up in bed, wide awake but very confused with her heart lodged somewhere near her larynx.

Five more pops quickly followed, almost directly under her window, sending her rolling to the floor before the details began to rush at her: She was in her childhood bedroom, not her first crappy apartment in that crack-addled neighborhood. There were no screams or cries or sirens blaring, just a low-pitched engine hum. . . .

The next *pop, pop, pop* brought clarity. That was a nail gun, not an actual gun, and that hum was the air compressor driving it. Good Lord, it was seven freakin' o'clock in the morning. Someone was about to die.

Grabbing Grannie's cotton robe off the back of the bathroom door, she wrapped it around herself and ran down the stairs, muttering threats the whole way. Sunlight blinded her as she jerked open the front door, only to be greeted by Ryan Tanner's backside as he bent over to send five more nails into Grannie's porch.

"What in the hell are you doing?" she shouted.

Ryan stood and had the audacity to grin at her. "Good morning, Helena. I'm building a ramp. What about you?"

"It's seven o'clock on a Saturday morning. I was trying to sleep."

"It's a good thing you're up now, then. The plumber is coming later today to run the pipes for the new tub, and I need to get in there to knock out that wall so he can."

"You're kidding me."

"No, why?"

"Did you not hear the part about it being seven o'clock and the whole 'I'm sleeping' thing?"

"There's a lot of work to be done. Are you really going to drag this out just so you can sleep late? Your neighbors aren't complaining."

Because this is Magnolia Beach. They are probably all awake already, eating their perfectly balanced breakfasts after their brisk morning walk. She, though, was a night owl, often working until three or four o'clock in the morning, but she wasn't going to defend her sleep habits, especially to *him.* But before she could answer, Ryan went back to work, attaching more boards to Grannie's new ramp and whistling a jaunty tune while he worked.

A quick survey told her Ryan had been here for a while. He was much further along than he'd been yesterday, when he'd been able to work for only a couple of hours before leaving for the football game. She guessed she should be glad he'd done quieter stuff first instead of greeting the dawn with that stupid nail gun.

She slammed the front door behind her—not that it made any impact over the din Ryan was creating—and went to the kitchen to start coffee. Even if she had been able to convince Ryan to find something quieter to do, the early-morning adrenaline rush was not going to let her go back to bed now.

Coffee on, she went to the little half bath under the stairs that Ryan was about to expand into the closet beyond to make room for Grannie's walk-in tub. The sight that greeted her in the mirror wasn't pretty. The mascara she'd forgotten to take off last night created dark smudges around her eyes, and half of her hair was sticking up as if she'd taken a WeedWacker to it. Even worse, her robe was gaping open at the front, exposing her chest, and the well-washed, oh so comfy tank she'd slept in was far more see-through than she thought, the darker circles of her areolas clearly visible.

Lovely. Just lovely. She'd just accosted Ryan Tanner on her front porch looking like a crazy, half-naked, bed-headed raccoon.

This day is off to a grand start.

Coffee in hand, she went upstairs to get dressed. The shades were partly open, but her attempt to close them and protect what little dignity she had left as she dressed was halted by the sight of Ryan wiping his sweaty face with the hem of his T-shirt.

Holy mercy, the boy had a nice set of abs. Toned and defined, with a little happy trail of dark hair leading to the waistband of khaki cargo shorts. The biceps she'd noticed the other day wielded the heavy nail gun with ease, and his shorts showcased his powerful quads and calves as he moved another set of boards into place on Grannie's new ramp. And when he bent over to grab his water bottle ... *whew.*

That kind of physique wasn't built in a gym. It came from good, old-fashioned hard work. Physical labor sculpted without adding bulk, creating musculature that was obviously for function, not decoration.

She had a sudden urge to fan herself. Stepping sideways, she was able to keep him in sight while ensuring that he couldn't see her if he happened to look up toward her window. She felt a tiny bit dirty, as if she were some kind of Peeping Tom, but the "hummina" factor was enough to easily trump that feeling.

In public, she claimed an attraction to smart, sensitive men, with varied and cultured interests she could connect to on an intellectual level, but this curling heat was primal, visceral, awakening something long buried in her DNA and long denied. She lived in an eclectic neighborhood in Atlanta, surrounding herself with artists and activists and hipster types, and while she did feel an attraction, it seemed muted and underdeveloped compared to the rush that Ryan was sending through her veins.

Which was completely insane.

Intellectually, she could tell herself that, but her libido wasn't listening. It was far too busy revving up at the sight of Ryan being all sweaty and manly with his power tools.

Ryan chose that moment to look up at her window, as if he felt her watching him, and Helena stepped back so quickly that coffee sloshed out of her mug and onto her foot. "Ouch, ouch, damn, ouch!"

She hobbled to her bed and sat down to inspect the damage. The top of her foot was red and sore to the touch. *That's what you get for spying, girlie.* The burn wasn't really bad enough to warrant rushing to the bathroom to soak in cold water, but it would serve as a painful enough reminder to keep her eyeballs off Ryan and his . . . assets.

He hadn't let himself go like so many former jocks tended to, and the intervening years had definitely been good to him. It would be crazy, though, to let her libido take over her higher thinking. This was Ryan Tanner. While he hadn't actually been the true bane of her existence growing up, she didn't exactly have fond memories of him, either. He and his crowd had been too "good" to associate with her and hers, making their interactions more like those of rival gang leaders than anything else.

But even she had to admit that he hadn't been *too* horrible these last few days. He hadn't called her Hell-on-Wheels since that first day, and he'd been kinder than required the other day when she was reeling from Grannie's new relationship. Sure, he still had some snark behind his words, but the snark had lacked teeth.

Whoa. She needed to stop this line of thinking right now. What was she trying to talk herself into, anyway? Permission to continue admiring his physique? Or a reason to get along with him? She didn't have to *like* him in order to appreciate his muscles, and maintaining a professional working relationship didn't require anything at all beyond common civility.

It was this town. It completely messed with her head. Made her crazy.

She heard the front door open, and then her name floated up the stairs. "Helena? I'm coming in."

Either Ryan was terribly efficient or she'd stood staring out the window for far too long, but either way, she needed to get some clothes on before she offered Ryan another gander at *her* assets. "I'll be down in a minute," she called. "Help yourself to coffee."

There was something strange, almost vulnerable-feeling, about changing clothes with a man downstairs in her kitchen. She didn't care much for that feeling, so she rushed, pulling on cutoffs and a T-shirt, opaque this time—she double-checked to be sure—before getting the tangles out of her hair and braiding it back out of her way. *Focus.* Ryan was probably going to be around a lot today, but today needed to be a work day for her, too. She still had to move all the boxes she'd cleaned out of the about-to-become-a-bathroom closet up to the attic, and make some progress on the sunroom that was going to be Grannie's new bedroom.

She got back downstairs just in time to see Ryan draping the kitchen in old sheets, leaving only a pile of sledgehammers and saws uncovered on the floor. With a dust mask over his face and goggles over his eyes, he looked ready to take down the whole house—or possibly reenact a slasher movie.

He didn't look up when she came in. "Grab some coffee if you want it, but if you're staying in here, you'll need a mask. Sheetrock is dusty stuff."

"Are you sure pulling out that wall won't bring the whole staircase down?"

"Still don't trust that I know what I'm doing, do you?"

She just shrugged as she refilled her coffee.

He sighed and pulled his mask down. "That wall isn't even in the original plans for the house. This whole thing was just a big closet until your grandparents decided to add the half bath." He nodded toward a mask and a pair of work gloves on the table. "You can help if you want. Supervise to make sure I don't accidentally destroy the house."

Put herself into a small confined space with Ryan after she'd already spent a good portion of her morning ogling him? Where she could watch those muscles do their thing all up close and personal? *Hell, yeah!* her libido shouted. "I'll pass. I've got my own manual labor to do."

She grabbed a granola bar out of the pantry and nearly tripped over her own feet in her haste to get out of there. A moment later, she heard a bang and figured the destruction was well under way. The noise—okay, the thought of those muscles—was going to distract her, so she needed to throw herself fully into her project. She turned the radio—technology also seemingly circa 1996—up loud and braced herself to face the sunroom.

Grannie might not be a hoarder yet, but Helena began to wonder if she might be teetering on the edge. Years' worth of magazines, the pages dog-eared to recipes or knitting projects, went straight into the recycling bin. Books were sorted into boxes and labeled so she could go through them with Grannie later and hopefully donate some to the thrift store.

Some of the furniture could be redistributed throughout the house, but most of it was going to end up in the attic. As she tugged Grannie's antique writing desk into the front room, a horrible, morbid thought landed on her shoulders out of nowhere. *The next time you do this, it'll be because Grannie is dead.*

She sat down hard as her feet went out from under her.

"You okay?"

She hadn't heard him come into the room. Hell, the hammering and sawing had become a background noise, and she hadn't even noticed it had stopped. His goggles were pushed up on the top of his head, and his dust mask hung around his neck. Fine white specks of Sheetrock dust stood out against the tanned skin on his arms and forehead, dusting his hair like snowflakes.

"Yeah."

"You don't look all right. Here." He handed her his water bottle, but she waved it away.

"I'm fine."

"You shouldn't be trying to move this stuff all by yourself."

She bristled, thinking there was censure there, but when she looked at Ryan's face, all she saw was mild concern. "That's not it."

"Then what's up?" He sat next to her and took a long drink of water as if the two of them sitting in the hallway chatting were just an ordinary thing. And though he was sweaty and covered in Sheetrock dust, he smelled like clean laundry and that hard-to-describe manly musk that came from physically hard work.

Down girl.

She certainly wasn't going to share her morbid thoughts, but Ryan seemed to be waiting for an explanation. "It's just the realization that things are only going to get harder. Grannie's getting older, and I'm so far away. . . ." She sighed. "I'm not sure how it's all going to work."

Ryan shrugged. "It'll work. Somehow. Ms. Louise is healthy and spry for her age, and she'll be fine once she's recovered from this."

Helena rubbed a hand over her face. "Yeah. But I have to start thinking ahead, because that's not always going to be the case. I feel bad, you know, not being here. It's just the two of us, and this"—she circled her hand to include the house and everything else—"makes me feel like I'm ignoring her." She couldn't believe she was admitting that to Ryan.

"You've got a life, Helena, and that's not a bad thing. And Ms. Louise is proud of you. Living far away doesn't make you a bad person. You're doing what you're supposed to be doing—living your life."

"So says the person with enough family to fill the high school gym. It's just me and Grannie."

A smile tugged at the corner of his mouth. "Good point. I knew Ms. Louise didn't have any other family nearby, but it didn't seem weird because she's got so many friends." He shrugged. "I guess I assumed there was more family somewhere else, though."

"No."

His eyebrows went up. "None? At all?"

Boy, he really couldn't wrap his head around that idea, could he? "My grandfather was an orphan and met Grannie in Virginia when he was stationed there in the military. They moved down here in the sixties. Grannie has a sister up in Wisconsin or Minnesota, maybe, but they had a falling-out twenty-something years ago and haven't spoken since. Honestly, I'm not sure if she's even still alive. My dad was an only child, so . . ."

"What about your mother? I heard she went back to Jacksonville, but she's still alive, right?"

There was a small moment of shock. She rarely thought about her mother anymore, and the benefit of time, distance, and therapy had taken the edge off the blade. Hearing Ryan ask, though . . . *That* was different, somehow, and brought back a wave of emotion she hadn't felt in years. It shook her composure.

But Ryan couldn't know that, could he? The idea of a nonmaternal mother had to be an alien concept to him. A deep breath brought her back into focus, dropping the emotional baggage and returning her to acceptance. And while the last thing she wanted was to overshare with Ryan Tanner, that acceptance meant she had no shame and nothing to hide.

"I'm not in contact with my mother." His eyebrows went up, and she saw the well-meaning but unwanted pity there. The questions would be next, so she cut him off at the pass. "She made it very clear when I was about fifteen that she wanted nothing to do with me."

She could tell he was weighing whether to ask more questions, and she was thankful he decided against it as her patience for explaining herself had limits. "I'm sorry," he finally said.

"Don't be. I'm not. That woman's so screwed up, she makes my life look like the Road Map of Good Life Decisions. I'm lucky she left me here with Grannie." Rubbing her hands against her legs, she moved on, putting an end to the discussion she knew she was going to regret having later. "So if there's family on that side, I don't know them. It's pretty much always been just Grannie and me. Which doesn't seem all that bad until situations like this where I'm the only one to handle things."

Ryan, smart boy that he was, took the hint and didn't ask more. "You can ask for help, you know. Ms. Louise has friends."

That fact had been thrown around one too many times, and it was beginning to sound like a slam against *her*. "Grannie is my responsibility, and I'm not looking to shirk it," she snapped.

Ryan held up his hands. "Whoa, there. No one said you were."

"Once the house is done, it will be much safer for her. I'm going to get her one of those I've-fallen-and-I-can't-get-up necklace things, too. That'll help ease my mind some, and we'll just take it as it comes, I guess." It occurred to her that no one—not even Grannie—had floated the idea of her moving back to Magnolia Beach, even though the thought loomed in the back of *her* mind from time to time, which just underscored the fact that even if she wanted to come home, no one really wanted her to actually do it. Whether she deserved it or not, Magnolia Beach had a hell of a way of beating up her ego. *Screw it.* She might not be wanted *here*, but she was wanted elsewhere. Intentionally brisk, she pushed to her feet. "Is the wall down?"

"Almost. The floor looks to be in good shape, so a coat of paint and a new light fixture is about all it needs. Cory texted me to say he'd be here in about an hour or so to run the plumbing. It's going to be a snug fit in there."

"But it beats having her climb the stairs to use the tub up there."

"Exactly. Now, do you need some help with this desk?"

She started to say no, but that was just habit and pride, both of which she was going to have to learn to let go of. "Please."

Those biceps flexed as Ryan lifted the desk easily, placing it carefully in a sunny corner of the front room. "Just yell for help next time. No sense in hurting yourself," he said over his shoulder as he walked away.

Yell for whom? Him? She thought of the furniture in Grannie's room that would need to come downstairs. There was no way she'd get a dresser or a mattress down here by herself. She could call Tate—he'd definitely come to help—but after hearing about all he was involved with the other night, she was hesitant to put more on his plate.

A wave of self-pity hit her hard. She wanted to go home. She might not have a large circle of friends in Atlanta, but she did have them. And they were good friends, the kind you could call to help move heavy furniture when necessary.

More importantly, they *liked* her. They *wanted* her around. They didn't carry decades-old grudges or judge her based on her mother's actions. She had nothing to live down or live up to in Atlanta—unlike Magnolia Beach, where no one seemed to think or care that she might not be the same person she was before. It was both frustrating and depressing.

She gave herself a strong mental shake. No time for pity parties. She'd let one morbid thought send her down a depressing spiral—but that ended here and now. She'd get Grannie settled and life would go back to the way it was, and when circumstances called for a change, she'd deal with that then.

There was no sense borrowing trouble. She already had plenty.

Chapter 6

At two o'clock sharp, Ryan was in his grandmother's parlor, properly attired in a collared shirt, khakis, and real shoes—not boots, not tennis shoes, but proper shoes. His grandmother had rules about attire and punctuality—just to name a few—none of which had relaxed in her golden years. In Gran's opinion, civilization rested on the foundation of the family, and Sunday lunch was the cornerstone of that foundation. Neither tardiness nor tennis shoes were acceptable.

Of course, there were so many freakin' people here, Ryan had yet to figure out how anyone took attendance. Aunts, uncles, cousins . . . They'd long outgrown the dining room, and satellite tables were set up in the kitchen, the parlor, and the den. If anyone else got married or procreated, they'd have to set up tables in the hall or on the porch.

His mother greeted him with a kiss, then wiped the lipstick mark off his cheek, simultaneously handing off silverware and napkins to his cousin Shelby to set the tables and directing Jamie and Adam to get the chairs from the attic. "Hello, sweetheart. I didn't see you at church this morning."

"I had a late night last night—at Ms. Louise's," he clarified as his mother raised a disapproving eyebrow. "We ran into some problems when the plumbing for her new bathroom went in, and I stayed late trying to get it straightened out."

She couldn't really claim disapproval of *that*. "Maybe next week, then."

"I'll try." They had the same conversation every Sunday afternoon, yet the thought of it was still not enough to pull him out of bed on Sunday morning. He knew it and Mom knew it, yet Mom still persisted, possibly just out of pure stubbornness. She gave him "the Look" as she went back to the kitchen.

Shelby shook her head at him as she set the table. "Your mother is only concerned about the state of your soul."

"Are you trying to tell me that you dragged yourself to church today?"

Shelby smirked. "Of course not. But I showed up last Wednesday, so I'm good. The trick is to show up more often than just Easter and Christmas. That way they know you're trying, at least." She tossed a blond ponytail back over her shoulder and smiled smugly at him. "And therefore, they leave you alone about it."

"I'll remember that. Nice dress, by the way." Shelby rolled her eyes and muttered under her breath, exactly as he intended. She, too, conformed to Gran's dress code, although under greater protest than most of the other cousins. Shelby was a proud tomboy, and her work at the marina catered to that choice, allowing her to live in T-shirts and shorts and deck shoes most of the year—except on Sundays, when she buckled to familial pressure and wore a dress. It really did look nice on her, though, not that she'd ever believe a compliment from him about it was sincere.

The tables were segregated by age—what had been his "children's table" had become a teenager's table, then an adult table of its own. He, Adam, Eli, Jamie, and Shelby made up the table for years, but Tucker had managed to squeeze in recently, despite the age difference, as the cousins who were closer to his age were off at college. Ryan often wondered what would happen when any of them eventually married and wanted to bring that spouse to lunch.

A smart spouse would have it written into the wedding vows that they didn't have to come.

Oddly, that made him think of Helena struggling to move that antique desk by herself. Since he could have at least twenty people at his house by just making one phone call, it wasn't something he could identify with. If Gran was in Ms. Louise's situation, he'd be lucky to even offer his opinion on what to do or make a single decision—much less *all* of the decisions. He might get frustrated with the constant intrusions, lack of privacy, unsolicited advice, and general meddling that came with his large family, but, hey, if he ever needed furniture moved or a barn raised, he had the manpower.

"Why are you smiling like that?" Eli asked.

"Just picturing a Tanner family barn raising." He got matching "you're crazy" looks from his siblings and cousins for that. "Don't worry. I'm not expecting y'all to actually come build a barn."

"Good," Jamie said, loading up his fork with ham and sweet potatoes, "because I really don't want to have to think of a good excuse not to."

Okay, make that nineteen people. Jamie didn't like manual labor. He barely tolerated being outside, which put him in the Tanner minority and really called the whole "nature versus nurture" argument into question.

"Great game Friday, by the way," Adam said. "Rumor has it there was a scout from Ole Miss there."

"Not that I know of, but I wouldn't be surprised. Scott Smith had a personal rushing best—"

"So," Shelby said loudly, effectively derailing a play-by-play rehash, "did you see the high school this morning? Someone bought the jumbo pack of toilet paper and had a good time."

"Not again." Ryan sighed and made a mental note to keep the principal and custodian off the agenda at the next town council meeting. He was not going to sit through another "kids today are out of control" diatribe. Then he noticed Tucker intently contemplating his collard greens. "Do you happen to know anything about this, Tucker?"

"It wasn't me this time, I swear."

Skeptical, Shelby frowned at him. "Someone's protesting a bit too much, I think."

"I have an alibi," Tucker insisted. "Anyway, I heard Mrs. Riley say at church this morning that someone should talk to Helena Wheeler about it."

Ryan nearly spit sweet tea across the table. *"Seriously?"*

Tucker nodded.

"Trust Mrs. Riley to give everyone the benefit of the doubt," Adam said.

Eli snorted. "Particularly at church."

Ryan shook his head. "Like an adult woman would have any interest in toilet papering the high school. Mrs. Riley has finally gone senile."

"She's got a grudge against Helena," Shelby said.

"Who doesn't," Jamie muttered.

"Grow up," Eli and Shelby said at the same time.

Jamie put down his fork. "Why does everyone keep saying that?"

"Because you really need to," Shelby said. "You were stupid enough to antagonize her, and you got what you deserved, so get over it, you big baby."

Jamie shot his sister an evil look. "Since when are you Hell-on-Wheels's champion?"

"I'm not. I just can't bear to see a thirty-year-old man whine over something that happened nearly fifteen years ago."

"She's got a point," Adam said.

"I didn't ask you," Jamie snapped in reply.

Maybe I am still at the children's table.

"Shelby was too young to be in Helena's direct line of fire," Eli said, trying to be the peacemaker as usual. "She doesn't really understand—"

"Oh, I totally understand. I caught my fair share, too. The girl has always been bad news—"

Ryan tried to focus on his plate as the bickering kicked

up. It was usually amusing to watch his cousins and brothers go at one another, but something about *this* conversation annoyed him. He'd gotten an unexpected glimpse into Helena's psyche yesterday, and it bothered him. He worked with teenagers, for God's sake, and he knew how easy it was to mess with their heads. That level of rejection from a parent could do all kinds of damage, and fifteen was about the age at which Helena had really gone off the rails. It was no wonder, really, that she'd been like that, and it was actually pretty amazing she'd managed to turn it around. And while that information might be something to shut down his cousins' escalating spat, it wasn't his place to tell Helena's business.

"You're just scared of her," Jamie snapped.

Shelby gave him a withering look. "Oh please, I'm an adult."

"So you two will be going to lunch, when, exactly?"

"Jesus Christ," he finally snapped. "Are you two listening to yourselves?"

"Ryan Ray Tanner, don't you dare blaspheme in this house."

The woman still has ears like a bat. "Sorry, Gran." He leaned forward. "First of all, all of you need to grow up, get over it, and act like adults. Second, is there *nothing* else for everyone to talk about other than the not-all-that-miraculous return of Helena Wheeler?"

Shelby actually seemed to think about that before shaking her head. "No, not really."

"Uncle Dave says the new cell tower you're all gung ho about will give us all brain cancer," Eli offered with a smirk.

"Jack McCleary got a new job, so he and the family are moving to Birmingham."

"Max Morris's dog had a litter of puppies and they're obviously mutts, so they're demanding the stud fee back."

His family was either insane or too insulated and in desperate need of wider experiences. "This is the best y'all can come up with?" he asked.

"I didn't realize we'd be expected to entertain you to-day," Adam said. "And since Shelby won't let us talk about football, Helena's about the only thing of interest."

Jamie leaned toward Adam. "He's just touchy because he's developing a little crush on Helena."

That got everyone's attention. *Gran will kill me if I get Jamie's blood on the carpet.* That realization was probably the only thing keeping Jamie alive after dropping that bombshell. At least he'd said it quietly enough so that his mother hadn't heard.

Tucker grinned at him. "Oh, that is excellent."

"Shut up," he growled.

"Hey, I'm on your side. I don't really remember her much from before, but I saw her at the store the other day, and she's hot."

"She's a little old for you, don't you think?" Adam said.

"I like cougars." Tucker was trying to sound suave and mature but failing miserably, and Ryan didn't have the patience right now.

Eli shook his head at Tucker. "She'd chew you up and spit you out without breaking a sweat. Don't even think about it."

"Thinking never hurt anyone," Tucker retorted.

"Any thought in your head would die of loneliness."

A horrified Shelby, who had been doing an excellent goldfish impersonation until now, finally spoke. "Y'all need to hush for a minute. Ryan Tanner, tell me that's not true."

"I can't see how that would possibly be any of your business either way."

"So you do?" Shelby said.

He was not going to participate in this conversation. Shelby needed to butt right out, and even the smallest comment on his part would have her all up in his business like she had a right to be there. "Anyone have any idea whose dog might have fathered the Morris's puppies?" he asked conversationally.

But Shelby wasn't having any of that, and since no one else jumped in to change the subject, he was forced to sit there under Shelby's increasingly intense stare. Finally she rolled her eyes in disgust. "Fine. Talk about football." She stood and picked up her plate. "I'm going to eat at the big table." Then she turned to Ryan. "You're insane. One day, I hope someone explains to me the allure of the Bad Girl. But this won't go over well, and you know it."

When she left, his cousins looked at him with varying degrees of interest and confusion, but he certainly didn't owe them explanations and he wasn't going to egg on this conversation by providing any. "So, the scout from Ole Miss . . ."

Adam picked up that conversational ball like a champ, thank goodness, since it was what he wanted to talk about in the first place. But as the meal progressed, Shelby kept sending him long, exasperated looks from across the room. She wasn't going to let this go, he realized, so he was going to have to come up with some kind of response.

Damn if he knew what that might be, though.

"You call that working?"

Helena looked up to find Molly behind her, staring at her laptop screen with undisguised interest. Not that Helena was surprised. The smorgasbord of bare chests, washboard abs, and smoldering eyes above sexy stubbled jaws should interest any red-blooded woman. "It's a tough job, but someone's got to do it."

"I am in the *wrong* business."

"Every job has its perks, and this is mine. Can you believe that my subscription to this site of gorgeous men is tax-deductible as a business expense?"

"If you tell me you get to bill by the hour for browsing, I might close up shop and go into business with you." Molly refilled Helena's coffee cup, then set the pot back on the counter. Helena was averaging at least an hour or two in Latte Dah every day, working her way through Molly's drink menu while she tried to keep up with her clients. There was something about Latte Dah that inspired her—probably that it was one of the few places in town that held no memories, good or bad, for her. Even though she could work at the house now that the Internet was hooked up, that lack of constant déjà vu let her mind work freely here. Plus, she enjoyed getting out for the short walk, fresh air, good coffee, and Molly's company.

Molly sat next to her. "So why are you downloading soft-core porn in my family-friendly establishment?"

"I'm putting together a media package for a small romance publisher—bookmarks, banner ads, all kinds of stuff—and I'm looking for pictures that complement their covers. Such pretty, pretty men to sort through. The real problem is not getting carried away in the search and losing hours ogling and drooling. Check this one out." She clicked open her favorite picture from today's search and turned the screen toward Molly.

Molly's low appreciative whistle was coupled with a quick fanning of her face. "I'm suddenly feeling a bit overwarm." She leaned a little closer to the screen. "That's got to be fake. There are no men who really look like that. Are there?" she added a little hopefully.

It was a bad time for Molly to be asking that question, since Helena had compared those abs to Ryan's abs about twenty times too many already today, and Ryan's abs were holding their own pretty darn well. They lived in a beach community for goodness' sake, and the human body was constantly on display. Surely people had seen Ryan shirtless at some point, so his assets couldn't be that much of a secret. But if Molly wasn't already familiar with Mayor Tanner's six-pack, Helena wasn't going to bring it up. "It takes a combination of good genes and a real commitment to the gym to get those kinds of results."

"I hate to add to the outrageous and artificial definitions of beauty our society has created, but . . . *damn.*" She fanned herself again. "I just want to lick him like an ice-cream cone."

"Right there with you." *The model's abs, not Ryan's. Really.* Unfortunately, that didn't stop the completely inappropriate image of her doing exactly that from flashing through her brain in high-def, Technicolor detail. *What the hell is wrong with me?*

"You sure you don't need an assistant?"

"It's not all sexy men, sadly," she confessed. "Next on my list is a brochure for a small beauty-products company—just pictures of soap and nature. That's not nearly as exciting."

"I'm not sure I could handle that much eye candy on a daily basis, anyway." Molly lowered her voice even though Latte Dah was empty except for the two of them. "A girl can buy only so many batteries before people start asking questions."

"Molly!"

She just grinned and shrugged, unrepentant. "A girl's gotta make do where she can. I love Magnolia Beach, but the singles' scene is almost nonexistent."

"That's a shame."

"It really is. Everyone talks about how Magnolia Beach is a great place for families, and I totally agree, but *getting* to the family is the hard part. Especially for imports."

"See, I think it would be easier. It's hard to see someone in a romantic light when you've known them since elementary school."

"But familiarity can help, too." Molly seemed to think for a minute. "I think I need to have a talk with Ryan."

"Ryan? Why?"

"As mayor, he's trying to keep Magnolia Beach relevant and moving forward. We need new blood and a reason for people to stay in order for that to happen. Single people are just as important to the overall health of a town as families."

That was very astute. "You're right. You know, maybe you should run for the city council."

"Bite your tongue."

"Why? You're smart, involved. . . . You'd be an asset."

"Yes, but I lack tact."

Cute little perky Molly? "I can't believe that's true."

"You haven't seen me mad or frustrated yet. I've been to council meetings where I was about to lose it and go off like a cannon, and I was just participating in back-row democracy."

"So what you're saying is that you have a low tolerance for bullshit."

Molly nodded. "And whining. And mindless complaining about minor stuff. Oh my God, you would not believe the great 'how to properly light a flagpole' debate that raged last year. I don't know how Ryan handles it."

"That's the job he signed up for. He must like stuff like that."

"I think it frustrates him, too. But it's because he really cares, and crap like that is really just a waste of time. He's done some amazing things that have really turned Magnolia Beach around. And that was before he was even elected mayor."

"Good for him." She didn't mean to sound sarcastic, but it came out that way regardless.

"Don't grump. Ryan has big ideas for ways to improve Magnolia Beach, and he ran for mayor so he could implement those plans."

"That had to go over well. Magnolia Beach as a whole doesn't like change."

"It didn't help. He had to really fight to get elected."

"You're kidding me. Ryan's 'Mr. Popularity.'"

"Oh, people like him, but they thought he was too young. Ageism is a real thing."

"I can see that. But it's probably more an issue of voting for someone to run your town when you remember them as that dumbass kid who was messing around one Fourth of July and accidentally set off the big fireworks show ten hours early."

Eyes wide, Molly asked, "Ryan did that?"

"No, that was actually me," she admitted, "but Ryan

did manage to drive one of the parade floats into Heron Bay the next year."

Molly laughed. "I don't remember that coming up in the campaign."

"I'm surprised."

"They were a little too busy arguing about a lodging tax increase on rental properties that Ryan wanted to use for infrastructure improvements. Dr. Crawford said it would have a negative effect on tourism."

"Dr. Crawford? The dentist?" When Molly nodded, Helena laughed. "He's got to be a hundred years old by now."

"And according to him, his age gave him wisdom that Ryan didn't have."

"But Ryan still won."

"Yes, and he's been proven right. Not only was there no negative effect on tourism overall, but the additions of Wi-Fi and the new pier have proven popular, and last year we were able to hire our first full-time firefighters and EMTs. Better quality of life, improved safety, and more jobs. All good things."

Helena had to admit that was pretty impressive. "That must make him a pretty popular mayor now."

"Of course, but he still gets pushback from the community, particularly the older population, but he says that's to be expected. Just between you and me, though, he's winning them over, too. The old men huff and puff because they don't want him to get too cocky."

That, she could believe. "How do you know all of this?"

Molly rolled her eyes. "I run a coffee shop. You wouldn't believe all the stuff I overhear in here."

"The thought kinda scares me."

Molly just laughed. "How's the work going at your place?"

"Good. Ryan seems to have it under control, so I'm feeling a little less stressed over the whole thing."

"Ryan's a good mayor *and* a good guy. If he says it's under control, you can believe it." Molly tossed that statement out almost as an aside, as her interest had been caught by Helena's screen again. Molly reached over and scrolled down a bit. "Oh my. Isn't he pretty?"

Helena was glad for the distraction. Molly was certainly a Ryan fan, but Helena couldn't tell how deep that appreciation went. Maybe Molly wasn't crushing on Tate after all. Or could she have a thing for both Tate and Ryan? Magnolia Beach did have rather slim pickings when it came to single men, so maybe Molly was hedging her bets, exploring an interest in more than one of Magnolia Beach's most eligible.

That kind of bothered her. And on several levels, not just out of loyalty to Tate. And since she hadn't seen Tate's abs in the last decade, she had no real clue what condition they were in. He was fit and firm, that much she knew, but *how* fit and *how* firm were questions she couldn't answer. But Molly's interest in the hotties on her screen made steering the conversation away from Mayor Tanner much easier. "So how many truly eligible bachelors is Magnolia Beach boasting these days? Feel free to set arbitrary standards and not include all the single men, just the quality ones."

"You looking for names?" A small sly smile curved up the corners of Molly's mouth. "Suggestions, maybe?"

"Oh, no, no, no. Just an estimate of the number."

"Why?"

"I'm curious. You at least have to have a top-ten list." Molly's look turned uncomfortable, so she retreated as gracefully as possible. "Ryan accused me of poaching Tate from the dating pool, and I was just wondering how big that pool was."

"So, you and Tate . . . ?"

"Are just friends. That's *all*. And I know there's probably going to be gossip because we're spending time together, so feel free to correct anyone who's speculating."

She was hoping for some kind of reaction from Molly about the nature of her relationship with Tate, but it was hard to tell. For Molly to be so open and friendly, she certainly was hard to read on this topic. And while she'd been happy enough to discuss her battery needs, she'd shut down when it turned to specific men. *Interesting.* That *might* be a look of relief on her face, but Helena couldn't say for sure, and she wasn't clear what else she could ask that wouldn't cross a line. So she changed the subject. "Hey, could I get another lemon bar?"

"Sure."

"At this rate, none of my clothes are going to fit."

"Not that I'm saying you need to, but I run almost every day. You're welcome to come with me anytime you'd like."

"Maybe one day. I'm pulling a lot of late nights right now, what with the work on the house and my job...."

"That reminds me. If you need help, please give me a call. I can paint, pack boxes, whatever you need."

"That's sweet, but ..."

"I'm just being neighborly. Your grandmother is a great lady and a loyal customer. It'd be my pleasure to help out."

Hadn't she just been bemoaning the lack of a circle of friends to help her through this? It seemed she might be building one. "That's sweet of you. And thanks. As soon as I figure out what I need, I'll call. Maybe plan a painting party." *I can invite Tate, too.* That brought back a memory that made her giggle.

"What?"

"The last time I got hold of paint, Tate and I took it up the water tower."

Molly nodded, impressed. "That takes guts. I'm afraid of heights."

"Me, too, actually, but it seemed worth it at the time."

"It always does. That's the problem with being a teen-ager. Stupid stuff seems so smart at the time."

"Oh yeah. Full development of my frontal lobe was the greatest gift of my twenties."

"Amen," Molly said. "I'm living proof God watches out for idiots and children. In a less kind world, I'd be in jail or dead."

Helena lifted her coffee cup. "Indeed."

"By the way, did you see the high school yesterday?"

"I did. That was impressive work. I imagine it took some time to accomplish, too, so I'm surprised no one got caught."

Molly shrugged. "Oh, they'll round up the usual suspects, put on some pressure, see who confesses."

"I know how that goes."

Molly gave her a stern look. "Do *you* have an alibi?"

"Ugh. I hadn't thought of that. Anyway, everyone in Magnolia Beach knows toilet paper isn't my style."

"I was always an instant-mashed-potato girl myself," Molly declared. "Delay in the gratification, but better chance of artistic display."

"With some added breathing room to get away as well. The timing's so tricky, though, especially if they don't have a sprinkler system. I never could quite get that right, so if you did, my hat's off to you."

Molly nodded regally. "Why, thank you."

"Nasty mess afterward, though, with all the flies and bugs . . ."

"Yeah, but that's where you get the real bang for the buck."

"Definitely." They both laughed.

Bonding over a delinquent past. That has to be one for the books.

The bell over the door chimed, and Molly pushed to her feet to greet her customers, patting Helena on the shoulder as she left. Putting her earbuds back in, Helena returned to the gallery of hunks, searching for a good image that fit the tone. She liked working here in the coffee shop. Sure there were distractions, but she actually enjoyed them. Back home, days would go by without her having a real, face-to-face conversation with another human being.

Hell, she didn't even have to speak to the baristas at her local shop anymore. They saw her coming and got her order ready, so she could just pay and leave with a minimum of human interaction. In fact, she'd had more conversations with people in Magnolia Beach in the last week than she'd had in the last month at home.

She finally found the picture she had in mind, and her focus narrowed as she mocked up image after image, finding her groove and staying in it. Finally, she had a whole package she loved and knew her client was going to flip for. After hitting Send, she sat up and pain shot up her spine. A glance at the clock told her she'd been hunched over the computer for the better part of two hours. The customers Molly had left her to wait on were gone, and Molly was on the computer behind the counter working on what looked like spreadsheets. Two more people had come in at some point and now sat on the puffy green couch reading the Mobile newspaper together.

The man didn't look familiar, but the woman certainly did, and Helena's good mood evaporated.

Perfect, pretty, prudish Amy Lee Huggins, with her holier-than-everyone attitude. Condescension and judgment were her forte. *I might have been a troublemaker, but she was just plain mean.* And while Helena got ostracized for that troublemaking and treated with derision, Amy Lee, the daughter of the pastor at Grace Baptist, was beloved and fawned over, held up as a model by parents who didn't know what she was really like.

Amy Lee must have felt Helena's eyes on her, because she looked up. Helena did her best to smile, but Amy Lee merely rolled her eyes and went back to the paper. *Yep, still a bitch.*

That was kind of the final straw. Her life wasn't some twelve-step program where she had to make amends to those she'd wronged in the past, but she didn't need to make new enemies or renew old animosities, either.

But seeing Amy Lee and remembering how awful *she* was reminded Helena that she was owed some apologies, too. While she might not be carrying grudges, she shouldn't have to slink around as if she were ashamed of herself, either.

She packed up her laptop, waved good-bye to Molly, and then went the long way to the door—the path that would lead her past the couch. "Long time, no see, Amy Lee. How are you?"

"Helena. How surprising to see you." Amy Lee wasn't even trying to fake it.

Helena noted with a little evil pleasure that Amy Lee wasn't looking as good as she might for her age. Obviously being that judgmental permanently carved lines into a person's face. It was shallow and mean of her to gloat, but Grannie always said that "you can't be pretty on the outside if you're ugly on the inside," and it seemed that was catching up with Amy Lee.

She put on her best smile. "Everyone keeps saying that. It's kind of flattering."

Amy Lee's eyebrows went up. "I don't—"

"I'd love to stay and catch up, but I've just got so much do. Maybe I'll see you around. Take care, okay?" Oh, the vapid perkiness made her head hurt, but it was worth it to see the look on Amy Lee's face. That alone buoyed her spirits as she settled her sunglasses on her nose and started back toward Grannie's house. This time, she made a point to smile and greet people by name, all the while waving like a pageant queen on her victory walk. Forget staying under the radar. She really didn't care what these people thought anymore, and she wasn't going to let them shame her for her past, either.

The visible shock and awe she left in her wake shouldn't have given her such pleasure, but it did. And she refused to feel the least bit bad about that, either.

Chapter 7

While it was the rare project that went exactly as planned, discovering rotten floorboards in the sunroom was the kind of issue that brought everything to a screeching halt and messed up Ryan's schedule something fierce.

Although Helena had been dismayed at the damage, she'd accepted his pronouncement and recommendation without comment, a real change from someone who'd worried he'd bring the whole house down around her ears by tearing out a useless wall just a few days ago. It was a bit unsettling.

At first he thought he was imagining it, but as the evening went on, he knew there was definitely a subtle change in Helena's attitude tonight. For lack of a better word, she was friendlier, less prickly. She hadn't invited him to a tea party or anything, but she wasn't ignoring him, either, nor was she shooting out barbs at every opportunity. He'd even deliberately left her a few openings, just to be sure he wasn't imagining things.

It was unsettling, but it was a relief, too.

While he'd been ripping up floorboards and examining the damage, Helena must have made fifty or more trips up and down the stairs, moving as much as she could into the attic to declutter the downstairs and remove tripping hazards. She was grumbling about it under her breath, and he caught the occasional word now and then when she passed, but honestly, the sight of Helena's long muscular legs on display in a pair of too-short cutoffs was distracting enough to keep him from making sense of what she was saying.

It was also distracting him from the project at hand. He tried to push the visual out of his mind and measured for the fourth time. Damn it, the joist had rot, too. He reached for his flashlight to examine the damage closer just as a yelp floated down the stairs, followed almost immediately by a hard crash.

He sprinted up the stairs two at a time. "Helena!"

"In here. I'm okay."

"Here" was a small bedroom, which, based on the decor, must've been Helena's childhood bedroom. Helena herself was in front of the closet, covered in clothes, books, and boxes, with a chair on its side behind her. It didn't take a genius to put together what had happened, but he asked anyway. "What did you do?"

"I leaned too far forward, and the chair slipped out from under me. I grabbed the shelf on my way down."

"You sure you're okay?"

"Yeah." She moved her shoulder experimentally, then winced as she shifted and rubbed a hand over her backside. "Just a little bruised."

He offered a hand and pulled her to her feet. Then he stuck his head in the closet. "It doesn't look like you pulled the shelf completely out of the wall. If you'll go get my screwdriver, I can get it back up easily enough."

"Thanks."

It was kind of weird being in Helena's bedroom. There were posters on the wall firmly freezing it in time at the turn of the century, and many of the clothes on the floor looked dated, even to him. He knelt, setting a half-opened box back upright, and was surprised to find the yearbook from their senior year on top. He couldn't imagine an eighteen-year-old Helena having enough school spirit to warrant buying one.

But the yearbook was just one of many mementos—

not that he understood what meaning these particular keepsakes would have, but they were definitely the odds and ends of high school.

"Oh Lord, I can't believe Grannie kept all that stuff." Helena stood in the doorway, his screwdriver in one hand and two bottles of beer held by the necks in the other. She passed him a beer and the screwdriver.

"Thanks."

She poked at a notebook with the toe of her shoe. "I told her years ago that she could throw all of it out."

"Why?"

"Because I don't want it or need it. I'm more of a minimalist. Mainly because my place is way too small for a bunch of crap."

"But you might want it one day." He tightened the screws she'd loosened and reset the shelf.

"If I haven't needed it or missed it by now, I think it's safe to assume I won't in the future." She took a sip of her beer and cocked her head to the side. "Wait. You still have all your high school stuff?"

"In a box somewhere." At her look, he added, "It's not like I sift through it on a regular basis reliving my glory days or anything."

"Good. Because that would just be sad." She sighed as she squatted. "This is quite the mess."

Maybe because she had been friendlier tonight and he figured it was safe, he went to help her, gathering up a few photos that had achieved distance in the fall. The one on top was of Helena—maybe about seventeen or so—seated on the tailgate of a beat-up truck, her usual crowd gathered around her. She looked at it as she took it from him. "Wow. That brings back memories. Tate and I look so young." After a pause, she added, "I wonder what ever happened to Paulie and Sid."

"You don't know?"

She shook her head. "I haven't talked to Paulie since he left for the Navy. I just assumed for all those years that Sid was still in town."

"He left not long after you did."

"Oh. Do you know where he went?"

"No. They were *your* friends. Why didn't you keep up with them? Or look them up at some point?"

She looked at him like he was a little slow. "Ryan, honey, when you're trying to forget your past, you don't go looking for it."

That was a good point, but it seemed like a lonely and scary way to start over. Before he could comment on that, though, she pulled a T-shirt out of the pile and held it up. "Oh, now *this* is awesome."

It was a simple black T-shirt with MAGNOLIA BEACH stenciled in bright red across the front. As Helena turned the shirt around, he remembered what was on the back. Still, the exaggerated hindquarters of the school's pirate mascot with YOU KNOW YOU WANT THIS BOOTY! written underneath made him laugh. It had been quite the scandal junior year, as no one really knew where the shirts came from and no one who had one had been willing to talk, claiming the shirts had just "appeared" in their gym lockers. The shirts, which had horrified the faculty and staff, had been confiscated on sight, and anyone wearing one on school property risked suspension. He hadn't gotten one, much to his dismay at the time.

"This brings back memories," she said with a laugh.

"That it does. I thought there'd been a bonfire of the entire stock. How'd you get one?"

The corner of her mouth twitched as she cut her eyes in his direction. "Who do you think designed them?"

Of course. There had always been suspicion that Helena was involved somehow, but never enough proof. In retrospect, that particular suspicion hung over everything that happened in Magnolia Beach.

"It was one of the few things I got away with." There was a touch of pride in her voice.

"I'm sure you got away with a lot more than that."

She sat and started putting things back into the box quickly. "You'd be surprised, actually. Shortly after this, people really started cracking down on me, watching me like a hawk. I swear, if I dropped a tissue accidentally on

Front Street, I risked getting hauled in for littering. I'm just lucky Grannie knew the sheriff so well. Otherwise, she'd have had to dig me out from *under* the county jail."

He couldn't argue with that. "Well, you seem to be an upstanding citizen now."

She cut her eyes at him. "If you're asking if I'm the one who rolled the high school last weekend, the answer is no."

"I never thought you were."

"Tell that to Mrs. Riley, then." The annoyed undertone said a lot about what Helena was facing right now.

"Mrs. Riley is completely senile. Everyone knows that." He paused. Helena's openness to confessing about the T-shirts brought up an old curiosity. "But I have to ask...."

Helena raised an eyebrow at him. "What?"

"How'd you manage to get the keys to the chief's police cruiser? I remember it hadn't been hotwired when they found it over in Bayou La Batre."

Face unreadable, Helena asked, "What makes you think I know anything about that?"

"Because." When she didn't say anything, he added, "Look, the statute of limitations is long past, so it's not like you could get into any trouble or anything. Come on, confession's good for the soul."

"Even if I had something to confess, I'm not Catholic. And neither are you, I might add."

"What if I confess first?" Helena didn't say anything, so he sat next to her. "Okay, senior year, I helped Toby Martin and Frank Holland steal the Parker High mascot."

She snorted and waved a hand, completely unimpressed with his confession. "Oh please. Tell me something I don't already know."

"How do you know about that?" He, Frank, and Toby had never said a word to anyone.

"*Everyone* knew it. But no one would rat out the great Ryan Tanner because even if we had, you'd never get hauled up the way others would in that situation.

And since the dog was returned in good health, there was no harm, no foul."

"Are you serious?"

"Yeah."

That kind of burst his bubble. Sure, he'd had a little guilt at getting away with it, but at the same time, it had given him a little kick that he had. "Well, that's annoying."

"Oh, you bet it is," she grumbled.

"No one ever said anything."

"Do you honestly think that any Tanner—especially you—was going to get into any trouble for anything less than being caught red-handed committing a felony? *Pfft.*"

She pushed to her feet and headed downstairs. He had to trot to catch up. "Don't pretend that any Tanner, especially me, was—or is—untouchable or anything."

Helena paused at the kitchen door, giving him that same look that called him simple. "But you were. All of you were. Hell, Jamie is the one who hacked into the school's e-mails and sent those pictures to everyone. All he got was a few hours of detention because they couldn't 'prove it.'" She included the air quotes disgustedly. "*I* got more detention than that—without solid proof, mind you—for hijacking the PA system at the game."

"That was epic revenge, by the way. Jamie is still sulking over it." Helena shrugged off his words, but not before he saw the beginnings of a smile. "And, if you ask me, Jamie totally deserved it, so good job. How'd you manage it, though?"

She seemed to be debating whether or not to tell him.

"The principal always thought you must've done it when he caught you breaking into the school."

She shook her head. "That's not why I was breaking into the school."

"It's not?"

"Of course not. I just liked to use the computer lab at night. The computer I had at home couldn't even handle simple Photoshop, much less the stuff I was trying to do. And hey, look at me now, so it was worth it, I think."

This was a whole new window into Helena's character. "Wait. You trained yourself for a career in graphic design by breaking into the school's computer lab? How many times did you break in?"

"Enough." With a grin, she pushed through the swinging door into the kitchen.

His entire brain was short-circuiting as he followed her. "Let's back up. If you didn't hijack the PA system by breaking into the school in the middle of the night, how did you manage it?"

For a minute, he thought Helena wasn't going to answer him. Finally, she took a long drink of her beer and shrugged again. "It's amazing how far a little side boob could get you with the A/V club back then."

"You flashed the A/V club?"

"Not completely. And it's not like I'm proud of it or anything, but you do what you have to do, sometimes."

"Oh my God."

"You said yourself that it was epic and well deserved. Epic things require extraordinary efforts." She lifted her chin. "I was willing to go the distance for that."

"You are one interesting woman, Helena."

There was that grin again. "Why, thank you."

"One last question."

"I think we've done enough for tonight."

"Just one more." With a resigned but amused sigh, Helena motioned for him to proceed. "How did you manage to start a fire in the football equipment shed?"

All the amusement on her face disappeared, leaving her shuttered and guarded. "That was an accident."

Something was off now. "I'm not implying that it wasn't. I'm just wondering *how* it happened."

Helena shrugged. "You get a little carried away, things happen. . . ." She wasn't making eye contact, and she looked uncomfortable. "Another beer?"

"Fires just don't start. There's got to be a story."

"Just being stupid, I guess."

All things considered, Helena's vagueness struck him as weird. It wasn't like she had anything to lose by telling the truth about it. So why the reluctance all of a sudden? He looked at her closely and realized the truth. "You didn't start the fire."

"I confessed and paid the damages."

"That's not the same thing."

Helena didn't say anything, essentially proving her innocence.

"So why would you take the blame if you didn't actually do it?" One more shrug from her, and he knew. "It was Tate. He's the only person you'd take that fall for."

She took a breath like she planned to argue, but she sighed instead. "It seemed easier. Everyone thought it was me anyway, and it would have been much worse for Tate. . . ." She picked at the label on her beer bottle as she trailed off.

Oh. Mr. Harris had been a mean son of a bitch, and everyone knew he often took it out on his kids and his wife. The cops and the state had made more than one trip out to the Harris place to investigate. Helena had probably saved Tate from one hell of a beating. It was a brave, kind thing to do, but looking back, she'd taken a big risk and gotten lucky. Tate had still been a minor at the time and legally, at least, he would have gotten off easy. But Helena had already turned eighteen, and the police could have easily thrown the book at her. Luckily, she'd just gotten community service and reparations instead of jail time. There was no way she could have known that when she confessed, though, so she'd taken one hell of a risk for her friend. "You're a good person, Helena."

She tried to shrug it off, but he saw the smile tug at the corner of her mouth. "It's what friends do. He was always there for me, and I owed him. But I'd appreciate it if you kept this information to yourself. No one needs to know the truth now."

Philosophically, he was all in favor of honesty and clearing someone's name, but since Helena wasn't interested in doing so, he had no reason not to agree. "Don't worry. Your secret is safe with me."

"Thanks. And anyway, it worked out even better than I could have hoped. Do you think Dr. Harris would be a pillar of the community today if people knew he'd once set the football shed on fire trying to light his own farts like a fool?"

Oh, he'd be hard-pressed not to casually drop that into his next conversation with Tate. "I guess it beats doing drugs or something. Youthful stupidity is forgivable."

She made a noise that sounded suspiciously like a snort, and it took him a second to figure out why. *Her* youthful stupidity was still being held against her. "If it makes you feel any better, Uncle Dave called you a real pistol."

Eyes wide, Helena went slack-jawed in surprise. *"What?"*

"He said you were just up to teenage mischief—and not even malicious mischief at that."

"*Your* uncle Dave? The same one who hauled me up in front of the city council when I graffitied the water tower?"

Now he knew what he'd looked like when Uncle Dave had dropped this info on him. "Same one. He told me to tell you 'welcome home.'"

Her mouth opened and closed a few times, but no words came out. Then she shook her head as if trying to clear it and laughed. "Well, I certainly wasn't expecting that."

"Neither was I, honestly."

"Hmm." She laughed quietly. "Wow."

"Hard to process, huh?"

"Indeed." She blew out her breath. "Well, that's far enough down memory lane for one evening. I need to get back to work."

"Aw, come on. I still have so many questions."

"What am I? *The Magnolia Beach Petty Crime Encyclopedia*?"

"It seems so." He grinned and she made a face at him. "Just one more. Mrs. Delaney's classroom—"

She cut him off. "That was not me. I liked Mrs. Delaney and wouldn't have done that anyway. *That* asshattery was courtesy of Rich Kendall and Mike Swenson. I'd have turned them in if I thought anyone would've believed me." She looked truly angry about it. "And before you ask, yes, that is why both Rich and Mike got their tires slashed, but no, I was not the one who did it. Wish I had, though. The little shits."

The vehemence in her voice caught him off guard. "But I thought you and Mike . . ." The look that crossed her face stopped his words.

"That Mike and I what?"

"That you two were . . ." Damn, she did not look happy. "Um, friendly."

"Friendly. Interesting." The words were clipped, and her lips pressed into a hard line. "Not really."

"Look, Helena, everyone knows. And we've all done people"—*damn*—"I mean *things* we're not proud of."

"You mean the sexcapades at homecoming? Featuring acts that are still illegal in several states?"

Hand me a shovel. He just wasn't digging this hole fast enough with his mouth. "Well . . . I figured there might have been some exaggeration."

"'*Some*'? Try 'all.' I know what he told everyone, but let me assure you, Mike Swenson wasn't even allowed anywhere near my ballpark, much less given the chance to run the bases."

Mike had lied? In retrospect, it made a hell of a lot more sense than his claim. Revenge for the tires, probably. "Why didn't you call him out on it?"

"Who would have believed me? Hell, you barely believe me now."

"That's not true."

"Good or bad, a reputation is hard to live down, and a bad reputation is nearly impossible to shake, so anything anyone decides to say is considered the truth, no matter how crazy it might seem, simply because it fits the narrative." She poured out the last of her beer into the sink and tossed the bottle at the bin. "And people wonder why I left town. I understand Julie believing it. She's always hated me and is arrogant enough to think I'd sleep with Mike just to hurt her. But I assumed everyone else would figure out the truth eventually, whether or not Mike ever 'fessed up to his lie."

"There's no way Mike would ever retract that statement. It made him a hero."

"Yeah, at my expense. It's a wonderful double standard. He wasn't the slut. I was." She looked at him and laughed—the dismissive, at-your-expense laugh he remembered so clearly. Then she plastered a fake, mocking smile on her face. "Well, wasn't this fun?" Sarcasm dripped off her words. "Now, you'll have to excuse me as I've got to get back to work."

Helena pushed past him, leaving the door swinging in her wake, and he was smart enough not to go after her. He owed her an apology, but he doubted if even a sincere apology would be received well right now. He'd been an ass and would have no one but himself to blame if she threw a well-deserved punch. Self-preservation kept him in place.

That conversation had been eye-opening, even if it had gone very bad, very fast. He now had to rethink everything he thought he knew about Helena Wheeler—both the Hell-on-Wheels she used to be and the woman she was now.

And that was an awful lot to think about.

Helena could practically feel her arteries hardening with each bite, but the famous Frosty Freeze bacon-chili-cheese hot dog might just be worth the heart bypass surgery later in life. When coupled with a strawberry-banana shake, the meal was both heaven on earth and hell on the waistline. And while diner's remorse was already setting in, making her feel a little ill as well as ashamed, it was still all she could do not to lick the last bits of chili off the wrapper.

Grannie would kill her for the display of bad manners, so Helena crumpled up the wrapper and tossed it toward the trash can before she could succumb to the temptation.

"Good shot. Two points." A red-faced and sweaty Molly swung a leg over the bench and sat across from her, breathing hard from her run. She took a long drink from her water bottle and swiped a hand across her forehead. Faced with Molly's healthy living, Helena felt even worse about the bacon-chili-cheese hot dog she'd inhaled. "I missed you this morning at the shop. Everything okay?"

"I spent all morning on the phone with a client," she explained. "And since I was not properly caffeinated, it took forever. Then I was supposed to meet Tate for lunch, but he texted to say he had to go deliver puppies and canceled on me. The day's been a bust all the way around."

"Puppies?" Molly's forehead wrinkled. "I thought dogs pretty much had that under control and didn't really need humans around, much less a vet."

"That's kind of what I thought, too, but maybe not." She rubbed her stomach. "Ugh. I shouldn't have eaten that."

"Chili-cheese dog?" Molly asked.

"With bacon."

"Mercy. Tasty, but . . ."

"Yeah, tell me about it. I think I'm going to go home and lie down for a while."

"I'll walk with you. I wanted to talk to you about doing some design work for me," she explained as she jumped to her feet. "Maybe tweaking my logo, helping me with my Facebook page, stuff like that."

Helena also stood, albeit far more slowly than Molly. "You're the only coffee shop in Magnolia Beach. Do you really need to worry too much about advertising?"

"I'm not looking to bust my budget with a massive campaign, but I do want to increase my visibility."

"That's smart thinking." The voice came from behind them, causing Helena to jump—which she immediately regretted.

"Well, hello there, Mayor Tanner," Molly said with a big smile. "Good to see you."

"Ladies," Ryan responded with a nod.

And this is one of the many reasons I hate small towns. The chances of running into people she really didn't want to see were just too high. But that wasn't the worst part. The *worst* part was that she even had a list of people she didn't want to see and that Ryan Tanner was sitting at the top. She thought she was long past caring what people believed or thought about her, but last night had stung. A lot. And that surprised her.

'Fessing up to the sins of her youth had been oddly liberating and sort of fun. Ryan's response had given her a tiny hope that things might be different this time. Instead, the staying power of Mike Swenson's lie—and that Ryan had accepted it at face value even after all this time—just drove home how things would probably never change. It hurt, and she hated that it could.

She hated that she'd let Ryan *see* that it hurt her even more, though.

She had her pride, and she wasn't going to let Ryan know that it still bothered her today. "Hi, Ryan," she said with forced casualness.

"Hey, Molly. Helena." Another man joined their little group, handing Ryan a Frosty Freeze bag smelling of chili. As the man looked a lot like Ryan, it was easy to tag him as a Tanner, but once again, it begged the question of which one.

Ryan saved her. "You may not recognize him all grown-up, but this is my youngest brother, Eli."

"Of course. How are you?"

"Good. Welcome home, by the way."

Eli seemed friendly enough and the "welcome home" seemed sincere, not snarky. If she remembered correctly, he was at least four or five years younger than she was, so any issues he had with her would either have to be those shared by the general population or grudges carried on behalf of his older brothers and cousins.

"Thanks."

"And please tell Ms. Louise we're all hoping she can come home soon."

"I will."

"How are things coming along?" Molly asked. "Anything I can do to help?"

"Not yet," Helena answered. "But Ryan's making a lot of progress, so I might be calling on you sooner rather than later."

"Just let me know and I'll be there," Molly promised.

"And I'll be by later today," Ryan added. "I want to try to get the floor finished, at least."

"No problem," Helena said. "I'm going to go see Grannie this afternoon, so let yourself in and do what you need to do. I'll be back around seven or so."

"I probably won't even get there until then."

"That works." *I'll hide in my room so we don't have a repeat of last night.*

"You'd better be careful," Molly said in a singsong voice. "All these evenings working together ... People are going to start to talk."

She knew Molly was teasing, so the words, however true, lacked any sting. "Well, I haven't done much else for people to talk about lately, so—"

"People like to run their mouths," Ryan interrupted, and if Helena hadn't known better, she'd have thought he sounded downright testy. It changed the whole tone of the conversation instantly, drawing surprised looks from all of them. "Sadly, this town's full of busybodies with nothing better to do than listen, and they should be ashamed of themselves for listening to rumors and gossip, much less believing or repeating it."

Ryan had been looking directly at her as he spoke, keeping an almost unsettling degree of eye contact. And coupled with that tone ... Was that some kind of apology?

"Amen to that," Eli said.

There was no sense pretending now that any of them didn't know exactly whom they were talking about in general, even if she thought Ryan might be speaking specifically about last night. She shrugged. "I'm trying not to let it bother me, y'all. I mean, really, what difference does it make?"

"You're a far bigger, better person than I would be about it, Helena," Molly said.

"Some things just aren't worth getting too upset over. People who want to believe the worst will, and I can't change that. I'm used to it, and either way, I don't care." *Who are you trying to convince? Them or yourself?*

"If you wanted to punch people for that kind of gossip," Ryan added, "I'd get your back. Make sure the charges didn't stick."

Helena fought back a smile. "It's tempting, but unnecessary. Fisticuffs might ruin my manicure."

"You sure?"

"Yes, Mayor Tanner. I'm sure."

"Let me know if you change your mind," Eli said. "I want to make sure to put my money on you. And I want a front-row seat."

Helena wasn't sure, but she might end up liking Eli Tanner. "I will."

Ryan gave her another of those heavy looks. "So we're good?"

"Yeah," she replied. "I'll see you tonight at the house."

Molly waved as Eli and Ryan walked back to Ryan's truck. Then she turned to Helena as they started back toward Grannie's house. "Okay, what the hell was that about?"

"What was what about?"

"Ryan staring you into the ground, talking about punching people who say mean things about you."

Helena hadn't noticed. She'd been too busy being stared into the ground by Ryan, as Molly put it. "It's nothing, really. Just a little disagreement we had last night about facts and fiction."

Molly laughed. "Oh, I'd have liked to see that. I assume you prevailed in the facts department."

"Of course." That might have come out a little smug, but Helena couldn't help it.

"I'd heard of you, you know, before you got back, and I've heard a lot more about you since you did. You are a legend."

"Um, thanks?"

"I knew it had to be mostly fiction. I mean . . ."

"Sadly," Helena interrupted before Molly could paint her as some misunderstood victim in this story, "it's probably safe to assume there's at least a kernel of truth to most of it."

"Then you're not just a legend. You are truly *legendary*. I feel both cooler and more badass just hanging out with you." Molly added a swagger to her walk, causing Helena to laugh.

"You'd better be careful. You could find yourself tainted by association."

"It goes both ways, you know. Folks might assume some of my stellar qualities are rubbing off on you."

Helena rolled her eyes. "Then alert the churches, because *that* would be a miracle."

Chapter 8

Helena's car was in the driveway when Ryan pulled up that evening. Much to his shame, it caused him to hesitate instead of heading directly inside. While Helena had seemed friendly enough this afternoon, she would be fully within her rights to still be mad at him.

He knocked and waited until he heard her call, "Come in," before opening the door. She was stretched out on the couch, her laptop in her lap, and her hair twisted on top of her head in a messy knot.

He must have paused too long at the door, because her mouth twitched. "You can come in. It's safe."

Ryan had to admire her straightforward attitude. She seemed genuinely fine, not repressing any hostility, and pretty relaxed overall. He looked at the glass that sat on the coffee table, but it looked like tea, so it wasn't alcohol-induced civility. It prodded him to be as straightforward with her. "I owe you an apology."

"It's okay. Really. It's not like you were the one spreading lies."

"Still . . ." When she didn't say anything, he sighed. "That is a very mature attitude."

She laughed. "Five years of therapy, dear. Anger gives too much energy to people who don't deserve it. Life's too short."

It seemed she was going to let it go and not even hold

a grudge against him. She really was more mature than half the people in Magnolia Beach. He came the rest of the way in. "I'll go on into the sunroom and leave you to work."

"I probably should be working, but I'm not."

"Do I want to ask what you are doing?" He'd heard about some of the pictures people had seen on her computer when she worked at Latte Dah.

"I am trying to look up some people."

"Who?"

"Sid. Paulie. That crowd."

Well, that was a change. He set his tools down next to the door and leaned against the wall. "I thought you weren't interested."

"Not exactly," she corrected. "I said that when I was trying to forget my past, it didn't make sense for me to look up the people who were a part of that past. But since I'm now sitting smack-dab in the middle of the past, practically wallowing in it, I got curious." She shrugged self-consciously.

"And what did you find?"

"Enough to thoroughly depress me. Not a lot of success stories."

He didn't know what to say to that. "Sorry."

She set the laptop aside, then stood and stretched. "It sounds horrible, but I can't say I'm all that surprised. Disappointed, yes, because I had hopes for those guys. But not surprised." Picking up her glass, she disappeared into the kitchen, leaving the door open.

"You did run with a rough crowd," he called after her.

Her voice floated out of the kitchen over the sound of ice clinking into glasses. "We couldn't all be student body president, you know. And not to sound indignant, but you didn't know them the way I did. They were my friends, and they were there for me."

"Tate turned out okay," he reminded her as she came back in, carrying two glasses and offering him one. When she sat, he did the same, taking the chair catty-corner to where she was on the couch.

"That he did," she said with what sounded like pride. "And it looks like the Navy turned Paulie around."

"That was a good choice for him."

"Definitely. Looking at his Facebook page, I think he may even have a couple of kids."

He couldn't tell if she sounded amused or baffled by the idea. "Did you send him a friend request?"

She shook her head quickly. "No."

"No? Why not?"

"He hasn't ever come looking for me, so he might not want to be in touch again. I can respect that."

"It's social media. It's not like you're asking to move into his house."

"You don't get it, do you?"

"Obviously not." When Helena didn't say anything, he added, "Why don't you explain it to me."

Helena thought for a second, then shrugged. "I don't think I can."

"Why not? I'm smarter than I look."

She made a face at him. "It's called being respectful of people's boundaries."

"You're saying I don't understand boundaries?"

"You live in Magnolia Beach, a place where no one understands boundaries."

He thought of his family. "You might have a point."

She blinked in surprise. "I must admit I wasn't expecting *you* to see it, though."

"Having people in your business gets tiresome. I don't think anyone would deny that. But that doesn't mean it's always a bad thing. It's just a part of what makes us a community, and that's generally good."

"Wow." She laughed. "You definitely sounded like the mayor just then."

"Good. I'd hate to think I couldn't do the job."

"Why do you want to?" she asked.

"Excuse me?" Helena looked genuinely confused, but her question still didn't make a lot of sense.

"I mean, is this a stepping stone? Do you have political ambitions like the state legislature or Congress? Governor, maybe?"

"God, no."

"So you just want to be mayor of Magnolia Beach."

"Yep." The look on her face was quite amusing. "Remember—I like living here."

"I can understand that."

There was a hook at the end of that line. He could tell by her tone. "Oh, you can?"

An eyebrow arched up. "I might like Magnolia Beach, too, if I were a Tanner."

The twitch of her lips told him she was teasing. "Oh, don't start that. As mayor," he said, putting on an official-sounding tone and straightening an imaginary tie, causing Helena to smile, "I can tell you that Magnolia Beach has a lot to offer."

"Such as . . ."

"Good weather, lovely beaches, all kinds of water activities, friendly neighbors—"

Helena held up a hand, stopping him. "That's a matter of perspective. Friendly is just a nicer word for 'nosy.'"

"Well, it's a safe community."

She shook her head. "That means boring."

"Charming?"

"Stuck in the past."

"Caring?"

"Smothering," she countered.

He racked his brain. "Moral, upstanding people."

"Judgmental. And possibly batshit crazy."

He laughed and held up his hands in defeat. "Okay, remind me not to hire you to head up our next tourism campaign."

She grinned. "Fair enough."

"And on that, I'll go to work."

"Do you need help?" His surprise must have shown on his face because she went on to explain. "I know you're working around other projects, and I thought maybe if I helped, you might be able to get home at a reasonable time tonight. But if I'd just be in the way ..."

He swallowed his surprise. "No. Help would be great. But don't you need to do some work tonight?" Normally, if she wasn't working on house-related projects, she was focused on her laptop.

"Yeah. But I'm not really in the mood. Hammering stuff actually sounds pretty good."

He stood and picked up his tools. "You can hold stuff, but not hammer it. I don't want to have to run you to the emergency room. No offense."

"None taken," she said as she followed him into the sunroom. "That's probably a wise decision. I'm not that experienced with tools."

In reality, he didn't need the help, but he should be able to give Helena a couple of smaller jobs that would make her feel like she was contributing. She was a quick learner, though, and soon enough, he was able to actually have her genuinely assisting. After a little while, they got into a groove, and he ran out of instructions to give. He went back to real conversation. "So how was your visit with Ms. Louise today?"

"Good. She's developed this new drive to get better faster and has become a model patient, according to the nurses."

"That is good."

Helena sat back on her haunches and ran a hand over her face, leaving a smudge across her cheek. "*I* think it has more to do with getting back to this side of the bay as soon as possible than anything else."

"Cal Parker Senior?"

Helena nodded. "That's my bet. I'm not questioning it, though. She looks great, she's getting stronger, and that's all good. Now, if we can just get her house put back in order ..."

"I'm working as fast as I can."

"That was not a criticism," she amended quickly.

"Good."

"I mean, do I look crazy enough to criticize a man

wielding a hammer? I may be foolish, but I'm certainly not a fool."

"You sounded just like your grandmother right then." Helena looked at him funny. "And now you look like her. You two really are a lot alike."

"Are you kidding me?"

"I meant it as a compliment," he explained.

"Oh, and I'm taking it as one. My grannie is an awesome lady. She drives me crazy sometimes, and I wanna strangle her on occasion, but . . ."

"That seems fair to me."

Helena's eyes narrowed. "Touché."

"I *meant* that because the two of you are so alike, it's understandable that you'd rub against each other sometimes."

Helena sat up, seemingly surprised at his words. "Oh."

He slid the last piece of new flooring into place. "And we're done."

"That was fast." She ran a hand over the new floor. "It looks great. I can't even tell where the damaged part was."

He accepted the compliment with a nod. "And I appreciate the help." He pushed to his feet and offered a hand to Helena. She grabbed it, and he hauled her to her feet.

She brushed her hands together and then slapped at her pants. "Man, I'm covered in dust."

"Occupational hazard."

"No, I'm just embarrassed the floors are so dirty. If I'd known, I'd have mopped before you got in there." She brushed at herself some more. "Jeez. Yuck."

"You've got a little on your face, too."

Helena rubbed a hand across her face, yet managed to completely miss the one spot on her cheekbone where that gray smudge ran up toward her hairline. "Better?"

Without thinking, he reached out to wipe it. He froze the second his fingers touched her skin, and Helena did, too, her eyes wide with shock. He had to decide quickly what he wanted to do. If he pulled away, it would only draw attention to the awkwardness of this moment, but while continuing on might make the action seem more casual, it might also get him slapped. He compromised by saying, "It's right there," as offhandedly as possible while still getting his hand off the woman as quickly as possible.

Helena's hand flew to her cheek and she rubbed it, removing the mark. Then she stood there for a moment, seemingly as uncomfortable as he was. Finally she cleared her throat. "Um, thanks. And . . . um . . . good job on the floor. I'm going to go in there now. And work. I've got a lot of work to do, so I'll leave you to, um . . . work, too."

"Actually, I think I'll make this my stopping point for tonight and get out of your hair."

"Okay, then." As if she belatedly realized how close she still was to him, Helena took a big step back. "And I'll see you . . . later."

That was weird. And awkward.

Helena wasn't on the couch when he came back through on his way out. Neither was her laptop, meaning she'd retreated upstairs. To avoid him, maybe?

Probably.

Things had been so easy tonight with Helena, just talking and working, that he'd forgotten himself for a moment. At the same time, Helena hadn't ripped him a new one, so either she'd forgotten herself as well, or else . . .

Or else what?

He wasn't going to deny that he was attracted to Helena. A man would have to be blind or dead—possibly both—not to be, and he was neither. But he hadn't finished thinking through what he might actually do about it, much less entertained the thought of Helena being open to any advance he might make.

And while he couldn't be completely sure, those few moments might be deconstructed to mean she *might* be.

Things had just gotten interesting.

Sitting on the jetty drinking beer with Tate in the moonlight was a date with déjà vu—only now she didn't have to worry about being busted for being underage, and Tate wasn't drinking.

She'd been slow on the uptake, only realizing tonight when she noticed the nonalcoholic beers in the bag along with the usual ones that she hadn't seen Tate touch a drop of alcohol since she'd arrived. Tate had shrugged it off with, "I quit a while ago." She didn't ask for an explanation and he didn't offer one, but if she'd borne the brunt of Mr. Harris's alcoholic rages, she might not be much of a drinker, either.

The concrete jetty wasn't that comfortable, and her butt was going numb, but it was a small irritation in an overall great night. There was a nice breeze coming off the water, and it felt good after being inside all day. The nights were getting cooler as they moved into the fall, but still not cold enough to put on the light cotton sweater she'd brought along.

It was peaceful and beautiful, and the view hadn't changed much over the years. She sighed. *Another one of those Magnolia Beach time warps.* But this one wasn't so bad.

Improvements on the Heron Bay shore had been done in the late sixties, adding the boardwalk and the jetties and widening the beach, but it couldn't compete with the sugar sands on the Mobile Bay side—at least for the tourists. The Shore was a locals' spot, and every inch of it held memories for Helena. And, oddly, she was feeling okay about that. It felt comfortable, right even, to be here.

Tate groaned and stretched. "Man, this was easier when we were younger. Sitting like this is killing my back."

"You sound like an old man."

"You lift a couple of Great Danes and see what it does to your lower back."

"Should have used your knees," she scolded.

"Oh yes, thanks. I'll remember that for next time."

A group of teenagers had a small campfire burning a couple of hundred feet away, and the high-pitched laughter of the girls carried over the sound of the water to their place on the jetty. It was a small crowd, but, then again, it was a school night. Not that there was much else to do on a Monday night in Magnolia Beach. The kids were just dark shapes moving around the fire, coupling and uncoupling, with the occasional couple wandering off toward the shadowy privacy under the boardwalk.

Tate pointed to the couple as they disappeared into the shadows. "Young love."

"More like young hormones. Something about the sea air must get them revved up."

"Hey, don't knock that. I lost my virginity under that boardwalk."

"So did most of Magnolia Beach." She thought for a minute. "I feel like we should warn them that's a bad idea. They're going to get sand in places sand really doesn't belong."

"Nah. That's a lesson you have to learn on your own." Tate leaned back on his elbows and looked at her. "I just realized that we're now the creepy old people sitting on the jetty watching us party."

That made her laugh. "I know. I think as long as we don't go over and try to join them, though, we're okay."

"Still, I remember being on the beach and watching the old people hanging out and wondering what they were doing."

"Quit calling us 'old.' It's depressing," she grumbled.

"How could you possibly be depressed on such a beautiful night?"

"And with such charming company," she added with a grin.

Tate tapped his can against hers in a toast. "Indeed."

"I've got a favor to ask you."

"Anything, sweetcheeks."

"Could you spare a couple of hours this weekend to come over and help me move some furniture and stuff around?"

"Did you not just hear me complain about my bad back?" he said teasingly.

"It's not heavy stuff, you wimp. And I'll even spring for pizza."

"In that case, then, of course I'll come help. This is the Saturday I've got a half day at the clinic, but I could come by after."

"That would be great. You're the best." She nudged his shoulder with hers. "And thanks."

"I haven't done anything yet."

"Yes, you have. You've hung out with me, taken me to dinner, and don't forget about that poetry reading. . . ."

Tate groaned. "If I could redo that night, I'd skip the poetry reading. That was pretty bad."

"Yeah, but I appreciate the outing anyway. Being back here would have been really rough without you."

"I'm just sorry I've been so busy and we haven't had more time together."

"You've got a life. I'm just happy you can squeeze me in when you can. And it's looking like I'll be here a couple more weeks, anyway. So we've got time."

"I'm glad to hear it. While I hope Ms. Louise's recovery is quick and complete, I'm not in any real hurry for you to leave."

"Aw, thank you." She leaned against him and rested her head on his shoulder. Tate's arm wrapped around her, pulling her snug up against his side. It was comfortable and familiar, and she sighed happily. She loved her grandmother dearly, but Grannie wasn't an overly demonstrative person. And while Helena had never doubted Grannie's love for her, she'd craved simple, nonsexual human contact, which Tate had always been willing to provide. She felt calm, serene even, for the first time in ages. *Bliss.*

The wind kicked up again, lifting her sweater off the ground and sending it toward the water. Tate jumped up to catch it, jostling her out of her Zen moment and nearly falling off the edge of the jetty in the process. She laughed, which got her a peeved look from Tate as he returned with her sweater. "That was graceful," she said.

With the wind behind her now, her hair was blowing into her face, and speaking gave her a mouthful of it. It was Tate's turn to laugh as she tried to gather the strands together into a makeshift ponytail, trying to twist it into something she could control. "I should have brought a barrette."

"Nah, windblown's a good look for you." A lock escaped her fingers and wrapped back around her face. Tate's finger brushed gently across her forehead as he corralled it and pushed it back behind her ear. Then his palm was on her cheek, his thumb stroking gently. "But, then, I can't imagine what isn't a good look for you."

The intimate touch, the half smile, the low pitch to his voice . . . It was unexpected but unmistakable, and she froze in shock.

Tate seemed to translate that as permission, and a second later, his lips were gently pressing against hers. They were soft and warm, the kiss hesitant at first. Then it gained confidence as his fingers threaded through her hair to pull her closer.

It was the touch of his tongue that snapped her out of her shock. Her hands flew up to press against his chest to keep him at a distance. "Tate!"

He pulled back, question and surprise written on his face, but his fingers continued to gently rub her scalp.

Helena's heart fell to her stomach, which contracted around it painfully. There was no way this wasn't about to hurt him. "You—I mean, we . . . *I* . . . can't."

His brow furrowed. "What?"

What were the right words? She pulled back a bit more. "This. I don't . . . I just don't feel—"

Tate's hand fell away as understanding dawned, and he stepped back. "Oh."

Her eyes started to burn, and she hated herself for causing that look on his face. "Tate, please . . ."

He shrugged. "No biggie, sweetcheeks." He smiled as he said it, but the smile was forced and the words were flat.

She reached for his hand. "I wish I—"

"Don't worry about it."

"But I *do*. I'm so sorry if I've misled you, given you the impression. . . ." Tate was shaking his head, and Helena hated herself more. "I've taken advantage of you. Of our friendship. I just needed someone to lean on, and I forgot that we're not kids anymore. . . ." She was making a muck of it—probably making it worse. "You are *so* important to me. I didn't really realize how much I missed you until I got you back, and I don't want to lose you again or mess this up. I'm flattered, *honored*, but—"

"But you don't feel that way. I get it, Helena. You don't need to belabor the point."

Damn it, damn it, damn it. "It's not that simple—"

He didn't seem to hear her. "Well, this is awkward and embarrassing." He shoved his hands in his pockets and looked out over the water.

"Please don't feel that way. If anyone should feel embarrassed, it's me, *not* you."

"Yeah. Right." His shoulders slumped. "I should probably go—"

"No. Please not like that." She sat and patted the ground beside her. "Come on, sit. Let's talk about this."

"Oh, I'd rather not. In fact, I'd just like to pretend it never happened."

"Done. It's already forgotten."

He looked down at her and shook his head. "I wish it were that easy."

"Then just tell me what you want me to do. I'll do it."

"Let me walk away with a bit of dignity, okay? I'll see you later."

She didn't really have a choice, as Tate took off and was quickly swallowed by the shadows. *Oh God.* Could she have made a bigger mess? She tucked her dress around her feet, wrapped her arms around her legs, balanced her chin on her knees, and sighed. A couple of tears escaped, and the wind chilled them as they slid down her cheek.

This was all her fault, and she hated herself for it. Tate was the one person in Magnolia Beach she could count on, the one person who genuinely cared for her, and she'd latched onto that, desperate for the support and acceptance. Now she realized she'd latched on a little too tight and crossed a line. *Damn.*

Tate was the last person on earth she wanted to hurt. Plus, she'd reacted badly, compounding the situation and making it worse.

But what was she supposed to do? Lead him on? Let him think she felt something she didn't? Take what he offered and worry about the lasting effects later—if at all?

Friends could be excellent lovers, but there was never a guarantee that the friendship would survive. And she didn't want to lose Tate as a friend. Not when she'd just gotten him back.

And what about new friends? She liked Molly, and the more she was around her, the more convinced she became that Molly might like Tate. Knowing that, there was no way she could ever sleep with Tate—even if she *wanted* to.

She was damned if she did, damned if she didn't.

The story of my whole sorry life.

Sitting here wasn't going to solve the mess she'd made of things, though. She pushed to her feet, grabbed her shoes, and walked back up to the road. As she brushed the sand off and slid her feet back into her shoes, she watched the kids down at their fire again. Even from here, seeing only the dark outlines of their bodies, she could recognize the teenage dating rituals—the playful shoves, the halfhearted chase, the ones standing off to the side, probably too nervous to make a move. . . .

It doesn't get any easier, kids.

Dear God, she really was getting old.

She walked back to Grannie's, trying to figure out how she could fix this with Tate—running possible scenarios, carefully choosing words. She was so lost in her own head that she was halfway up the front walk before it registered that the lights were on inside the house and Ryan's truck was parked in the driveway.

She cursed, fighting the urge to just sit on the grass and pout. Ryan Tanner was the very *last* thing she needed right now.

She'd been enjoying his company lately, feeling flirty and liking the attention. It had made her feel normal, less on edge, which was nice. Plus, the ideas her libido and overactive imagination kept throwing at her seemed merely crazy now instead of flat-out insane.

But she couldn't deal with that tonight—especially not after what happened with Tate. Hurting Tate was bad enough for one evening. Coming home to someone she shouldn't want and couldn't have was just salt in the wound.

She desperately needed a drink.

Deep breath. Chin up.

Ryan was on all fours, installing a ramp over the threshold from the front room to the kitchen. While usually she'd appreciate that view, it just made her grumpier tonight.

Sitting back on his haunches, Ryan seemed surprised to see her. "You're back early."

She dropped her purse into a chair and kicked off her shoes. "Yeah." She had to shimmy past him to get to the kitchen, but she needed that drink. "Excuse me."

The words came out sharper than intended, and Ryan's eyebrows went up. "You're in a bad mood. You and Tate get in a fight or something?"

Argh. "Shut up." Condiment bottles rattled in the fridge door as she jerked it open. She looked inside, then cursed. *Why* was there no alcohol in her fridge?

"Whoa. I was just kidding."

"I'm not in the mood." Oh, thank God, there was a bottle of Chardonnay in the vegetable crisper. She grabbed the corkscrew as if her life depended on it.

"Obviously," he said quietly. "I'm almost done here, so I'll finish up and get out of your way."

"I'd appreciate that." She sent the corkscrew in crookedly, and the cork split and broke. "Damn it!"

"Would you like some help?"

The need for the wine outweighed everything else. She took a deep breath and closed her eyes. "Please. I'm a little ham-handed at the moment."

Ryan reached for the bottle, unscrewed the corkscrew, and examined the damage to the cork. "Are you sure you're all right?" he asked casually. *Too* casually, actually. What was he getting at?

"What do you mean?"

"You come back from a date—"

She nearly interrupted him to correct that it wasn't a date, but it rather seemed like she was the *only* person who didn't see it that way, so she kept her mouth shut.

"And you're upset, your hair's a bit crazy—"

A hand automatically went to her hair, smoothing it back into some semblance of order. "It was windy on the shore."

"All things that might be signs that . . ." He paused as if searching for the right words. "Signs the evening didn't quite go as planned."

There was no real sense in denying it. "No, it didn't."

Ryan got the cork out, poured a good-sized glass of the wine, and handed it to her. "Would you like to talk about it?"

In a way, she did want to, just to get an outside opinion. She could call Misha, but Misha didn't know all the backstory or Tate and the wider implications. . . . But Ryan wasn't really the right person, either, even though he did have that background knowledge. Anyway, even with all the time they'd been spending together recently, they weren't exactly *friends*. Telling Ryan something private about Tate seemed disloyal to the one person she *knew* was her friend—even though Tate might not be feeling too friendly toward *her* at the moment. She took a long drink of wine, while Ryan waited patiently for her to decide. She sighed. "Ever been caught between a rock and a hard place?"

"Yep. It's not fun." He motioned toward the bottle, seeming to ask if he could have some, and she nodded.

"Are you sure there's no way out?" he asked as he poured.

"Not without hurting someone."

"Including you?"

She rolled her eyes. "I'm hurt no matter what I do. It's only a matter of deciding who I want to share that pain with."

"Well, that does suck, then."

"Yep. There's no way around it, though. At least not that I can see." She stared at her glass. "I shouldn't have given Grannie a choice. I should have just made her come to Atlanta."

Ryan snorted. "I can't imagine that would have gone over well."

Since just the mere suggestion had been met with a flat-out refusal by Grannie, demanding it would have been a disaster. "You're probably right. But at least I wouldn't be in this mess. I'm not sure which I'd prefer."

"Tate will get over it, you know," he said quietly. She looked at him in surprise, and he shrugged. "It's not all that hard to figure out what you're not saying. Tate's always had a thing for you."

Ryan made that statement matter-of-factly, as if this were something she was supposed to know already. She was still recovering from the fact he'd known what she wasn't saying, so *that* little bombshell of info sent her mind reeling. How was that even possible? After all those years and everything they'd been through? She stared into her glass again, hoping the wine might have an answer. "Well, it's news to me."

It was Ryan's turn to look surprised. "You're kidding. The only real question was how you felt about him."

"*I* thought we were friends. Now I have to face the fact I've either been leading him on for years, or else he's been banking Nice Guy credits in the hope they would one day pay off." She leaned against the counter, suddenly needing the extra support. "Sweet Jesus, this is a mess."

"Do you honestly think either of those things is true?"

"No," she grudgingly admitted.

"Then give him—and yourself—a break."

"But—"

"Tate's a big boy. It can't be the first time he's been rejected by a woman, and while rejection stings, it doesn't do irreparable damage."

"Well, since you're so damn smart, tell me how to fix this."

Ryan seemed to think for a minute. "You don't. You give him space until he gets over it."

"Give him space. *That's* your advice?" She didn't know whether to laugh or bemoan the ignorance of the entire male species.

Ryan nodded.

"What if he doesn't get over it?" She pushed off the counter and started to pace. She had to do something or else she'd start to cry. "I'll have lost one of my best friends. I can't—"

Ryan reached for her arm, stopping both her pacing and her words. Leaning close to meet her eyes directly, he spoke quietly. "He will, Helena. I promise."

She wanted to believe him, and she needed that promise. Ryan sounded sincere, and the warm hand on her elbow reassured her. She took a deep breath. "Thank you."

Ryan smiled slightly and nodded, then gave her elbow a little squeeze. She still felt guilty and bad for hurting Tate, but she was calming down now, the fear she'd done serious damage abating.

It took another couple of seconds to realize that Ryan hadn't released her yet, and she was more bothered by the fact she hadn't noticed than by the fact he hadn't. Hard on the heels of *that* thought came the realization she didn't mind, and might, in fact, actually like it.

That was a little confusing. And while she might have liked the casual flirting and spent way too much time thinking about that moment when he touched her face, she wasn't sure now was the right time for her to try to decipher any signals Ryan might or might not be sending her way.

That *could* be something more than concern and re-assurance in his eyes, but it also could be wishful think-ing egged on by a revved-up libido. At least she was smart enough to realize that she was a little too raw and unstable right now to distinguish simple human courtesy from something else. And while Ryan seemed convinced no one could actually die from rejection, the embarrass-ment of reading this moment wrong could possibly kill her.

She stepped back, removing her arm from his grasp and putting space between them before she could screw up tonight any worse than she already had. That *might* have been a flash of disappointment she saw on Ryan's face, but it was gone so quickly, she couldn't say for sure.

This is the safer choice. The better *choice.*

"I appreciate the pep talk."

"Feel better?"

"I do. Thanks. But I am suddenly exhausted and think I should just call it a night." That wasn't a lie—the emo-tional roller coaster had drained her—but it was a handy escape route out of this, too.

He nodded toward the door ramp he'd been working on when she came in. "Give me fifteen minutes to finish this, and I'll be out of your hair."

"No rush. Whenever's fine." She forced herself to walk slowly and calmly out of the room and up the stairs.

Lying in her bed, she stared at the ceiling for ages, even long after she heard Ryan leave, trying to make sense of everything that had happened since she set foot in Alabama. The world had gone crazy around her. It was a lot to process.

Tate—her friend, champion, and partner in crime—was carrying some kind of torch for her. It was hard to picture, and she could only hope Ryan was right and Tate would get over it.

And Ryan . . .

If he was sending out signals of interest, it would be

very tempting to take him up on it. She wasn't going to lie to herself and say she wasn't interested in seeing some of those muscles up close and personal.

Oh, good Lord, what was she even thinking? Ryan couldn't be interested in *her*. He was the freakin' mayor, for goodness' sake. Were mayors even allowed to have casual sex?

Argh. She pulled her pillow over her head. Nothing made sense.

This wasn't Magnolia Beach. It was the freakin' *Twilight Zone.*

Chapter 9

At least he'd made up his mind.

Choosing to make a pass at a woman shouldn't feel like a monumental decision worthy of pride, but Ryan fully admitted these were unusual circumstances. Twice in the past few days he'd given Helena reason and opportunity to rip his head off and hand it back to him, and she hadn't done it either time. That was definitely a promising sign.

While that low-grade simmering attraction in his belly had been getting harder and harder to ignore, hearing Helena say she *didn't* want Tate had turned that up to a boil.

The problem, though, was that while Helena did not seem completely averse to the idea, she hadn't exactly given him any encouragement, either. It was enough to give any smart man pause.

But while he might be cautious, he wasn't going to chicken out.

If he hadn't been so distracted by simply talking to Helena, he'd have finished working on the house days ago. Not that he minded the delays, but he only had a few piddling projects left to do, so one way or the other, he'd be finished tonight.

His plan of action still wasn't fully formed when he got to the house. He vaguely planned to finish up as quickly as possible, maybe sit and have a beer, and then he'd ask her to dinner or something.

But even those few vague ideas went straight out the window when he got there, because Helena was anything but predictable.

Usually, Helena would either be on her computer or she'd be working on something in another part of the house, and he'd see her briefly in passing. Tonight, though, he found her sitting cross-legged in the new recliner she'd bought for Ms. Louise. She wore a light yellow dress that looked more like an oversized T-shirt and had the hem tucked under her feet to create a sling for a big ball of green yarn.

And she was knitting.

The domesticity of it brought him to a screeching halt.

Helena had looked up when he opened the door, and she greeted him with a smile. "Hey." The smile faded. "Something wrong?"

"You're knitting."

"Yes." She frowned at the yarn. "Not very well, though. I'm a little rusty." She cut her eyes back up at him. "Is that look on your face surprise that I can knit or fear because I'm armed with pointy metal sticks?"

"A little of both," he confessed. "I just never pictured you as a knitter."

"Well, I'm full of surprises."

"I happen to agree."

Her eyes narrowed. "Is that a compliment?"

"Since you're currently armed and I'm not ... yes." When she laughed, he decided it boded well for his master plan, and he whistled as he went to work.

The swinging door between the kitchen and the living room was a hazard for a person using a walker and had to come down. He'd wanted to install a pocket door, but there wasn't enough room, so he was replacing it with a pretty folding door Ms. Louise would be able to open out of the way with one hand. He felt eyes on him and looked up to see Helena sitting at the bottom of the stairs watching him. "Am I in your way?" he asked, already starting to climb down the ladder.

"No."

When she didn't elaborate, he asked, "So, are you supervising me or . . . ?"

"Where'd you learn to do this?" she asked instead of answering.

"Hang a door? It's not hard. You just—"

She waved that away. "I mean all of it. Replacing floors, tearing out walls . . ."

"Trial and error, mostly." He laughed as he sent another screw into the track, but Helena didn't join in. "Wait. That was a serious question?"

She nodded.

"Some of it I taught myself. I did a lot of work on my parents' house when I was growing up."

"With or without permission?"

"Both, actually." He went back to work, but since Helena seemed to expect more, he continued. "I worked for Harvey Meadows's company on summer breaks and then full-time after college until I was ready to go out on my own about five years ago. I think I've worked on every building in Magnolia Beach at one time or another."

Helena's head cocked to the side. "So why go study business at Auburn?"

He grinned at her. "Mainly to figure out I'd rather do this any day."

"So you like it?"

"Of course. I wouldn't do it otherwise." After tightening the last screw, he climbed down and popped the door into place. "Why all the questions?"

"I'm just curious." She shrugged a shoulder. "It seems strange to go to all the hassle and expense of getting a degree like that and not use it."

"Well, I can say I have it. And it made my folks happy."

"Ah." She nodded in understanding. "It's *their* degree."

"Well, they did pay for it. But it's not like I regret getting it, mind you. I had a very good time in college."

"If that's true, then why'd you come back here?"

The answer to that question had always seemed so obvious, but then, Helena had never been the one asking. "My family and friends are here," he tried by way of explanation, then decided it sounded weak. "And I couldn't think of anywhere I might like better." Since that answer was also rather lame, he turned the tables. "Why *didn't* you come back?"

"Because I could think of a hundred places I might like better."

"Like Atlanta?"

"That was one possible place. Mainly I wanted a city where I had options and there was always something exciting going on."

"You kept things pretty exciting around here."

"Let's not go there. I'm still within arm's reach of my knitting needles," she teased. "I just didn't want to be bored, because yes, boredom is a proven breeding ground for Hell-on-Wheels-style shenanigans," she conceded sarcastically. "But then I discovered the joy of anonymity, and that was the best thing *ever*."

"That was actually one of the things I didn't like about Auburn."

"You like being a big fish in a little pond, huh?"

She made it sound bad, somehow, and it put him on the defensive. "It doesn't suck, you know."

"That depends on the fish."

She'd said it matter-of-factly, but it landed hard, making him realize he'd never really given it much thought. "Helena—"

"Sorry," she interrupted with a shrug. "I didn't mean for that to sound so judgmental. I think it's great you have that big family and are so happy here in Magnolia Beach. Being happy is what's important."

This evening had gotten odd, shaking his willingness to follow the original game plan. And while he'd made his name as both a quarterback and coach by being able to read the other team quickly and adjust accordingly, he was, unfortunately, without an alternate plan. Still, he had to try something or else abort entirely.

But with the door now hanging, he was, for all intents and purposes, finished with his work here. He started cleaning up. Carefully casual, he said, "Well, that's the last of it. I'm done."

"Seriously?" Helena looked around. "I guess you are. I can't thank you enough."

"You're welcome."

"I'll get my checkbook." She stopped to test the door on her way into the kitchen. "That's nice. Grannie will like it."

He debated with himself as he picked up his tools, but a second later he heard Helena ask, "How about a beer? I think we should celebrate."

Well, that made things easier. "Sounds great."

Two hours and he didn't know how many beers later, he and Helena were sitting on the rug in the living room. She had her hand pressed against her side, fighting a stitch from laughing so hard, as he told her about the time Eli and his dumbass friends decided to streak through the ribbon ceremony of the county fair—something that happened five years after she left town.

"So then Eli trips and ends up sprawled on the ground in front of the stage, wearing nothing but the Batman mask Mom made him in sixth grade. His friends, of course, just left him there, and as he tried to get up, he got tangled in the bunting hanging off the stage and sprawled flat again."

Helena seemed to be fighting for breath. "Oh my God, that's priceless."

"No," he corrected, "the *priceless* part was watching Mom walk over there, seemingly as cool as could be, and placing the quilt she'd just won second prize for across his genitals before walking away."

Helena howled and nearly fell over. Righting herself, she wiped at her eyes. "See, Grannie *never* tells me the good stuff."

"I doubt Ms. Louise found it amusing, as she was on-stage getting her blue ribbon for her jam at the time. It kind of stole her thunder."

Helena snorted as she pushed to her feet. "Another?" At his nod, she headed for the kitchen, and he followed.

She was still chuckling as she opened the fridge. "Public nudity. That's not even on *my* long list of sins."

"Pity."

Helena's jaw dropped as she turned to look at him.

"Hey, you could have made a lot of teenage boys really happy."

"I'm going to pretend you didn't say that," she said primly.

"Why? You may have had half the county boys scared to death of you, but it wasn't because of your looks. You, unknowingly of course, were the star of many a fantasy of the senior class. Juniors and sophomores, too. Hell, probably even a few freshmen."

She leaned against the counter and crossed her arms over her chest. "You're kidding me."

"Why would I? You were gorgeous even then."

"Including you?"

"Including me." He'd said it without thinking, but Helena was now looking at him funny, and he regretted the confession. *Ah, hell.* At the same time, wasn't this kind of his plan?

A small smile pulled at the corner of her mouth. "You thought I was gorgeous?"

"You don't need to fish for compliments. You know you were. Still are."

There was a long, heavy moment as the whole mood shifted and the air turned thick and hot. "Careful there," she warned.

She'd started it, so he didn't see the need. And while her tone had been casual, the pulse point in her neck was fluttering, and her chest was flushing pink. That might not have been his best, most suave move, but she was thinking about it now, and that was what counted. "Why? It's true."

There was a long, disconcerting silence as Helena studied him, and it kept him in place, waiting for her to decide.

The deep breath she took stuttered in her chest, and she licked her lips, sending a bolt of heat through his blood as it rushed south so fast, he felt light-headed.

Then she smiled at him.

That smile was a match dropped on gasoline.

Helena took a step forward, closing the space between them. Her mouth was under his, an almost gentle kiss that clashed with the fire racing through him. Then she sighed against him, twining her arms around his neck and pulling his head down to hers, and the kiss went from gentle to hungry in a heartbeat.

There was a disconnected moment as his brain rushed to catch up, trying to make sense of Helena, here, in his arms, kissing him. As her lips moved to his throat, though, brain and body clicked, narrowing his focus to this, *now*. A tug on her hair brought her mouth back up to his, and her knees buckled under the onslaught.

He let her anchor against his arm while his other hand traced the flare of her hip and curved around the indentation of her waist. Her rib cage heaved under his fingers, and her head fell back with a sigh as he traced the curve of her breast and palmed her through the thin cotton.

"Ryan . . ."

The sound of his name, breathy and broken, on her lips caused his pulse and temperature to spike.

Good Lord, he wanted to take her here and now, up against the refrigerator, and the slide of Helena's hands down his back, up under the hem of his shirt and around to play across his chest wasn't exactly helping him gain control. With a groan, he hauled her up, wrapping her legs around his waist, and pressed her against the cold metal door.

Helena gasped and arched against him, her nails digging sharply into his skin.

There was no way he was going to make it up the stairs to her bedroom. He dug his fingers into her hips to steady her, then covered the short distance to the kitchen table, setting her on the edge.

Helena fisted a hand around the neck of his T-shirt, pulling him down on top of her as she lay back. The table, built of solid pine with sturdy legs, held steady, accepting their weight with only a tiny creak.

Her dress rucked up nearly to her waist, giving him full access to those lean thighs that squeezed around him with surprising strength. Slowly, savoring each inch of skin, he slid the dress the rest of the way up and over her head, leaving her only in two pieces of silk before leaning down to kiss her again. He felt her hands on the hem of his shirt, pulling it up, until he had to break the kiss to remove it. She locked her ankles behind his back and trailed her hands over his chest and arms.

Trapped between her thighs, he balanced on his elbows to look at her. Eyes closed, hair rioting around her head, lips swollen from his kisses . . . "God, you're beautiful."

He hadn't really meant to say it aloud, but when her eyes opened and she trailed her hand across his jaw, he was glad he did. The sexy, appreciative smile nearly did him in. She grabbed his belt buckle and tugged. "Come here."

He held back, shifting his weight to one arm and tracing the smooth swell of skin above the edge of her bra with his fingertips. Cupping her through the silky fabric, he retraced his path with his tongue, feeling her nipple pebble against his palm. He flicked his thumb across it, causing her to gasp in pleasure.

Helena writhed under his mouth as he eased down her torso, and gooseflesh spread across her body. The whimpers timed perfectly with the skin and muscles jumping under the touch of his tongue. He wanted to explore, take his time, but he was too on edge and those sexy sounds were priming the pump, leaving him feeling like a teenage boy who'd never touched a woman before.

He licked a trail along the edge of her panties to her hip, then pressed his tongue against her center through the already damp fabric.

Helena cursed and bucked and grasped for purchase on the tabletop. When that failed, she sat up, grabbed his jaw, and pulled him to his feet. Hot kisses branded his chest as she worked his belt and zipper, and then it was his turn to cuss as she palmed him.

He stilled her hand with one of his own, fighting for a single ounce of self-control. It nearly killed him.

He put a finger under her chin and tilted it up. The desire in her eyes nearly sent him to his knees. *Slowly. Slowly.* "If you continue like that, this will be over before you know it."

"I think I can keep up." She pulled his forehead down to hers. Her eyes met his as her hand started to move again. "Next time. We'll go slow next time."

That was all the permission he needed. As he pushed Helena back flat on the table, everything became a blur of hands and lips and skin. She wasn't shy, and between her eager participation and moans of approval, Ryan was shaking with need as he steadied her hips and pressed inside.

Her breath hissed out, and her eyes met his evenly as she locked her legs around his waist to hold him in place. He leaned forward for another kiss and slid the last inch, his groan mingling with Helena's sigh as their hips met. Twining his fingers through hers, he began to move, watching the pleasure play across Helena's face until her eyes rolled back in her head and she nearly arched completely off the table with a keening wail.

The world went fuzzy around the edges as he exploded, and he collapsed atop her, sweating and heaving. When he was able to think again, he became aware of Helena's fingers tickling softly down his spine.

Pants around his ankles, naked ass in the air, sprawled on Ms. Louise's kitchen table . . . He probably looked ridiculous, but, *damn*, he didn't care.

He wasn't sure where he found the energy, but he managed to lift his head a few inches. Helena was flushed and mussed, her hair damp around her temples, and her face was rubbed slightly red from his five o'clock shadow.

But she had a smile on her face. A damn satisfied one, he noted with a touch of male pride.

"Not that I'm complaining," she said, "but can we move upstairs now?"

Half a second ago, he'd felt half-dead and would have claimed he'd never be able to move from this spot. But that smile . . . Well, it felt like pure adrenaline shooting straight into his veins.

"Grab the wine."

Helena no longer had control of her major muscle groups. She was precariously hanging half off the mattress, her right arm and leg brushing the floor, but she couldn't seem to actually move anything in order to change the situation. She was a noodle. A sated, sweaty noodle.

Fortunately, Ryan reached for her and slid her back onto the bed, spooning her against his front. Where he found the strength, she had no idea. He'd done everything short of turn her inside out in his efforts over the course of the evening. She knew from his work on the house that he was a thorough, inventive, patient perfectionist, and she was currently grateful—ever so grateful—for those traits.

For the first time in, well, *ages*, Helena felt like her head was clear and the tension she'd gotten so accustomed to carrying was actually gone. It seemed the phrase "Sometimes you just need to get laid" might actually hold some merit.

But that didn't make this less crazy. It was one thing to toy with the idea, maybe even ponder it deeply, but actually sleeping with Ryan was just short of insane. And it wasn't like she could blame it on the beer; she'd had enough to give her a buzz and relax her, but not enough to obliterate her higher-thinking skills.

The simple fact was that she'd wanted Ryan, wanted *this*, and she'd made the choice.

But now what?

Ryan, it seemed, was a postcoital snuggler, and it almost felt *too* intimate—which was absurd, considering what they'd just done with and to each other. She was definitely okay with the sex; the snuggling, though, she wasn't quite sure about. She groaned as she pushed up to a sitting position and moved her hair out of her face. It felt like one giant tangle, and she didn't even want to imagine what it might look like.

Ryan rolled to his back and draped his forearm over his eyes. "Honey, I'm done. I don't think I could get it up again if my life depended on it."

He'd said something similar an hour ago and ended up recanting the statement. Ryan must have remembered that as well, because he lifted his arm far enough for her to see one eyeball. "And this time I mean it. You may have killed me."

"Actually, I'm going to get some water. If I can get my legs to work, that is."

"Good luck with that. I may not move until next week sometime."

"And exactly how would I explain your campout in my bed to the good people of Magnolia Beach?" she teased.

"Maybe they won't notice I'm missing." There was a tiny note of hope in his voice.

She shot it down gleefully. "Fat chance."

"I can dream, can't I?"

"You can't set yourself up as the big fish in the little pond, Mayor Tanner, and then complain about it."

"Watch me, Hell-on-Wheels."

The nickname didn't bother her this time, and since she'd kind of started it by calling him "Mayor Tanner," she just snorted as she slid carefully to the edge of the bed and tested her legs. They were wobbly but working. Her quads, though, launched a major complaint as she went down the stairs.

She drank the first glass of water as if she'd been in the desert for a week. Her initial thirst sated, she sipped at her second glass and stared out the window. Magnolia Beach was small enough not to cause much light pollution, so the stars were visible—unlike the view of the sky from her apartment in Atlanta. In a way, seeing the stars made her feel disconnected and small. Unimportant. She had a small circle of friends in Atlanta, but a certain amount of disconnect was important and expected in a city that size. Otherwise, it was too easy to get overwhelmed with it all.

Here, she knew almost everyone over the age of thirty—their families, their histories, their biggest hits, and their most embarrassing moments—but she wasn't really a part of any of it anymore.

Anonymity could be great. But feeling small in a small town wasn't fun.

And it drove home the fact she really didn't belong here, making her wonder if her rush to jump into the sack with Ryan had been born just as much from a need to connect with someone—*anyone*—as from physical attraction.

But that didn't make sense, either, because, if so, she would have been more receptive to Tate's advances.

Tate.

Damn it, what *was* she going to do about Tate? If this hit the grapevine, her rejection of his advances might look like she was holding out for Ryan. That would just add insult to injury.

Oh yeah. This was complete insanity.

And now she needed to get Ryan out of here before she became grist for the rumor mill again.

She filled a second glass of water for Ryan and made the slow, painful trek back up the stairs to her bedroom.

The little shepherdess lamp on her nightstand, long ago defaced with a marker to give her a more acceptable gothlike appearance, cast just enough light to be flattering. And it certainly flattered Ryan, giving his tanned skin a nice glow and creating defining shadows around the musculature of his chest and arms.

Goodness, he was just *pretty*. She might make bad

choices, but she had damn good taste in whom to make them with.

He was staring with a frown at the Wolverine poster that hung on her wall opposite the bed. "I find it disconcerting that Hugh Jackman just watched me have sex. It's like he's judging me or something."

She snickered. "Maybe he was. You get high marks, though."

"Thanks. But still . . ." He took the glass she offered and drank deeply.

"So I had a Hugh Jackman crush. He was really hot in 2001." She looked around. "This room is a little bit like a time capsule, though, isn't it?"

"You should redecorate."

"In all that spare time I have?" She grabbed her robe and pulled it on, suddenly modest now that they were just talking. "I guess I could at least pull down the posters and put away some of the junk. You don't know how creepy it was to come home and find my room almost exactly as I'd left it."

"That's creepy, but not as creepy as an adult man having sex in a room that looks like it belongs to a teenager. I almost feel dirty."

"And judged by Hugh Jackman."

"You gave me high marks, though, so Hugh's opinion doesn't really matter." Setting the glass on the nightstand, he lay back down with a sigh.

It was a small opening, but she'd have to take it. "But the neighbors' do."

"What?"

Perching on the foot of the bed, safely far enough from Ryan's impressive chest to resist temptation, she said, "Your truck is still in my driveway, and you know half the neighborhood has made note of that. People will start to talk because there's no good non-naked reason for you to be here past midnight."

"I don't really care."

"Well, I do."

"Since when?"

"Since now. It's nobody's business who I sleep with."

"You think I'm going to go bragging or confirming any rumors?" he asked.

"No," she admitted, "but I'd rather it not even be an issue."

"You do know how hard it is to keep a secret in this town, right?"

"I do. Which is all the more reason to get on top of this before anyone gets suspicious."

"It's not their business."

"Oh, like that's actually ever mattered to anyone." She rolled her eyes. "And since you're Magnolia Beach's favorite son, this will be front-page news. I can see the headline now. 'Mayor of Magnolia Beach Seduced by—'" A chill ran down her spine. "Oh, *shit*. You're the mayor." She got up and started to pace as she realized the ramifications of this.

Ryan looked at her like she was a little slow. "Yes," he said carefully, "but you knew that already."

"I knew it in theory, but it wasn't real. *Christ*. Magnolia Beach will lose its collective mind if they find out Mayor Tanner had sex with Hell-on-Wheels." She tossed him his clothes. "You need to get out of here."

"I'd think I'd remember if celibacy had been part of my oath of office." He laughed, but Helena didn't find any of this funny. "I'm allowed to have sex."

"Not with me." The look on Ryan's face questioned her sanity. She leaned against her dresser to explain. "I will destroy your career."

"Intentionally?" Ryan laughed again. "Jeez, Helena, I didn't know you were so displeased with my performance."

"Be serious. *Think* about it for a second, will you? I'm Magnolia Beach's reigning Bad Girl and Poor Example. Sleeping with me shows pretty poor judgment on your part."

"I disagree—"

She didn't let him finish. "Your image, your *credibility*,

will be damaged by any association with me. People will lose respect for you. If you like your job as mayor, I'm a bad choice for recreational activities."

"I think you're overreacting. And, not to burst your bubble, but I don't think you're so bad that your reputation could harm mine." She started to interrupt, but he didn't let her. "And anyway, if you think I care what small-minded busybodies think, you're mistaken."

"Those small-minded busybodies voted you into office," she reminded him.

"And if they think my personal life is adversely affecting my mayoral duties, they are welcome to elect someone else to the job."

It sounded very logical, and it was a bit flattering, but if she'd learned anything about Ryan in the last few weeks, it was that he loved being mayor and took the position seriously.

"I'm not ashamed of myself," he continued, "but it sounds like you are."

"I'm trying to be realistic here." She motioned to his clothes. "If you don't care about your reputation, that's fine, but I still think it's best that you get dressed and go. I don't want Grannie to have to face another round of people gossiping about her granddaughter."

He finally started to get dressed. "So you're worried about me and Ms. Louise, but not yourself. How altruistic."

"I am thinking of myself, too. I don't need that crap on top of everything else. And Tate doesn't—"

"Tate?"

"You think the fact I chose to sleep with you but not him won't hurt his feelings? And if, as you say, everyone knows he 'always had a thing for me,' then that would be doubly hurtful and embarrassing for him."

"Ah, well, we wouldn't want Tate to be embarrassed." He pulled on his shirt and reached for his shoes. "Don't worry. My lips are sealed."

This conversation had not gone as planned, but it had

been effective. Ryan was getting dressed and leaving, and that had been the whole point. She should be glad. They could sort the rest of it out later—in daylight hours, when it wouldn't look questionable for him to be there at all.

The tension and ill mood radiating off him bothered her, though, and left her feeling conflicted.

But *that* wasn't something she wanted to examine too closely right now.

Chapter 10

"What did you do last night? You look like hell."
Ryan looked up from his phone as Shelby
flopped into the seat across from him. He'd landed on
the front step of Latte Dah at one minute past opening
time so Molly could load him up on her high-octane coffee in hopes that he might be able to face the day. He
was bone-tired from lack of sleep, sore in muscles he'd
forgotten he had, and more than a little pissed off about
the way Helena had all but hustled him out the door. He
had every reason to look like hell, but that didn't mean
he was going to tell his cousin about it. "Well, we all can't
be as naturally gorgeous as you first thing in the morning."

"Don't be an ass."

"Learn to take a compliment."

Molly materialized with a coffeepot and topped up
his cup, scolding them at the same time. "No bickering in
my shop, y'all. Especially this early in the morning." She
then turned a bright smile on Shelby. "The usual? Or do
you want to try something different?"

Shelby looked over at the menu board like she might
be considering it, although Ryan knew it was just an act.
It was a good act, though, perfected through years of
practice until even the family could sometimes forget
that it was just a cover. "The usual." Molly nodded and

went behind the counter, and Shelby eased back in her chair. "Seriously, you look exhausted. Are you getting sick? I could run you over to the clinic."

There was an almost hopeful lilt in her voice that he sincerely hoped he was imagining. "I'm just tired. I was up late."

She smirked. "Doing something fun, I hope."

He nearly spit his coffee, earning him a strange look from Shelby. "I was working. Trying to finish up at Ms. Louise's," he added, getting ahead of the gossip. If people had noticed his truck in Helena's driveway that late, it would be better to go ahead and proclaim the information far and wide before any type of innuendo could become attached to it.

"Are you almost done there?"

It was hard to say, considering how things had changed so dramatically last night, but also not something to discuss with Shelby. "I think so."

"Good." She smiled at Molly as she set coffee and a bagel on the table in front of her.

"Why?" he asked carefully.

"Because it's been eating up what little free time you have."

There was no way Shelby would be concerned about his free time unless she had another idea in mind of how he should fill it. He was almost afraid to ask because he was afraid he knew. "And?"

"Have you met Kathryn Kendall? The new physician's assistant at the clinic?"

Christ, he was *not* in the mood for Shelby's attempts at matchmaking. But it explained why she'd been so eager to take him to the clinic. "Can't say that I have. I haven't been sick lately."

"I *told* your daddy that he needed to do something to introduce her around and make her feel welcome. All of her family is up north somewhere, and she doesn't really know anyone here yet."

"She obviously knows you, so there's that."

Shelby ignored him. "I was thinking of getting a group

together, maybe at my place, for a little potluck or something, just to introduce her to some folks."

Be vague. "That's very nice of you."

"So you'll come?"

Okay, try noncommittal. "If I'm available."

"Ryan . . ."

Direct, then. "I'm sure she's a lovely person, but I'm not going to let you set me up with her just because you feel like playing at matchmaking."

Shelby pouted. It was a fake pout—not that it would have worked on him even if it were genuine—and it looked a little silly on the normally straightforward Shelby. "She is lovely," she insisted, "inside and out, and you'd probably have a lot in common."

"Such as . . ."

"Such as . . ." She thought for a minute, then shrugged it away. "I'm sure you'd find something."

Shelby might like to consider herself a bit of a matchmaker, but she wasn't very good at it. Mostly because it was hard to make matches in a town where almost everyone knew everyone else and would have made their own connections if the chemistry was there. "Thanks, Shel, but no."

"When was the last time you went on a date with a woman?"

Did last night count as a date? He hadn't been planning on proposing marriage or anything, but he'd considered it something like a date until Helena had brushed it off so easily.

Shelby misinterpreted his silence. "See? This is what I mean. You're good-looking, successful, charming. . . . There's no reason for you to be single."

"Your brother is single. Hell, so are both of mine. Why are you not setting them up?"

"One Tanner boy at a time." She grinned. "You're the oldest, so I'm starting with you."

"What about you?"

She licked cream cheese off her fingers. "What about me?"

"You're single, too. We seem to have an entire generation of single Tanners, much to our mothers' dismay over the lack of grandchildren."

"That's a completely different situation." She tried to sound flippant about it, but he noticed her squirming a little in her seat. "The pickings are rather slim since I'm related to most of the single men around here."

"Surely there's someone we could invite to your little *Love Connection* potluck." As Shelby got increasingly uncomfortable, Ryan realized he should have turned that table years ago.

"Well, let me know if you happen to come across an eligible bachelor."

"How about Tate Harris?"

"Oh, I wish." Shelby sighed, making him regret he'd even brought it up. "He's definitely a hottie. But I think if he had any interest in me, he'd have made a move long ago."

Well, he's been too busy carrying a torch for Helena.

Shelby shrugged. "But you, on the other hand, are an all-around good-looking, genuinely nice guy—at least as far as anyone not in the bloodline knows," she added cheekily. "You'll be much easier to pair off than I'll ever be."

"Not true. Who in his right mind wouldn't adore you?"

Shelby made a face at him. "You're real funny."

"I'm serious."

"You have to love me. Your mother would kill you if you didn't."

Poor Shelby. She was so used to being dismissed as "sweet, but not too bright" that she believed it. That, coupled with her natural tomboy leanings, made her socially awkward outside her small group of friends. It probably was hard for her to date, and he was rather ashamed of himself for not realizing it sooner.

Not that he was going to let her get by with this stunt just because of that. Paybacks were hell. "Hmm, I think my next official act as mayor will be to declare a Shelby Tanner Appreciation Day—" He had to dodge the coffee Shelby spit in shock across the table at his words. "We'll have a parade, with you riding in a convertible in front, showing you off. We'll get kids with clipboards along the route as you pass to sign up eligible men to compete for a date with you."

"Shut up."

He leaned back in his chair, warming up to the topic now as Shelby's face turned amazing shades of red. "We can test their skills at rebuilding engines and cleaning fish, their familiarity with tidal schedules, maritime laws, Game and Fish regulations. . . ."

Shelby started wrapping up her bagel. "I kinda hate you," she said as she stood. "Stay single. See if I care."

"Oh, if only any of that were true. Bye, Shelby," he called at her back as she walked away. She stopped at the counter to speak to Molly, then stuck her tongue out at him before backing out the door.

That was fun. Of course, if she told either of their mothers about it, he was in for a chewing out for teasing her, but it might be worth it.

Molly came over a minute later. "Shelby told me to give this to you."

It was the bill for Shelby's breakfast.

Leveling a look at him, Molly added, "And that was a paraphrase. I won't tell you which unflattering adjectives she used to describe you."

He laughed and reached for his wallet. "I can imagine. I seem to be bringing that out in a lot of women these days."

"I don't know about that. You've certainly put a smile on Helena's face."

He fumbled his wallet. *"What?"*

Molly picked it up and handed it to him. "She's singing your praises. Says you're amazing. Much faster than she expected and she's more than satisfied."

The world went a little cock-eyed. What the . . . ? Molly knew already? And from Helena? *Faster?*

Seemingly unaware of his brain melting down, Molly kept talking. "I figured as much, of course, but now I can't wait to see it with my own eyes." Then she winked at him, and his last brain cell misfired.

"What did she . . ." No, he wasn't going to ask that. "When did you talk to Helena?" he managed to ask.

"Yesterday. We were making plans for me to go over there Saturday and help with the last bits of painting, hanging some curtains, and moving some furniture."

Okay, things made sense now. He just had a dirty mind. Or too much Helena on the brain. "The *house*."

"She's so impressed with the work and how quickly you've gotten it all done. I know it's a big relief for her." Her brows pulled together. "You okay, Ryan?"

"I'm fine. Just tired and the brain isn't quite awake yet."

Molly was instantly sympathetic. "More coffee?"

"Please. To go." He had to get his head screwed on straight before anyone else noticed.

She frowned as she handed over a steaming to-go cup. "Are you *sure* you're okay?"

That was a loaded question.

But all things considered, it was easier just to say yes.

Having a friend who owned a coffee shop might just be the best thing ever, Helena decided, because when Molly showed up bright and early Saturday morning, she brought an enormous carafe of coffee and a selection of pastries fresh from the Miller's Bakery delivery to Latte Dah that morning.

It certainly made facing a day of manual labor a bit easier—even if she did immediately delay the start of any such labor to properly enjoy the goodies while sitting on Grannie's front porch.

Molly, it seemed, was well liked, as everyone who walked past had a smile and a wave for her, and a couple of people even ventured all the way up to the porch to chat. Helena did her part, even if it boiled down to the same three sentences: "She's much better; thanks"; "She hopes to come home very soon"; and "I'll tell her you said hello."

Molly finally stood and brushed the croissant crumbs

off her shorts. "We should bolt inside before anyone else shows up. We'll never get finished if we have to have the same conversation with every person on the block."

Helena swallowed the last bite of her bagel. "That might be the most conversation I've had with people since I got here—barring the chitchat with the checker at the grocery store. It's a little freaky, actually."

"See, people are coming around."

"Only because *you* were sitting here."

"Nah. They just needed to get used to the idea of your being back and get over who you used to be. It takes time, but it does happen. You just have to give people a chance to give you a chance."

"Oh yeah?" So far, she was zero-for-two, as both Ryan and Tate seemed to be avoiding her.

"Yeah, you need to be more positive, Helena."

Helena leaned against the porch railing and crossed her arms. "And exactly how often do *you* go home for a visit?"

Molly made a face. "Hush."

"That's what I thought."

"We're not talking about me," she said primly.

"Oh, but let's *do*."

Molly opened the screen door and pushed her inside. "Let's not and say we did."

Serious now, Helena looked at her. "Was it bad?"

Molly hesitated for a second. "It wasn't great, that's for sure."

Helena didn't want to pry too much, but at the same time, she needed to know how bad the scars were so she didn't poke them too hard accidentally. "Like 'burn it and salt the earth on your way out of town' bad?"

Molly seemed to be weighing that as she eyeballed the curtains waiting to be hung in Grannie's new bedroom. "More like therapy-approved burning of bridges for the sake of my mental health."

"Fair enough." It somehow seemed easier to have this kind of conversation if they were busy doing something else, so Helena climbed the stepstool so Molly could pass up the curtain rods. "You know, I can actually relate to that. 'We have permission to let go of that which hurts us, even if we mourn what might have been,'" she quoted from memory.

"That's from *Exorcising Your Own Demons*. I have that book, too!" Molly said. "Although I think *Finding Your Path to Happiness* is much better. It really helped me come to terms with my mother."

"See, I didn't find that one as helpful. My mother made it clear she never wanted me to begin with, and we're certainly not in contact now, so I had to work out my mommy issues differently."

"Trust issues?"

"And anger. And doubting my own self-worth. I got the trifecta."

"Your mom sounds like a real gem."

"It's been fifteen years since I've seen her. I think I'm safely over it."

"That's why I like the *Happiness* book better. *Demons* makes too many assumptions and tries to spread out the responsibility." Handing Helena the screwdriver, she added, "You should really read *Loving Yourself When Others Won't*."

"That sounds like porn."

Molly blinked but then nodded. "You know, in a way, it is exactly that—self-help porn. It tells you all the things you need to hear to help yourself feel better. It's what you read when you've read all the other books and are convinced you're just too screwed up to be fixed."

"Ah, that was when I started therapy and Prozac."

Molly sighed. "God bless Prozac. Better mental health through chemistry."

"Amen. But now that I'm off it, why do you think I need so much caffeine?"

Molly gave her a look. "And why do you think I opened my own coffee shop?"

The absurdity of this conversation seemed to hit them both at the same time, and they burst into laughter. The curtain fell as Helena collapsed against the wall, tears rolling down her cheeks. Molly leaned against the dresser, holding her ribs and gasping for air.

It took Helena a few minutes to find enough breath to speak. "Oh my God. We are so messed up. You're like my soul twin."

"I know." Molly fanned her face and coughed as she calmed down. "It's so refreshing. I love this town, but I swear everyone seems so mentally healthy, it's just downright weird."

"Oh, trust me, they're not. Scrape away the Mayberry frosting and you'll find Magnolia Beach is a nutty fruitcake underneath. And it's not the cute, small-town eccentrics you see on those made-for-TV movies, either. I could tell you tales of dysfunction that would make you feel like the poster child of good mental health. We just don't talk about them in public."

"Interesting." Molly smiled at her. "Don't take this the wrong way, but I kinda wish Ms. Louise weren't healing so quickly. I'm going to miss you when you go back to Atlanta."

"I'm going to miss you, too. But I have a futon in my office that's yours anytime."

"I've never been to Atlanta. Maybe I'll take you up on that offer."

"You'd better."

Molly grabbed the curtain rod at her feet. "Come on. Let's try this again."

They hung the curtains up this time without incident. Helena stepped back to admire their handiwork, when she heard the screen door open and someone knock before coming in.

"Anybody home?"

"Tate?" Helena looked and saw him standing in the front room. *Thank God.* She'd sent him a text yesterday asking him to call or come by so they could talk, but he hadn't responded. Unfortunately, she still wasn't sure what to say. "I wasn't sure you'd still come."

"I said I'd be here to help. So, here I am."

"I know, but . . ." This was much more important than

the house. She moved farther into the room and lowered her voice. "Can we talk?"

He shook his head. "No need, sweetcheeks."

"Can I apologize, then?"

"What for? If anything, I should apologize to you."

"Not for that. Never that. But I do want to fix this somehow."

"There's nothing to fix. I'm over it. We're good. We go on like it didn't happen."

She wished it could be that simple. And while Tate was talking a good game, she wasn't necessarily buying it. But what could she do? Force him into awkward conversations that only rubbed his nose in it? "Are you *sure*?"

"One hundred percent." When he smiled at her, she felt better. That wasn't a "one hundred percent fine" smile, but it was definitely in the "fifty percent fine" range. Maybe the other fifty percent would come with time. She wrapped her arms around him, and he returned the squeeze.

"Um, sorry." She heard Molly behind her. "I didn't mean to interrupt."

"Hey, Molly." Tate kissed the top of her head and let her go. "You're not. I just brought my big manly muscles over to help this poor little weak lady move heavy things." He struck a pose, flexing his biceps—which weren't too shabby, Helena noted, sneaking a peek at Molly to see if she was checking them out, too. She couldn't quite tell if she was or not.

She poked him. "Then get your butt upstairs and grab the headboard. I'll be up in a second."

"Oh, yes *ma'am*," Tate said, his voice husky and filled with innuendo. Molly laughed, and Helena's mouth fell open as she realized what she'd said.

Maybe they'd be all right after all.

Midway through the third quarter of the Auburn game, Ryan's doorbell rang. He debated not answering it. He'd ignored several phone calls today already and found it immensely satisfying, so ignoring the door should be even more so. Plus, Auburn had just gotten hold of the ball on their own fifteen-yard line....

The bell rang again, followed by a rather insistent knock.

He paused the game and went to the door. *There'd better be blood. Or fire. Or a hurricane on the way.*

Instead, he found Helena. Which, depending on why she was here, could easily equal the catastrophe of all three.

"You left a screwdriver at the house the other day," she said by way of explanation. "I thought you might need it."

He took it. "Thanks. You didn't have to make a special trip."

She shrugged. "Well, we have some unfinished business, too, so ..."

"I think you made yourself pretty clear the other night. So we're all good."

Helena's eyebrows pulled together. "I meant the money." She reached into her back pocket and produced a checkbook. "I never got around to paying you the other night."

"Oh." Now he felt like a fool. "There's no rush."

"Well, I'd like to take care of the bill now, if that's okay. I don't like owing people."

"Fine." He opened the door wider to let her inside.

She looked around as she came inside, far more intently than what would normally be expected. He looked around as well, not sure what had her so curious. It was a basic house, probably exactly what would be expected from a single male living alone — recliner, big-screen TV with the cheerleaders frozen midjump, the room tidy enough not to be embarrassing, but not immaculate, either.

Tank came off his pillow to greet her. Tank didn't like most people, but he'd taken a liking to Helena pretty quickly. "Cute shirt," she said, giving him a pat.

Tank was wearing the Auburn jersey his mother had made. "Game attire. Plus, it's a little chilly tonight, and he gets cold easily."

"I didn't realize there was a game tonight. Do you want me to come back later?"

Really not. "This is fine. This is yesterday's game. I recorded it."

"What's the score?"

"Fourteen to six, Auburn."

"Go, Tigers. Okay, I'll make this quick." She perched on the edge of his sofa, pen poised over the checkbook. Tank jumped up beside her. "I can't thank you enough. I realize you probably don't need references or testimonials for your business around here, but if you ever do, I'd be happy to tell folks how good you are." She snorted. "I'll leave it to you to decide if my recommendation would be a positive in the long run or not."

He leaned against the chair. "I'm glad I was able to satisfy you." That came out slightly double entendre-ish, which he hadn't intended, but when Helena tensed up a fraction, he wasn't sorry that it had.

She shot him a look out of the corner of her eye, then went back to writing. There might have been a small twitching of her lips. "Oh, I'm more than satisfied."

"Glad to hear it. I thought you were, but it's hard to tell sometimes, you know."

"Yeah, well . . ." She cleared her throat and scribbled a signature before ripping off the check and setting it on the coffee table. Then she stood. "I know there were some unexpected things that came up, so if this doesn't cover it all, just let me know."

"Don't worry about it."

"But I do. I'm not *that* good in bed." As he choked, she leveled a wicked look at him, and he almost regretted teasing her in the first place. He'd forgotten whom he was dealing with. Helena's look clearly put the ball in his hands, and he had to decide whether to play or punt.

Well, he might be foolish, but he wasn't a coward. "I didn't realize you were willing to work this out in trade. You should have brought that up during the initial negotiations."

To his surprise, Helena laughed at his crudeness. "I'll remember that next time. But for now, we'll just stick to money. Thanks to your 'friends and family' discount, I'm still under my budget," she finished with a grin. Then she stood and put the checkbook back in her pocket. "I guess I'll go and let you get back to the game."

Wait a minute. This was all just a little *too* odd. Helena moved toward the door, and he stepped in front of her, blocking her way. "Why are you here, Helena?"

"I told you. To return your screwdriver and pay the bill."

"Neither of which require you to come by my house at eight o'clock on a Sunday night. You could have brought them to the office tomorrow morning, or just left them on my porch...."

"That sounds like a good way to get your stuff and your check stolen."

That was a lame excuse. "In Magnolia Beach? Really? You know better."

"You're right." She shrugged. "I guess I've just been away too long and forgot that would work."

"No other reason?" It might be just hopeful thinking on his part, but he didn't think it was.

"I don't know what you mean."

He stepped aside and extended a hand toward the door. "Then I guess you should go."

"I will. Good night, Ryan." She took a step, then turned to face him and crossed her arms over her chest. "Look, I give up. Why are you mad at me?"

"I don't know what you mean." He tossed her words back at her, earning him a frown.

"When I asked you to leave the other night, it was because I didn't want the whole damn town knowing my business."

"And I thought you just didn't want Tate to know."

"I don't. But it also wasn't personal. There's no need for you to be all bent out of shape over it."

"I'm not."

"Could've fooled me. If you weren't, you would have come by and picked up that screwdriver sometime in the last couple of days."

"I have lots of screwdrivers. I didn't even know it was missing."

"Oh." Her mouth twisted. "My mistake, then."

This was confusing, yet somehow he still thought he wasn't completely off base in his hope that she was here for something else. "Did you *want* me to drop by?"

"I expected you to come get your screwdriver, but when you didn't, I thought your feelings might be hurt." She lifted her chin. "I'm glad to know they're not. So we're good, and I'll be on my way."

Oddly, though her words were brisk, her feet weren't moving toward the door, solidifying his hopeful thoughts. But since she wasn't saying anything, he didn't quite know what to do or say next. He wouldn't have thought Helena was one to hesitate or second-guess herself—and Lord knew she wasn't one to mince her words—so, this weird, uncomfortable standoff had him at a loss. He guessed he could *ask* her to stay. The worst she could do was say no. And then he'd know for sure. "Want a beer?"

"You're watching the game...."

"I told you. It's taped."

"Then yes, I'd like a beer. If it's not any trouble."

He went to the kitchen and returned with her drink to find her leaning against the back of the couch. He joined her there, copying her pose. The mirror on that wall reflected Helena and the TV behind her. It was a little less awkward to talk to her reflection. "Slow night?"

"I'm a little bored of my own company today, tired of working, sick of dealing with the house, but Tate's in Mobile at his sister's and Molly's at her book club meeting.... So, yeah."

"So I'm third on your list?"

"Don't get offended now. I thought you were pissed at me, remember?"

"Hardly. I wouldn't have dared believe I ranked so high."

Helena's mouth twitched, but she covered it by taking a drink. "Amazingly enough, I've enjoyed your company."

"Ditto."

"Are you surprised?" she asked.

"That you've enjoyed my company or that I've enjoyed yours?"

She chuckled. "Either. Both."

He had to consider that. "Strangely enough, not really."

"Well, *I* am," she muttered.

"Gee, thanks."

She turned to look at him. "No, thank you."

Carefully, slowly, he set his beer down. This could be a mistake. This could be a trap. But the alternative was continuing to stand here like two awkward wallflowers at the junior prom.

He held his hand out for her drink.

There was a moment's hesitation, but Helena gave it to him. He set it next to his, then turned to face her. "Well?"

That was a loaded question with a very obvious answer, and Helena nearly bolted for the door.

She hadn't really planned for this.

Actually, that was a bit of a lie. She hadn't planned on this *exactly*, but she had hedged her bet by shaving her legs once she'd decided to deliver Ryan's check in person tonight.

Just in case.

Why was this so awkward? He was an adult; she was an adult. They'd had toe-curling, sweaty, athletic sex just a couple of nights ago. It wasn't out of the realm of reason to want it to happen again.

Since she wasn't exactly the shy, retiring type, the fact she wasn't being up-front and direct with what she wanted really bugged her. No wonder Ryan wasn't making any bold moves. In his place, she'd be looking for the bear trap she was about to step in, too.

Well, she could either stand here like a fool, hoping, or she could just make the move. Ryan had come more than halfway; she could close the distance.

She pushed off the couch slowly, closing the space between their bodies. Ryan sucked in his breath. She could feel the heat from his skin, see the pulse in his neck jump to double speed.

And, *damn*, he smelled good—like soap and clean laundry and sunshine and . . . Ryan. She let her hand rest on his chest, enjoying the way the muscle leapt under her palm, then tightened her hand, fisting the fabric of his shirt to give herself an anchor.

Because if memory served, she was going to need it.

Ryan's kiss was hot and hungry, enough to make her knees wobble, yet unhurried, like he had no place he'd rather be. One hand threaded through her hair, his fingers gently massaging her scalp, supporting her without the feeling he was holding her in place. There was a freedom implied there, one that allowed her to break away without resistance at any time, but there was no mistaking that he wanted her, either.

Damn.

The kiss worked magic on her body, awakening every nerve ending and priming them for his touch. And when his hands did begin to wander, they left a sizzling path in their wake.

She wanted so much more, attacking the buttons on her shirt until she could shrug it off and stepping out of her shoes. Ryan paused long enough to pull his shirt up and off, then slowed down to trail his hand from her chin to her navel with a deep, appreciative sigh.

A slow sexy smile made her want to climb him like a tree, but she grabbed the hand he offered instead and followed him down a short hallway.

Ryan's bedroom was as masculine as his living room—neutral colors, clean lines, and no frills, bordering on minimalistic—but organized and tidy. Definitely a bachelor's house, but a grown-up one with real furniture and some sense of decor beyond neon beer signs and dirty laundry.

It suited him nicely.

More importantly, it had a bed. A king-sized bed, with high-thread-count sheets that felt almost as amazing against her back as Ryan did against her front. The slatted headboard gave her something to hold on to as he peeled her jeans off and began a careful, thorough exploration of her erogenous zones that left her keening in pleasure and moist with sweat.

But it was the incoherent mumble in her ear and the kiss pressed against her forehead when she finally collapsed atop him and they both fought for breath that struck the deepest chord in her, forging an intimacy that seemed far deeper than the sex itself.

It was certainly worrisome, and that worry must have shown on her face. "You okay?" Ryan asked.

"Yeah," she lied, unsure of how convincing she was being.

"We'll work it out," he assured her, making her feel better even though she wasn't sure what he was assuring her about. He gave her that half smile. "Sneaking around is one thing. Being discreet is something else. I can handle discreet."

"Oh. Good."

"Did you drive or walk over here?"

Huh? "I walked."

"See, we're already being discreet. The neighbors can't talk about what they don't know about, and I won't have to kick *you* out of bed for several more hours." Naked and tousled with an obvious postorgasmic glow, he lay back, hands stacked behind his head, and grinned at her.

"Hours?"

"Hours," he said, attempting a leer—which didn't *quite* work for him, not with those wholesome boy-next-door looks.

But it certainly worked on her.

Chapter 11

Grannie was released on Wednesday.

Helena got the call on Monday afternoon. Grannie had told her during that morning's call that it would be happening, but she hadn't believed it until the doctor called later that afternoon to make it official. She very much wished she'd had a bit more notice, as being faced with Grannie's imminent homecoming brought to light many things she'd forgotten or assumed she still had time to accomplish.

Monday and Tuesday passed in a blur of cleaning, laundry, grocery shopping, and calls to doctors and physical therapists. When Ryan showed up on her porch unexpectedly Tuesday night with burgers from the Frosty Freeze, she was exhausted and on her last nerve. But the burgers and the company gave her a second wind and an attitude adjustment, and Ryan hadn't left until very late.

But Grannie was in high spirits and thrilled to be going home. After Grannie's lack of cooperation there for a while, Helena had been expecting a "run her out on the rails" kind of departure and was pleasantly surprised to see the hugs and best wishes bestowed on Grannie from the staff and the other patients as she left.

"Well, that was a nice send-off," she said as the convalescent center disappeared in the rearview mirror. "You obviously made some friends while you were there." *Other than Cal,* she added to herself.

"I made the best of it that I could. I've always believed you just have to bloom where you're planted."

She knew Grannie too well not to know what she was hinting at. "I'm blooming just fine in my temporary flower box. I've spent a lot of time catching up with Tate and am really enjoying getting to know Molly better." There was no sense in bringing up Ryan.

"Molly's a sweet girl," Grannie said, "and I'm glad it hasn't been too hard on you. I knew a little time and distance would help things blow over. Now people can see the real Helena."

The optimism was nice. "I love you, too, Grannie."

She caught Grannie up on what little local news she knew, like the questionable parentage of the Morris puppies, and the new cell tower going up. Everything seemed back to normal.

It was a little surprising to see a group of about twenty people milling about as she turned onto Grannie's street, and the surprise only grew when she realized the people were milling in Grannie's yard.

As she pulled into the driveway, the people started clapping and waving, and Helena saw a large Welcome Home banner stretched between the columns of the porch.

"How wonderful!" Grannie reached over to squeeze Helena's hand. "How did you manage to arrange this?"

Helena was saved from answering as Grannie already had her window down, calling and waving to the crowd like the queen. Ryan came over to open Grannie's door and extended his hand to help her get carefully to her feet as Helena ran to get her walker out of the trunk.

Ryan made a gesture with his hand, and the Wilson twins appeared from out of nowhere to unload Grannie's luggage from the car. Then Ryan helped Grannie on her slow walk up her new ramp, with Mrs. Wilson and Mrs. Blatty from the bridge club hovering close by to supervise and encourage. Helena brought up the rear, carrying only her purse and water bottle.

Once inside, Grannie settled into her recliner with her feet up and a cold glass of tea. A fresh bouquet of flowers sat on the sideboard along with small boxes, which, even without looking, Helena knew contained cookies, chocolates, and other homemade goodies from the ladies of Magnolia Beach.

As Grannie happily held court, Helena snuck into the kitchen, only to find Ryan in there talking quietly on the phone. He waved her in when she started to back out.

"Thanks," she said when he finished his call.

"For what?"

"For setting all this up. Did you see the smile on her face?"

"I didn't actually do anything. I just mentioned to Mrs. Wilson that today was the day. She did the rest."

The fresh pitcher of tea on the table hadn't been there when she left this morning—but then, neither had the loaves of fresh bread or that jar of homemade pickles—but she didn't have any problems with helping herself to a large glass of it. "Well, thank you for thinking about it. It didn't occur to me."

"Mrs. Wilson seemed disappointed you hadn't mentioned it to her."

"Ah, yes, I'm surprised it didn't come up in one of our regular long chats."

Ryan frowned at her. "You know, maybe you should give people a chance to give *you* a chance."

That was the second time she'd been told that. "Oh?"

"Many of the people out there mentioned how you've been a hermit since you arrived."

"That's completely untrue. I'm at the coffee shop pretty much every day, plus I'm always all over town running errands." She looked in the fridge, and sure enough, the shelves were nearly overflowing with casserole dishes and plastic containers. That trip to the grocery store had been totally unnecessary. "And I haven't been hiding, for God's sake. It's no secret that I'm here."

"But you haven't exactly been participating in local life, either."

"I've been a little busy, you know, with work and the house and everything. And I'm *so* sure there's an opening in the Tuesday afternoon book club for me."

"How do you know there's not?"

She snorted and shot him a look.

Ryan held up his hands. "I'm just saying that you can't get bent out of shape that people don't want you around when you've made it clear you don't want to be here yourself."

"I *don't* want to be here. And I wasn't real popular when I *was* here, remember?"

"You changed my mind," he reminded her with a wink. "Just something to think about."

"Well, since I now have to write thank-you notes to the entire female population of the county for all this food, everyone will be hearing from me. How's *that* for an outreach program?"

That got her a grin. "It's a start. By the way, my mom sent her fried chicken. It's amazing stuff." Ryan leaned in and gave her a quick kiss. He stepped back quickly, though, when the door opened a second later, and Molly backed into the room, her hands full.

If Molly found it strange that she and Ryan were alone in the kitchen, she didn't show it. Instead, she seemed amused. "When I heard you were on your way back with Ms. Louise, I loaded up some goodies to welcome her home."

Ryan gave Helena a little smile before nodding to Molly and slipping out through the back door.

Molly surveyed the spread wryly. "It seems I wasn't the only person in town with *that* idea."

"I am capable of feeding my grandmother. She's not going to starve, you know," she grumbled.

"I know." Molly patted her on the shoulder. "And I'm sure no one is trying to imply otherwise."

"My refrigerator rather belies that." She leaned against the counter and sighed. Rationally, she knew Molly was right, and that the food was just an outward show of love and support for Grannie. She should be glad Grannie was so well cared for and looked after. But still . . . "Did you bring lemon bars?"

"Of course."

"Good. I'm going to need them."

Even knowing Helena would most likely be occupied with getting Ms. Louise settled didn't keep Ryan from wanting to see her. And while it might be the height of immaturity—and would probably get him sent straight to hell—he couldn't help but be disappointed that Ms. Louise's homecoming would put a crimp in this new development with Helena. If he'd known Ms. Louise had the regeneration powers of Wolverine, he would have made his move sooner.

Helena was going to be coping with a lot over the next few days, and he should really leave her to it. Knowing that hell would probably freeze over before she asked anyone for help worried him, though.

And *that* was why he was headed to her house, of course.

The front porch lights were off and the windows across the front of the house were dark. Light was peeking around the side of the house from the back porch, however, and the gentle creak of a swing led him in that direction. Helena was lying stretched out in the swing, head back on a cushion and eyes closed. The foot on the ground keeping the swing in motion was the only sign she wasn't asleep.

He was about to retreat when Helena opened one eye. "Hey. I thought I heard someone."

"I just came by to check on you. You look exhausted."

"I am. I got Grannie settled in about an hour ago, and she's sound asleep, thanks to her pain meds."

"Maybe you should do the same."

"I will. Eventually. I needed some time to unwind first." She groaned slightly as she got up to unhook the screen door. "Come on up. Are you hungry?" she asked as she let him in and went back to the swing. "I can offer you any kind of casserole you want."

"I'm good. What about you, though?"

"You could get me a beer."

He started to go into the kitchen, only to have Helena stop him. "They're in the cooler."

He flipped open the top to see a partial six-pack and a bottle of wine swimming in an ice bath. "Out of room in the fridge?"

"Now that you mention it, yes. But, more accurately, Grannie doesn't allow alcohol in the house. This is what you might call a compromise."

He handed her the beer and sat next to her on the swing, putting it into motion. "You just said she was asleep."

"I am not going to jinx my life by defying her behind her back like that." He must have given her a funny look, because she added, "Oh please. Like you don't obey your grandmother's rules regardless of how inane or arbitrary they are."

"Point taken."

"Anyway, it forces me to experience the pleasure that is a screened-in porch on a lovely fall evening."

"Be glad we live in south Alabama, or the winter could be rough."

She laughed. "I will be long gone by winter, regardless of Magnolia Beach's wonderful climate."

"I think that's the first nice thing you've said about Magnolia Beach since you got back."

"I've got nothing against the geography. I'm even starting to get used to the peace and quiet again."

He didn't say anything, and they sat quietly, swinging gently. It wasn't a cozy scene—there was a good foot of space respectably separating them—but it was comfortable.

Which was kind of odd, considering they weren't really friends—regardless of the benefits. From the tired pinch around her eyes, it was obvious Helena wasn't in the mood to exercise any of those benefits, but he wasn't bothered by that. In fact, he was quite happy to sit here quietly enjoying her company. Helena seemed okay with it, too.

His life had taken a strange turn.

Helena sighed again. "I'm not sure how this is going to work."

"How do you mean?"

She rolled her head to look at him. "I'm afraid I've already bitten off more than I can chew, just with caring for Grannie. I can't leave her alone right now for any length of time. . . ."

"It will work itself out. You've only had half a day to adjust. You'll find your rhythm."

"I'm just warning you. I've had a great time the last few days, but I don't see a lot of that in my immediate future."

He wondered briefly if he was getting the brush-off, but Helena sounded genuinely disappointed about the prospect. "Don't worry just yet. Give it a couple of days to settle down. Things won't look so out of control once you know what you're in for and can make a plan."

"You're such an optimist."

"No, I just don't worry about problems until they present themselves. Then, it only becomes a matter of forging a plan of attack." He reached for her hand and gave it a squeeze. "And *I'm* not above asking for help."

She yawned. "I'm not usually so pitiful and mopey."

"You're tired and overwhelmed. Things will seem more manageable after you've had some rest."

She cut her eyes sideways at him. "Are you sending me to bed?"

"Maybe."

"No one's sent me to bed since I was in middle school."

"No wonder you're so tired, then."

"You're funny."

"And you're about to fall asleep right here."

She shrugged. "It wouldn't be the first time I've slept on this porch."

Helena continued to shock him. "I would not have thought you were the type to like camping."

"You'd be very right," she said with a laugh, "but

Grannie did not tolerate crawling in at any old hour of the night."

General perception had been that Ms. Louise had lost control of Helena, letting her run wild because she had no choice. This was an interesting development. It seemed Ms. Louise had tried to keep a hand on the reins. "Ms. Louise would make you sleep on the porch if you were late?"

"Yep. I had to be inside by eleven o'clock or she put the chain on the door and there would be hell to pay the next morning. She was usually nice enough to leave a blanket out for me, though. Needless to say, I may have been a hellion, but I was a hellion with a curfew I didn't want to miss."

The thought of Hell-on-Wheels tearing through town with one eye on the clock was almost absurd. "Eleven o'clock? Even I got to stay out until midnight."

"Weren't you the wild thing?" she teased. "Grannie always said that there was nothing good to be doing after eleven o'clock. And it served as a handy alibi a couple of times. In fact, the night the chief's car was stolen, my grandmother was able to testify that *my* happy ass was safe at home."

"So you really didn't have anything to do with that incident?" The mystery might never be solved, then.

Helena stood and stretched before sending a coy smile his way. "Oh, I didn't say that."

"Then how . . . ?"

"I'm going to plead the fifth and go to bed." She drained the last of her drink and tossed the bottle into a small bin. Taking the not-at-all subtle hint, he stood as well. To his surprise, Helena rose to her tiptoes to plant the sweetest, softest kiss on his lips. With her hand on his cheek, she looked him right in the eye and said, "Thank you. For everything. And I mean that."

He was a little shell-shocked by both the kiss and the tone of her voice, but before his brain could fully process what had happened, Helena was inside the house.

That kiss had done something to his brain, and he had

the distinct feeling he needed to think about things. He just wasn't exactly sure what those "things" actually were. Specifically.

He let himself off the porch, careful not to let the screen door bang shut behind him, and headed through the side yard to the street.

As soon as he hit the sidewalk, the porch light went off.

She'd watched him leave.

I love my grandmother. I love my grandmother. A period of adjustment is normal and expected, and this adjustment is complicated by her health limitations and frustrations. I love my grandmother. My grandmother loves me.

Helena took a deep breath, breathing in the peace, and exhaled slowly, releasing the tension on the out breath.

I will not strangle my grandmother in her sleep.

As far as mantras went, that one probably wouldn't pass muster with her yoga instructor, but it was helping. A little bit. They were both still alive, and that was something. Helena would take what she could get.

It was probably a very good thing that Grannie didn't allow alcohol in the house, or else she'd be walking around in a constant state of intoxication. The last three days had shown Helena where her lines were drawn and how far past them she was now.

She wasn't used to living with another person, much less a person she had to care for. And as much as she wanted to take care of Grannie, she was slightly overwhelmed by it all.

Her phone was constantly buzzing with alarms for Grannie's many medications, and she had to time meals appropriately so that some pills could be taken on an empty stomach, others with food, and one that was to be taken an hour after she ate.

Get up, get dressed, get Grannie up and dressed, fix breakfast, clean up breakfast, take Grannie to physical therapy, fix lunch, clean up lunch, play cards and entertain Grannie until her soaps come on, try to squeeze in some work, tidy up and run errands, entertain Grannie some more, fix dinner, clean up dinner, get Grannie ready for bed, try to work some more ...

Plus, Grannie wasn't used to being idle, and short of duct-taping her to the chair, Helena wasn't sure how to keep the woman from getting up to putter around for no specific purpose, causing Helena to not only have to help her up and down, but to also follow her around—without seeming to hover—to make sure she didn't fall. On top of that, Grannie didn't care for being "coddled like a child," so tempers were a bit short in the Wheeler residence.

Smilin' Cal had come down with a cold and hadn't come to visit, leaving Grannie grumpy from missing her honey. In fact, Grannie seemed more concerned about his recuperation than her own, and she snapped at Helena when she wouldn't drive to Bayou La Batre to deliver chicken soup.

Helena had exactly one nerve left and *that* had nearly snapped it in half.

Quietly, and admitted only to herself in the privacy of her room, Helena decided that caregiving was a job best left to professionals. She obviously lacked the necessary skill set.

She'd fallen behind on work in the past couple of weeks, but she'd told herself she'd get caught up once Grannie was home. That hadn't worked out. Instead, she had an in-box full of messages from unhappy clients, many of whom had already found someone else to take on the project since she was so far behind. That sucked. She'd worked so hard to build a satisfied client list in a business that lived and died on word-of-mouth recommendations, and while her clients claimed understanding of her situation, they still needed their stuff yesterday, and she couldn't deliver. She didn't blame them, but it still sucked.

The phone rang with people calling to check on Grannie to the point where Helena was about to yank the thing out of the wall. Plenty of people stopped by, which, in a perfect world, would have given Helena a respite, but they only stayed ten to fifteen minutes at a time, claiming they didn't want to wear Grannie out. That was nice, and very considerate of them, but the "Come in, nice to see you, can I get you a drink" was barely finished before it was time for the "Thanks for coming and you take care." Then twenty minutes later, she got to start it all over again. Helena never had a chance to settle anywhere for longer than a few minutes and was developing an eye twitch from the constant interruptions.

She'd seen half the church's congregation, Grannie's entire bridge club, and every neighbor in a four-block radius, but she hadn't seen Tate or Molly—much less Ryan, although the fact she included him on that list was a whole other issue of craziness she didn't have the energy to explore right now—at all. And while they sent support via text message, they didn't have any more experience with this kind of thing than she did, so she kept her full frustration and looming breakdown to herself.

It's a period of adjustment. I'll adjust.

On Monday, when Grannie had been home for five days and after another e-mail from a client pulling their project had her taking a hard look at her bank balance, Helena reached her breaking point. She needed advice, guidance, help. She needed an actual grown-up. Leaving Grannie napping in the recliner with the phone close by and a note of her whereabouts, she went next door to see Mrs. Wilson.

She took a deep breath and rang the bell before she could chicken out.

Mrs. Wilson didn't look happy to see her. Helena's initial instinct was proven wrong, though, as Mrs. Wilson opened the screen with a concerned, "Is everything all right?"

"Grannie's fine. She's resting right now."

"That's good," she said, and sighed audibly with relief. "She needs to rest to get her strength back. And, no offense, Helena, but you look like you could use some rest, too."

The kindly tone nearly broke her composure. "I'm in over my head," she confessed.

"Of course you are."

Helena's jaw tightened. She should have known better. *Screw this.* She was about to walk away when Mrs. Wilson opened the door farther and stepped out onto the porch. "It's a hell of a system when a patient has a whole team of trained professionals looking after them while they're in the hospital, yet as soon as they're released, suddenly a couple of family members are supposed to be able to handle it. I remember when Jack came home from the hospital after his bypass. After a day or two, I was about to run screaming into the streets. Come on," she said, heading toward Grannie's. "We'll have a glass of tea and talk this through."

Helena was still frozen in place on Mrs. Wilson's porch.

"Well, come on. I'll need to see what the situation is before I can help you. That is why you came to me, right?"

"Right." Could it really be this simple? She still felt uneasy about the whole situation, but she felt better at the same time. She might be a failure, but at least she wasn't going to fail spectacularly and damage Grannie in the process. She followed Mrs. Wilson back toward Grannie's porch.

At the door, Mrs. Wilson paused. "You've come a long way, Helena, and proved a lot of people wrong. You've done the right thing by your grandmother, and that means something." Helena started to nod, oddly touched, when Mrs. Wilson continued. "You've still got a long way to go, though."

She squared her shoulders. "I do need help, and I'm not too proud to ask for it. I can't change the past, but I don't have time now to worry about what other people think of me. My only concern is for Grannie and making sure she gets what she needs. I'll do whatever it takes to ensure that, and if I'm proving people's assumptions about me wrong at the same time, that's great. But that's a side benefit, not the goal."

Mrs. Wilson's eyes widened, but then she nodded, seeming to accept that statement at face value. "That's not the approach *I* would take, but it's fair enough. People will come around eventually, I guess."

It wasn't exactly a rousing endorsement for the new Helena Wheeler, but it did feel like a milestone of sorts. Mrs. Wilson had always disapproved of her, but as Grannie's friend, she hadn't outright condemned her. As she followed Mrs. Wilson inside, Grannie was just waking from her nap.

"Margaret! So good to see you. Come in and have a seat. Would you like something to drink?"

Taking her cue, Helena headed for the kitchen and poured two glasses of tea, and returned to the living room with Grannie's afternoon pills as well. Mrs. Wilson was seated at Grannie's antique writing desk, pen in hand.

"Oh, Margaret, we don't want to be a bother to anyone," Grannie was saying.

"That girl is run ragged, Louise."

Grannie looked up at her. "Is that true, Helena?"

Damn. That was a hard question to answer when Grannie was looking at her like that. "I'm just really behind on work and such. . . ."

"Then go do some work, honey. I'll be fine right here."

"Grannie, it's—"

Mrs. Wilson laid the pen down and smiled sweetly. "Helena, why don't you run down to the diner and get your grandmother a piece of Maude's cherry pie?"

Even though there were three different kinds of pie still in the fridge, Helena didn't have to be told twice. She recognized that sweet smile for what it really was—a warning. *She* might not be able to take her grandmother to task, but Mrs. Wilson sure could. Grabbing her phone and wallet, she bolted for the door.

She felt a tiny bit guilty, but not guilty enough to stay.

She'd give Mrs. Wilson twenty minutes or so to get Grannie on the right page, and then they could come up with a plan.

For the first time in five days, she felt like this might actually work out okay.

Chapter 12

This is plain foolish.

Ryan wasn't the sneaky type. He never had been. Never really saw the need. Yet, here he was, a grown man sneaking around to Helena's house at nine o'clock at night.

And all because she'd sent him a text. It didn't exactly speak highly of his maturity level that a simple text reduced him to behavior most teenagers had outgrown, but his hormones were running the show, canceling out higher brain functions and reasoning abilities at the prospect of getting naked with Helena again.

Mrs. Leary's poodle poked his head over the fence and began to raise the alarm as Ryan cut through the side yard into the shadows of Ms. Louise's backyard. The Learys' porch light flipped on, but he was safely past its reach. Nonetheless, he still sprinted the last few yards to the back porch. Pausing to catch his breath, and feeling utterly ridiculous, he tapped quietly on the back door.

Helena had the door open almost immediately, and he slipped inside. "You are not at all stealthy," she whispered, shaking her head at him.

"My apologies. It's not a skill I felt the need to hone before now."

She rolled her eyes. "Pity, but you'll need to try harder. Grannie's on pain meds, but she's still not the heaviest of sleepers. So *quietly*, please. Oh, and the third stair squeaks."

The door to Ms. Louise's bedroom was closed, but a thin strip of dim light shone under the door. A nightlight, maybe? Following Helena's lead, he tiptoed past, carefully avoided the third stair, and crept down the hall to Helena's room.

After carefully closing the door, Helena launched herself at him, wrapping her legs around his waist and pressing her lips against his in a hot, hungry kiss. Just as quickly, she released her legs and landed on her feet to grin up at him. "I'm glad you came." She was already tugging at his shirt.

"Missed me, huh?"

"Oh, don't get all cocky," she said as he took over, pulling the shirt up and over his head and grinning at her, happy to hear her admit it. "A woman has needs, you know."

"So you think you can just snap your fingers, and I'll come running to take care of those needs?"

Helena leaned against the door, arms crossed over her chest, and slowly surveyed him from head to toe. That eyebrow went up and her mouth twitched. "You're here, aren't you?"

He braced his hands outside her shoulders, caging her, and leaned in. "Oh, now who's getting cocky?"

Eyes locked on his, Helena placed a hand in the center of his chest, then trailed it slowly down over his stomach to the bulge in his jeans. "I'm still going to say it's you."

The steady pressure and gentle, purposeful movement pulled a groan from deep in his chest. It seemed he had needs, too.

"Shh." Her hands worked the snap and zipper quickly, releasing him into her grasp. He dropped his forehead to hers as he sucked in his breath.

A hand under her chin easily lifted her face to his for a kiss. "Well, I missed *you*."

He got a smile for his honesty, followed by kisses that seared a path down his neck, then over his chest and belly as Helena slid to her knees.

The ringing of a bell snapped both their heads up. Helena cursed under her breath and scrambled to her feet, adjusting her clothes and running a hand through her hair. "I'll be right back," she said, slipping under his arm and out the door. He heard her feet on the stairs, then indistinct voices as Helena answered Ms. Louise's summons.

No wonder Helena had been shushing him. Sounds carried a little too well in this house.

There wasn't anything to do but wait, so he sat on the edge of Helena's bed and ran a hand over his face to try to compose himself. Thank God Ms. Louise had called out now, because a few minutes later, Helena's sudden but required departure might have killed him.

At least Ms. Louise was unable to climb the stairs, unable to open the door and find her granddaughter on her knees. . . .

What the hell was wrong with him? Sneaking around, glad Ms. Louise's injuries kept her to the first floor? Grumbling because an injured woman's needs trumped his wants?

Good Lord. This was crazy.

He'd spent too much time over the last five days thinking about her. While he'd hauled ass over here like a teenage boy on a booty call, *that* hadn't been the only focus of his thoughts. The simple fact was he liked her. Liked talking to her, sparring with her. . . . She was funny, equally prickly and sweet, and while the sex was good, he'd have jumped at the opportunity to come over, regardless. He wouldn't admit it to Helena, though.

If she wasn't so worried about what everyone else might think about what they might or might not be doing, he wouldn't have had to wait five days to see her *and* be forced to cut through backyards in the cover of darkness in order to do so.

Helena was definitely messing with his head, and tonight just proved it.

He zipped his jeans and reached for his shirt. A moment later, Helena returned. "Sorry about that. She just needed some water, but the meds are really kicking in now, so she'll be fast asleep in no time. . . . Why are you getting dressed?"

"This is insane, so I'm going to go."

"But—"

"This is insulting to both of us." Helena motioned him to be quiet, and he lowered his voice. "We're adults, for God's sake, and I really have no desire to hone my stealth skills so you can grab a little nookie behind everyone's back."

"What? You want me to tell my grandmother that I'd like to have a boy up to my room to have sex? Jeez, she just got *out* of the hospital. I don't want to send her back right away. I thought we had an understanding."

"I agreed to discretion. I didn't realize it would equal skulking. I've got too much respect—for you and myself—to keep this up."

"Respect." She sounded confused.

"Yes, respect. I'm not asking you to marry me. Hell, I'm not even asking you to go steady. I just refuse to act like I'm ashamed of myself when I'm not."

That seemed to suck the wind out of Helena's sails. She opened and closed her mouth a few times before perching on the edge of her bed and studying him. "You don't want to . . . see me anymore?"

"Of course I do. But not like this. It's ridiculous."

"So . . . what, then? You want to go on a date?" she said sarcastically.

He hadn't really thought about it, but . . . "Yes."

Helena blinked in surprise. After a moment, she finally said, "People would freak."

"I think you're wrong."

"Suspicion and rumor are one thing. Flaunting it is another."

"I'm talking about dinner, Helena, not public sex acts. That's hardly 'flaunting' anything."

"That could be worse, actually," she argued. "Just sleeping together could be explained by my wicked seduction skills. A date really calls your judgment into question."

"But not yours?"

"For once, people would think I was making a good choice. But the thing is, you have to live here. I don't. You'll be dealing with the fallout long after I'm gone."

That set him back a pace. "You're really worried about me?"

"Duh. Have you not been listening to anything I've been saying? You may be golden in this town, but you're not untouchable."

That wasn't exactly an admission of affection, but it was pretty damn close. "Why don't you let me worry about my next election."

"Heads will explode. You know that, right?"

"Then think how much fun it will be—both watching them lose their minds *and* rubbing my nose in the fact you were right all along."

She laughed softly, then shook her head. "You really are a nice guy, aren't you?"

Helena made it sound like a bad thing. " 'Fraid so."

Helena mumbled something. He couldn't say for sure, but it sounded like "Frickin' Boy Scout." She sighed. "Fine. But I don't want to make a big deal of it. We just go about our business, and people see what they see."

He sighed. "I wasn't planning on hiring a skywriter, Helena."

"Good. Those are annoying."

"So, tomorrow night, then. Seven o'clock."

Helena's eyes widened. "That soon?"

"I know women can take a lot of time to get ready for a date, but surely you can shower and dress yourself in the next twenty hours or so."

"Smart-ass. Now you have to pay for my dinner."

"It never occurred to me that I wouldn't."

She shook her head. "You're getting some kind of weird kick out of this, aren't you?"

Most men would take offense at Helena's distinct lack of enthusiasm and the most begrudging acceptance of a dinner date in the history of mankind, but he wasn't most men and Helena wasn't like any other woman. He laughed. "Oh, absolutely."

She rolled her eyes and flopped back on the bed, muttering under her breath.

Reaching for her hands, he pulled her to her feet and kissed her until she stopped grumbling and sighed against him. "I'll see you tomorrow."

"You're leaving? *Now?*"

He fought to keep a straight face and nodded.

"But I agreed to dinner."

"I know. I'm looking forward to it."

"Withholding sex until you get what you want? That's practically extortion."

"It's absolutely extortion." At her gasp of outrage, he reached for her waist and pulled her close to nuzzle that sensitive place on her neck that he knew would give her goose bumps. "Maybe I'm not quite the Boy Scout you think I am."

"Obviously," she grumbled.

"Seven o'clock. G'night, Helena."

He was down the stairs—skipping over the third one—and out the door before Helena could mount a stronger counterargument. Like by getting naked or something. He was proud of himself for making a stand, and pleased he'd gotten his way, but he wasn't made of stone.

He headed home for a cold shower.

This was utter, complete insanity. Helena wanted to hit her head against something hard for allowing Ryan to bully her into going out with him. She'd made what she thought was a pretty convincing case against the idea, but Ryan was proving to be far more stubborn than she ever would have guessed. After shooting down all of her reasonable, practical objections, he'd left her with only the ridiculous and embarrassing ones, and she'd be damned before she admitted any of those to *him*. She could only barely tolerate admitting them to herself—and only then when she couldn't distract herself with something, *any*thing else.

So now she was going to dinner. With Ryan Tanner.

God help them both.

Mrs. Wilson had volunteered to take Grannie to physical therapy this morning, supposedly freeing Helena up to work for a few hours, but this dinner with Ryan pushed more important things into that time slot.

So while she dreaded it, her first stop today was the office of Dr. Tate Harris—which, on first glance, still looked remarkably like the office of Dr. Masters.

Helena hadn't been inside since before Grannie's Yorkie, Guinevere, died, and that had to have been at least twenty years ago. She remembered the office as a dank place, with yellowing tile and questionable smells, but she was pleased to see that while the outside hadn't changed much, the inside was completely redone to be both cheerful and professional looking, and smelling clean but not of disinfectant.

A few people were seated around the room, two holding cat carriers that emitted ominous hissing noises from their depths, and a small child cuddled a clearly obese guinea pig in his lap. An old, gray-muzzled Labrador lay at the feet of his equally old owner, and a puppy bounced at the end of his leash.

I should have called first. The habits of Magnolia Beach drop-by visits had infiltrated her brain so much that she'd forgotten Tate would actually be working while at work. She turned to leave.

"Can I help you?" the young woman behind the desk called out, waving her over.

"I dropped by to talk to Tate for a second, but he's obviously busy—"

"Actually, I think we're in a bit of a holding pattern at the moment. Want me to see if he's got a minute or two for you, Helena?"

The sound of her name brought her up short. Carefully, she searched the woman's face, but she didn't look familiar. Even the name tag JENNY didn't help shake anything loose. "I'm very sorry, but I don't remember who you are." *Just please tell me I didn't do something mean and horrible to you.*

Jenny laughed. "Oh, there's no reason you should remember me. I was just a kid when you left."

Jeez, you're still a kid. Why did she suddenly feel as ancient as the Labrador and his owner?

"I'm Jenny Blake. My grandmother plays bridge with your grandmother."

The last time she'd seen Jenny Blake, Jenny had still had most of her baby teeth. Helena could almost hear her joints starting to creak with age. "Oh my, I didn't recognize you at all."

"Well, you haven't changed a bit," Jenny said, picking up the phone and hitting a button. "Whatever your skin care regime is, please share it with the rest of us. Tate, Helena's here and wants to know if you have a minute."

She'd automatically braced herself after the "you haven't changed a bit" comment, only to have it followed by what had to be the nicest phrase that had ever followed those words. Helena was feeling pretty good as Jenny waved her around the counter. "End of the hall. Welcome home."

Tate was at his desk, scrolling through something on a tablet, a little concentration crease between his eyebrows that she remembered well from before. He looked so grown-up and professional, it was almost adorable: bottom of his tie tucked into his shirt, white lab coat with his name embroidered in script above the breast pocket. He looked up as she got to the doorway, and a Great Dane the size of a pony, wearing a cone of shame, lifted his enormous head off the pillow beside Tate's desk.

"Come on in. Everything okay?"

"Yeah." Helena sat, and the Great Dane's head landed in her lap. He hadn't even needed to stand up to reach her. Figuring Tate would stop her if she shouldn't pet the dog, she carefully rubbed his muzzle. "You are ginormous."

"That's why he's in here. Sultan won't fit in any of the cages in the back. And while it's lovely to see you, I've only got a couple of minutes. What's up?"

Crap. Now that the moment was here, she wasn't sure how to say it. But she didn't have the luxury of time to go think about it, as she only had about nine hours until everyone in town would know. "I've got to tell you something, because I want you to hear it from me first."

Slightly worried, Tate leaned forward. "Okay . . ."

"Ryan Tanner asked me to dinner."

"Really? Wow." He laughed, but when she didn't join him, his eyes widened and he sat back in his chair. "Wait, are you going?"

"Yeah. I am."

Tate blinked. "Can I ask why?"

"That's a good question." Pity she didn't have a good enough answer. She couldn't admit that she'd been sleeping with Ryan; to Tate, any Helena-and-Ryan connection was a brand-new development. And since she was only a temporary Magnolia Beach resident, "dating" seemed to be a silly thing to do. "I want to, but I'm not sure why I do." That wasn't a complete lie, just a different way of viewing the truth.

There was a long, uncomfortable moment. "Are you asking for my permission?"

"No."

An eyebrow went up. "Fashion advice?"

"No."

"Intel on Ryan's likes and dislikes?"

"No."

"Then why the hell are you telling me this?"

"Because . . . well, because you're my friend, and I wanted to be the one to tell you."

He shook his head. "Why on earth would you feel the *need* to tell me about it?"

Damn it. "You know, beats me. I guess I was afraid you would misunderstand and get your feelings hurt."

"There's not a lot to misunderstand, Helena." He shook his head. "Well, congrats. You must be thrilled."

"What?"

"What better way to prove you're no longer Hell-on-Wheels than by dating Mayor Tanner?"

"I'm not dating him. It's just dinner. And I'm certainly not out to prove anything."

He laughed at her. He *actually* laughed at her. "I know you well enough to know *that's* not true."

Now she was getting annoyed. "And I know you well enough to tell you to shut the hell up and quit acting like a baby," she snapped.

There was a moment of silence where Tate just stared at her. "Have fun at dinner." With that, he grabbed his tablet and left her sitting in his office with a dog's head still in her lap.

"That did not go well," she told him as she scratched his ears. Sultan just stared up at her with no understanding but in complete sympathy for whatever her problem might be.

But what had she really expected? Things with Tate weren't supposed to be this complicated, yet somehow they were. She could only hope that Tate would get over it once the initial shock wore off. Hell, this thing with Ryan was only temporary, anyway; she had time to rebuild things with Tate—phone calls, e-mails after she went back home. She vowed she would get their friendship back into a good place for them both eventually.

With a final pat for Sultan, she got up and headed out. Jenny waved as she passed through the reception area, where a different selection of animals and people now waited. She recognized two of them, and surprisingly, they smiled at her as she left.

She stopped by the pharmacy to pick up Grannie's blood pressure medication, and not only did the pharmacist—Lucy Harrow, who'd been three years behind her in school—make genuine and pleasant conversation, but so did two of the waiting customers. She recognized them as Mrs. Abernathy, the former Spanish teacher, and Mr. Colley, one of the Sunday school teachers at Grannie's church. She'd grown accustomed to going about her business with only the required levels of Southern small talk, and this sudden change seemed odd.

When Beth Mayers stopped her in front of the makeup

counter to ask about her prices for design work, the world officially skewed sideways. She stammered through an answer, offered a business card, and dialed Molly's number on her way out of the store. "You busy?"

"Not really," Molly replied. "What's up?"

She headed toward home. "Has the world gone crazy?" The Rileys were on their porch swing, but instead of just a hairy eyeball, Mrs. Riley gave her a tiny, reluctant wave.

"Like how? You're going to have to be more specific."

"People are talking to me. Being nice to me. They're freaking *waving* at me. It's weird."

"And?"

She gave Molly a quick rundown of her morning's conversations, intentionally leaving out the part about Tate. And Ryan. First things first.

"You said you wanted people to just get over everything and move on. It sounds like they're starting to. How is this bad?"

"I didn't say it was bad. I said it was weird. Beth Mayers never liked me, and Mr. Colley told me flat-out when I was nineteen that I was probably going to hell. Yet all of a sudden, today everyone's being all nice and friendly."

"Again, I ask, how is that bad?"

"Because it's freaking me out. What the hell is going on?"

Molly laughed, then cleared her throat. "Look, as the proprietor of a place where people congregate and converse, I often overhear conversations—"

That stopped Helena in her tracks. "About me?"

"While I normally would treat what I overhear with the sanctity of the confessional—"

"Yeah, yeah, yeah. Spill."

"I've noticed a turning of opinion recently." Helena felt her mouth drop open. "People have been really impressed at the way you've rallied for your grandmother. It shows maturity, personal growth. . . ."

"And that means . . . ?"

"You're garnering some goodwill, chickie."

She nearly dropped her phone. "That's the craziest thing I've ever heard."

"Crazy or not, you might be turning the tide."

"Impossible."

"Yet still true. Run with it, honey. Don't question it too much."

"I question everything." She sighed. "That's one of the reasons why Mr. Colley was convinced I was going to hell."

"Ah, come on. There's nothing better than a reformed sinner."

"Just last week no one believed I *could* be reformed."

"Isn't this what you wanted? Acceptance?"

"I guess."

"Then quit worrying about it. Accept it graciously and move on."

Molly had a point. "Fine. It's still really crazy, though."

"Aren't you on record as declaring all of Magnolia Beach certifiable anyway?"

"Pretty much."

"There you go."

If Molly didn't think it was too crazy, maybe it wasn't. It was just more than she was ready to deal with right now.

"By the way," Molly added, "there's a band I like playing at a bar up in Tillman's Corner tonight. Want to go with me?"

Time to tell Molly. "Well . . ."

Molly took her hesitation the wrong way. "Jeez. Surely you weren't so bad that the people of Tillman's Corner have issues with you, too."

That rather depended on exactly where she wanted to go and how strictly "lifetime bans" could legally be enforced. "That's not it," Helena hedged. "I actually have dinner plans for tonight."

"You and Tate?"

"No." She took a deep breath. "I'm going with Ryan."

"Ryan Tanner?" There was surprise in her voice, but

a normal level of it, considering it was coming out of left field as far as anyone in Magnolia Beach knew.

"Yeah."

"Whoa. That is . . . new."

"It's not a big deal."

"Yeah, it is. When did this happen?"

"We spent a lot of time together when he was working on the house, and we've gotten to know each other. He thought it might be nice to go to dinner." She tried to sound very casual and let half-truths do the work.

"And . . . ?" Molly prodded.

"And what?"

"You don't exactly need a free meal, Helena."

"Are you calling me fat?" she teased.

"You know what I mean. I got the feeling you didn't like Ryan all that much."

"Like I said, I've gotten to know him better recently. And since I'm expecting everyone else to move past old high school crap, I should probably do the same. Why? You don't think I should go?"

"Of *course* you should go. Ryan's a hottie. And a sweetie, too. Smart, funny, successful . . . You could find far worse dinner companions. Go for it." She lowered her voice. "And then tell me *all* about it."

That she couldn't quite agree to. "We'll see. I'm going to let you get back to work, and I'm going to do the same. Talk to you later."

Now she just had to find someone to come sit with Grannie tonight while she was gone. Which meant she would have to tell Grannie she had a dinner date, and Grannie would definitely want to know with whom.

Things were about to get *really* weird.

Chapter 13

Weird turned out to be a major understatement.

Helena sat on the sofa in the front room, dressed and ready to go, making small talk with Smilin' Cal and Grannie while waiting for Ryan to show.

In the end, she didn't have to find a sitter *or* feel guilty about it, as Grannie had come home from physical therapy to inform her that not only did she have company coming over that evening, but that she'd appreciate it if Helena could find somewhere else to be during that time.

Just to be difficult, she'd agreed, but decided to hold back on the fact that she, too, had plans. So she'd poured tea for everyone, helped set up a table for Cal and Grannie to eat on, and participated in the social requirements.

Finally, Grannie pinned her with a heavy stare. "You certainly look lovely. Where are you headed out to this evening?" *Translation: When are you leaving?*

"Dinner. I'm not sure where, though. But Ryan will be here soon."

"Ryan Tanner?"

She just loved how everyone responded with Ryan's first and last name and a question mark. There weren't exactly a lot of Ryans in her age group. The field was sufficiently narrow. "Yes, Grannie. Ryan Tanner."

"That's wonderful. I had no idea you'd gotten so close to someone since you arrived."

"Yeah, well . . ." Helena cut her eyes at Cal—just enough for Grannie to notice. "I guess I just forgot to mention it."

Grannie frowned at her impertinence but recovered quickly. "Ryan Tanner is a very nice young man. I must say that I'm quite pleased."

"I knew his grandfather well," Cal added. "He comes from a good family."

"Yes, he is very nice," she answered Grannie, "and while I don't know his family well," she told Cal, "I do know they're good people."

"Still, a dinner date with the mayor is quite an achievement," Grannie added.

"He's the mayor of Magnolia Beach, not New York City."

"It's still impressive, dear."

"I guess so. Especially for me. We all know I've never been popular with Magnolia Beach's mayors before. Or the police. Or any authority figure, for that matter," she added.

Cal looked a little surprised at her words. It seemed her reputation hadn't reached the over-sixty-five group of residents of Bayou La Batre, nor had Grannie filled him in. How refreshing.

Before he could say anything, though, the clock chimed seven, and, hard on that, the doorbell rang. "Mayor Tanner is very punctual. Excuse me." She went to open the door.

Mercy. Ryan looked . . . well, "hot" was the only word that came to mind. Nice slacks, a button-down shirt . . . It wasn't anything particularly fancy or high fashion, but it totally worked on him. Sexy without effort. Stylish without a hint of metrosexual. Small-town alpha-male casual without the good-old-boy, redneck vibe. There was a sweet spot, and Ryan was dead center of it.

And, *boy oh boy*, was it working on her. If only her grandmother weren't twenty feet away.

Then he grinned, causing a disturbing little fluttering deep in her stomach. "Hey."

"Hey," she echoed. Ryan leaned in like he might give her a kiss, but she stepped back quickly. "Come on in. Grannie wants to say hello."

Ryan straightened up immediately, a mix of surprise and caught-in-the-cookie-jar written across his face.

"It's nice to see you, Ryan."

"And you, Ms. Louise. You're looking like you feel better."

"I do. Thank you."

"And this is Grannie's friend, Cal Parker."

Cal stood, extending his hand to Ryan, who shook it, and Helena bit back a giggle as Cal gave Ryan a very parental look. "What plans do you two have for the evening?"

Ryan cleared his throat. "I thought I'd take Helena to Bodine's."

Grannie raised an eyebrow, impressed, as Cal nodded. Helena was impressed, too. Bodine's wasn't cheap, and their seafood was known to be some of the best on the Gulf Coast.

"And what time should I expect you back, dear?" Grannie asked casually.

"I'll be home in time to help you get to bed. Say around tenish? Do you mind staying with Grannie until then, Cal?"

"It will be my pleasure," he answered. "I'd love to hear how you enjoyed Bodine's. Tell the hostess that you're friends of mine, and they'll take very good care of you."

The subtext was so clear, it practically hung in the room like closed-captioning. *We will wait up. We will know if you don't go where you say you are. Behave yourselves.* Helena felt seventeen.

Ryan shifted uncomfortably under the unmasked stare. It seemed he was feeling a little adolescent as well. "Thank you," Ryan said awkwardly. "We'll do that."

Before this could regress any further, Helena grabbed her purse and Ryan's hand, pulling him toward the door. "Good night. Y'all have fun."

"You, too," Grannie and Cal chorused behind them as she shut the door.

"Man, I haven't done the 'meet the parents' small talk in years," Ryan said as they walked to the car. "I'm out of practice, and I think it showed."

"It did," she assured him. At his look, she defended herself. "Hey, *you're* the one who wanted to do this 'properly.' Therefore you get to come in, meet the parental units, squirm a little. . . ."

He shook his head. "So that's Ms. Louise's new boyfriend? Maybe you should be making him squirm a little, too."

"Unfortunately, that's not how it works. And, anyway, I really don't like to think about it too much. I just tell myself it's a good thing and assume they'll play cribbage all night. Otherwise, my head explodes." She stopped at the car and leaned against the door. "You're really taking me to Bodine's?"

"Well, I kind of have to now," he grumbled halfheartedly.

"I'm flattered."

"Why?"

"It's a nice place."

"You're worth it." He leaned in to kiss her. She kissed him back briefly, feeling that little flutter in her stomach again, before pulling away and placing a finger against his lips.

"Don't get all sappy on me. I'm only letting you buy me dinner so that we can have sex later. Consider this the foreplay."

Ryan shook his head again and opened her door. "You are the strangest woman I've ever met."

"Thank you."

"But, since I have to have you home in three hours . . ."

"We could go to your place first," she offered, a little ashamed at the eagerness in her voice she couldn't hide.

Ryan looked both amused and disappointed. "Our reservations are at seven thirty."

She grabbed her seat belt. "Then I guess I'll just have to eat fast so we'll have time after. Get in."

He was laughing as he closed the door.

But he wasn't going to be laughing when he found out she wasn't kidding.

That gave her a laugh as well.

Overall, Ryan would give his date with Helena high marks.

They'd cut it close getting Helena home on time, but they'd made it, and the early night meant he'd actually gotten some much-needed sleep. The trade-off, though, was the pulled muscle in his back, but that was only proof that he was too old to be getting hot and heavy in the cab of his truck. There wasn't enough room, and he wasn't nearly as flexible as the event required. He probably still had the imprint of the gear shift on his ass.

But the sense of satisfaction this morning was unexpected. In a way, he felt like he'd accomplished something big, which was strange, because he'd never had a hard time getting women to go out with him before. But somehow, getting Helena Wheeler to put on a dress and go out with him in public—even if she did claim to do it only in order to sleep with him—was almost something he felt he should put on his résumé to prove he could accomplish the nearly impossible.

That "I'll only go out to dinner with you if you agree to have sex after" stereotype reversal was something he'd think about later. Or maybe never. It would only lead to headaches, as he couldn't decide whether his ego was being stroked or dented by the idea.

Possibly both.

Helena wasn't boring or typical in any way, and that was definitely part of her charm. She had plenty of other positive qualities as well—smart, funny, kind, sexy; all of which were on display last night—but she kept him on his toes, providing a challenge, as if he had to earn her company while at the same time she was offering it freely and without strings or games.

And there was the headache. He could feel it forming behind his eyes as he tried to untangle the infinity knot that was Helena. It was far better and easier to just accept her for exactly what she was and exactly what she presented—which was also part of her charm and somehow refreshing and easy.

It was all very strange.

And then it got downright weird.

Getting out of the shower, he heard his phone go off as a text came in. It went off at least twice more in the time it took him to dry off, and it was alerting him to voice mail messages before he had his clothes on.

Figuring someone had to be dead or dying, he finally went to the kitchen and unplugged it from the charger to see.

Every message was from Shelby in her typical concise text style—Call me. Since the missed calls were from Shelby as well, he didn't need to listen to the voice mails. Something was up; what, exactly, was the question. He wasn't going to panic, though; if someone really was dead or dying, he'd have messages from multiple family members—and probably at least one person banging on his door. So whatever was going on with Shelby couldn't be *that* life-threatening.

Shelby answered her phone on the first ring and skipped right past any and all of the usual pleasantries. "It's about damn time you called me back."

"What's gotten you all riled up this morning?"

"You and Helena Wheeler? Really?"

It seemed Shelby wasn't going to beat around the bush. "We went to dinner. So?"

"*So?*" He couldn't see the look on her face, but he knew exactly what it was. "I thought you were just doing some work for her."

"I was, and I did. And then I decided to ask her to dinner."

"Was it just dinner, or was it a date?"

"What difference does it make?" He remembered Helena's comeback to *his* comment on her and Tate's dinner plans and added, "Unless *you* have a thing for Helena, I don't see why you'd care."

"I care that *you* might have a 'thing' for Helena."

"Why?"

Shelby made a few noises that may or may not have been the start of sentences. Finally, she took a deep breath. "You shouldn't get involved with her."

"Not that it's any of your business either way, but I'll go ahead and let you tell me why."

"She's not right for you."

"You don't even know her, Shelby."

"I know enough about her."

He'd thought the same thing, but now he knew better. "You'd be wrong."

She wasn't one to back down, even though his tone had been sharper than intended. "I know she's bad news. She's a troublemaker."

"And what has she possibly done to prove that's the case?"

"You're asking *me* for her greatest hits?"

"What has she done *recently*?" He waited. "See? Nothing."

"I should have known. When you were championing her cause at Gran's that day, I should have known. What are you going to tell your mother?"

"I don't plan to tell her anything—because there's nothing to tell," he added quickly. "I took a woman to dinner. We had a nice time, but I'm a long way from having to tell my mother anything."

Shelby laughed at him. "Oh, good luck with that. If she doesn't know already, she'll know by lunchtime."

"You know, *you're* quite possibly the only person who cares. And since you were just trying to set me up on a date with that woman at Dad's clinic, I would think you'd be happy that I'm dating at all."

"So it *was* a date."

Helena might give him headaches, but no one could bring on a full-on migraine like Shelby. "Let it go, Shelby. It's not a big deal. She's only here for a short while, anyway." That truth actually pinged him in a different place than it had before. A not-nice place. He wasn't quite prepared for that.

"Well, there is that, I guess," she conceded. "I can't believe it, though."

"You've made that quite clear. Now, can I go to work?"

"Sure. Just be careful, okay?"

"I'm going to the office and then to the Millers' to install their cabinets. There's nothing remotely dangerous on my agenda today."

"That's not what I meant." Her voice lost its indignant edge. "You're a good guy, Ryan. I want you to be happy. And I don't want someone like Helena Wheeler to hurt you."

As irritating and wrong as Shelby might be, he had to appreciate the sentiment. It was hard to get mad over someone's good intentions—not impossible, of course, but hard. "I'll keep that in mind."

"You should."

Now running late, Ryan grabbed his stuff and his coffee and headed to his truck, only to see that Helena had left footprints on the inside of the windshield last night.

He had to go back inside to get something to clean it off with. He didn't have time, but he'd never hear the end of it if someone noticed.

It was a good thing he did, because his mother was waiting for him at city hall.

Grannie was up fixing coffee when Helena came downstairs the next morning. "Grannie! What are you doing? Why didn't you call for me?"

"I'm not an invalid," she snapped.

"Actually, you kind of are." Helena took Grannie's elbow and led her to a chair. "Sit. I'll get it."

"I'm going crazy having people hover over me."

"Well, if you don't take it easy, you'll end up back at the New Day Center." She took Grannie a cup of coffee, poured one for herself, then stuck bread into the toaster. Fortunately, Grannie wasn't much of a breakfast eater, so Helena didn't have to attempt eggs or anything, but she got butter and jam and one of Grannie's pretty china plates ready. "I'll make you a tray."

"I'm going to eat at the table like a human being. And I might just slap the next person who brings me a tray," she warned.

"So, I guess we're feeling better today, then." Helena had her doubts Grannie was really as better as she claimed— there were already signs of strain around her eyes just from getting herself out of bed and to the kitchen—but it was a good sign of progress, nonetheless. Grannie wasn't a fan of idleness, so the chafing against restrictions was to be expected. "Promise me that you won't overdo it. Slow and steady, okay?"

"I don't think I can promise anything. Thank you," she added as Helena served her some toast. "We didn't get much of a chance to talk last night after you got home. Did you have a good time?"

Helena refrained from mentioning that last night's exhaustion might be a sign she wasn't really as recovered as she might hope, but she kept those words behind her teeth, taking the chair opposite her and cuddling her coffee instead. "I did. What about you? Did you and Cal have a nice evening?"

A little smile tugged at the corner of Grannie's mouth. That, plus the fact Grannie had been a little disheveled upon her return last night, told Helena that Cal was more than just a platonic friend. She still didn't want to explore that too much, but it was nice to see Grannie in the flush of a flirtation.

"We did. We had a light dinner, watched a movie.... You?"

"Dinner was fantastic. The chef at Bodine's is a genius."

"Did you try the crab cakes?"

"I did. They were amazing. Then we drove around for a little while so I could see some of the changes in town, the places I haven't been in ages." That was basically true. They'd passed several new things on their way to the back side of Bayside Park, and she hadn't been to that lover's lane since high school. Now she was fighting back her own little smile. She'd thought the pleasures to be found in the cab of a pickup truck were long in her past, that her tastes and standards had evolved beyond that, but she had been proven wrong quite quickly last night. Who knew that hard, fast, and stealthy could be so good? Thank God the police hadn't cruised by and decided to investigate.

"Well, I'm so glad to see you with a nice young man like Ryan Tanner for once."

Helena pressed imaginary pearls in wide-eyed mock shock. "Are you saying you didn't like the boys I went out with in high school?"

That earned her a frown. "You are well aware I didn't. I always knew you could do so much better."

She fought back a smile. "Like Ryan Tanner?"

Grannie shook her head. "Not *specifically* Ryan, but a polite boy from a nice family, one with a good future ahead of him. Someone who'd treat you right, take care of you—"

"Take *care* of me? How very medieval, Grannie. I can take care of myself quite well—in fact, I already do."

"I know you *can*, but it's nice to have someone else on the team, too. And Ryan Tanner is that kind of man. No offense, sweetheart, but you tended to drag the net when you went fishing."

"Grannie . . ."

"So I think it's wonderful to see you with someone like Ryan. Will you be going out with him again?"

"He hasn't asked, but I kind of assume he will." She hadn't agreed to more than one date, but Ryan had been right about one thing: She'd gotten a bit of a kick out of the rather shocked looks on people's faces last night. "And, before you ask, yes, I probably will go if he does."

"Good."

Uh-oh, she didn't like that smile. "Don't get ahead of yourself, Grannie," she warned.

"Oh, I wouldn't dare."

Yeah, right. She was an over-thirty single woman who'd caught the eye of Magnolia Beach's favorite son—if Grannie *wasn't* already planning the wedding, Helena needed to call the doctor and make sure that concussion hadn't caused permanent brain damage.

She was saved, though, when her phone rang and Molly's name popped up, so she left Grannie with her newspaper—and her imaginary wedding bells—and took her coffee with her to the other room to answer it. "Hey."

"Did everything go okay on your date last night?" Molly sounded genuinely concerned.

"Yeah. Why?"

"Then why was Shelby Tanner just in here trying to set *me* up on a date with Ryan?"

Helena nearly spit her coffee out. "You're kidding me."

"Hand to God. I just got an earful about all his good qualities and how it's just so hard for him to go out with women because of his schedule and his position in the community, blah, blah, blah."

"Wait. Shelby said what? Why?"

"Shelby thinks she's Magnolia Beach's yenta or something these days, so that's not really the weird part," Molly said dismissively. "But, I mean, he went out with *you* just last night. So unless something bad happened . . ."

"Everything was great. Maybe she just doesn't know that we went out."

"Oh, honey, she knows. *Everyone* knows."

"Everyone?" *Jeez.* But then, she really shouldn't be that surprised. The sheer speed at which the news had spread *was* pretty impressive, though. "Was there a press release or something?"

"Not that I saw. All I know is plenty of people are talking about it this morning. I mean, *I* got the news at six thirty with my pastry delivery."

Helena leaned her head against the couch and groaned.

"But," Molly added cheerfully, "I heard you looked great, if that makes you feel any better."

"Oh, that makes it *much* better, thank you."

"Look, I just wanted to make sure nothing bad had

happened on your date. If you think it went fine, I wouldn't worry about it."

"But Shelby—"

"Is a busybody." Molly dismissed it easily. "She's sweet, and I like her a lot, but she's a bit of a meddler."

"Who doesn't want me going out with her cousin, it seems."

"Well, it's a good thing she doesn't get a vote, then, isn't it?"

"Well . . ."

"Okay, enough of this. We're moving on now. *So . . . ?* How was it?".

She was constantly amazed at Molly's ability to just move past things. She, on the other hand, needed a second to shift gears. "Great. We went to dinner at Bodine's. . . ."

"Ooh, fancy."

"And then we went for a drive. I had to be home by ten to look after Grannie, so it was a short evening."

"But fun, yeah?"

"Yeah," she answered honestly, but she could feel her smirk, and she was glad Molly couldn't see it.

"You had sex with him," Molly declared flatly.

"Uh, *what?*" Was Molly clairvoyant?

"Oh my God, I'm *right*. It was wild guess, but I was right!" she crowed.

Damn it. "Um . . ." *Great, now I sound like a slut.* As far as everyone knew, last night had been their first "date," and there was no way to defend herself from what was the truth. Even if it wasn't really like that at all.

"Oh, honey, I'm not judging you for it. Well, actually I *am*," she amended, "but in a good way, because it shows you have excellent taste. I won't ask for details because you've already said everything went great, so that answers the most important one. I am slightly jealous, though."

Helena was slightly dizzy from trying to keep up, but she did catch that last bit. Now was her chance. "Maybe you should give—"

"Oops. I gotta go. Bible study at Grace Baptist just let out, and here they all come. We'll talk later, okay?"

"Oh, okay, bye." But Molly had already hung up.

Helena leaned back and rubbed her eyes. So the entire town knew. It was interesting that while Molly said everyone was talking about it, she hadn't reported the tone or content of those conversations. That fact alone spoke volumes.

Shelby's reaction, though, was just strange. Matchmaker wannabe or not, why would she be trying to set Ryan up on a date just hours after he'd had one? Try as she might, Helena couldn't think of a reason for Shelby to dislike her. Shelby had been too young—and if anything, she'd have been merely adjacent to any happenings that occurred, not in the middle of them. Shelby hadn't done anything to her; therefore it was very unlikely she could have done something to Shelby. Unless Shelby was acting out of solidarity with her brother, Jamie, who was still holding a grudge.

It was weird, sure. But what was even weirder was that she found it more amusing than insulting.

Either she was completely twisted or remarkably mature.

Oddly, she felt she might be both.

The slide of chair legs across linoleum had her on her feet and headed back to the kitchen to get to Grannie before she overdid it and hurt herself.

Mature Helena had things to do today. She'd worry about what Shelby and the rest of Magnolia Beach thought later.

Chapter 14

Dinner at Bodine's had been nice, as it was a real "first date" kind of place, the kind of restaurant a man took a woman to when he was trying to impress her. But for a second date, Ryan decided the Frosty Freeze would work nicely. After all, it was exactly the place he'd have taken her if he'd screwed up the courage in high school.

Helena, though, had balked. Not at the food or the idea that it was a big step down from Bodine's, but that it would be very public. The small portion of Magnolia Beach who *hadn't* heard about their first date—or hadn't believed the reports—would know about it soon enough. Since Helena was sticking with her argument that this could somehow come to bite him in the ass, it had taken some convincing—and more than one prod between her shoulder blades.

He'd dealt with less recalcitrant mules. But, once again, he'd ended up with a great sense of accomplishment once Helena was seated at one of the battered picnic tables. There had been a few curious looks from some of the other diners, but they'd gawked, nodded, and gone back to their own lives and food.

Helena was nearly halfway through with her burger before she finally seemed to loosen up.

"See, it's not so bad, is it?"

"The burger is great. I know it's so bad for me, but I just can't manage to care all that much."

"I meant coming here."

"It's everything my teenage heart ever dreamed about."

He could have called her on the sarcasm, but instead he grinned. "So you used to dream about me, huh?"

"Only that time I ate bad scallops from the old Tanker restaurant. It was a long night."

"Funny."

She grinned and daintily ate a French fry. "But in answer to your first question, it's fine. I'll never be elected prom queen, but no one's flinging holy water in my direction, either. That's good enough for me. Let's talk about something else, though. I can't be the only thing of interest in Magnolia Beach."

Hadn't he gotten onto his family for exactly the same thing? Helena, though, *was* the main thing of interest in Magnolia Beach for him—albeit for different reasons entirely. Still, surely there had to be something for them to talk about that didn't include the past, her ongoing reentry into Magnolia Beach's society, and her grandmother's house or health. It took him a second, though. "How's business? Are you getting caught up?"

"I am. *Finally*. Mrs. Wilson has proven herself to be quite the community organizer, and I'm back to having at least part of my day to myself to work. She's also very adamant that I get out of the house and go do fun things—like this, for instance—because she says it's unhealthy not to."

"I remember when Mr. Wilson was sick. She probably knows all about caregiver's fatigue."

"Exactly. I'm also being careful to limit the number of jobs I'm taking on right now. It's less money overall, but I'm keeping my clients happy, so that's probably more important at this point. Mrs. Wilson says it's all about balance."

"I didn't realize you and Mrs. Wilson had become such confidantes."

"She's been a godsend. I wish I'd gone to her sooner for advice."

He was having a hard time processing that statement, but Helena said it so offhandedly and naturally that it had to be true.

"I'd like to do something nice for her, just to partly say thanks," Helena continued.

"I doubt she's expecting anything. Mrs. Wilson loves giving orders and advice. That you're following any of it is probably thanks enough."

Helena laughed. "I know. But I also know she was recently elected president of the historical society. I was thinking I could design a new header for the Web site or something. What do you think?"

The historical society. He hadn't thought about them in days, and it had been quite nice. "I'm sure she and the rest of the ladies would appreciate it."

"But ... ?" she asked. When he didn't answer, she added, "I know they're not thrilled with you right now, but I'm not sure why. From the look on your face, it goes both ways."

"How do you know they're unhappy?"

"It's a small town. I hear things." She shrugged. "I don't always understand what I'm hearing, but I hear it nonetheless. What did you do?"

"Why do you assume *I* did something?"

She laughed. "Because a bunch of sweet little old ladies are upset with you. You had to have done *some*thing, and you're too old for it to be mischief or foolishness."

"It's complicated." Helena drank her milk shake and waited for more. He sighed. "The historical society wants to pass a historic overlay that would cover a good portion of Magnolia Beach. The Chamber of Commerce does not like their regulations. The council is divided. The historical society feels I'm not supporting them strongly enough."

"Do you not want the overlay restrictions in place? Magnolia Beach seems like the perfect place for that."

"It's complicated. The quaint old-town charm is part

of our attraction to tourists, but the breadth of their regulations could stifle businesses."

Helena nodded in understanding. "So that's why the Chamber is against it."

"No one is really against the idea of historic overlay, but the Chamber doesn't want it applied so widely. They feel business owners can be trusted to walk the line between preservation and innovation without municipal oversight."

"What about the businesses that are primarily dependent on tourism?"

"It's a mix of support, some for, some against. Most aren't totally against it, but they also want some leeway to keep us attractive to tourists in the future."

"And where do you stand on this?"

"Somewhere in the middle—which is not really acceptable to either side."

"But that's the proper place for the mayor to be. Trying to find a compromise that benefits everyone and keeps the best interests of Magnolia Beach as a whole in mind."

"I wish everyone else thought that."

"I'm sure they do. But in a negotiation, your opening stance *has* to be extreme. It gives you the chance to relent on some things to make you look reasonable while you protect the core demands you know you *won't* cede. A clever mayor just needs to tease out what those core demands are and build a compromise around them. Let them bicker and argue for a while, and when you present your middle-ground solution, you'll look like a sensible, grounded, in-everyone's-best-interests hero."

It seemed Helena knew about more than just graphic design. "That's basically my plan. We're just not there yet. Right now, it's just endless meetings and e-mails flooding my in-box."

"I did some work for the Chamber of Commerce for a small town in west Georgia last year. At the time, it reminded me a lot of Magnolia Beach, but they had some really neat ways of incorporating the new into the old and keeping it all harmonious and aesthetically pleasing. If you want, I could send you their links and info. Seeing how it works somewhere else might help both sides envision something like that working here."

"That'd be great, Helena. Thanks."

"No problem." She cut her eyes at him. "If you want, I can even casually mention it to Mrs. Wilson—in the context of designing new headers and such."

Helena caring about—much less getting indirectly involved—in Magnolia Beach business? What was next? Pigs flying? Ice skating in hell? "It couldn't hurt."

After one last suck on her milk shake to make sure the very last of it was gone, Helena gathered up her trash off the table. "I've got a little time before I need to be back at the house. Want to walk down to the Shore?"

Strap on the skates and check the skies for swine. Forget dinner at Bodine's. *This* was now an official Magnolia Beach date.

And he hadn't had to prod her into it.

When Ryan pulled in to the parking lot and cut the engine, Tank knew where he was and sent a warning growl at him from his perch on the center console.

"Necessary evil, dude," Ryan said before scooping him up. There was no way Tank would go into the vet's office on his own four feet, and dragging him through the parking lot on a leash was beneath their dignity. Tank continued to growl low in this throat, his lips curling up into a snarl that showed his teeth, showing his displeasure to everyone they passed in the parking lot.

"Hey, Tank. Who's a good boy?" Jenny Blake asked as Ryan signed in. Tank's tail wagged once to acknowledge her; then he went back to snarling in everyone's general direction. "And how are you, Ryan?"

"Great."

"Good. Tate will be with you in just a minute."

"No problem."

"Uh, Ryan . . ." Jenny looked downright uncomfortable. "Can I talk to you for a second?"

"Sure."

"Privately?" This was weird, but he nodded, and she waved him around the counter and into one of the exam rooms. "This is kind of awkward, but . . ."

It wasn't like Jenny to beat around the bush. "What's up?"

"You're a wonderful guy, and I'd really like us to be friends."

Huh? "I thought we were already."

"Yeah, but, you see, I have a boyfriend. He goes to school in Mobile, but we've been together for about six months now."

Okay. "Congratulations."

"So, I'm flattered. I really am. Maybe we can just stay friends instead."

"Jenny, I'm lost. What *are* you talking about?"

"Well, Shelby came in with Cupid this morning and we were talking and she said that *we* should . . . I mean, she kind of implied that you thought I was . . . Wow, this is really awkward."

The realization hit him like a truck. "I'm going to kill her. Jenny, you are lovely, and your boyfriend is an extremely lucky man to have you. Shelby, however, has way overstepped her boundaries and is meddling without permission. I'm sorry she made you feel awkward, but . . ." *Damn, there is simply no good way to tell a woman you aren't interested in her without making it sound like an insult.* "I'm happy for you to forget she said anything at all. In fact, I'm begging you to forget it."

"Oh." And there was the mixture of relief and insult. "I'm glad to hear it. I did think it was a little strange since you just went out with Helena Wheeler. . . ."

So Shelby was telling him he could do better *and* taking it upon herself to find that "better" woman for him. He really was going to strangle her this time. Good Lord. And while there was nothing particularly *wrong* with

Jenny Blake, there was *definitely* something wrong with dating anyone you used to babysit. He repressed a shudder. "Shelby isn't Helena's biggest fan."

"That makes sense, then." Jenny sighed. "I feel much better. Not that you're not a great catch," she quickly added.

"Can we just stop now? Pretend this didn't happen?"

"Done." She opened the door again, then paused and looked at him and smiled. "But I think it's great about you and Helena."

Not knowing whether Jenny was the type to feed grist into the rumor mill, he went with the far safer disclaimer of, "It's just a couple of dinners. Let's not get carried away."

"Fair enough." She held the door for him. "Have a seat. It'll be just another minute."

Fortunately, there weren't a lot of patients in the waiting room, so Ryan wasn't going to be forced to make small talk with the owners or try to keep Tank from picking a fight with a Rottweiler. As Tank sniffed around at the end of his leash, Ryan took the time to text Shelby.

Stop it. Now. Do not try to fix me up.

He put the phone away as he didn't expect a reply. Shelby didn't text unless she had to, but maybe this could prevent any further embarrassment until he had the chance to call her. Lord knew, it wasn't a conversation he wanted to have in the waiting room of the vet clinic.

Jenny called them back into an exam room a few minutes later, and he lifted Tank up onto the table over the dog's protests. While Tank may have put up a small fight with him, the vet tech—a young blonde he vaguely recognized as one of the Masterson girls—won Tank over quickly, cooing at him until Tank rolled over for a belly rub.

"What a sweet boy," she said, rubbing Tank's chest. Then, looking at Ryan, she added, "I'm going to take him to the back for his shots, and the doc will bring him back when we're done for any questions you might have. He looks great to me, but you do need to get him scheduled for a teeth cleaning. He's got some tartar buildup." She handed him a brochure on doggie dental care, scooped up Tank, and left.

Oh, Tank is going to just love having his teeth cleaned. He flipped through the brochure, surprised to find out he was supposed to be brushing Tank's teeth with a special toothbrush and paste every other day. Who had time for that?

The scrabbling of tiny toenails against the tile told him Tank was returning, and when Tate opened the door, Tank limped over to him, drooping his head pitifully and favoring his front foot.

"He's fine, I promise," Tate said. "That's not even where he got the shot."

"He's a bit of a drama queen." But he picked Tank up anyway and rubbed his nose.

"Everything looks fine. He's starting to edge up to the upper end of his weight class, though, so you might want to watch his food intake. Otherwise, he's good. Any questions for me?"

Tate was being very professional, but not his normal self, and Ryan had no question as to why. Everyone in town seemed to know about him and Helena, and he had to assume that everyone included Tate. It wasn't a subject he could just broach with Tate, though. Not without seeming insincere or gloating. But it felt like *some*thing needed to be said nonetheless.

Surprisingly, Tate broached the subject. "I should probably tell you that Shelby was in here this morning."

"Yeah, I know. I've already apologized to Jenny. Shelby really needs to find a new hobby."

"We had an *interesting* conversation as well."

Whoa. Had Shelby really lost her mind? Bitching about Helena to the one person in town who was definitely on her team? "Then maybe I should apologize to you, too."

Tate snorted. "At least she didn't try to fix me up with you."

The amusement caught Ryan off guard. *Maybe this is not a big deal.* He laughed. "You're not my type."

Tate's humor died. "Neither is Helena, and that didn't stop you."

So, no, then. And since Tate didn't see the need to beat around the bush, neither did he. "I know how things are between you and Helena, but that really has nothing to do with me."

"Actually, it does. Friends look out for each other, and first and foremost, Helena's my friend. I watched her back for years, and that won't change now."

Tank, either bored or picking up on the tension, wiggled around, and Ryan let him jump back to the exam table, where he trotted over to Tate for petting before settling in the middle to thoroughly lick himself. Ryan looked at Tate. "Are we going to have a problem?"

"That depends on whether or not Helena gets hurt."

"I assure you I have no intention of hurting her."

"That's nice to hear, but it doesn't exactly ease my mind. Being back here has been hard enough on her. Getting mixed up with you probably wasn't the best choice she could make in order for things to be easier for her."

He hadn't thought about that. Helena's objections had never included how she might be hit from the fallout. "I think she's strong enough to handle it."

"Of course you do."

The words were simple, but the tone was snide. "What the hell do you mean by that?"

"Like she doesn't have enough on her plate to deal with right now with Ms. Louise's injuries and coming back to a place that treats her like the devil's spawn? Hell, your cousin was in here this morning trying to fix you up with my receptionist and any other single woman who happened to be in the waiting room simply because the two of you have been doing dinners. Do you think that's going to be *good* for her ego?"

"I'll take care of Shelby—"

"Really? Because she asked me to see if I could get

Helena to back off. She tried to couch it in the nicest possible terms, but in reality it was all about *you* and your reputation being sullied by hers."

"I'm going to kill her."

"Yeah, well, in the meantime, someone has to look out for Helena's best interests. You might be surprised to hear that I agree with Shelby, albeit for different reasons. Helena is probably better off without you."

"Helena's a big girl. She can decide for herself what's better for her."

"And when this goes to hell and you go back to your regularly scheduled life, *I'll* still be the one helping her pick up the pieces, because that's what friends do."

Tate's defense of Helena would have been heartening *if* Tate hadn't been painting him as the bad guy. He felt unfairly vilified. In a moment of clarity, he knew it was a small taste of Helena's life, and it was pretty damn bitter and hard to swallow. "I happen to care about Helena."

That was a news flash, even to him. Oh, he knew he liked her well enough and was certainly having a good time, but he wasn't aware it had shifted to *care*. Or when it had. But the weight in those words was obvious even to him, and it left him reeling a little in the wake of that truth.

"Good." Tate didn't sound fully convinced, though. "Then we won't have a problem." He gave Tank one last pat, completely changing the subject and moving on. "And we'll see you in six months for his Bordetella booster."

Tank walked out under his own steam, which was nice, as Ryan had a lot to think about. Helena had always been a force of nature and about as predictable as one, but he hadn't fully prepared himself to embrace that hurricane. And he certainly hadn't thought about the blowback on Helena—mainly because she didn't seem concerned about it as she would be leaving soon enough anyway.

Hmm, that idea wasn't sitting quite as comfortably on him as it had before.

And while it was no surprise that Tate would champion Helena and get indignant on her behalf, Tate knew

Helena better than almost anybody. If *he* worried Helena could get hurt, it gave Ryan pause and reason to believe it. That meant Helena wasn't as tough as she claimed to be.

It meant that he had the power and possibility to hurt her.

Which meant she might care.

And that changed everything.

Flashlights, batteries, beer. Yep, pretty much all we'll need.

On second thought, she grabbed a can of insect repellent. It got swampy out by the Neville place, and it could be buggy even this late in the year. Part of her wanted to grab some snacks for a mini picnic, but that was just too sappy to fathom.

Helena's quick dash through the Shop 'n Save had taken less than ten minutes, so she still had time to run by Latte Dah for a coffee to-go and get home in time to make Grannie's dinner.

I might just be getting the hang of this. Finding my groove.

The thought of a groove made her chuckle quietly to herself, but that died quickly as she left aisle six and ran straight into Shelby Tanner.

Shelby at least had the good grace to look a little guilty as well as surprised. "Hi, Helena. Good to see you."

How she'd managed to go nearly a month in Magnolia Beach without running into Shelby before now was a great mystery. Shelby hadn't changed much at all—she was taller and her features had matured, but the feminine version of the Tanner looks was impossible to deny.

Her initial amusement had given way to irritation and finally insult as Shelby's attempts to find Ryan another woman picked up steam. *Be the bigger person. Say something small-talkish and move on. Or just walk away.* Maybe if Shelby hadn't opened with "Good to see you," Helena might have managed it. "I find that hard to believe, Shelby."

I am petty and should be ashamed.

Shelby accepted the snark with a nod. "I guess that's fair enough."

"I won't keep you, then. I need to get home to Grannie."

"Please give her my best."

"I will." *Grannie will be proud.* She'd covered the basics of required politeness and could now leave without looking more petty and bitchy. "Bye, Shelby." Head high, she turned away.

"Helena, wait."

Christ. "What can I do for you?"

"Ryan's beyond pissed at me, and I know you think I'm horrible, but I just want you to know that it's nothing personal."

Nothing personal? It was all she could do not to gape like a goldfish. "I don't know how I can assume it's anything but. What I don't understand is why. What did I ever do to you?"

"Nothing. Which is why it's not personal. It's about Ryan, not you. I just want him to be happy."

It was galling as hell, and Helena had no idea how to respond.

"Ryan has a good life here. He's respected and loved, and you—"

"Are not. I know that." She sighed. "We've talked about it, and he doesn't think it's a problem."

"Of course he wouldn't. Call it ego or arrogance or naïveté, but whatever it is, Ryan just has blinders on when it comes to you."

"He's a big boy. It's his choice."

Shelby shook her head. "But Ryan needs a nice, sweet girl who'd be happy here in Magnolia Beach being a mayor's wife. I think we both know that's not you."

That stung. It was the truth, but that didn't make it sting less. It also gave a stir to all the feelings and insecurities she'd been deliberately squashing. *Damn it, I'm not letting Shelby Tanner undo years' worth of therapy.* "Since he hasn't proposed to me and I'll be leaving anyway, it's not an issue. And I don't think he'll have a problem finding that nice, sweet girl once I'm gone."

Shelby leveled a look at her. "But after he's been with you, do you think a nice, sweet local girl will ever measure up?"

Ouch. Or maybe it should be *thanks*. Compliment or complaint? It was a hard comment to unpack. "I'm sure one will. As you said, that's what Ryan needs." She was done discussing Ryan with Shelby. It was time to try that dignified exit again. "Now, if you'll excuse me, I need to get home and fix my grandmother's dinner."

Shelby nodded and let her leave without another comment.

Man, that was irritating as hell. Especially because Helena didn't have a good counterargument. Nothing Shelby had said was wrong, and half of it she'd argued herself with Ryan. She couldn't force him to care about something he didn't. And maybe he was right. It wasn't her problem, and she was frankly happier leaving it alone.

She was deep in thought, causing her to nearly run down another woman as she pushed through the glass doors to the street. She grabbed the woman to keep her from falling, recognizing her in the same instant as Pastor Thorpe's wife. *Lovely.* "I'm so sorry, Ms. Jane."

"Be careful, Helena. You'll hurt somebody rushing around like that."

"Yes, ma'am."

"How's your grandmother?"

"Getting stronger every day," she answered automatically.

"Margaret Wilson says you've offered to freshen up our Web site. That's very kind of you."

Helena hadn't known Jane Thorpe was part of the historical society. "It's my pleasure."

"Well, watch where you're going so you don't fall, and tell Louise I said hello."

"Will do." She held the door open for Ms. Jane, thinking that if Ryan wanted to win over the ladies of the historical society, all he had to do was offer to redo their media presence.

It wasn't until she got home that she realized *she* might have won over the historical society. If that wasn't a coup, she didn't know what was.

Chapter 15

"Helena, just admit you're lost."

This was not what he'd expected when Helena showed up at his house. Even when she'd told him to change into boots and jeans, he couldn't have imagined she planned to march him through the backwoods of the outskirts of town for some as-yet-unexplained reason.

She turned and shone her flashlight in his face. "I am not lost. I just got turned around for a minute. It's been a while since I've been out here, ya know."

He pulled out his phone and checked. He had a signal but only two bars. It would be embarrassing, but he could call for help if she'd gotten them truly lost. "And where exactly is 'here'?"

"You'll see."

He opened the map app. Maybe it could find them. "We've got to be on private property by now. So we're trespassing."

"Put that away. You'll ruin the surprise. And don't be such a goody-goody."

"I coach teenagers. I'm the mayor. I'm supposed to set a good example."

"Then keep your voice down."

The pin finally landed, and the map told him where they were. "Jesus, we're on the back side of the Neville place. That's just great. Forget arrested. We're going to get shot at."

She dismissed that with a wave of her hand. "Hank Neville is a terrible shot. He couldn't hit the broad side of a barn."

He pointed his flashlight at her. "I am not going to ask how you know that...."

Grinning, she said, "That's probably a good idea. Come on." Reaching for his hand, she pulled him along. "I can't believe you don't know where we're going."

"Well, you haven't told me, remember?"

"But you would recognize where you were if you'd ever been out here. Jeez, what did all you good little boys and girls do in the evenings?"

"Hung out at the Frosty Freeze. Went to the beach. Obeyed the laws. You know, the usual kid stuff."

"Loitering, underage drinking, taking glass containers onto the beach ... yeah, real law-abiding."

"It might not have been Bible study, but I certainly didn't trespass onto property owned by crazy rednecks who shoot first and ask questions later."

"Good for you. You get a cookie," she said sarcastically. Then she pushed through a bush and pointed with her flashlight. "Here we are. Look."

A cinder-block lighthouse just a little taller than a one-story house, stuck up in the middle of the woods. Red and white stripes circled the tower. All that was missing was the light on top. "It's real."

"Of course it's real."

That lighthouse was a local legend—everyone claimed to have been there, yet no one would ever tell exactly how they got there. The story was that some Yankee tourist had gone crazy when his wife drowned in Heron Bay, and he built her a lighthouse with the idea she'd find her way home. When she didn't, he climbed up to the top and shot himself. Supposedly his ghost still haunted the lighthouse, shooting at anyone who approached who wasn't his dead wife.

He'd thought both the story and the lighthouse were

just silly local lore. He didn't know if kids today had even heard the story. But sure enough, that was a lighthouse, in the middle of nowhere, and in the last place anyone would look for it. "No, I mean, I always thought it was just a joke, a reason to get drunk kids to wander around in the middle of the night once they were too smart to go on a snipe hunt."

"It is a bit of a snipe hunt." She laughed. "A lighthouse should be on the water, so most people don't think to come eight miles inland to look for it."

"How did you know where to look?"

"Do you want the truth, or something that won't horrify your mayoral and coaching sensibilities?"

Although he might regret it . . . "The truth."

Helena laughed again as she cleared out the plants that grew in front of the small door. If the legend was still going around, that alone was proof the current generation wasn't having any more luck finding it than he had. "Old Mr. Neville used to grow pot back here in the seventies. The lighthouse started off as just a lookout—inside it's just a platform on scaffolding—which is why folks got shot at when they got too close. When the old man died, Hank Neville decided to make himself a lighthouse and built the cinder-block tower around it. I have no idea why, but he was always eccentric, you know. It used to have a place for a light up top, but that disappeared in the summer of 'ninety-seven or 'ninety-eight. We couldn't exactly ask, so I never found out what happened to it."

"I know I'm going to regret asking this, but how did you learn of its location?"

She tossed a couple of rocks out of the way, then stood and brushed her hands off against her jeans. "Paulie's older cousin used to help with the harvest. He told us about it."

That was about the best answer he could hope for. "I've lived here my entire life. I can't believe I didn't know about this."

"Well, even you can't know everything, can you? Come on, the view is really cool from up top."

"We're going in?"

"Of course. Why else would I drag you a mile off the road into the woods?"

A quick glance over the door showed it was held shut by a rusty hasp and ancient padlock. "It's locked."

"You give up too quickly." Helena gave the hasp a jiggle, and it released from the wall, leaving the door hanging drunkenly at an angle. "Things aren't always what they seem," she said as she ducked inside.

With no other option, he followed her in. The cinder blocks had been built around a metal ladder and scaffold, creating a circle with maybe a five-foot radius. While it smelled earthy and damp, the floor was clear of trash, meaning people didn't come out here often. The ladder itself led straight up to what looked like a converted tree stand overhead. "Well, this *seems* to be a death trap."

Helena gave the ladder and each of the supports a hard shake, but it didn't move much. "It *seems* pretty sturdy to me." She tucked her flashlight into her waistband, adjusted her backpack, and started to climb.

Ryan held his flashlight on her to provide light and hovered underneath her, waiting to catch her if the whole damn thing gave way. When she got to the top, he finally released his breath.

She looked down at him. "You coming?"

Ryan climbed slowly, pausing to listen carefully for creaks or the sounds of rusted metal about to collapse. Even with his added weight, it seemed like it would hold, but he tried to convince himself that if it did collapse, the fall wouldn't be far enough to kill either of them. Once on the platform, he couldn't stand up fully without bashing his head against the ceiling, so he sat.

Helena dug into her pack and set up a battery-operated camp lantern, which illuminated the area nicely, but as far as he could see, it was simply a cinder-block column, and he said so.

She sighed. "Well, give me a hand." She put her hands against the ceiling and motioned for him to do the same. "Now push."

Like a giant skylight, the ceiling swung back on protesting hinges, opening them up to the night sky and allowing them to stand up completely. Helena pointed
toward the southwest. "On clear nights you can see almost all the way to the Coast Guard station. You can't
see the boats, but you can see the lights from the helicop-
ters taking off and landing." Then she sat and leaned
back to look up at the sky. "It's pretty, huh?"

Honestly, he didn't see much difference between the
sky here and in the rest of Magnolia Beach, but he figured he probably shouldn't offer up that information. He
sat beside her. "It's nice."

"I know it's the same ol' sky, but being up here makes
it feel closer. Plus, it's so quiet and dark out here. In
town, you've got the lights and down by the beach there's
the sound of the water, but out here . . . about two o'clock
in the morning, it's like you're the only people on earth."

"That's cool. Wait. I thought you had a curfew you
had to be home for."

"I did."

"Then how were you out here at two in the morning?"

Helena gave him a pitying look. "I never said I *stayed*
home."

"Wow. I'm beginning to think your grandmother deserves a medal for not strangling you."

Helena sighed. "The woman's a saint, that's for sure."

"How is she doing, by the way?"

"Better. She invited her bridge club to the house tonight to play cards. She's showing progress every day, so
maybe we're turning the corner toward the home stretch.
Or at least, the my-going-home stretch," she corrected
with a laugh. "She's going to need help for the foresee-
able future, particularly with the cooking and cleaning,
so if you know anyone who'd do a good job for a reasonable amount of money, send them my way."

There was that unpleasant pang again. *Don't ask
questions you don't want the answers to.*

Helena reached into her backpack and pulled out two
cans of beer. After passing one to him, she returned to

her earlier position. The lantern and the moonlight cast competing shadows and light across her face and body.

"So why'd you bring me out here?" he asked.

She smiled at him, and she seemed almost shy. "I thought you might like it." Then she shook her head. "You're right. It's stupid. We can go."

"No," he corrected quickly, "I'm glad you brought me. It's nice."

That seemed to please her, and they lay there quietly for a few minutes watching the stars. When she sighed, he looked over and noticed the wrinkle between her eyebrows. "You okay?"

"Yeah, just thinking."

"About . . . ?" he prodded.

"You, actually."

The honesty of that shocked him. He wanted to be pleased, but . . . "From the look on your face, I don't think they're very good thoughts."

"They're good thoughts, I promise."

"How good?" He hoped he'd laced the words with enough innuendo to cover the naked curiosity.

"They're not *those* kinds of thoughts."

"Oh?"

"I was just thinking that you've been really great."

"You sound surprised."

"You weren't what I was expecting; that's for sure."

"It's another question I'm sure to regret, but what were you expecting?"

She seemed to consider it for a long moment, and that made him nervous. She sat up, leaned against one of the metal supports, and crossed her arms over her chest. "Ryan Tanner, of *the* Magnolia Beach Tanners, a good, God-fearing, established, and well-connected family. Good-looking, charming, local hero and football legend. A popular, well-liked, forward-thinking and respected mayor, successful businessman, role model for the youth of Magnolia Beach . . ." Somehow Helena made those descriptions seem less than complimentary. "You should be smug, self-assured, self-righteous, married to the former head cheerleader with two-point-five kids and a picket fence. But you're not, so color me surprised."

Helena wasn't one for easy compliments. "I'm not sure whether to say 'thanks' or 'bite me.'"

"I'd go with 'thanks.' I meant it as a compliment. I'm *pleasantly* surprised."

"It goes both ways."

"Really?"

"Yeah. Who'd have thought Hell-on-Wheels would grow up to be you? Responsible, sensible . . ."

"Ugh, stop," she interrupted. "My inner child is horrified."

"Those were compliments."

A small smile tugged at her lips. "I know. And thanks." Helena leaned onto her side and propped her head on her fist. With a waggle of her eyebrows, she asked, "So, you wanna make out?"

He leaned in to give her a kiss. "No."

Shock, outrage, a touch of insult . . . The reactions played across her face. *"No?"*

"Don't get all offended. Believe me when I say I want to, but I'm not sure we should get this thing rocking too much. It seems sturdy enough, but it's probably best not to risk it."

She frowned. "Hmm. It does seem like a good way to get tetanus, too. It's certainly rusty enough. Boy, the wisdom that comes with age puts a real damper on the idea of reliving your youth."

It didn't make sense, nor did it speak highly of his maturity levels, but the thought of Helena bringing him to a place where she'd had sex as a teenager just didn't sit right. Aside from the ick factor, his feelings also smacked of jealousy, which he really didn't like admitting.

"You know, we'd come out here—me, Tate, Paulie, Sid, Jack Wilson sometimes—to drink and hang out. It was like our own private clubhouse. At the same time, I always thought it was a very romantic spot, and I would have these silly daydreams about bringing a boy out here for a picnic under the stars."

"But you never did?"

She snorted. "None of the guys I dated were really the romantic-picnic sort. So . . ."

"I'm flattered I made the cut."

"Don't flatter yourself too much. Your competition isn't exactly stiff. Look at the guys I dated."

He searched the back of his brain, and the results did—without any egotism needed—put him at the top of the list. "Well . . ."

"Exactly," she said. "I swear, if there was a loser in a twenty-mile radius of Magnolia Beach, I could find him. I had pretty low standards back then."

"Why?"

"Because none of the high-quality boys from 'good' families were interested in me. Aim low and you don't get disappointed, you know."

"You should have aimed higher. You probably could have had your pick."

She took a drink and shook her head. "No way."

"You might have been bad and scary, but the boys would have tripped all over themselves to get to you if you'd given them the tiniest bit of encouragement."

"Oh please."

"It's true." Helena shot him a look, so he added, "Did you ever try?"

She thought for a moment. "Guess not. I just assumed. My self-esteem wasn't real high back then."

Funny how she lacked self-esteem when everyone else thought she was überconfident. *Funny how I work with teenagers and am just now figuring that out about her.* "So what about that guy you ran off with?"

"Charlie? Oh, now, he was a doozie. He fed me a bunch of lies, but they were exactly what I wanted to hear." She leaned back and stacked her hands behind her head. "Things had gotten really tense here, with everyone always expecting me to screw up or do something terrible. I was unhappy and looking for a way out of town. I wouldn't admit *that* to anyone, though. Charlie told me all about the houseboat he had on Lake Lanier, the cool apartment in Atlanta, and all the great parties he went to. It sounded amazing. Completely different from the life I had and exactly the life I wanted. I thought I'd landed in a fairy tale and the prince had come to take me away." She sighed.

He had to admit that would be attractive to most any small-town girl. "But wasn't he working as a hand on one of the charter boats?"

She laughed. "Yes, and the wisdom of my age now tells me that detail was a big warning sign. But at the time, I believed him when he said he was just doing something he'd always wanted to do. Oh, don't look at me like that. I was twenty years old, living in a Podunk town, with nothing but more of the same on the horizon. Logic didn't figure into the decision much. I wanted to believe, so I did."

"And?"

"*And*, it only took about three days for me to find out it was all BS, but by then I was already in Rome, Georgia, with no car, no money. . . . I left him a month later."

"Why didn't you just come home?"

"Pride, of course." She chuckled. "It's a dangerous thing. And that was all I really had left. I wasn't going to slink back home in shame, looking like a fool. I decided then that I wouldn't come back to Magnolia Beach until I could come back under my own terms with my head held high."

"And how has that worked out for you?"

"I think it worked out pretty well. I've built myself a good life, started my own business. I've got no reason to be ashamed of who I am now."

"You're right." When she smiled at him, he added, "So why do you act as though you are?"

"Excuse me?"

"You're certainly still worried about what people think."

"Old habits die hard," she confessed. "And let's face it, I'm still cleaning up the debris of who I was then. It's not just the trouble I caused, either, although that would have been bad enough. I could have been kinder to people. I always had a bit of an attitude, I fully admit that, but I could've been less defensive and angry and reactionary."

"But it's understandable, considering what you went through with your mother."

An eyebrow went up. "Please don't try to psychoanalyze me."

"You're saying that didn't screw you up?"

"I'm saying that I don't need an amateur armchair psychologist. I'm well aware of my issues and problems and their manifestations, but that's in my past."

"From what I see, it's still in your present."

Helena's spine stiffened. "What the hell are you talking about?"

"You still seem very concerned with what people think of you."

"You're wrong," she said, shaking her head. "I don't care."

"You keep saying that, but it's not ringing true. You keep saying that *I'll* somehow suffer fallout from being with you, but it's only because of what people say and think about *you*. I think you care very much and it makes you mad."

Instead of answering to that, she deflected the statement. "I think you're thinking too much about this."

"Well, I'm not the only one. Tate says—"

Helena's eyes widened. "*Tate?* You and Tate are talking about me?"

"Yeah," he answered, realizing his mistake in admitting that a second too late. "He worries about you."

"Tate needs to worry about the impact of his own hellish childhood and butt the hell out of my issues," she snapped.

"At least you admit you do have issues."

That made her mad. "I'm not having this conversation." Helena pushed to her feet and grabbed the rope attached to the trapdoor, pulling it closed with a bang and nearly bashing him in the head with it in the process.

Grabbing her pack, she was halfway down the ladder before he could blink. "Where are you—"

"I'm leaving. I didn't sign up for Psych 101 with Mayor Tanner, and I refuse to participate." From the bottom of the ladder, she looked up at him. "Now, unless you're sure you can find your way out of here on your own, you'd be smart to follow. *Silently*," she warned.

Jesus. "Helena, wait." Even jumping the last few feet off the ladder, Helena was outside before Ryan's feet hit the ground. He ducked out the door and jogged to catch up with her. Damn, she could move fast when she wanted to. Finally, he managed to grab her arm. "What is the problem?"

"I'm tired of fighting with you."

"I wasn't trying to pick a fight."

"Well, you succeeded nonetheless." She shook off his hand and started walking again, almost making it to her car before he caught her.

"How? I'm just trying to understand you. Why is that bad?"

"Then understand this. All I want is acceptance. A simple 'live and let live.' Not understanding or tolerance or even forgiveness. Just acceptance. I thought you had that much figured out about me. I am who I am, and that's *because* of who I was."

"So I can't even be curious about what makes you tick?"

"Only if it goes both ways." She crossed her arms over her chest.

This conversation had gone way off course. "What?"

"Fair's fair, right? Riddle me this, then," she challenged. "Why, when you've had every advantage possible in life handed to you, have you never left the pissant little town you grew up in? What are you afraid of? Is life outside Magnolia Beach's town limits too scary, or is the pond out there just too big for the little fishy?"

Helena knew how to go right for the jugular with uncanny accuracy. "Whoa, there. Let's not . . ."

"Aw," she mocked, "it's not fun when people go poking into your psyche uninvited, is it?"

"I wasn't trying to poke. I'm not going to deny that I'm interested in what makes you tick, but that's only because I happen to care about you." He shouted it to keep from shaking her.

Helena pulled back as if he'd slapped her. After a confused second, she asked, all the heat gone from her voice, "How can you possibly care about me? You barely know me."

It seemed he'd hit her in a sensitive place without even trying. That made him feel a little better about his declaration. And since he had already made the big step, he had no reason to pull the punch now. He shrugged. "But the fact remains that I do."

Helena was silent for a long while, and it made him very nervous. "That's probably a big mistake."

"I'm willing to take that chance." It felt like he'd thrown down a gauntlet with that statement, and in a way, he probably had. The words just hung there in the air between them, and he realized he was very worried about what she might say next.

She was standing in the middle of the Nevilles' back forty, in the middle of the night, with a good chance someone might pop off a shot in their direction at any moment, with Ryan Tanner confessing he cared about her just minutes after she'd yelled at him for butting casually into her psyche like he had some kind of right to do so. And to top it all off, Ryan was staring her down in a way that made her terribly antsy and uncomfortable.

Because he said he cared about her.

And while she couldn't quite believe that—they were little more than friends with benefits, after all—the fact that he thought he might was a big problem. But it wasn't the biggest.

The biggest problem was that *she* might believe it. And if she did, she might end up returning the sentiment.

And she simply couldn't let herself care for him. That was just a disaster waiting to happen. He might be blithely ignoring what was being said about them—

about *him*—but she couldn't. For his sake, she had to care about that. He had no idea what was waiting for those who stepped outside the lines. Her earlier conversation with Shelby came back to her. She'd pushed it aside, not wanting to think about it, but if Ryan cared about her—or thought he did—then Shelby might have a point. It was one thing to have a fling and go your separate ways, but if this became more for him . . .

No wonder Shelby was running interference.

The only reason all this worried her was because it meant she was already starting to care about him, and that was just a bad idea no matter how she looked at it. When this thing ran its course, she didn't want to end up hurt.

This was just insane. A recipe for disaster. And since she was the new-and-improved Helena Wheeler, she wouldn't leave that kind of debris behind again. She got in the car, and after a moment, Ryan got in the passenger side. She could feel him watching her as she pulled out, but it was easier now that she didn't have to look directly at him. But he wasn't saying anything, letting his words just hang there ominously as if he were waiting for her to make up her mind about what she wanted to say. As she turned onto his street, she raked up her courage to say what needed to be said. "You know, now might be a good time to end this. Before anyone gets hurt."

"What?" She could tell he hadn't been expecting that.

In his driveway, she shifted into park and faced him, forcing a polite smile and an even tone. "It's been fun, and I do really appreciate everything—the dinners, the conversations, the work on Grannie's house, all of it. But since this can't go anywhere anyway, why stir so much up? It'll just be harder for you in the long run. And for me, too. The simple fact is that I'll have to make more trips to Magnolia Beach in the future, and there's no sense setting those up for failure."

It sounded both reasonable and mature to her ears, but Ryan didn't look like he was buying it. "So is this really about me? Or you?"

She could answer that truthfully. "Both. I'm a big believer in quitting while I'm ahead."

"You forget I'm a football coach. Quitting while you're ahead is a good way to end up losing in the end."

"I'm not the one with something to lose. You are. You're the one who has to live here."

"You keep saying that, but you touched on something earlier without making the most important connection of all. I *am* a big fish in the tiny Magnolia Beach pond. With that comes the luxury of not having to explain myself or worry too much about what other people think."

"That's a little arrogant." *Unsurprising, but arrogant.*

"Yes, but it's also the truth. Why do you think I came back to Magnolia Beach? It's not that life was too scary out there. It's that I didn't like feeling unimportant. Call it arrogance or a character flaw of some sort, but I chose to come home so I could take advantage of what I have here. I'm not going to deny I like the benefits."

Could she blame him? She'd probably like Magnolia Beach, too, if everyone liked and respected her. He wanted to come home to quit feeling unimportant. She wanted to leave for exactly the same reason.

"But you can't reap all those benefits if people lose respect for you. You need their support. I know you have all kinds of great ideas for Magnolia Beach, and I know you were getting pushback even before I came to town. If you piss these people off, or give them any reason to question you, they'll fight you just because they can. Trust me, I *know.*"

"I doubt that." She shook her head, meaning to interrupt him, but he put his hand on her arm before she could. His voice softened. "I like you, Helena. And I think, contrary to your protestations, that you like me, too. So what's the problem?"

"You know the problem." She couldn't keep the sigh out of her voice. Damn, she was tired. Tired of fighting the world. Tired of trying.

"No problem is unfixable. It just takes time and a little

effort." He smiled at her, and that smile nearly had her folding like a cheap card table.

"I don't have the luxury of time, and I don't want to put in any more effort. Which is why I really do think it's better to just end this now. That way, we can still part friends."

"Friends? I think we're more than just friends."

Stand strong. "I'm sorry if I've misled you somehow." At least the lie sounded better than it felt saying it. *It's for the best.*

The look on Ryan's face morphed into something inscrutable, and she had no idea what he might be thinking. Then he nodded once and got out without speaking.

It was odd and somehow deflating. She didn't know what to make of either feeling.

But she did know it sucked.

Which meant it had been the right thing to do.

Chapter 16

The next few days passed mostly uneventfully, which was good. Grannie was showing real signs of improvement and getting stronger every day, and Helena began to see the light at the end of the tunnel. She still had help coming in from Grannie's friends, even though it was less necessary now than in the early days, and she was almost caught up on work again. She'd even taken on some new clients to replace the ones she'd lost.

Of course, she had a lot more time on her hands now to work. Celibacy certainly freed up large blocks of her schedule.

It made her antsy, though. She'd seen Ryan a couple of times in town, but he hadn't done more than nod in her general direction. On the one hand, that was exactly what was supposed to happen, but on the other . . . No one wanted to be so easily forgotten.

The more it bothered her, the more she knew she'd made the right decision. The achy feeling in her stomach would pass as soon as she got Ryan out of her system. It didn't help, though, that every time she took a break, she'd look for a text from him. And on top of that, the evenings seemed longer and more boring now that she wasn't trying to see him.

It was enough to make her keep the cooler on the porch filled with alcohol. *Too bad it's too early in the day to start drinking.* She shook off the self-pity and focused on the banner she was designing for Lannie Hanley's flower shop's Web page. Lannie was the third hometown client she'd picked up, and while they were small jobs, it made Grannie very happy to see her working with local businesses.

She jumped when her phone beeped as a text came in. Tate. *Speaking of things that require alcohol . . .*

U still mad?

She'd called Tate the day after that night at the lighthouse, planning to chew him a new one for butting in where he didn't belong and discussing her with Ryan. Her anger, though, had opened a pressure valve for Tate, and the conversation had devolved rapidly into a shouting match over who belonged in whose business, who had hurt whom more, and God only knew what else. The bad thing about fighting with someone you knew that well was that all kinds of stuff could be dug up and flung around, and you both knew where to aim for the hardest hits. All the things Tate had been holding in for years came out, and it had gotten ugly.

Intellectually, she knew it would be good in the long run to have all those things said, and that their friendship would be stronger going forward with all the old hurts healed, but it had been really hard at the time to hear them.

But this was Tate, and that alone made it impossible to stay mad.

Not mad, but still pissy.
But you still love me :-)
Of course. I also still want to kill
you a little.
Ditto.

That, as weird as it was, actually felt like closure—more so than anything else Tate had said. She'd hurt him, but he really was getting past it, even if his pride was still a little dented. Then we're even?

Guess we have to be, he answered. I miss you.

Miss you, too. She thought for a second and then added, Come over for dinner tonight? 7ish?

Sure.

She sent another text to Molly, offering the same invite, and when Molly replied in the positive, Helena got a little rush of satisfaction. No wonder Shelby tried so hard to match up people: The feeling was almost a power trip—a *good* kind of power trip, of course.

At least she—unlike Shelby—didn't try it with folks who were already seeing someone, however casually. *Jeez, I can't believe how catty I am about that.* She really needed to let that go and get over it. She'd just hope that was something else that would come with time. Meanwhile, she was going to quietly, *unobtrusively* encourage Molly and Tate to see the best in each other. She was feeling pretty pleased with herself until she realized she had nothing to actually serve for this impromptu dinner party. Cursing, she shut down her computer and started making a shopping list.

Molly showed up early for dinner and brought a pie for dessert. When she saw the table set for four, she asked, "Is Ryan coming?"

"No. Tate is."

"Oh."

"Is that okay?" she asked, pulling the chicken out of the bottom oven and setting it on the back of the stove.

"Of course. Tate's great."

Helena tossed the pot holders onto the counter, then leaned against it. "He *is* great, you know. Sweet, funny, kind, smart, good-looking . . ."

"Yes, I know. And I think your rolls are burning."

"Damn it!" She grabbed the pot holders again and rescued the rolls, which were a little too brown but not destroyed. *And double damn. I should just ask her.* But without knowing Tate's feelings toward Molly, she risked stepping in something Molly didn't want. *I kinda suck at this.* Matchmaking wasn't going to be as easy as she thought.

Tate opened the door a crack and stuck his head inside. "Something smells good."

"Come on in."

Tate kissed her cheek, and things felt back to normal. Then he turned. "Hey, Molly. Good to see you. How's Nigel Kitty?"

"Fat and sassy."

He nodded, then asked, "Where's Ryan? I figured he'd be here."

"Why?"

"Because you two are . . . ," Tate began, but he trailed off when Helena shot him a look.

She'd known the question would come, but that didn't make it easier to brush off. "We had a couple of dinners together. We weren't going steady or anything."

Molly and Tate exchanged a pointed look. " 'Weren't'?" Molly asked. "As in past tense?"

Nonchalant was impossible, but casual was doable. "Yeah. We decided it was better all the way around to just be friends." As Tate and Molly gave each other that look again, she added, "Anyway, I wanted to have my two besties over for dinner and an enjoyable evening. Is that a problem?"

"Of course not, but . . . Are you okay?" Molly asked.

"Yes. Totally."

"Are you sure?" That was from Tate, whose eyebrows knit together like he was planning on avenging her in some way if she said no.

"One hundred percent. We had a good time while it lasted, and we parted on good terms. No worries."

"But—," Molly started, but the sentence never got finished because Grannie came shuffling carefully into the kitchen. Tate jumped up to offer her an arm.

"Thank you, Tate, but I've got it. I'm slow, but I'm stable."

"Physically, maybe," Helena muttered under her breath.

"I heard that, young lady," Grannie said, causing Helena to busy herself at the sink while Molly stifled a laugh.

"Let Tate get your chair, Ms. Louise, and I'll get you a glass of tea while Helena finishes up," Molly said as she passed on her way to the fridge. "Tate, do you want some, too?"

It was a ridiculously normal evening. She and Grannie hadn't entertained much when Helena was growing up, and when they had on the rare occasion, it was normally one of Grannie's friends. That had tapered off as Helena got older and in more trouble, and Helena regretted denying Grannie that simple pleasure now. Of course, of all her friends, only Tate had ever eaten dinner with them. Grannie had summarily banned the others from the house. Not that Helena really blamed her.

"So," Grannie asked, "who is Magnolia Beach playing for homecoming?"

Helena shrugged and looked to Tate who rolled his eyes at her ignorance. "Baldwin County," he answered. "Mack Raider is the head coach over there now, so it's a bit of a grudge match between him and Ryan. It should be a good game."

Grannie turned to Helena. "If you're wanting to go to the game, sweetheart, I'm sure Margaret will check in on me." Grannie had been the first to notice she and Ryan weren't seeing each other, and her disappointment had been palpable. But it seemed Grannie wasn't giving up without a meddle or two first.

"That's okay. I'm still not much of a football fan."

"Aw, come on Helena, go to the game with me," Tate coaxed. She shot him a "shut up" look, which Tate ignored. Grinning, he added, "It'll be fun."

Helena nearly choked on her green beans. "What makes you think that?"

Tate grinned. "Because you always have a good time when you're with me. Please? For old time's sake?"

"You should go," Molly added.

Helena swallowed and pretended to think. "Only if you'll come with us."

It was Molly's turn to choke. *"Me?"*

"Yes, you. If we're doing it for old time's sake, then we need to do it old style. And if I remember correctly, that means going as a group."

"Three is not a group. Three is a couple and a fifth wheel," she said.

"Then we need to find Molly a date," Grannie said. "That way she won't feel like a fifth wheel."

Molly blinked and turned an interesting shade of pink.

"Fine. I'll go. *Stag*," she added emphatically before rolling her eyes.

"Great," Tate said. "Kickoff's at six, so I'll pick Helena up about quarter after five, and then we'll come get you, Molly. By the way, we just had a litter of kittens dropped off at the clinic. Anybody want an adorable tabby?"

Helena wanted to kiss Tate for adeptly changing the subject away from relationships and football with the allure of kittens. As Grannie and Molly debated the best way to keep kittens from shredding the furniture, Helena shot Tate a grateful look. He just shrugged.

After dinner, Tate helped Grannie get settled in the front room while Molly helped clear the last of the dishes off the table.

"By the way," Molly said, "Mary Ellen Mackenzie is looking for some part-time work. She's a good kid, nineteen, and going to cosmetology school over in Pensacola. She used to nanny for the Jones family until their youngest started school this year, and they speak very highly of her. I told her you were going to need someone to come help cook and clean for Ms. Louise once you went back to Atlanta, and she asked me to give you her number."

"That's awesome. Thanks." Helena dried her hands and stuck the piece of paper with Mary Ellen's name and number on it on the fridge door with a pig-shaped magnet.

"You think you'll be heading back soon?" Molly asked.

"Probably, barring any backtracking on Grannie's part."

"Well, I think Mary Ellen would do a good job. And Ms. Louise knows her already, so it's not like bringing in a stranger."

"Oh, I'll be calling her."

"Hey, she might be at the game tomorrow night. I can introduce you." Molly rolled her eyes. "I can't believe you're making me go, too, by the way."

"Are you kidding me? I can't believe *I'm* going to the game."

"I don't even like football."

"Neither do I, and I didn't want to suffer alone." Now that the kitchen was tidy, Helena grabbed her drink and backed up to the kitchen door. "I was kinda hoping I'd still be banned from the premises or something," she admitted.

Molly perked up. "Are you sure you're not?"

Helena laughed at the hopeful note in Molly's voice. "Short of asking the principal, no. And you'll have to pardon me if I don't wave a red flag at the bulls unless I have to."

"And Ryan?"

"What about him?"

"Are you really okay?"

"Yes. I really am. I appreciate the concern, though." Then, to change the subject, she added, "I'm more concerned about surviving three hours at the game. Do they sell beer at the concession stand?"

"I don't think so." Molly took a deep breath and put a smile on her face. "You know, maybe it will be fun. It's just a game. How bad could it actually be?"

Opening the door, she let Molly pass through to the hall. "You know, I'm almost afraid to find out."

Well, that sucked.

It was a good game, well-played and close—until

Magnolia Beach's defense got cocky and let Baldwin County run the ball through a hole the size of Texas to score a touchdown in the last three seconds of the game.

The boys had gone off to the locker room dejectedly, but Ryan knew the traditional bonfire on the shore would blaze on regardless of the game's final score.

Amid the handshaking and fifth-quarter coaching taking place on the sidelines, he looked up and saw Helena in the stands. *Helena at a football game? Someone must be holding her hostage.* But there was no masked bad guy at her side, only Molly and Tate. They were animatedly discussing something as they made their way down the stairs to the field, and they seemed to be having fun with the topic.

He'd been mad the other night, smarting from the hit Helena landed on him. Being told he wasn't worth her time or effort had hurt—and he hadn't seen *that* coming. It had been a one-two punch, in that not only did she not feel the same way about him, but she'd left without even a second glance back. He'd been left hoping that a couple of days to calm down and recover from the shock of his confession might have her feeling differently. Needless to say, that hope had been fading fast, only to be rekindled at seeing her here now.

She wasn't heading in his direction, though, so he wound through the crowd until he was right at the bottom of the stairs.

Tate noticed him first and came over, Helena and Molly in tow. At least Helena wasn't avoiding him. "That was just heartbreaking. So close . . ." Tate shook his head.

"It's a tough way to learn the lesson," he said, "but the boys now know the danger of celebrating too soon."

"Still . . . ," Molly said.

"Yeah, it's a bit of a bummer for them."

"How many laps will they be running on Monday?" Tate asked.

"I'd assume as many as Coach Hopper can get away with legally."

That made Helena smile. "They should just let Coach

Hopper retire and let you take over," she said, finally joining the conversation. "You're a great coach. Those boys really look up to you. They respect you and want to make you proud. And you're really good with them. You yell at them, but it's not mean-spirited, and it's easy to tell that you believe in them. They're lucky to have you. Especially since the other voice yelling at them is Coach Hopper." She made a face.

The praise meant a lot coming from Helena. It also meant she'd been watching *him*, not the game, the whole time. That improved his mood considerably.

"Uh-oh, speak of the devil," Tate muttered. Ryan looked over to see Coach Hopper approaching. As one of the football team's boosters, Tate was getting respect from Coach these days, but it seemed Tate was still holding a grudge from high school when he'd been scrawny and an easy target for Coach during gym class.

"Well, Hell-on-Wheels, I heard you were in town, but I'm surprised to see you here, of all places."

Helena's smile turned fake. "No more than I am, Coach Hopper. Believe you me."

"I trust you'll stay away from the equipment shed this time?"

Helena didn't even blink. "Of course, Coach. I learned my lesson."

"Good." Coach Hopper slapped Ryan on the back. "Good game. I'm going to go talk to the boys. Tate, Molly." He nodded at the pair.

"Go yell at the boys is more like it," Tate muttered as Coach walked toward the locker room.

Helena rolled her eyes. "Let it go, Tate. He has every reason to dislike me, and I'm not worried about it at all."

"I've got my own reasons to dislike the man," he reminded her.

"Coach is mellowing in his old age," Ryan said. "Plus, times have changed, and so have the rules about how we have to treat students."

"Glad to hear it," Tate said.

"Amen," Helena added.

"So, what do grown-ups do after a game?" Molly asked. "I doubt our presence would be welcomed at the bonfire."

"I say we go grab a drink," Tate offered. "The Tackle Box should be open."

"Sounds good to me," Molly said. "Ryan? You in?"

He jumped at the invite, even as he saw the look Helena shot Molly. "Sounds like a good idea. Let me finish up here, and I'll meet you guys by the gate." He might not be totally back in Helena's good graces yet, but she hadn't objected outright, and that was a start.

Helena groaned as she rubbed her back. "I'm going to need more than one beer. I'm too freakin' old to sit on bleachers."

"Quit talking about how old we supposedly are," Tate grumped. "Jeez, Helena."

"Well, we *are* old."

"Speak for yourself," Molly said.

Ryan watched them as they disappeared into the tunnel under the stands, bickering good-naturedly.

It took him about ten minutes to get his stuff together, and the stands were still full with people milling about as he walked out.

He spotted Tate's head first over the crowd, and as he got closer, he noticed the three of them were surrounded by a decent-sized group. All were faces he recognized, most from high school. Popularity and notoriety were often hard to tell apart, and Helena's notoriety had always attracted attention, if not a crowd. She had her hands stuck in the pockets of a battered leather jacket, and leaning against the fence like that, in jeans with her hair loose around her shoulders, she looked like she was still in high school.

But while Helena looked relaxed, if not particularly engaged with the group, something seemed off even as she spoke with Anna Grace from the post office. Her body language was all wrong, like she was *trying* to look relaxed, but not succeeding very well. It wouldn't have been noticeable if he hadn't gotten to know her so well recently, and seen how she interacted with Tate and Molly when she *was* comfortable and relaxed. This wasn't exactly an excited reunion of peers, full of hugs and squeals, but it wasn't a mob, either—very reserved with a veneer of friendliness across the surface. She wasn't being ignored outright, but she certainly wasn't in the midst of everything. The tension was noticeable, even from the outside.

He'd known that Helena would have a hard time settling in—or even fitting in, for that matter—but that didn't make it easier to witness, and the full realization hit him hard in the gut. Even worse, he'd quit thinking about it, even when Helena mentioned it; once he'd gotten to know her, he had arrogantly assumed that everyone was getting past her past simply because *he* had.

He couldn't decide whether that made him an idiot or an ass. Or possibly both.

She'd made some headway—that much he knew just from the chatter around town—but it obviously wasn't enough. No wonder Helena constantly planned for the day when she'd leave Magnolia Beach again. He couldn't blame her for that. There was no real way to start fresh from a clean slate when everyone knew exactly what you were trying to leave behind and judged who you were *now* solely by who you were *then*. In that scenario, there was no real way *not* to come up lacking.

And it made him mad. As he got closer to the group, he was greeted by the same "tough game" comments—like he'd actually been playing it—and hindsight quarterbacking, along with the usual polite questions about the general health and well-being of himself and his family. Completely normal and banal, but made strange by standing near Helena, when it was obvious no one really cared about the family; they really wanted to know about him and Helena, but were too polite to ask. Which was good, because he sure as hell didn't have any answers.

And while Helena had acknowledged him when he arrived, she kept a good twelve inches of distance between them—a respectable gap for someone who didn't want to give gossip legs. Despite the distance, he felt the sudden change in her attitude—a tiny stiffening of her body, a swing in her mood. A moment later, he heard someone call his name, and he turned to see Mike Swenson coming toward them. Julie was nowhere to be seen, but Mike's residual high school posse was still backing him up.

"The whole defensive line should be running laps after that giveaway, Ryan."

He really didn't want to hear Mike's opinions on anything, but he forced himself to be polite. Mike owned several small businesses in Magnolia Beach, and Ryan would need his support as president of the Chamber of Commerce for both the historic overlay and an upcoming rezoning plan. "It happens. They're probably feeling bad enough as it is."

"They should feel bad. There's no excuse for that kind of sloppiness."

Mike liked to talk a big game, but he had zero credentials to back any of it up. Hell, although he'd somehow managed to letter, Mike had spent more time on the bench than on the field, and any coaching he was doing these days was strictly from his recliner. But he certainly looked the part of a former football player—a bulky and barrel-chested good ol' boy stuck reliving what he saw as his glory days from a stool at a local bar.

While he liked Julie Swenson just fine, he and Mike had never been good buddies to begin with, and knowing his lies about Helena gave him an additional reason to dislike him. And Mike's "Well, hel-*lo* there, Hell-on-Wheels. You're lookin' *good* these days," verbal leering didn't do much to help that.

"Wish I could say the same about you, Mike," she retorted, flipping her hair over her shoulder before looking him up and down. Her nose crinkled. Then, in a pitying tone, she said, "You might want to consider laying off the longnecks and pork rinds. The older you get, the harder it is to lose that belly fat."

Chuckles could be heard around them at their sparring. "Oh, it's just more to love, darlin'. Just more to love."

"Well, it's good to know you're still not letting your deficiencies affect your self-esteem. But you keep thinking positively, sport," she said with sarcastic cheerfulness. "Maybe one day you'll actually accomplish something worth stroking your ego over."

"Everyone already knows how much you like stroking my *ego*," he sneered.

There was a sharp gasp. Helena opened her mouth to respond, but Ryan was already reacting. Between the name-calling, the crudity, the insinuations everyone would take as true again . . . he just snapped.

He didn't realize he'd even thrown the punch until he heard the satisfying sound of bone cracking against bone, and Mike dropped like a rock into the dirt.

Helena was the first to recover, grabbing his arm. "Have you lost your mind?" she hissed into his ear.

Mike was flat on his back, eyes wide, a lovely red mark already showing where the bruising would be across his cheek.

"What the hell?" he said, rubbing a hand over his face and wincing in pain.

"Come on, tough guy, get up. Somebody should have beaten your ass years ago, you lying little piece of shit."

Tate stepped between them and turned to Mike. "Stay down," he ordered. Helena still had hold of his arm, pulling him back, but he shrugged her off. Seeing that, Tate grabbed his shoulders and pushed him backward, keeping his body between him and Mike. "Back *off*, Tanner. That's enough."

Julie had pushed her way through the crowd. Kneeling next to her husband, she inspected the damage, then turned to him and shouted, "What the sweet hell is your problem?"

Before he could respond, Tate got his attention. "Do you think you're the only person in all of Magnolia Beach who's ever wanted to beat him to a pulp?" he said quietly. "I'm glad you threw the one punch, but I can't let you throw another."

"*Let* me? Don't make me land the next one on you, Harris."

"Would you listen to yourself? Jesus, get a grip. You're an *adult*. There are a hundred kids here who just saw you attack another man over some trash talk. Way to lead by example."

Tate was right. Damn it.

"And since Helena basically started it," he continued, "you just look like an ass with anger-management issues right now. And anyway, even if you did beat the truth out of him, it won't change the past."

Ryan didn't like that, but he'd have to be satisfied with that much. And punching Mike—as juvenile as it had been to do it—was far more satisfying than he'd expected, even if he *was* going to be denied the pleasure of a complete ass kicking.

Mike was being helped to his feet, the look on his face clear evidence he knew exactly what Ryan was angry about.

"Man up, Swenson," he warned, "or next time I *will* kick your ass."

The murmur racing through the crowd grated across already irritated nerves, and even as the rational part of his brain yelled at him to stop, his mouth was already moving. "You all need to grow up. Every single one of you has something stupid or horrible in your past you'd rather forget, and the rest of us are simply nice enough not to constantly throw it in your face. It'd be nice if y'all extended the same courtesy to Helena." The guilty looks, lack of eye contact, and intense cuticle inspections told him he'd made his point. But to drive it home, he added, "You act like she's got to prove she's changed, but y'all aren't even willing to give her a chance."

With that, he turned to find Helena and get her out of there, but she wasn't standing behind him anymore. He scanned the now-dispersing crowd: nothing. His questioning look at Molly was answered with only a shrug.

Helena was gone.

Chapter 17

Fury, embarrassment, shock, disbelief—the combination of emotions was hard to process, but they definitely kept her feet moving. There was no way she could stick around and watch that circus unfold even further.

She should've known better. She shouldn't have gone to the game at all. Just when she was starting to make inroads, she'd been sucked back into all the high school drama with a cringe-inducing display of immaturity. It was infuriating. And embarrassing.

And then Ryan had thrown that punch. *Oh sweet Jesus.* That was its own level of disaster. Mayor Tanner brawling? Like anyone wouldn't believe that wasn't a result of her bad influence on him. There wasn't a person in that crowd who hadn't heard—and probably believed—Mike's conquest story, so it was glaringly obvious what had set Ryan off. Especially since they'd been seeing each other recently. She didn't know which of them it would be worse for—him for doing it or her for corrupting him.

Either way, any ground she'd gained with these people was probably lost now.

Besides, if anyone was going to throw a punch at Mike Swenson, *she* should be the one doing it. God knew she'd *wanted* to do it for years, but to see Ryan do it ... As shameful as it was to admit, she almost found it *flattering*, somehow. Of all the things she'd felt when Ryan's fist hit Mike's face, the little flutter in her chest was the most difficult to explain or understand.

And that was just all kinds of messed up.

She heard the rumble of the truck's engine long before it coasted to a stop at the curb. She kept her head up, staring straight ahead, and kept walking.

"Helena, wait!"

She didn't even bother to look back, much less stop. "Go away, Ryan."

There was a sharp curse, followed by the sound of the truck's door slamming. Then Ryan was trotting at her side, holding her elbow. "At least slow down, okay?" he joked.

Now she wanted to throw a punch at Ryan. "I can't talk to you right now."

"Look, I'm sorry. Really sorry about that."

"And you should be."

He shook his head. "I should have shut his mouth for him sooner."

That stopped her in her tracks. "Wh-what?"

Ryan smiled crookedly in apology and took her hands gently in his. "I'm sorry I let it go that far."

She jerked her hands away. "No, you should be sorry for making a scene like that. Are you just completely insane, or do you want to try to explain that ridiculously immature display of testosterone poisoning some other way?"

Ryan blinked twice, then cleared his throat. "Mike was way out of line."

"Maybe. But so were you. So was I, for that matter. But, it's not *your* place to swoop in like some kind of redneck Avenger because Mike Swenson is being his normal asinine self."

"I thought that—"

"You thought what? That I needed you to defend my honor or some such?" Her head felt like it was about to explode. She fought to stay calm. Or calm-*ish*. "Go home and cool off, and just pray that Mike doesn't decide to press charges."

"He deserved it."

"Good Lord. 'He had it coming' isn't a valid legal defense for assault—not even in Alabama. Do you *want* to spend the night in jail?"

Ryan looked so confused, she almost felt sorry for him.

She took a deep breath. "While your gallantry is kindly noted, it's very misplaced. If you want to beat the crap out of Mike Swenson, then do it. But find your own reasons. Don't do it because of me or something that happened years ago."

"The fact he's never been called on it before doesn't mean he shouldn't be now."

"Why? What possible purpose could it serve?"

"I thought you just wanted to be accepted here."

"Your punching Mike Swenson doesn't exactly advance that cause. It only makes both of us look foolish."

Ryan waved that away. "Mike's an ass. Everyone's wanted to take a swing at him at some point."

"Great. They can form an orderly line. That doesn't change the fact you shouldn't have done it."

"I'd have thought that you, of all people, would be glad someone finally did. And better I do it than you."

"I'm not some meek little miss who needs the big strong man to defend her or jump to her rescue because some guy's being a jerk."

"Is that why you're mad? That I beat you to the punch? Literally?"

She was about to pull her hair out. "*Argh*. Why couldn't you just leave it alone? Do you have no sense of self-preservation? Mike Swenson might be an ass, but he's an *influential* ass around here. As mayor, it behooves you to stay on the good side of the president of the Chamber of Commerce. That act of immaturity—regardless of why you did it or what he did to deserve it—does not bode well for your future dealings with him."

"Why do you even care? You'll be gone soon enough, and life will go back to normal. Isn't that the song you've been singing this whole time?"

Why did that feel like she'd been hit between the shoulder blades with something sharp? She lifted her chin. "You're right. And that's only all the more reason for you not to go mucking around with the current state of affairs."

Ryan's face was stony and expressionless except for the muscle twitching in his jaw. If she hadn't felt like pulling her own hair out, she might have felt bad about it, but honestly, she just needed to get home and be alone. "Just go home, Ryan."

He started to say something, then stopped as if he'd changed his mind. After a deep breath, he stepped back. "Come on. I'll drop you off on the way."

She was not going to get into his truck. She felt too raw, too on edge to put herself into that kind of close proximity. Not at least until she had time to think it all through. She didn't want to do or say anything else she might regret tonight. "No, thanks. The walk will do me good."

Wisely, Ryan didn't argue with her. He just nodded and walked away, instead.

Helena deliberately started walking, even before she heard his engine rumble to life. After a long moment, Ryan put the truck in gear and drove away, leaving her in a picture-perfect setting for an evening walk.

For the next block, she tried to focus just on the peaceful sounds of a quiet town, the cool gentle breeze, and the sound of her own deliberately slow breaths. Instead of heading straight home, she walked down to the water. Not the Shore where the kids had gone to party, but the sandy beach on the Mobile Bay side. This time of year, she could pretty much guarantee it would be quiet and nearly deserted. It was a long walk, but she needed the time to calm down.

When she got to the boardwalk over the dunes, she kicked off her shoes and left them on the bottom step, letting her toes sink into the sand. A small dinghy was overturned down by the high-tide line, and it made a perfect bench. The sound of the water was relaxing, and she leaned back to stare at the sky. Wispy clouds moved over a full moon, but it was clear enough to see all the way across the bay to the lights of Bon Secour on the other side. A cool breeze blew her hair into her face, but it felt good, as though the wind could clear some of the cobwebs and confusion out of her brain. It worked— kind of—to calm her, giving her the mental space she'd need to sort through the events and reactions of the evening in some kind of organized manner.

Yes, watching Mike hit the ground had been immensely satisfying. She gave herself one small minute to remember that moment and enjoy it.

Regardless of Ryan's assertion that everyone had wanted to punch Mike at least once in their lives, the fact remained they'd think Ryan was acting out of jealousy, not justice. There wasn't much she could do about that. It would always be her word against Mike's, and launching a protest this late in the game seemed rather ridiculous anyway.

If Ryan thought a fistfight at the homecoming game wasn't going to be all over town by morning, he was deluding himself. And once again, she'd be swimming upstream to try to counter any gossip, as the truth was never as interesting as the speculations.

And there would be gossip. Lots of it.

That was what was so infuriating. While it was galling to admit, somehow in the last few weeks she'd bought into the idea that she didn't just have to *survive* this trip; that it might actually be possible to reconnect and yes, even redeem, herself. And the ground she'd just lost made her sad and angry at the same time, because starting over again was just too much to contemplate. Getting involved with Ryan was a double-edged sword: people might see her differently—better—based on Ryan's acceptance of her, but they might also resent her for the bad influence on him—as Ryan had just demonstrated in bone-cracking detail. She had a sinking feeling it was that side of the sword that was about to cut her deeply.

If she acted like she didn't appreciate Ryan's white

knight routine, she'd be making him look like a fool for defending a woman who didn't appreciate his efforts or concern. Of course, if she did show appreciation for it, he'd *still* look like a fool for defending the honor of someone whose honor didn't deserve defending.

There was no way for either of them to win on this.

What was even worse, though, was the fact that she *did* appreciate it, even though she couldn't—and didn't want to—admit it. It made her feel special, and that was definitely a first.

Because the reality was that *she* wasn't special. Ryan was the kind of guy who'd probably do something like that for any woman in that situation. That was what white knights *did*. Letting herself believe otherwise— even for a second—was a good way to get her feelings hurt.

According to Ryan, his life would go back to "normal" once she was gone. She was a disruption, a distraction from the way things were supposed to be.

So why did knowing all of this—reasonably, rationally, knowing this—make her feel a little sick?

Because you fell for him, you idiot.

Oops. When had that happened?

In a lifetime littered with bad choices, that could possibly be the stupidest thing she'd ever done. She didn't have a future in Magnolia Beach. She didn't have a future with Ryan. Falling for him was pointless.

He said he cared about you.

That actually made things worse. The "if"s and the "but"s and the "maybe"s were too tempting to ponder, but every conceivably realistic scenario played out like a bad movie.

Wow, she'd walked right into this. Set herself up to get hurt, engaging in a semipublic fling to somewhat disastrous results for one or both of them.

Was she stupid or just a masochist? Good Lord, she wasn't really helping herself much.

The facts were simple. It didn't really matter if Ryan cared for her or not; she would never be good enough in anyone's eyes for him to be serious about. Regardless of what he said, wouldn't that eventually be too much to deal with? And would she even want to put him in that position? Caring about someone meant doing what was right for that person, even if it meant being disappointed in the process.

Of course, if Ryan was mistaken and really didn't have feelings stronger than friendly, friend-with-benefits, fling-type ones, then she was setting herself up to get smacked down hard.

Damn.

Simple facts didn't make it any easier to hold conflicting emotions, but facts didn't lie, and staring at the stars didn't provide answers other than the obvious.

She'd gotten the house done, and Grannie was getting stronger every day, pretty much at the point now where she needed a support staff more than a commander in chief. She'd accomplished what she set out to do.

It was time to go home.

Oh, he'd known he'd hear from his mother. There was no way in hell she wouldn't hear about what happened after the game, so there was no sense pretending it was a surprise to find his mother at his door with an annoyed frown on her face. The only real surprise was that he hadn't heard from her sooner than this. It had been twelve whole hours since he'd landed the Punch Heard Round the Bay.

"Hi, Mom. Come on in," he said as Tank growled a greeting from his cushion by the window.

Mom seemed to be looking him over, searching for damage. When her eyes reached his right hand, her frown deepened. "Let me see that hand."

"It's fine," he assured her, but he placed it in hers anyway. There was some swelling around a knuckle and a mild bruise, but he'd done worse to himself fighting with his own brothers.

Still, she manipulated the fingers, looking for injuries with the expertise only a mother of three boys could have. "I don't think anything's broken, but you should probably let me take you to the clinic and let your father x-ray it, just in case."

"Really, I'm *fine*," he assured her. "If the swelling doesn't go down today or if the pain gets worse, I'll call Dad."

"Pain?"

"Nothing some ibuprofen can't handle."

"Good. Keep ice on it and consider yourself lucky." Mom set her handbag on the side table, then spun to face him, the frown of concern replaced by the mask of an angry, unhappy mother. "Now, Ryan Ray Tanner," she snapped, "explain yourself."

"Well—"

"You are a grown man, with a position of authority and respect in this community, and you're brawling—in *public*, no less—like an adolescent thug?" So much for doing that explaining himself. She wasn't shouting, but it was awfully close to it. Tank jumped to his feet as her voice started to rise, barking and growling. "Tank, hush. Now," she snapped in the exact same tone, and Tank went back to his bed. Quietly.

He couldn't blame Tank. He might be a grown man, but his mother could make him feel fifteen again with just her tone of voice. "It wasn't actually a brawl—"

"I don't care what you want to call it. I raised you better than that."

"I was defending the honor of a lady. Surely that's a suitable reason."

"Helena?"

He went back to the couch and sat with a sigh. "Yes, Mother. Helena. But you knew that already."

A tiny shrug acknowledged that fact. "And you couldn't have done it in a more civilized manner?"

"Not really. Mike Swenson deserved a hell of a lot more than he got. He's been spreading rumors about Helena since she was seventeen." That would put his mother in an awkward position, he knew, weighing justice against propriety.

Instead, she skewered him with a look. "Exactly how serious are things between you and Helena?" She lifted a finger in warning. "And don't try to feed me cow patties and tell me it's pudding. If you're taking on the whole town for her, then you've come quite a long way pretty fast, considering that dinner the other night was just 'a casual, friendly outing.'"

Never lie to your mother. It will come back to haunt you. But that didn't stop him from contemplating a half-truth, even though he couldn't come up with one. He leaned his head against the back of the couch and sighed. "Honestly, at this point, I don't even know."

"How can you not know?"

"You've met Helena, right? Or at least heard of her? She's not the easiest puzzle to solve."

She came to sit beside him. "I mean, how can *you* not know how you feel?"

That seemingly simple question backed him into a very uncomfortable corner. Tank, jealous of their proximity, jumped up onto the arm of the couch and cuddled close to his shoulder. Petting the dog gave him a much-needed moment to think before he tried to answer. "I like her. A lot more than I thought I would. But it doesn't matter. We're not seeing each other anymore."

He could tell that news surprised her. "All of this over a woman you're *not* dating?"

"Well, that's by her choice, not mine. So I can relieve your mind on that much, at least."

"You can't possibly assume to know the state of my mind about anything—especially since I haven't come to my own conclusions yet."

"Then you're the only person in town who hasn't."

"Don't get fresh. If you really like this woman, then I must not have full understanding of who she is. For the *most* part"—she glanced pointedly at his hand and rolled her eyes—"you have a good head on your shoulders. And you're not one to be blind to the obvious or jump in over your head. If you truly care for her, then there's more to her than I know."

"That's the problem she seems to be facing all over town. No one seems willing to give her a chance."

"I think you'd be surprised. I've heard some rather good things about Helena recently. Even if you think she's not getting a fair chance from people, she's making it work."

"Well, it's not enough. Plus, she's determined to head back to Atlanta as soon as possible."

"I won't deny that Helena's got a tough row to hoe, but if you care about her and she returns that sentiment, you'll figure out a way to make it work."

She made it sound so simple, like he could wave a magic wand and just make it so. "How?"

"I don't have a single clue." Then she smiled. "I'm not promising it'll be easy, but few things worth having are. And while there are some attitudes that will need to be overcome, your family will have your back."

"Yeah, right." He couldn't keep the sarcasm out of his voice, even though he knew his mother wouldn't like it. "Shelby's busy trying to set me up with every woman in town. Jamie's horrified I'd even go near her. Adam and Eli are—"

She waved her hand, dismissing all of that like she had been crowned Queen of the Universe. "Shelby needs a new hobby, Jamie needs to grow up, and Adam and Eli will support you in your decisions because it is the right thing to do. Just like your daddy and I will."

Because if they didn't, Mom would kill them.

"Everyone else will come around eventually," she added.

It sounded good, but . . . "You seem to have forgotten the small but important fact that Helena broke up with me."

"That's something else entirely, and you'll have to sort that out between the two of you. But once you do, maybe you could bring her over for dinner sometime and let us meet her properly. In the meantime"—she leveled a chastising look at him—"we will use our words, not our fists, to make our point, correct?"

"Yes, ma'am." Although he couldn't promise he would never hit Mike Swenson again, he at least wouldn't make the mistake of doing so publicly.

Mom reached across him to scratch Tank's head. He reveled in the attention. "I found an adorable new pattern for a sweater for Tank. We don't want him to get cold this winter, do we?" she cooed. "He doesn't have a light green one yet, does he?"

That might be one of the few colors Tank didn't have. "Mom, I have the best dressed dog in Magnolia Beach already—much to my embarrassment," he added. "Don't feel like you have to do it."

She smiled sweetly at him. "Oh, I would much rather be knitting booties and hats for a pack of adorable grandbabies, but my sons seem determined to deny me that joyful chore."

Boom! He'd left an opening, and she'd effortlessly landed the hit like a pro. At least his mother was a gracious winner and didn't belabor the point. She gave Tank one last pat, kissed him on the cheek, and left—still smiling.

He picked up his phone with the idea of calling Helena, but then changed his mind. Helena probably wasn't in the mood to talk, and he had some serious thinking to do anyway.

Helena draped the chain and its pendant around Grannie's neck. "Now, you have to wear this *all the time*, even in the tub. You can take it off when you go to bed at night and leave it on the nightstand, but you have to *swear* to me you won't set one single toe on the floor unless you're wearing it."

Inspecting it, Grannie frowned. "It's ugly, Helena."

"It's not a fashionable accessory, I know, but it means you'll be connected to help every second of the day just by pressing that button. Trust me. It's the most beautiful thing *I've* ever seen."

The setup was impressive, and the peace of mind did make it worth every penny she'd spent. She'd even hooked the house's smoke detectors into it for extra protection. "Anytime you need help, you just press that button and start talking. The operator on the other end can call an ambulance, the police, the fire department, or even a neighbor. I've already given them a slew of phone numbers, including mine, so you tell the operator what you need and they'll help. Twenty-four hours a day."

Lord, I sound like the commercial. But she had to sell Grannie on the idea.

"Well, if it will make *you* feel better . . ."

"It will, Grannie. Otherwise, I can't go home because I'll worry about you the whole time."

An eyebrow went up. "So if I say I won't wear it, you'll stay?"

"Grannie . . ."

"I'm not going to apologize for wanting my granddaughter around."

"I love you, too. But I've got to get back to Atlanta."

"Is something wrong?"

She dodged the question. "You are, of course, welcome to come with me," she offered, knowing full well there was no way Grannie would agree. "Two single girls living life in the big city . . ."

Grannie shook her head. "I'll pass, thank you. Atlanta's not my kind of town."

And Magnolia Beach isn't mine. "Mary Ellen is coming over this afternoon to talk to you, work out a schedule, and get acquainted with where everything is. You'll have her for only a few hours each day, but she'll cook and clean and run errands for you. Whatever you need."

"She's a sweet girl and quite capable, I know."

"Mrs. Wilson and the others are still going to be around as well."

"Helena, darling, I'm an adult, and I've been living without you for twelve years now."

Guilt nibbled at her.

"I'm not foolish, and I'm capable of asking for help." Leveling a knowing look at her, Grannie asked, "Who are you trying to convince this is a good idea? Me or you?"

"Both. I hate leaving you here —"

"But you've been here long enough. It's your life and you need to go live it." Helena started to protest, but Grannie shook her head. "One day, I won't be able to live on my own anymore, and you can take care of me all you want. But until then, make decisions that make *you* happy."

"That's what I'm trying to do."

"I know this has been hard for you—coming back to Magnolia Beach, I mean. But I couldn't be prouder of you. Not only are you an amazing woman, but you've also handled your return with grace and dignity." Grannie patted Helena's cheek and squeezed her chin. "Now everyone's had a chance to see the Helena I've always known."

Her eyes started to burn. "Thanks, Grannie."

"Just don't leave your room in the same disgraceful condition you left it in last time."

Grannie wasn't one to let things get overemotional, which Helena greatly appreciated. "And how would you even discover the condition of my room if you're not supposed to climb the stairs?"

"Don't get cheeky with me," Grannie warned. "So, how much longer do I have you for?"

"If everything goes well with Mary Ellen today, I'm thinking I'll head out tomorrow or the day after."

"That quick?"

Like ripping off a Band-Aid. "No sense in dragging my feet."

"Are you sure there's nothing wrong?"

"Positive."

"What about Ryan?" Grannie asked carefully.

"What about him?"

"I thought you two were—"

"It wasn't meant to be a big deal. We were just having some fun."

Grannie made a *harrumph*ing noise, obviously disapproving of what "fun" might entail but not willing to commit to believing it. Ignorance was bliss, after all.

And Helena was more than a little jealous of that skill.

Chapter 18

The problem with snap decisions was that there often wasn't enough time to carry out the necessary plans to make those decisions work.

But it all came together better than she could have hoped, and pretty soon Tate was loading her luggage into her car as Molly hugged her on the porch. "I stuck a box of lemon bars and a thermos of coffee in the front seat," she said. "It'll keep you fueled while you're on the road."

"Maybe it's a good thing I'm leaving. I'm barely fitting into my jeans these days. Do me a favor and check on Grannie every now and then, will you? Especially over the next few days. Just make sure things are settling in all right and Mary Ellen is working out."

"Of course." Molly smiled, but her eyes looked teary. "Call me, okay?"

"I promise. And you have an open invitation to come visit me. Anytime you want."

Molly wrapped her in a hug. "So do you. Come back soon."

She'd said her good-byes to Grannie inside, so that left only Tate, who was standing by her car, waiting. Molly went back inside, presumably to give them some privacy.

As much as Helena had wanted to have a long good-bye with Tate, there simply wasn't enough time. On the other hand, the time crunch almost made it easier because it couldn't be painfully drawn out.

"I'm really going to miss you," he said.

"I'm going to miss you, too. But I'm not disappearing this time. I expect you to e-mail me and call me and text me on a regular basis. I'm even going to set up a Facebook account so I can post pictures of LOLCats that I will expect you to like."

Tate smiled.

"And I have a very comfortable futon that you are welcome to crash on anytime."

"Stay out of trouble, okay?"

"You, too." She hugged him tight. *Oh God, this hurts.*

"Drive carefully. Text me and let me know you made it home safe."

"Will do."

Grannie, Molly, and Tate waved from the porch as she pulled out. After she turned out of sight, she pulled over and thought for a minute. She'd been able to put Ryan out of her mind the last two days just due to the number of things she had to accomplish before she left. Last night in bed, she'd even convinced herself that she could leave town without going to see him. Hell, she had the letter she'd written to him in her purse, ready to drop off at his office where he'd get it first thing tomorrow morning.

But she wasn't a coward. And she definitely wasn't the kind of person who could just disappear on someone. *Well, not anymore, I'm not.* That was rude and mean and unnecessarily hurtful. She pulled out her phone and sent a text to Ryan:

> Are you someplace we could talk for a minute?
> At home. Come on over.

It was almost perfect. She'd been afraid he'd be somewhere, like on a jobsite, where not attracting an audience would be difficult. On the other hand, now she had to go to his house, which would offer privacy and the opportunity for a whole different kind of awkwardness.

Maybe she should have just dropped off the letter.

It was a two-minute drive to Ryan's, and he answered the door within seconds of her ringing the bell. Helena cursed her lack of foresight as she blankly stared at him, not knowing what to say.

"Come on in." His smile was understandably cautious, considering how they'd last parted ways, but he was obviously pleased to see her.

Damn. Now this was going to be really difficult. "Actually, I can't. I've only got a minute. I don't want to get caught in traffic on my way home."

He chuckled at first, but the realization of what she meant came quickly after. Several expressions played across his face, but they were fleeting and she wasn't able to identify any of them. "So, you're really leaving, then?"

She nodded. "Grannie is doing better than I expected, and it makes me feel a little superfluous. I realized I could finally go home."

"I see."

His terse words were making her purpose both harder and easier at the same time. "So I came to say good-bye and thank you for everything. It's been fun."

Ryan seemed to find her words vaguely amusing, but he didn't have much to say. It was extremely unnerving and rapidly became irritating.

"Take care of yourself, Ryan."

"You, too, Helena."

She stuck her hand out. It was awkward and ridiculous, but what else was she supposed to do?

Ryan gave her a long, unreadable look, then shook her hand. "Drive carefully. Bye."

Then he closed the door, leaving her on the porch gaping like a goldfish.

You got exactly what you wanted. It was easier than you could have hoped. Why are you so perturbed about it?

Because there was no denying that she *was*. Ryan had claimed to like her, but if that had been true, he would have said something instead of closing the door nearly in her face. Instead, when it was time to say good-bye, he'd done so as if she were a tourist who'd overstayed the summer season and was finally checking out.

Dazed and a little confused, she fled to her car.

They were done and dusted and moving on without messiness or melodrama. Which should have been exactly what she'd been hoping for.

Then why did it hurt so much?

She kept turning it over in her head as she drove past the familiar landmarks of Magnolia Beach: the softball field, the high school, the library where Grannie had taken her for story time as a kid and where she'd hidden in the old research room to read romance novels behind the dusty encyclopedias as a tween. She passed Wilson Park, where the little kids scurried around on playground equipment and older kids snuck behind the tree line to smoke and make out, and the Civil War monument, which still had a chunk missing from the pedestal from the time Grady Unger got drunk and drove his truck into it. Every place in Magnolia Beach had a story—public and personal— and she knew every one of those stories, good and bad.

The difference between leaving this time and the last time couldn't be more stark. She'd been giddy with good riddance before, and she'd rather expected to feel the same this time around. Instead, she was bummed and confused about what she should be thinking or feeling.

She stopped at the gas station just outside the Magnolia Beach city line—funny how she still knew exactly where Magnolia Beach's police jurisdiction ended and the Mobile county sheriff's began. A redheaded teenage boy came trotting out. She didn't know him, but she'd lay down money that with that hair and that nose, he was a twig on the Anderson family tree. Unlike Atlanta, Magnolia Beach still offered full-service gas stations, and she left the boy to pump her gas, clean her windshield, and check the oil and tires as she went inside for a cold drink to take with her in the car.

In the drink aisle, she heard, "Helena?"

Turning around, she found a cute and very heavily pregnant brunette staring at her. Although her brain did a frantic search, the face simply wasn't familiar. *Crap.* "I'm so sorry, but—"

The woman laughed. "I'm actually flattered you don't recognize me." After that confusing statement, she added, "Jessie Floss?"

Whoa. Talk about transformations. In high school, Jessie Floss had been chubby and heavily goth—white makeup, too much black eyeliner, combat boots, and moodily sulking in the back row of class. Helena was at a loss for words, opening her mouth and closing it without managing to say anything.

"I know," Jessie said. "I look back at pictures and wonder what the hell I was thinking."

"Well, you look great now."

"So do you. I heard you were in town, but I've been in Biloxi the past few weeks with my aunt. My uncle passed recently, and she's been having a rough time. I'm glad I ran into you."

"I am, too, but I'm actually on my way out of town."

"So Ms. Louise is better?"

"Getting there." Gesturing toward Jessie's stomach, she added, "And congratulations. When are you due?"

"A couple of weeks. That's why I'm home now. Duncan was getting antsy with my due date looming and my being away."

"Duncan *Hollis*?"

Jessie nodded. "We've been married nearly five years now. This is our first," she added, rubbing her belly.

A year older than Helena and Jessie, Duncan had been the prom king and the student council president, not to mention making the all-state basketball team three years in a row. And hadn't she seen something in the paper about Duncan taking over the bank as president or some such? Jessie Floss and Duncan Hollis? *Mind blown.*

Her thoughts must have shown on her face, because

Jessie laughed. "Go ahead, take all the time you need. It's a lot to process."

Horrified, Helena tried to cover her rudeness. "No, um . . . it's just . . ."

"It's fine," Jessie assured her. "We get that all the time. Hell, you should have seen the look on *Duncan's* face when I came home from college minus forty pounds and all that eyeliner."

"I can only imagine."

"I'm so sorry I've been out of town. I'd have loved to have caught up. Duncan says you're some kind of artist now?"

"Graphic designer," she answered automatically, wondering how she'd managed to even ping on Duncan's radar.

"Well, you're certainly a Magnolia Beach success story. Claire was telling me—"

She searched for a Claire in her memory banks. Only one popped up. "Claire Montgomery?" *Prom queen Claire Montgomery?*

Jessie nodded. "It's Kingston now, though. She lives over in Bayou La Batre, but she said you just swooped into town and took over, getting everything sorted out for Ms. Louise like a general on a battle march. Of course, you shook everyone up, but Magnolia Beach needs a good shaking every once in a while."

"I didn't mean to shake anything."

"Oh, honey, I'd have paid cash money to see the looks on people's faces when they realized their former cautionary tale was now a role model."

She shook her head. "I'm hardly—"

"You know what I mean. Everyone loves a good redemption story, and yours is great."

Helena's head was starting to hurt. Jessie had just said more words in the last five minutes than Helena had heard from her in all four years of high school. The content of that flood of words would take time to process, and the Mini Mart was not really conducive to that depth of thought.

At that moment, the redheaded boy stuck his head inside to tell her that she was filled up, checked out, and ready to go, giving her the excuse she needed to go pay and get on her way.

"It was really great seeing you, Jessie. Congrats on the marriage and the baby, and good luck."

"You, too. And don't wait so long to come back, okay?" Jessie gave her a brief squeeze. "Drive safe."

"Okay," she answered as the theme song to *The Twilight Zone* played in her head. "Take care."

In her car, Helena took a deep breath. *That was surreal.*

It was also another very good reason to get the hell out of Dodge before she got sucked deeper into the crazy. As the Mini Mart and Magnolia Beach disappeared in her rearview mirror, she expected to feel relief, a lessening of the tension that had been camped across her shoulders for the past week.

Instead, the weight in her shoulders shifted to her chest. She couldn't figure out why, though.

Everything was the way it should be. Everything made sense.

So why did it still suck?

She'd left. Just up and left. Like it wasn't anything.

Even after a week, Ryan was still unable to get past that fact. He'd rolled it all around in his head repeatedly, from the day she'd arrived until the moment he'd closed the door, unable to figure out what any of it meant or what he should have said when she'd come by out of the blue with a blithe good-bye.

She hadn't even thrown him a "We can still be friends" bone. The "Have a nice life" had merely been implied. It was infuriating.

But it still smarted.

Magnolia Beach heaved a collective sigh of relief as word got around that Helena had left, but honestly, things felt stale and bland now. Helena added a bit of color to life in Magnolia Beach and an energy that was now absent.

Or maybe it was just him. Everything went back to normal within hours, and though his life hadn't changed dramatically from its pre-Helena state, the satisfaction he used to feel was lessened somehow.

He was suddenly bored by it all.

Here he was, back in his usual spot at the Sunday dinner table in his grandmother's house, surrounded by his family, wearing a proper shirt with a collar and eating his peas like a good boy. His brothers were arguing about something—he'd long lost interest—while Jamie lectured a now-sorry-he-asked Tucker about the pros and cons of low-interest financing versus taking a cash-back dealer incentive on a new car.

Shelby leaned over. "Hello? Earth to Ryan. What's with you today?"

"I've just got things on my mind."

"Things that aren't sports or money?" she said, rolling her eyes at the conversations going on around them.

"Believe it or not, yeah."

"Everything okay?"

He still owed Shelby a shouting-at over her interference in his life, but this was neither the time nor the place. And he wasn't in a safe mood for that anyway. He might say something to really hurt Shelby's feelings or otherwise come to regret later. He settled for a safe topic instead. "I've got a meeting tonight with the ladies of the historical society and members of the Chamber of Commerce."

"Well, punching the president of that association probably doesn't help your case with them."

"Trust me, I think everyone's glad I did, even if they won't admit it. I'm more worried about the historical society."

"Yeah. Don't let the lace and cookies mislead you. Those historical society ladies are tough. They'll be loaded for bear."

"Exactly. It's a waltz through a minefield."

"Better find your dancin' shoes, then," she teased. "But I wouldn't worry too much if I were you. Those little old ladies love you."

"I don't need them to love me right now. I need them to trust me. They can love me later."

"They just fear change. They like Magnolia Beach just the way it is, and they're worried. You just have to sell them on your ideas."

"I like Magnolia Beach, too, but I've got to figure out a way to convince them of the difference between 'tradition' and 'stagnation.' "

"It's the curse and charm of all small towns."

"Yeah, well, I don't have a lot of patience for it right now. Excuse me." He pushed his chair back from the table, walking to the kitchen as if he were after something, and went straight out the back door into the yard.

Shelby, of course, followed him. A man couldn't get a moment's peace around here.

"Ryan, what's wrong? And don't say the historical society, either."

"Nothing."

Shelby sighed. "It's Helena, isn't it?"

"What?"

"Hey, don't take my head off. You've been a real bear ever since Helena left town. I don't have to be psychic to see there might be a connection between the two events."

"Could you butt out for once?"

"I could," she admitted with a shrug, "but I know my butting in made some problems for you two in the first place, so I might as well stay in trouble and give you a friendly ear to vent to."

"I don't need to vent. I need to think."

"She's been gone for a week already. How slow do you think?"

"You know, maybe I don't want to have this conversation with you."

"Sorry." Then her forehead wrinkled in concern. "So this wasn't as casual as you two led everyone to believe, huh?"

He couldn't stop the sigh. "For Helena, it was."

"I can't believe that. A woman would have to be a fool to not snap you right up. What did she say?"

He didn't want to have this conversation, but since Shelby just stood there, blinking and waiting for him to talk, it seemed he didn't have much of a choice. "Very little actually. 'Thanks for everything. It's been fun. See ya.'"

Shelby winced in sympathy. "Ouch."

"Tell me about it."

"So what did *you* say?"

"There wasn't much to say. *Ouch*," he added when Shelby punched him in the arm. "What was that for?"

"The girl's not a mind reader. If you didn't tell her how you felt, no wonder she left you like that. She made the sensible choice based on the information at hand."

"But she knows I care about her."

Shelby rolled her eyes. "That's not enough. She's not going to fight the tide because you vaguely 'care' about her. You'd be a fool to even expect it."

"Wait, so now you're suddenly okay with me and Helena being together?"

"She wouldn't be my first choice for you, no, but that horse has already left the barn. Does she make you happy?"

He wasn't used to this level of honesty. "I'm pretty sure she could. I know I wanted to find out."

"Do you love her?"

The baldness of the question caught him off guard. "What kind of question is that?"

"A rather important one," she explained in a tone that called him dumber than a bag of hammers. "Helena's come a long way in people's eyes, but she's still got a ways to go. If you love her, you'll have to be willing to fight those old prejudices with her and deal with the consequences."

"I am."

"Then tell her that." When he hesitated, she sighed in exasperation. "Jeez, on behalf of women everywhere, I should hit you again."

He gave her a warning look, and she unclenched her fist. "I'm going home," he said. "Make my excuses to Gran and the family?"

"Of course. But what are you going to do?"

"I don't know," he confessed. "But I need to do something."

"Just be sure you know what you want—and are willing to live with the consequences—before you do anything rash or crazy."

"Once I figure out what I want, then I'll do what I have to do."

"That's kind of what I'm afraid of," Shelby said quietly. "But good luck."

"We're talking about Helena Wheeler. I'm going to need a hell of a lot more than luck."

Chapter 19

This was her life. A few of her plants had died and there was an abundance of dust waiting for her on the furniture, but otherwise, it was as if she'd never left. Yoga on Monday, Wednesday, and Friday, book club on Thursday evenings, and plenty of time to devote to her clients to keep them happy. She'd caught up with the news of the neighborhood and the happenings in the lives of her friends and gone to see the new exhibition at the Museum of Design with Misha.

This, indeed, was her life—everything she'd missed and longed for the six weeks she'd been in Magnolia Beach.

So why wasn't she happier now that she was back?

There was something seriously wrong with her these days. If her life hadn't changed, the fact it didn't feel right or satisfying meant that *she* had. Only she couldn't see how it had happened.

Maybe it was because she still had one foot in Magnolia Beach. She'd called Grannie every day in the beginning, but after the first week, Grannie had gotten frustrated with the long-distance hovering and told her to stop calling so much. She had Mary Ellen sending her e-mail updates, Tate teasing her on Facebook, and Molly texting her at least once a day with jokes and gossip and info on life in Magnolia Beach. Molly had even called the owner of the coffee shop here in Helena's neighborhood to give them the special recipe for her rocket fuel to surprise Helena on her morning coffee run.

But every last one of them had been silent on the topic of Ryan Tanner—so completely silent that it was glaringly obvious it was intentional and calculated. That kind of hurt, which was strange, because she hadn't expected to *want* informational updates on Ryan. What disturbed her most, though, was that the silence worried her. They didn't want her to know what Ryan was doing, which her brain readily twisted into meaning that they didn't want her to know *who* Ryan was doing. On the most obvious end of the spectrum, though, was the high probability that Ryan had gone right back to his life without a blink, as if nothing had happened at all.

Somehow, that thought hurt more.

And *that* was why her wine budget had gone right through the ceiling.

She missed him. A lot. A hell of a lot more than she thought possible.

It wasn't fair. In fact, it was *sick*. Twisted. Simply *wrong* in more ways than she could comprehend.

She wasn't supposed to fall in love with Ryan Tanner.

Hell, it wasn't even *possible* to fall in love with someone that quickly—especially without even knowing you were doing it.

Was it?

No, it couldn't be. Life wasn't a made-for-TV movie.

This would pass in time. She'd get over this and move on, and she'd be fine. Ready to smile at whichever nice, sweet local girl Ryan eventually settled on as the right one to be Magnolia Beach's First Lady when she went to visit Grannie.

Even more pull-her-hair-out frustrating was the knowledge that if not for the whole Ryan situation, she wouldn't be dreading the next trip back. After she'd friended Tate and Molly on Facebook, she'd received friend requests from other Magnolia Beach residents—most of whom hadn't given her the time of day in high school. Hell, she'd even picked up a few new clients after the historical society uploaded its new banner. She certainly wouldn't win any popularity contests, but she wasn't the worst thing that could roll into town for a visit, either.

So it all boiled down to Ryan, and the fact she had to get over him. And she would. It would just take time.

But all the rational pep talks didn't really help all that much. Which was why she'd invited Misha over for an exciting Friday night with movies, chocolate, and wine.

"Death by serial killer, cancer, apocalypse, terrorism, natural disaster . . ." Misha looked up from scanning Helena's Netflix queue in disgust. "What is wrong with you? I thought this was going to be a fun night. Chick flicks, rom-coms . . . I was thinking less of tales of blood and destruction, and more of Bradley Cooper's abs. Are you PMSing or something?"

Helena tried to picture the calendar. "Maybe. It would explain a lot, wouldn't it?"

Misha refilled both glasses and handed one to Helena. "Drink. You need it. Seriously, what is wrong? You've been all weird since you got back. I'm starting to wonder what the hell they did to you down there in the hollers." Misha was a transplanted midwesterner still carrying a deep distrust of the South outside of the urban areas.

"Hollers are for hillbillies. You have to have a mountain to have a holler, and there are no mountains or hollers in south Alabama," Helena explained. "And no one 'did' anything to me." That was arguable, but she'd done it to herself more than anything. "Anyway, Magnolia Beach doesn't have a decent Thai restaurant, so there were some serious *phat si io* withdrawal issues I had to deal with. Going cold turkey like that really messed me up."

"Then I'm going to call Charm Thai right now and tell them we need an emergency delivery. You can clean out your queue and find something with a shirtless hot guy in it. Chris Pine, Josh Lucas, Ryan Gosling—take your pick, as long as they're not dying horrible deaths." Misha jumped off the couch and went into the kitchen where the menu hung on the fridge door.

"Bring another bottle back with you," Helena called after her. She had to shake this off. She couldn't stay miserable forever.

The knock on her door was unexpected, and Helena groaned as she moved the laptop to the coffee table and went to answer it.

Ryan.

She blinked, sure he was a drunken hallucination, but he was still there when she opened her eyes. A slew of emotions rocketed through her far too quickly to identify any of them, and then her heart fell to her stomach. There was only one reason Ryan would appear on her porch unannounced. She braced herself as she asked, barely able to get her voice above a whisper, "Is it Grannie?"

Ryan looked shocked and confused until understanding finally dawned. "No, no, she's fine," he quickly assured her.

"Oh, thank God." She had to grab the doorframe for support. "I think my heart stopped beating there for a second."

"I'm sorry. I didn't realize you'd jump to that conclusion."

"Why *else* would I think you were here?" Now that the shock had passed, she was being hit from all sides with all kinds of emotions and reactions, and her words came out sharper than she intended.

Ryan smiled crookedly. He looked tired, she noticed, with a two-day stubble and his hair sticking up all crazy as though he'd been running his hands through it. But it only made him look yummy, and a wave of longing hit her hard. Fast on that, her heart started to hurt—both from missing him the last few weeks and seeing him now. All this was still doing battle with annoyance for scaring the daylights out of her, and the adrenaline from both the shock and excitement kept her blood pumping at high speed. She was an overstimulated wreck at the moment, yet she still took a nanosecond to bemoan standing here in pink pajama pants, a ratty tank, and a hoodie.

"Like I said, I'm sorry about that."

She waved away the apology as she opened the door wider to let him in. As he passed, she took a deep breath, inhaling his scent. It sent a pang through her. "So, why *are* you here?"

Ryan looked uncomfortable, squashing the hope that was fluttering to life in her chest. "Well, I—"

"Hey, Helly, it's *so* not on my diet, but would you eat rangoons if I got some? Oh—" Misha stopped short in the kitchen doorway. "I didn't realize someone was here." She looked Ryan over carefully and smiled her approval.

She'd totally forgotten about Misha in the eternity of the last minute and a half. "Ryan, this is my friend Misha. Ryan is a . . . Um . . . He's a . . . He's from Magnolia Beach."

Misha looked at Helena with raised eyebrows asking and answering a dozen questions even as she held out a hand to Ryan. "Well, you've come a long way to visit."

"This obviously isn't a good time. . . ."

"Actually," Misha interrupted, "I just remembered that I have a really important phone call I need to make, so I'm going to run home and do that." She grabbed her purse off the floor by the couch and slipped her feet into her shoes. "You can talk to Ryan"—she smiled at him again—"and we'll postpone our evening to another time. I'll call you later." She waved and pulled the door shut behind her.

There was a long, very awkward silence.

Ryan finally cleared his throat. "It's Friday night. I should have known you'd have plans."

She couldn't believe Misha had just bailed on her like that. She had to fight back the urge to chase after her and drag her back in here for moral support. "Just a girls' night in. Nothing important."

"Maybe I should have called first."

She was about to scream in frustration. Her nerves felt like tiny knife blades cutting into her skin. She tried hard to keep that frustration out of her voice. "Well, you're here now, so . . ."

"How are you?"

Argh. "Good, thanks. Settling back in. How about you?" She tried to sound casual. "Everything okay in Magnolia Beach?"

Ryan's smile was wry. "About the same. You know how it is."

"Good." This conversation was so inane, it bordered on farcical.

"You look great."

Oh. Dear. God. "Ryan Tanner . . ."

He laughed softly and ran a hand through his hair, creating more spikes. "I had seven hours in the car to plan this and thought I had it all worked out, but now it just sounds stupid, even to me."

"Just say whatever it is you came to say. The suspense is killing me." That was the understatement of the year. She was swinging wildly from one possible explanation to the next, and she needed to know where to park.

"I missed you."

That was neither what she'd hoped nor thought he'd say, landing smack in the middle of the spectrum of possibilities and not giving her strong ground to plan her next words. "Is that why you came all the way here? Just to tell me you missed me?"

Ryan rolled his eyes heavenward, then shook his head as if clearing it. "I know this is crazy, and I know it's coming out of left field, and I don't really expect . . . Actually, I have no idea what I expect—"

The tenuous grasp she had on her sanity snapped. "Damn it, Ryan. Spit it out."

His hand cupped her cheek. "Isn't it obvious? I came to tell you that I love you."

The room skewed sideways, and Helena had to sit. "Oh."

Ryan knelt in front of her. "I know it's crazy, but that's the way it is."

It was hard to process, harder to believe, even as her

heart began to beat faster and the cloud that had loomed over her lifted. "You hardly know me."

"Technically, I've known you my entire life. I'm just slow on the uptake," he joked, taking her hands in his so tenderly that Helena's heart cracked a little. "The last few weeks have been . . ." He paused as he searched for the right words. "Dull. You're one of a kind, Helena," he said with a smile. "You've got a good heart and a sharp tongue, and the combination is irresistible. You make me laugh. You keep me on my toes and constantly surprise me. I keep looking for you now, expecting to see you somewhere in town, and I'm disappointed every time I don't. I'm grumpy and foul-tempered, and that's solely because I don't have you." He blew out his breath heavily. "So I came here to tell you that I love you and I miss you and I need you."

Her eyes began to burn. The words weren't fancy or flowery, just straightforward and honest, exactly like the man saying them. It felt real, and she believed him, making this the single most amazing moment of her life. She wanted to revel in it.

But as wonderful as it was to hear, it hurt, too. The situation was doomed, and in that moment, Helena decided she might rather have never known. It would have been easier in the long run.

"Well?" Ryan caught her eye. "Say something."

He'd been honest with her. She owed him the same respect. "This is crazy and very romantic, like something from a movie."

"And . . ."

She took a deep breath. "I love you, too, but—"

He cut her off with a finger against her lips and smiled at her. "Let me enjoy that first part. We'll get to the 'but' in a minute." Then he kissed her. It was both gentle and passionate and filled with something she couldn't bear to face. That knowledge didn't stop her body, though, from cranking its engines, and a little shiver ran over her skin. It was a long, wonderful moment, one Helena really didn't want to end, but the kiss finally slowed and broke, and Ryan rested his forehead against hers. "Now you can finish."

She had to unscramble her brain and backtrack the conversation before she could. "This won't work."

He moved to sit beside her and laced his fingers through hers. "Because you don't want to live in Magnolia Beach, right?"

She nodded. "It wouldn't be good for *you* for me to be there. There will always be someone who holds my past against me, and they'll hold it against you and start to judge you for my sins. They did it to Grannie, and they did it to Tate. I won't let them do that to you. I won't be responsible for that." She squeezed his hand. "It hurts, but it's the right thing to do."

"That's very mature and insightful of you, Helena."

"Thanks." *That doesn't make it suck any less.*

Ryan sighed. "You like this neighborhood?"

The change in topic threw her and was a bit deflating after such a dramatic moment. "Yeah, it's all right."

"Because I noticed a sign on the building next door that there's an apartment for rent. If you'll let me crash here tonight, I'll go tomorrow and fill out the paperwork. Do you know if they take pets?"

This made no sense. "What the—"

"If it's vacant at the moment, I can be in by the end of next week."

The meaning of his words finally dawned. "You can't move to Atlanta."

"Of course I can. My job skills are very portable. Between my savings and whatever I can get for the house in Magnolia Beach, I'll be fine until I get established here."

"You'd be miserable here. You love Magnolia Beach. It's where you belong."

"I'd rather take the chance, because I *know* I'll be miserable at home without you. Magnolia Beach isn't going anywhere. It'll always be there, and I'd pick you over a place any day."

The shock nearly left her sputtering. "You'd leave Magnolia Beach because of me?"

"Not 'because of,' but 'for,' yes. Absolutely."

"But your whole life is there."

"I can always visit. I know you'll be wanting to go see Ms. Louise as often as you can, so I'll go then, too. We can split the driving." He smirked. "You know, it might actually be good for me to move. My family is way too far up into my business. It would be a refreshing change."

She threw out her last, desperate idea. "But you said you *like* being a big fish in a little pond. Atlanta's the damn ocean."

An eyebrow went up. "Are you saying my ego couldn't handle it?"

"I honestly don't know." She didn't know *anything* right now. Her whole worldview was shifting, for God's sake.

"That hurts, Helena." He clutched his chest in mock dismay. "Maybe my ego needs adjusting. It'll be a character-building experience."

She kept waiting for the punch line, but it never came. "You're serious."

"That's what I've been saying."

Helena wasn't sure her system could take many more shots tonight. Ryan loved her—loved her enough to not only stand beside her proudly in Magnolia Beach, but also enough to jeopardize his place in the community to be with her. Loved her enough to make an ass of himself and risk arrest by punching Mike Swenson. Loved her enough to leave Magnolia Beach for her.

He loved her. Loved her a lot.

And that changed everything.

How long it took her to work all of that out, she didn't know, but Ryan was still staring at her, waiting patiently for her to respond.

"I can't believe this."

"Which part?"

"Any of it. *All* of it."

She could see him sucking it up, regrouping, ready to

start in again with a fresh set of arguments. "So how do I convince you?"

"You already have."

Ryan perked up, question written all over his face. At her nod, he grabbed her and pulled her into his lap. Everything seemed so up in the air and strange, but it all felt completely right and good at the same time. They could make this work.

It took a long time to get the kiss she needed to give him out of her system, but it was nice. No rushing, no trying to get to the next, naked, part. She'd have plenty of time for that, and reveling in this moment was more than enough.

"It'll take a while for me to get things completely sorted at home, but I promise I'll be permanently settled up here as soon as I can."

"It will be easier if I go home with you. I've got less stuff, and I already have a place to live."

Ryan looked at her as though she'd lost her mind. "I'm not sure I'm following you."

It was hard not to laugh at the look on his face, but then, he had every reason to be confused. "I'll give Magnolia Beach a chance, see how it works. If it doesn't work out and it all goes to hell, Atlanta will still be here."

"You'd come back to Magnolia Beach for me?"

"Yes. And that answer surprises me as much as it does you."

"Why?"

The happiness on his face made this worth a try. "Because you really do love it there. And I'd rather you not give all that up for me if you don't absolutely have to. Hell, if Jessie Floss can reinvent herself and marry Duncan Hollis, maybe there's hope for me. It's worth a shot first, I think."

"I do love you, Hell-on-Wheels."

She rubbed his jaw. "And I love you, Mayor Tanner." She giggled. "And now I'm actually looking forward to it."

"To what?"

"Me and you, together in Magnolia Beach. The possibility that I'm back for good *and* I've bagged the town's favorite son will definitely stir up some excitement. Oh, and heads will explode all over the county at the mere speculation that Hell-on-Wheels herself could very well be the First Lady of Magnolia Beach one day. It'll be better than having the circus in town, and I don't have to do a single thing except show up and breathe."

Ryan laughed and shook his head. "You are far too excited about that idea. It's a little scary."

She grinned. "Yes, but doesn't it sound like *fun*?"

Epilogue

Ryan parked the truck and turned off the engine, but Helena stayed put, not even unbuckling her seat belt. The light from the streetlights was enough for him to see her eyebrows pull together as she stared at the school. Then she shook her head.

"This is not a good idea. Actually, I think it's one of the *worst* ideas ever. I can't believe that I—or anyone else for that matter—agreed to it for a second."

"Helena . . . ," he began, but she interrupted.

"You go on. I'll come back and get you later," she offered.

Helena's return to Magnolia Beach—this time in a moving truck—had certainly caused a buzz, but mainly because everyone knew the reason why she'd come back had little to do with Ms. Louise. But since the big shock had happened back in September when she'd first arrived, a second return, less than a month after she left, felt a little redundant and lacking oomph. She'd moved back into her childhood home—using reasons of "appearances" and "propriety" and "respect" to explain why she wouldn't just move in with him—and by the time everyone got through the hustle and bustle of Christmas and New Year's, it was old news. There'd been a couple of rough patches, and there were some folks who still held grudges and several who held to leopards-not-changing-their-spots opinions, but for the most part, the foundations of the town remained unshaken and Helena was settling in fine.

Well, *most* of the time. She had a few grudges of her own to carry—but really no more than people who had spent their whole life in the same place—and she wasn't always comfortable in certain situations. Tonight was turning out to be one of those situations, but hell if he knew why.

"That's not happening." He opened his door, and the music escaping out the gym doors—a heavy bass thumping that he knew would give him a headache long before midnight—floated into the cab of the truck. "Come on. We're late."

She pinned him with a look. "This is insane. I *cannot* chaperone the Sweetheart Dance."

He decided to intentionally misunderstand. "It's not hard work. Just stand around, give kids an evil eye if they start grinding or twerking, and make sure no one spikes the punch—"

"Then burn in hell for my hypocrisy?" she asked.

"Honey, if you're going to hell, the devil has bigger sins to choose from."

Her eyes narrowed. "You're real funny."

With a sigh, he said, "Look, we all grow up and get self-righteous with the next generation. It's not hypocrisy." She wasn't buying it, and he tried to think of something else. "It's . . . It's sharing the knowledge *we* acquired the hard way in the hopes *they* won't repeat our stupid mistakes."

Helena snorted. "That's one way to spin it."

"Anyway, I *want* you to come with me."

"Because misery loves company?"

"Well, that and . . ." He reached into the backseat and got the small box he'd stashed earlier. He'd felt a little silly about it all day, but it was worth it when Helena opened the box and her jaw fell open.

She laughed. There was a note of disbelief in it, but he could still tell she was touched. "You got me a corsage?"

"Helena Wheeler, will you go to the Sweetheart Dance with me?"

Helena pulled the corsage out of its box and paused to sniff the orchid before sliding it onto her wrist. "You make it very hard to say no," she admitted.

"So that's a yes?"

There was a long pause. "Yes."

Ridiculously pleased, he gave her a quick kiss, then hurried around to the passenger's side to open her door. She reached for his hand as they walked through the parking lot, and every now and then she lifted her wrist to her nose for another sniff. He shortened his stride to match hers, but he noticed pretty quickly that her pace was slowing the closer they got to the building. Before they made it to the sidewalk, she stopped completely.

"Good God, does this mean I'm supposed to be some kind of role model now?" He couldn't quite tell whether she was shocked or horrified by the idea.

"Of course not. Just try not to give the kids any ideas, okay? *Ouch*," he added, rubbing his arm where she'd punched him.

"You deserved that and you know it," she said primly.

He leaned in and kissed her again, hard and long and uncaring of who might see.

A little breathless, Helena needed a second to recover. "What was that for?"

"Because you deserve it." When she smiled, he tugged on her hand. "Let's go, Hell-on-Wheels. Time to set a good example for the young ones."

"Now *that's* something I never thought I'd hear. Usually it's 'Be good' or 'Don't make trouble.' "

"Well, that, too."

"Don't worry, Mayor Tanner," she said, sliding a hand down his chest seductively. "I'm saving all that for later tonight."

"I'm looking forward to it."

"You should be." She arched one eyebrow up at him, then turned and walked into the gym, head held high like she owned the place.

A little while later, he pulled a protesting Helena onto the dance floor, totally ignoring the shocked faces of the high school set who moved aside to give them room. With an appropriate, school-sanctioned distance between them, they swayed gently to the music. "I should have done this years ago," he confessed.

"Gone to the Sweetheart Dance? I believe you did. With Melody Herman, if memory serves."

"Jealous?" he teased.

"Maybe," she confessed. "But you're here with me now, and that's what's important, right?"

"I'd like to think so."

He pulled her closer, dropping his head to kiss her, which caused Coach Hopper to blow his whistle and motion them to move apart—much to the amusement of the students.

"Tsk, tsk, Mayor Tanner," Helena scolded. "So much for setting an example."

"It's an excellent example to set, thank you very much. Meet the perfect girl, wait fifteen or so years to make your move, and then live happily ever after."

Her eyes widened. "Happily ever after?"

"Yeah, that's pretty much what I'm thinking. You game?"

"I'm game." She rose up on her toes, plastering herself against him, and kissed him hard, causing him to wrap his arms around her and lift her off her feet.

And Coach Hopper could just keep blowing that damn whistle all night long.

Acknowledgments

There are so many people I need to thank:

My fabulous agent, Beth Miller, for telling me this was the book I needed to write and not strangling me while I did;

Liz Bistrow for loving it and buying it;

Christina Brower for her amazing editorial notes;

Linda Howard and Linda Winstead Jones for their wisdom and guidance;

Pamela Hearon, Kira Sinclair, Andrea Laurence, Dani Wade, and Marilyn Baxter for cheering me on and keeping me sane all these years;

Darling Geek, Amazing Child and WonderMom for their unwavering support, endless patience, and contortionist levels of flexibility when I'm on deadline. (*No, you still cannot have my jelly beans*.);

The copy editors and cover artists and everyone at New American Library who worked on this book and made it better and beautiful;

And all the readers, who make it possible for me to do this.

Read on for a sneak peek at the next book
in Kimberly Lang's charming
Magnolia Beach series,

EVERYTHING AT LAST

Available from Signet Eclipse in
January 2016.

It's nearly impossible to keep a secret in a small town.

But *nearly* impossible meant it was still possible. Damn hard, though.

Molly Richards felt like she knew most of the secrets in this particular small town. She wasn't a therapist, a preacher, a bartender, or even a hairdresser, but she ran a coffee shop—the *only* coffee shop in Magnolia Beach, Alabama—and that had to come close. People didn't have to tell her secrets. She overheard them at Latte Dah—whether she wanted to or not.

But she wasn't a gossip. She never repeated what she'd heard, never even dropped hints, because everyone had something they'd rather other people not know.

But she also never forgot those overheard tidbits, either, and it gave her a more complete picture of this town and the people in it than most of the folks who'd lived here a lot longer than the two and a half years she had.

In a way, it made her love Magnolia Beach all the more. Not only did she know *what* was going on, but she also knew the *why*, the *who*, and often the *whoa-you-won't-believe-this-part*. This was a quirky little place, and the key to appreciating it fully was understanding it.

The buzz today was all about the engagement of Sophie Cooper and Quinn Haslett, but that was *news*, not gossip—literal news, as Quinn had announced it himself on the front page of the *Clarion*. *That was one benefit of owning the paper*, Molly thought with a giggle.

There were sighs over the romance, speculations over the timing—they'd been together less than a year, after all—and a bit of jealousy from the younger, single set now that Quinn had been taken off the market, but it all made Molly smile. It was spring and love was in the air.

And, she was a sucker for a love story. Even after everything, she still believed that everyone should get a happily ever after. And she had gotten to see lots of relationships start, grow—and occasionally end, too—over cups of coffee in the overstuffed chairs of Latte Dah.

Jane, who'd been with her from almost the day she opened her doors, blew her blue-streaked bangs out of her eyes as she passed, carrying a trayful of dirty coffee cups. "There are three applications under the register. Hire someone, or I'm going to quit."

"I will," Molly promised. In addition to Jane, Molly had two part-timers, but they were high school kids and the hours they could work were limited. And while it was very nice to be busy enough to need another employee, she was enjoying the security of the extra cash after two years of just making ends meet. She'd invested in the shop and padded her savings a little bit, but that cushion could deflate quickly. But she couldn't risk losing Jane, either, and they'd only get busier once the summer season started. She tugged the envelope with the applications out and opened it as she followed Jane into the kitchen. "Any of these you particularly like?"

Jane didn't look up from loading the dishwasher, but Molly saw the triumphant smirk. "Samantha Harris or Connie Williams. Patrice is a little flighty."

Molly knew *of* both Samantha and Connie, even if she didn't know them well or personally—Magnolia Beach was pretty small, after all—and didn't have a strong feeling either way. "I'll call them both back for interviews, and if they're good, I'll see who can start next week."

"*This* week," Jane insisted. "I'd like to have a life, too."

Molly sighed. "Fine. Can you call them and see if they'll come in this afternoon? Maybe one at four and one at five?"

"Thank you. Now I won't have to poison your coffee today."

Molly grinned. "Then thank *you*." A glance around told her the rush was officially over for the morning. "I'm going to run out for a while. I'll be back before the Bible-study group arrives."

"Bring back change," Jane called from behind her. "We're low on fives and ones."

Molly nodded as she hung up her apron and then held the door for a mother pushing a stroller with a sleeping baby. Outside on the sidewalk, she took a big breath of non-coffee-scented air and turned her face up to the sun. Late spring was quite possibly one of the best times of year here, weatherwise: warm, but not hot, days and nights that were just cool enough to require a light jacket.

It might be a quirky little place, but there sure wasn't much prettier than Magnolia Beach on a bright spring afternoon. The town was practically a movie set labeled "small-town Americana"—tidy buildings set along clean, narrow streets and flags waving lazily in the breeze. Even the newer buildings intentionally had that older aesthetic, giving the impression the town wasn't necessarily stuck in the past but rather gently resisting change where and how it could.

That feeling was part of what drew tourists to the area. That and the water, of course. Magnolia Beach was locked in on three sides by water: Mobile Bay to the east, Heron Bay to the south, and Heron Bayou to the west.

The Yankee snowbirds had already left town for their Northern cities and climes, but in a few more weeks, the town's population would nearly double in size as all that water would draw folks down to the coast. The Mobile Bay shore—called "the Beach" by the locals—had white, sandy beaches, perfect for sandcastle building and long walks along the water, while the Heron Bay shore—called "the Shore" to avoid confusion—offered fishing off the jetty and a boardwalk along the rockier man-made beach. Add in a marina full of boats to charter, airboat tours into the bayou, and long, hot sunny days, and Magnolia Beach was a summer paradise.

While the tourists looking for wild parties would head over to the east side of the bay to Gulf Shores and farther along the Florida panhandle, families and those wanting a more low-key vacation would come to Magnolia Beach. And when they weren't on the water, tourists had a full selection of restaurants, quaint shops, and family-friendly activities right at their doorstep.

Trapped as it was between the water and unable to sprawl, the town was rather compact, making pretty much everything within walking distance. The tourists loved that perk, and Molly liked it herself, leaving her car at home except on the most miserable of days. Since she tended to nibble at the pastries—strictly for quality-control purposes, of course—she needed all the exercise she could get. That would be another perk of a new employee: She could possibly find the time to start running again before the winter weight became permanent.

More important, though, she liked the walk. In the early mornings on her way to open Latte Dah, the whole place felt quiet and still, and that was better for clearing her mind and relaxing her soul than any meditation. In the afternoons, the streets were busy and active but not stressed and crowded, and there was always someone to stop and speak to, making her feel like a real part of the town. Making it feel like *home*.

Only better. She had no desire to really go home.

Fuller, Alabama, was only six hours away, but as far as she was concerned, it might as well be on the other side of the planet. Eventually she'd have to go back—her day of reckoning would come—but until then, it was easy enough to forget Fuller even existed. *This* was where she wanted to be.

The bank, post office, and grocery store were quick, easy errands and she made it back to her place, a tiny guesthouse beside Mrs. Kennedy's house, in plenty of time for her own lunch and maybe a short nap. Even after over two years, that five a.m. alarm was still hard to handle sometimes.

She dropped onto the couch and kicked off her shoes, and Nigel jumped into her lap with a purr. Threading her fingers through his soft gray fur, Molly closed her eyes with a sigh.

And, of *course*, there was an immediate knock at her door, followed by Mrs. Kennedy calling, "Molly?"

Nigel hissed in the general direction of the door, expressing Molly's feelings quite nicely. While the place was clean, cozy, and affordable, her landlady had boundary issues and a rather interesting interpretation of tenant-landlord relationship boundaries.

Grumbling, Molly moved Nigel off her lap and rolled off the couch. Knowing Mrs. Kennedy could see her through the glass window in the door, she pasted a smile on her face as she opened it. "Hello, Mrs. K."

Eula Kennedy was welcoming warm weather with a bright fuchsia sundress and a color-matched faux hibiscus in her carefully coiffed white hair. Molly could only hope that forty years from now she'd have the nerve and ability to carry off something like that. "Hello, dear. I'm *so* glad I heard you come in. I was about to head to Latte Dah to find you."

"I just came home for lunch." *Like I do most days.* It wasn't a secret or anything.

"Well, I won't keep you but a minute."

Molly had no choice, really, but to open the door wider for her to enter. Mrs. Kennedy was carrying a bulging grocery sack from the Shop 'n Save, but it didn't look like groceries. As she set the bag on the coffee table with a sense of satisfaction and purpose, Molly had a bad feeling she wouldn't like the explanation of that bag.

"I got a call from Jocelyn last night."

Jocelyn was Mrs. Kennedy's niece, currently pregnant and living over near Destin. Molly nodded absently while she eyeballed the bag. Oddly, it looked like it was full of notebooks. "I hope she's doing well."

"The doctors have put her on bed rest. Worries about an incompetent cervix."

That got her attention. Molly had no real knowledge what that diagnosis might mean, but Mrs. Kennedy looked worried, so it probably wasn't good. "I'm sorry to hear that. Please let me know if there's anything I can do," she said automatically.

"I'm so glad you said that," Mrs. Kennedy said in a tone that had Molly wishing she'd stopped talking after "sorry." "There's no way Jocelyn can rest the way she needs to with two other little ones running around, so I'm going to go stay with her and help until after the baby is born."

"I'll keep an eye on things at the house, no problem." Molly often looked after the place while Mrs. Kennedy traveled. It was one of the reasons her rent was so cheap.

"I know you will, and I appreciate it, but the house is really the least of my issues. I've got my Sunday School class and volunteer shifts at the library covered, but there's no one to take over the Children's Fair on Memorial Day weekend."

She couldn't possibly be thinking that I should . . . No. Memorial Day marked the official start of the summer tourist season, and Magnolia Beach always went all out with a weekend of concerts downtown, an arts-and-crafts fair downtown, a fireworks show over Heron Bay, services at the War Memorial, a parade, and of course, the Children's Fair, which was Mrs. Kennedy's idea originally and her pride and joy. More important to *this* conversation, it was a huge undertaking, with a dozen different parts. Not to mention all the screaming children. "Oh, Mrs. K., I couldn't. *Really*. I wouldn't know where to begin, and I'd hate to mess it up."

Mrs. Kennedy waved that away. "It's impossible to mess it up. Most of the heavy lifting is already done, and the folks involved are old pros at it by now, so it will mostly just roll along on its own. I just need someone to keep an eye on it."

Oh, crap. Think. "But . . ."

"Have you already agreed to volunteer somewhere else?"

Molly wished she could lie. "No, but . . ."

"Then this is perfect. A great way for you to get your feet wet."

Get her feet wet? This would be like jumping into the deep end. With dumbbells strapped to her legs. And the pool would be full of small, screaming children.

"I don't—" Molly started her protest, but Mrs. K. just patted her on the arm—firmly, but kindly nonetheless.

"Everything you'll need to know should be in those notebooks, and if it's not, just ask Margaret Wilson or Tate Harris for help. They'll know. Now . . ." Mrs. Kennedy started unloading the notebooks as she talked, placing them in Molly's hands so that she was forced to accept them or end up with bruises on her feet from dropping them.

Molly was being steamrolled and she knew it, but damn if she knew how to stop it. Mrs. Kennedy kept talking like it was a done deal, with or without Molly's agreement, and Molly couldn't bring herself to interrupt a sixtysomething-year-old woman. And since Mrs. Kennedy never seemed to stop to take a breath, she had no place to interject an objection.

The flood of words and instructions rolled on, interspersed with assurances of Mrs. Kennedy's confidence in Molly's ability to pull this off. Molly was still blinking in confusion and formulating her plan of resistance when Mrs. Kennedy gave her a quick kiss on the cheek and was out the door.

Leaving Molly with the Children's Fair literally in her hands.

"Damn it."

Nigel blinked at her from his perch on the back of the couch, then stretched out his neck to sniff disdainfully at the load in her arms. A second later, he pulled back quickly, ears lying flat against his head.

"My thoughts exactly."

She didn't have time for this. She had a business to run, and they were shorthanded right now anyway. Equally as important, she didn't *want* to do this. She, too, was from a small town, and *this* was exactly how people got sucked into the volunteer pit, never to surface again. She was all for community spirit and pulling together, but there was no way she wouldn't screw it up somehow. And since it was a big fund-raiser for ... Damn, she didn't even know where the money raised actually went. It had to raise a lot, though. Christ, she was going to mess this up *and* be the reason some deserving charity couldn't make its budget this year.

This was insane.

She was still standing there, trying to figure out a graceful way to decline the honor, when she saw Mrs. Kennedy come back out carrying a suitcase. She hurried to the porch, ready to claim illness, insanity, incompetence, any reason not to be in charge of this, but Mrs. Kennedy was very spry for her age and was already driving off with a honk and a cheery wave.

Damn it. She was well and truly stuck now.

Tate Harris stood under the shower and let the hot water beat the tiredness from his shoulders. After a long spell of nothing but checkups and routine procedures for weeks, it seemed every pet in a twenty-mile radius had decided today was the day for illnesses and accidents. He'd been on his feet all day without even a lunch break and gone through multiple changes of clothes, due to sprays of pretty much every bodily fluid an animal could emit, and Mr. Thomas's Pomeranian, Florie, had taken a bite out of his hand.

It was days like today that made him wish he still drank.

With that option off the table, though, he stayed under the spray until the water ran cold and forced him out. He scrubbed a towel over his hair to dry it, then grabbed clean jeans and a T-shirt.

Now that the animal smells were washed away and out

of his nose, he caught the faint scent of lemon furniture polish and bleach floating through the house, meaning Iona had come today—a day earlier than usual. Suddenly hopeful, he went to the kitchen and opened the fridge. There, in neatly wrapped and labeled packages, were his dinners for the next several nights.

He'd been not exactly dreading, but not looking forward to either, a cold dinner of ham sandwiches, so the sight of Iona's pot roast made his mouth water. Feeling better already, he stuck it into the microwave to heat.

A fresh pitcher of tea sat on the counter, holding down a note from Iona explaining that she'd come today because she had a doctor's appointment tomorrow, and if he'd text her a list of any personal items he might need from the store, she'd take care of those on her next trip.

But the fact that she'd signed that note with just an initial and a small heart, well . . . that was a little disconcerting.

When he'd hired Iona last year, he'd been drowning, overwhelmed by a busy practice and trying to have some kind of life while still having clean clothes, decent food, and a house that didn't look like the Health Department needed to intervene. Iona had laughed at her interview and said he actually needed a wife. He hadn't disagreed with her. And she'd been an absolute godsend, taking over and running this part of his life with ease. Unfortunately, the feeling that Iona might be wanting to take on that title as well as the job had grown stronger over the last few months.

It'd first become really noticeable when Helena Wheeler had moved back to town last fall. The amount of time he'd spent with her ignited Iona's jealousy. He'd faced weeks of bland food and scratchy, wrinkled clothes. Once Helena had started dating Ryan Tanner, his life had gone back to normal.

And Iona had starting making him cookies, saying he was too skinny and needed fattening up. Mainly, her supersecret-recipe peanut butter–chocolate chip ones, which he loved. He rubbed a hand over his belly absently. Those cookies would do it for sure.

Last week, he'd found a lacy pair of Iona's panties "accidentally" mixed in with his laundry, and now she was leaving notes signed with a heart.

Iona danced perfectly right along the line of inappropriateness, never really crossing it and making it impossible for him to call her on it.

He was going to have to do something. Soon. And he was selfish enough to not want to do it simply because Iona took such good care of him, and he didn't want to hire someone else.

The thing was, there wasn't anything *wrong* with Iona Flemming. Cute, sweet, kind—she'd make some man very happy one day. But that man wasn't going to be him.

He'd have to face that music at some point, but for now, the price of domestic tranquillity and delicious food was ignoring innuendo and playing dense as a tree when she flirted.

Working long, unpredictable hours didn't hurt, either.

He burned his fingers on the plate as he took it out of the microwave, nearly sloshing the rich gravy off the edge. The smell made his stomach growl as he carefully carried it to the table. Now ravenous, he grabbed a fork, only for his phone to ring before his first bite.

Almost any other ringtone would have been ignorable, but not Sam's. Since her divorce last year had brought her home—and back to Mom's house—she'd been a little fragile. And he could talk to his sister and eat at the same time, rude or not. He answered with a "What's up?" and shoved a forkful of pot roast into his mouth.

"Guess who got a new job today," Sam singsonged, obviously in a good mood.

"That's great," he mumbled around tasty bliss, then finished chewing and swallowed. "Where?"

"Latte Dah. I'm a barista now." She rolled the *R* with gusto.

"But you don't even like coffee."

"Doesn't matter. I know how to make it, and that's far more important."

He put his fork down. "What about the library?"

"I'll still have that, too. But Molly's offering more hours and better money. That means I'll have the money to get my own place even sooner."

Sam didn't like living with their mother—not that Tate blamed her a bit there—but she wouldn't move into his extra bedroom either, however temporarily. He sighed and rubbed his forehead. "I told you I'd give you the money so you could move out."

"And that's very kind of you, but no. I don't want your money," she insisted.

Stubborn girl. "Then why don't you come work at the clinic instead of picking up part-time jobs all over town?"

Sam snorted. "Besides the fact that I don't want to work for you?"

He sighed. "Yes, besides that."

"If I had any training or experience in the veterinary business, or even any interest in learning, I'd consider it. But I don't want a pity job from my big brother."

It was times like this when he wished Sam was more like their sister, Ellie: sweet, quiet, and much more persuadable—at least when he was doing the persuading. But Sam . . . Sam often made him want to pull his hair out. They were too much alike. "It wouldn't be a pity job."

"Then what would it be, exactly?"

He thought for a moment, then grinned, since she couldn't see it. "Nepotism."

"Because that's *so* much better." He could almost hear her eyes rolling. "Thank you, but no," she added seriously. "I need to do this myself."

"Sam . . ."

"Tate . . ." she echoed in the exact same exasperated tone. "I called you because I wanted you to be happy for me."

"And I am. I just don't want you killing yourself when you don't have to." He wasn't rich, but he could certainly help his sister through a bad time. If she'd just *let* him do it, for God's sake. *Maybe if he . . .*

"Put your cape away, Superman. I don't need rescuing

tonight," she said, as if she could read his mind. "Look, I know the offer's there," she continued in a much kinder tone, "and I promise I'll take you up on it if it all gets to be too much or goes rocketing into hell. But let me at least *try* to fix my life myself first, okay? I got myself into this mess, and well, I have my pride, too."

It nearly killed him, but he agreed. Then he ate more pot roast to keep himself from arguing more with her as she moved on to other topics. He'd just start hanging out at Latte Dah more when she was working and make sure to tip well. He could at least slip her a little extra without her being able to refuse it without making a scene.

He heard his mother in the background, followed immediately by a muttered curse from Sam before she said she'd talk to him later, and then left him holding a dead phone. Sam's pride really *was* running the show; otherwise she'd be begging him for a loan to get her out of that house.

Hell, he knew that's why she'd gotten married so young, but since she'd been burned by that choice, she was being more careful this time. And here he was with the money to help assuage his guilt for leaving her and Ellie there with their parents while he went to school, and she wouldn't take the loan from him. It was frustrating.

Ellie, at least, seemed happy enough up in Mobile, married to a marine biologist she'd met when he'd been down here studying fish or shrimp or something like that. He couldn't complain about Doug—much—and she had the kids and some volunteer work to keep her busy. She'd warned him that it was best to let Sam find her own way, but at the same time, she wasn't here, dealing with their mother or watching Sam barely keep her head above the water.

He ate more pot roast, but his irritation at the orneriness of all women in general had sucked all the enjoyment out of it now. He swallowed the last few bites and stuck the plate in the dishwasher.

There was nothing he could do about Sam or Iona or

anyone else tonight, and in a way, that felt good to just accept. Anyway, after today, he deserved a lazy, brain-dead evening of doing nothing. He grabbed a couple of Iona's cookies and took them to the other room with him.

He'd certainly earned them.